BONE MARROW STEW

by Tim Curran

B lake dunked his coat into the warm Caribbean Sea, squeezed out the excess water and then wrapped it around his head and shoulders. "No, but you're gonna tell me anyway."

Fulco laughed. "He cuts the gull's throat with a piece of coral and drinks its blood. Blood is mostly water, right? It can keep you alive."

"Good idea, if we can get a gull to land in this boat."

Fulco nodded. They saw gulls from time to time, flocks of them flying in the distance. At first Fulco got all excited, thinking that birds meant they were near land...then Blake told him that gulls, like many sea birds, often flew hundreds of miles out to sea.

Just like Blake to stomp down a guy's hope.

Fulco looked down at Howe, wrinkled his blistered nose. Guy was starting to stink like the pig's straw.

Blake had been mothering him since the wreck. Did no good, of course, what with his head sheared open like that. He was a dead man. Anyone could see that. Ever since that freighter rammed the charter fishing boat, splitting it in two like a matchstick, he'd been like this. A hatch cover popped free from the impact, slamming into his head like a discus. Only good that came of that clusterfuck was that the collision had ripped the dingy free from its davits. Fulco made for it as the fishing boat sank with all hands. Five minutes later, Blake clawed his way aboard, dragging Howe with him.

CONTENTS

REIGN OF THE EATER

(Stygian Articles #2, 1995)

The Eater is a chopper of souls, a licker of bones.
The Eater is hungry but he shall have no food.
Starvation is the way, good fellow, cold, empty, wanting starvation that clears the muddled mind of debris and the heart of filth. Jesus fasted, did he not? And the Eater is a martyr of souls and suffering, so he, too, will fast.

Blessed are the bleak, the Eater has said with jeweled tongue, for they will inherit this infertile womb. As it was in the beginning, so it shall be at the end, Our Father, Lord of Cadavers, Cannibals, Death-Houses, and Drainage Ditches. Hear my prayer, oh most cruel and concupiscent one.

As the Eater walks the last dust-choked and godless mile through the curving, snaking, slippery bone-strewed byways of the City of No Regrets, he watches the onlookers, the sainted sinners in their crumbling flesh houses and gulags of despair. They watch him with desperate Roman predator eyes that loll and spin and roll in red-rimmed sockets of hate-love. They chant and sing and spit at the sun. On the horizon, said sun flickers and coughs and succumbs in its tangerine and crimson ash pit death bed, leaving a trail of shimmering blood opalescence.

Toothless and eyeless, the crowds gather in jeering, crying, endless throngs that dance to hideous, vapid melodies of pale brass. It is to these sunless and barren songs that the weak and worthless and would-be are dipped in oily vats of black tar grease and impaled on blood-browned stakes and set aflame. God shall light our way. Praise she who laughs in the highest, cower and quicken in the cold lamp glare of her eyes. She who stalks mortuary and crypt, dust-eater and master-embalmer, Queen of the Dead. Count the holes in her face and nibble at the winding shroud of her moldering sacraments.

"Got any Fish?" the Eater asks, shambling slowly, zombie of the ages.

The Eater likes fish. He likes to catch them, clean them, eat them with teeth that are filed to rabid points. The younger the better, the softer the sweeter. And all around the Eater, a sea of fat-bellied swimmers with Pisces eyes stroking in a contaminated yellow pond.

"I'll eat you up," the Eater promises them. "You are my food, your blood my drink. Prepare a shaved and eviscerated table of your infants for me. I bless them with my rows of ripping teeth."

With this in trembling mind, see the Eater as they see him: a hollow-eyed stalker from the Reptile House with a dead and knowing smile; a lizard-tongued and spike-fingered butcher of dreams; a night gaunt in flapping, fashioned rags of stitched slave flesh, salted and cured, chewed and licked, his flaking throat scarfed with ropes of sun-dried viscera from the guts of babes. The Eater, cannibal of souls, member in good standing of the Vivisectionist Society. Walking pestilence. Praise the Lord of the Flies for His time is at hand. Forever and ever. Alpha and Omega.

The Eater in a desert voice: "I shall dwell in the House of the Sterile and Infirm forever, Amen, Omen. Got any fish, burning one?"

The impaled ones have no answers, they burn and flicker, their flesh an oily stink that blots the sky in blackness. Their screams only vapors of memory in the twisting, seething, cremated air. Sacred balm of human ash.

"I was like you once," the Eater proudly proclaims, "meat for the beast. But no more: I go not to my death screaming but rejoicing with a bloated belly of boy-meat, my shredded lips hot with their flowing juices. Kill me, murder me, put me out of my grand misery, roll said stone before my tomb, vicar, for I am a thing of midnight fogs and nightmares. Forty days, sinners, forty days hence I rise from the fungous, rotting black blanket of death and walk amongst you once more to feed upon you in dark alley and wind-blown sepulcher. Oh, brother can you spare a dime for a fellow hell-raiser who's going down on his luck? Dance with me, Piper of Chaos, now and at the hour of my eternal, blessed damnation…"

The Eater has said his piece, walking cadaver, dead eyes deader than death, wench-eater and flower-pisser, grave-robber and sin-eater. Up to the splintering, creaking gibbet he goes. A braided snake-rope encircles his pulsing, bloodless throat, tighter, tighter, constriction at its finest, the snake's ready bifurcated tongue licks salt trails from his eyes.

Under a black and hopeless sky of crying children and whimpering, wondering elders, the trapdoor releases with a groaning benediction of worse things waiting, the scalped serpent rope snaps and the Eater's rawboned neck gives with a resounding crack that's heard in every dark tomb and rustling grave.

But his eyes, bird of prey raptor orbs, alive and smirking, dripping with tears of joy, say to all: In the Midnight hour, ghouls and hangmen, I am you and you are me.

RED SEA

(The Edge #8, 2000)

Five days at sea.

No food, no water in nearly seventy hours.

Fulco started going crazy.

Desperate? Two days ago he'd been desperate, now he was simply mad: talking to himself, whispering to people who weren't there, grinning constantly.

The ocean was flat, dead calm, a mirrored surface reflecting the burning sun above. There were three of them in the little ten-foot dingy. Howe's head was split open, dried blood crusted over his face like fingers of dark fungi. He lay in the bottom of the boat where he'd lain since the other two had hoisted him aboard. In five days he had not regained consciousness.

Never would as far as Fulco was concerned. "Hey, Blake?"

From the bow, Blake looked up at him. His face was baked red, peeling, his lips swollen and split-open. "Yeah?"

"I read once where this guy was stranded on a desert island," Fulco said, his voice low and scratchy like an old 45. "No food, no water. Just rocks, sand. But seagulls kept landing on the beach, picking in the dirt. So this guy, he gets this idea. Next seagull lands, he pegs it in the head with a stone. Kills the little prick. You know what he does then?"

Blake dunked his coat into the warm Caribbean Sea, squeezed out the excess water and then wrapped it around his head and shoulders. "No, but you're gonna tell me anyway."

Fulco laughed. "He cuts the gull's throat with a piece of

coral and drinks its blood. Blood is mostly water, right? It can keep you alive."

"Good idea, if we can get a gull to land in this boat."

Fulco nodded. They saw gulls from time to time, flocks of them flying in the distance. At first Fulco got all excited, thinking that birds meant they were near land...then Blake told him that gulls, like many sea birds, often flew hundreds of miles out to sea.

Just like Blake to stomp down a guy's hope.

Fulco looked down at Howe, wrinkled his blistered nose. Guy was starting to stink like the pig's straw.

Blake had been mothering him since the wreck. Did no good, of course, what with his head sheared open like that. He was a dead man. Anyone could see that. Ever since that freighter rammed the charter fishing boat, splitting it in two like a matchstick, he'd been like this. A hatch cover popped free from the impact, slamming into his head like a discus. Only good that came of that clusterfuck was that the collision had ripped the dingy free from its davits. Fulco made for it as the fishing boat sank with all hands. Five minutes later, Blake clawed his way aboard, dragging Howe with him.

Blake was handy, sure. First few days they'd used up most of his survival knowledge, though. Things like drinking the water from the spines and eyes of fish. That had been easy enough, what with flying fish diving right into the boat the first night. But there'd been no fish in three days now.

Fulco's mouth was full of blowing sand, his tongue like a dried-out sponge. His hands and arms were a mutiny of saltwater boils and pustulant red sores, hurt like all hell. Had to be careful, too: you brushed up against something, they burst open like egg yolks. And the pain? Like somebody had stuck the blade of a red-hot screwdriver in you.

"I wasn't talking about no fucking gulls," he told Blake, still studying Howe. "That's not what I was talking about at all."

Blake caught his meaning, did not like it. "I don't want to hear that, Fulco. You got me? I don't want to hear crap like that."

Fulco kept grinning. Blake. Who was he, anyway? Fulco had to concentrate a minute. Yeah, Blake was...Blake was his brother-in-law. That's right. Married Fulco's sister Katherine. Try as he might, he couldn't even remember what she looked like. No matter, even if Blake was married to her, that didn't give him the right to boss people around. To make the decisions.

"I ain't gonna die like this, Blake. You better understand that right now."

"Stop it, for chrissake! Use your head! Do you hear what you're even saying?" Blake asked him. *"Do you?* It's the heat, the dehydration, the hunger…it's getting to you."

Fulco shook his head. What the hell was Blake even talking about? He was fine, his brain was clear. His thoughts were crystal clear as a mountain stream. He took out his folding knife. "Way I see it, whasisname…*Howe*…he can't make it much longer. He ain't gonna wake up. What good's it do us to die, too? What does that solve?"

"You're a ghoul," Blake said. He had his own knife out.

Fulco started giggling. "Better a living ghoul than dead fish bait. Way I see it."

"You touch him and I'll kill you."

Fulco eyes were bulging now, flaking lips pulled back from yellowed teeth. Knife in hand, he started inching toward Howe.

"Don't," Blake said from the bow. "Don't do it."

But Fulco was going to do it, goddamn right he was. He needed something wet in his mouth, needed a drink in a bad way. He didn't care what it was. He would've sucked piss by that point. He lunged and landed on Howe, brought his knife up to strike. Blake dove at him, slashed with his own knife, opening up a line of saltwater boils on Fulco's arm. And, oh Jesus, the pain. Fulco fell back, knife clattering to the hull plating. Blake stabbed out again and Fulco saw the blade pass bare inches from his eyes. Balling his fist, he struck out with everything he had, caught Blake in the mouth, felt his fat lips smash against his teeth. He hit him three more times, the boat rocking like a whore's bed. Finally, Blake's eyes rolled back white.

Breathing hard, Fulco found his knife. He took hold of Howe and pulled him up into a sitting position, his head dangling over the gunwale. It was easy then. He located the weak pulse at his throat, stuck the knife in his carotid. Blood came spurting out like water from a slit garden hose. Fulco pressed his lips to the wound and let the hot liquid fill his mouth, wash down his throat. It was salty, too warm, made him want to vomit, but, oh Christ, it was good, so very good.

Then, motion behind him.

He turned, blood running from his mouth. Blake sank his knife in Fulco's shoulder. Fulco staggered back, flipping over a seat and landing in the bottom of the boat. Full of animal rage, he pulled the knife free. There was pain, yes, but it came from far away like maybe it was happening to someone else.

He pulled himself up and saw Blake there, catching the blood in his cupped hands, lapping it up like a kitty with a bowl full of milk. "You won't have him!" he cried out, his teeth red and dripping. "I won't let you have him!" He had Fulco's knife now, brandishing it wickedly.

Fulco's belly was full of boiling oil, veins thrumming with electricity. *His kill. That sonofabitch was stealing his kill.* He came at him with the knife. Drenched with blood, painted red savages, they faced each other, snarling, snapping. Blake made another charge with his knife, slitting open Fulco's chest. But Fulco brought his own up in a deadly arc, slashing at Blake's outstretched fingers. Blake screamed as his index finger was nearly severed, hanging by a thread of meat. He retreated into the bow and Fulco, wounded and hurting, crawled back to the stern to lick his wounds. The cut on his chest wasn't too bad, but his shoulder was bleeding pretty good. He figured neither were fatal, though.

The sea began to pick up with gentle swells, a mild breeze blowing. Water began to slap against the side of the boat. It would be dark in a few hours.

"I wouldn't close your eyes if I were you," Fulco said.

"Oh, I'm a light sleeper, Fulco. You just try me and find out. I'll cut your fucking balls off." He chuckled deep in his throat. Using his knife, he slit the fiber of gristle that held his dangling finger. He tossed the digit at Fulco, stuck the stump in his mouth, sucking at it, still talking, garbled words pouring out.

Fulco picked up the finger and stuck it in his shirt pocket. No sense wasting a good piece of meat. A guy could stay alive nibbling on something like that. Protein. He settled back in the stern, watched the sea, the sky, but mostly he watched Blake.

Blake had bandaged up his finger with a strip of his shirt.

Yeah, you gotta sleep sometime, mister, then I'll get you.

"Murdering fucking animal," Blake told him. "Well, there won't be no more. I'll see to that. Next thing an animal like you does is start thinking about meat. Blood was good, you think. Why not the meat? It won't happen, see? I won't let it."

Fulco kept grinning. He realized then that he wasn't alone. In fact, his father was sitting next to him. Tough old wop, he thought he'd died years ago, drank himself into a fugue and wandered out in front of that bus.

"Lookit that puke over there," Fulco's old man said. "Never should've let him marry Katherine. *Blake?* What is that? Fucking *limey* or something? Not Italian, you know that much. Greedy asshole. We'll fix 'em, eh, boy?"

"Fucking right we will," Fulco promised him.

Blake was muttering to himself. Knife at the ready, he slid over to Howe's corpse, favoring his bad hand. "Not gonna eat him. No sir. I won't allow it." He took hold of Howe's legs, heaved him overboard. Howe's body was drawn up to the crest of a wave, pulled into the trough between another, began drifting away. Blake stared at Fulco, dared him to try something.

But he didn't.

Fulco was patient like a lion watching a stray gazelle. His time would come and he knew it. What he didn't get was that his old man was gone again. There. Then not. Must've gone below or something. Except…there wasn't any below. No matter, he'd be back.

About ninety minutes later as the sun began to sink low in the western sky, painting up the horizon orange and red, a gray chill mist began to rise off the water. Blake, his belly full, began to slip lower in the bow, his eyes getting heavy. Fulco pretended to do the same. Waited, waited. Blake kept fighting himself awake. But as the shadows began to grow long, his chin dropped to his chest and he went out.

Fulco slipped over there real quiet. Silent as a snake into a shoe. When Fulco was inches from him, Blake's red eyes snapped open, hazed over, then went wide. Fulco stabbed him in the throat four, five times. Blake flopped and jumped and squealed like a prize hog. But in the end, he simply died. Limbs stopped twitching, eyelids closed, mouth fell open.

Fulco gorged himself on the man's blood, filling his belly to bursting.

What with that cold fog moving in, the hot blood tasted real fine. Like a broth really. Maybe beef. Salty beef. Warmed Fulco up just fine. He lapped at Blake's throat, remembering his mother's kitchen, big pot of beef barley simmering on the stove, filling the house with good, hungry smells that just about turned your mouth to water.

Fulco was jarred back to reality when he saw something bearing down on the dingy. A big sailing yacht. Had to be a sixty-footer at least. He saw no one on deck. As it got closer he made out the dim form of a woman at the wheel, but she wasn't paying attention. Maybe she was sleeping.

Fulco's heart pounding madly, he pulled Blake's cadaver down into the bottom of the boat. He crouched over it, hid it with his own body. He had to be careful. That woman on the boat saw what he had, she'd want some, too. Greedy, miserable bastards always trying to snap up another guy's kill. What was the world coming to?

The yacht passed and vanished into the dusk.

Fulco felt his body relax, the tension running out of him. Looking about to make sure there were no other poachers around, he took out his knife and slit open Blake's jeans, began cutting strips of flesh from his thigh. It was good and salty like the blood, very tender. Little bit of oregano, maybe some sage, fry it up in a pan with butter, be damn good.

Wasn't bad raw either.

As he ate, he looked down at the man's dead face, wondered who he was.

Behind him, a voice said, "You ain't gonna hog all that, are you boy? Don't forget about your old man over here."

And the night passed slowly, hideously.

THE EYES OF HOWARD CURLIX

(Horrors Beyond, 2005)

"I have harnessed the shadows that stride
from world to world to sow death and madness."
—H.P. Lovecraft

I met Howard Curlix at a pizza parlor just off campus.
Given the subject of this little narrative of mine, I'd like
to say I met him in a brooding, gothic house in a deserted, rat-
infested neighborhood down near the wharf. You know, a place
of wild rumors and unspeakable truths. Alas, it is not so. And
let that serve as a lesson for us scribes, scribblers, and creative
hacks—the true vein of aberration and gnawing terror runs
deepest in the most prosaic settings. I'd gotten a call from Curlix
and he'd dropped a bomb on me—would you, he asked, like
to know of the connection between theoretical physics and an
ancient, banned witch book out of the twelfth century?

Well, of course, I would.

Now if I told you my name was George J. Kramer, that
wouldn't carry much weight. But, if I told you I was a senior
editor at the *Weekly World Examiner,* you might begin to see the
connection and my interest. The *Examiner* is one of those tabloid
rags you see at the grocery store checkout. The kind you laugh
at: *College Girl Raped by Bigfoot, She Sez It Was Love* or *Was Elvis
Hitler's Stepson? Shocking New Evidence.* Yeah, no point in going
into it any further than that. You've heard all the bad jokes,

seen the stories—pregnant aliens and first ladies possessed by demons, mothers eating their babies and radioactive jellyfish devouring ocean liners, the face of Jesus on Mars...that sort of highbrow stuff. The *Examiner* is not exactly *The Washington Post*, but we have something like five times the circulation of any of the nation's largest and most prestigious newspapers put together. And we're always on the lookout for offbeat stories. Sometimes we create those lurid stories from whole-cloth.

That's right, we make 'em up, just like you thought all along.

Other times, well, we look for odd headlines, weird occurrences and extrapolate the living hell out of them, fill their wagons with so much bullshit they would tip straight over if we didn't hold them up. The radioactive jellyfish? Japanese fisherman claimed they saw it. Only it was a fishing tug and not an ocean liner and I threw in the bit about radioactivity. It seemed fitting in a Bert I. Gordon sort of way.

So, I'm always looking for something I can twist and warp completely out of shape. I did a fourteen-week series on the Squid-Baby, people, so trust me, if there's any blood in it, I'm the guy to squeeze it out.

But Howard Curlix?

No, that particular yarn came fully developed and all I'm going to do here is write down what he told me...and the aftermath of it.

Curlix was sitting in the back at one of those tables with the red-and-white checked vinyl tablecloths on it, the candle in a wine bottle with the wicker net around the bottom. Along with violin music playing, it was supposed to create a genuinely ethnic Mediterranean atmosphere. But it was about as Italian as my Hassidic Jewish grandmother.

Curlix was a tall, sparse man with a long, angular face, a touch of silver at the temples. He wore a midnight-blue suit without a tie. A cravat or ascot would have fitted him just right. He seemed very precise, meticulous, polished. The sort of man who could spill the gravy boat all over his crotch and make it look socially acceptable. Make you want to do it, too, so you could look half as good as he did. He was wearing an outlandishly large pair of black sunglasses—think Yoko Ono—and a white cane was leaning up against the table.

"Mr. Curlix?" I said, knowing it was him, all right. "Howard Curlix?"

He nodded. "Sit down, Mr. Kramer. Can I get you something? Wine? Food?"

I shook my head and he said that was probably for the best, since he could recommend neither.

It was past the supper hour and the place was dead. I looked at those sunglasses, never realizing he was blind. And, at that moment, the way he seemed to be looking around, I didn't actually think he was.

"First off, Mr. Curlix, tell me a little something about yourself." My voice-activated digital recorder was rolling.

He did. Curlix was a research fellow at Brown University's Electron and Optical Physics Division and ran the reflectometry facility there. He was forty-eight years old, unmarried, and childless. He had won both the Mott and Holweck Medals for his work in experimental particle physics and his paper, *Light-Speed Reduction in Ultracold Atomic Gases*, was considered required reading in theoretical physics circles. And if that wasn't enough, he was also a regular guest lecturer at the Niels Bohr Institute in Copenhagen. Wow. Of course, it meant nothing to me being that I'd flunked general science in the ninth grade, but it sure sounded impressive. If you took into account some of the nuts I dealt with, believe me, he was really something. Howard Curlix, PhD, ScD, was the real item.

"Impressive. Now tell me what you do at Brown," I said.

He smiled thinly, continued looking about through those gargantuan sunglasses of his. "We conduct experimental research with laser, electron, ultraviolet, and x-ray radiation, determining the fundamental mechanics by which electrons and photons transfer energy to gaseous and condensed matter. With, of course, specialized attention given to nonlinear interactions of light and matter."

I scratched my head like an ape looking for a tasty nit. "Okay. Let me rephrase that, Doc. What do you guys *really* do over there...and without the gobbledygook this time, please."

"We freeze light," he said.

Just like that. As if light was something you could pour into an ice cube tray and cool your scotch-and-soda with later on. "What do you mean?" I asked.

He told me that they were involved in slow-light experimentation at Brown. In a vacuum such as empty space, he explained, light travels at a speed of nearly 300,000 kilometers per second. In their experiments at the Optical Physics Division, they had slowed light down to something less than one mile an hour.

"You mean I can walk faster than a beam of light?"

"Precisely."

It was wild stuff. I'll admit I was impressed, but none of that was selling any newspapers or contributing to my George-Bush-is-the-Antichrist scenario I was playing with back at the office. I didn't have all night. "And what does slowing light have to do with an ancient *witch book* as you called it?"

If I could have seen his eyes, I'm sure he was looking at me like something one step up the evolutionary ladder from *Homo erectus*. Which, at that point, I surely was.

"What do you know of light?" he said.

I told him I turn them off and turn them on, end of story. So he enlightened me, so to speak. He told me the sun emits light, so-called *white light*, in radiation waves at a visible range that our eyes interpret as the colors of the rainbow. These colors— red, orange, yellow, green, blue, indigo, and violet—are called the visible spectrum. For something to be seen, it must reflect, transmit, or absorb light waves. But other waves, many others, exist above and below the visible spectrum.

"The electromagnetic spectrum is composed mainly of waves that fall into the *invisible* spectrum, waves we cannot see without specialized instrumentation," he told stupid me, "and even then, we can't actually *see* them, we only record them and harness their capabilities for our own uses. But it's interesting, isn't it? The idea that there are vast worlds we cannot see with the naked eye."

He was boring me. "Okay, got it, now tell me about freezing light and witch books."

Curlix looked around as if he had x-ray vision and could see through the uniforms of the waitresses, mostly college girls.

There was a tic in the corner of his lips and his hands trembled slightly. He looked...well, he looked frightened.

"Are you okay, Doc?"

"No," he said, but would not elaborate.

He paused, lit a cigarette and flicked his ash dead-on in the ashtray. Real good for a blind man. He sat there, smoking, his fingers shaking. I moved the ashtray and he found it on his next flick of ash without hesitation. Pretty good, that.

"Now, as I said, we were doing experiments in freezing light, freezing the waves they are composed of. We were following certain paths set at Stanford in electromagnetically-induced transparency. How this works is fairly simple: A laser beam with a carefully designated frequency shines on a cloud of atoms and changes it from being opaque as a bank of fog to a field clear as glass for a second laser beam to pass through."

This is how they went about freezing light waves, he said. Basically, they would chill sodium atoms with a combination of lasers, magnetic fields, and radio waves. The lasers cool the atoms into sort of a cloud of optical jelly, then the lasers are turned off and the electromagnets turned on and their combined fields hold the cloud of atoms in stasis. When the cloud is cooled to 500 billionths of a degree, it forms a Bose-Einstein condensate, an ultra-cold atom cloud suspended in a vacuum and, ultimately, the coldest place in the universe.

"There are all kind of applications for this research," Curlix said excitedly. "Quantum computers and nonlinear optics...but what we were interested in were condensates produced in a vortex state. When the super-cold gas rotates—like water going down a drain—a pulse of slowed light finds itself dragged along with the gas...bent, subverted, turned inside out. This is very similar to the phenomena expected to occur near black holes. And it was during this line of investigation that we first saw what we called Green Matter, a sort of superfluid field created by the bending and slowing of light in a vortex. Green Matter is essentially an unknown frequency in the electromagnetic spectrum between ultraviolet and x-rays, a lens of sort into the invisible spectrum."

"Meaning?"

He looked at me with those dark, shining glasses of his. "Meaning, with the aid of Green Matter, we were able to look into the invisible spectrum with the naked eye. Look into and *beyond* it. Like using an electron microscope of sorts, we made the unseen and unseeable reflect light so that we *could* see it. In essence, Kramer, we had poked a hole between this dimension and the next."

Suddenly, I was interested. "Another dimension? That's incredible…what, what did you see?"

"We saw only vague, obscure forms at first…fluxes and pulses, shimmering mists and elongated fields of rarified gas. Nothing solid, nothing truly tangible…like looking through a dirty window, I guess. Just bizarre energy patterns and drifting bits of dark matter that reminded me of dust motes. The lab was pitch black—had to be for our experiments—and we were looking at something nobody would really believe later on. We had accidentally hit upon a random series of variables. Had we been off slightly in either direction, we would have seen nothing."

He said it was like a religious experience, like seeing Moses coming down from the mountain or Jesus walking on water. They stood there in that darkened lab at Brown, awed and slack-jawed, beyond themselves. All knowing and knowing full well, that even with the most sophisticated computerized controls, that it could take a lifetime to artificially bring about what they had struck upon by pure chance.

My throat felt dry. It wasn't much in the telling, but you could see by how Curlix told it that it was big. Like splitting the atom. It was something that could have transformed physical science as we understood it.

"Yes," he said. "That vortex had given us the key. Light had been subverted, matter disrupted, time turned on its ear…our instruments told us that much. We had created a visual wormhole between this dimension and whatever lies beyond. And in our vortex the space between our plane and the other was incalculable—our computers couldn't even speculate beyond saying infinity squared—yet, *yet*, Kramer, it was close enough to touch. The barrier had been broken."

"What happened then?"

Curlix sighed. He did not look excited all of a sudden. In fact, he looked tense and worried. "Then there was an accident..."

While that vortex field was held in stasis, something happened. Maybe it was an accident or maybe somebody at the optics table got a bright idea. The entire thing was still under investigation. The best that they could ascertain was that the vortex was hit by gamma rays. And then the shit hit the fan.

Curlix grabbed my wrist, squeezed it as he told me. "There was an explosion...no, not some huge theatrical conflagration here, but something a bit more subtle. Gamma rays...we're still guessing it was gamma rays...flooded our cloud chamber and somehow, the vortex dragged them in, funneled them to a place where gamma rays do not exist naturally. The result was like matter and antimatter coming into contact." He was breathing hard now, all that polish wiped right off. "A rending explosion...a brilliant flash of light. Even with our protective goggles, it blinded us all. I've never seen light like that in all my days...a primal and chaotic pulse of illumination that flickered but an instant and in colors I could not identify. But I recall thinking as it burned through my vision that it was the light of creation, the ancient spark of primary cosmic generation. Cold fusion maybe. The very thing stars are born of. The hand of the Almighty..."

Curlix was breathless, panting. I had to order a carafe of wine because the waitresses were looking at us funny and maybe wondering when we were going to vacate the table. But nothing could have gotten me away by then. I had to know, I just had to know. Because I knew there was more.

And I was right.

He said, "That blinding flash only robbed us of our eyesight for maybe ten seconds, if that long. Had we not been wearing goggles, we would have been permanently blinded. But it didn't end there, you see. For as my eyesight returned, something was coming out of the vortex and it hit me dead on...me and Paul Shepard, another physicist." Curlix licked his lips, lit another cigarette. "Well, how can I explain it? I was struck by a shimmering pulse of freezing blue light that numbed me to my bones. It was light and yet *not* light in the ordinary sense, but more like a spill of agitated particles. It had form and substance and solidity, yet it was no more substantial, I felt, than a cloud of helium or methane. I could feel it *crawling* all over me like ants, billions of ants inside and outside of me and it felt like my eyes were being ripped out of my head. It trapped me and held me and then it died out and I went out cold."

I had to ask him something. I tried to phrase it delicately. "That blue light, that blue stuff...was it what blinded you? Really blinded you?"

He nodded. "Yes and no. Maybe I was blinded and maybe my eyes were truly opened."

I let that go. "How long did it last?"

He laughed with a cool, emotionless tittering. "It seemed to me, as I was trapped in that cloud, that flux of energy, that it went on for at least five or ten minutes, maybe longer. I was literally paralyzed. I could not move or breathe. It was like being in suspended animation...drowning in a viscous, buzzing sea. But the others there that did not get hit by the light, they said it lasted maybe two or three seconds. The gamma rays hit the vortex, there was that flash, the integrity of the vacuum was compromised, and then the blue light hit Paul, then me. It happened very quickly."

"And that other guy? Shepard?"

"Dead," Curlix said grimly. "He was standing in front of me. The blue light hit him first, then me. He took the brunt of whatever it was. The others said it knocked him through the air and right past me. That he became *transparent*, that they could see his bones and insides as if he'd been x-rayed from within. He flew through the air, flickering with that awful phosphorescence, they said, and *passed* through a table, Kramer. Not fell into it or broke it, *he passed through it like it was made of fog.* A solid oak table. They found him lying under it, dead." Curlix was having trouble with this. His mouth was trembling. "An autopsy revealed that Paul's entire anatomy had been *reversed* and that he had *two* left hands, not a right one to speak of. They listed his death as radiation exposure, left it at that."

Curlix said for one moment there, as both Shepard and he were trapped in that field of extradimensional ether, it had changed the both of them. It had rendered Shepard's atomic structure diaphanous, allowed him to pass momentarily through solid objects.

"What did it do to you?" I asked.

"It blinded me."

He gave me another lecture. He told me we can see colors and the like because our eyes have light and color photosensitive receptors, rods and cones, tiny cells lining the back of the retina.

"I don't have them anymore," he told me. "I have something else now."

He was completely blind for nearly two months. Brown brought in the very best ophthalmologists when they realized what they were dealing with, the change Curlix was undergoing.

"My rods and cones began to mutate almost immediately, they became alien things roughly shaped like spindles and nerve ganglia," he told me. "The specialists they brought in, they did everything they could. They even tried preventive surgeries—laser and cryo—but it did no good. Like a tumor, once they toyed with my new receptors, the faster they grew."

"What did you do?"

"I took a leave of absence, I had to get away, away from those doctors. I knew what they wanted, they wanted me on a slab so they could put my new cells under a microscope. In their shoes, I'd have wanted the same." He drank some wine, winced, decided a cigarette would be better. "Yes, I had to get away before they found out. Before they found out I could see again, because what I was seeing…dear God in Heaven."

"What *were* you seeing?" I didn't smoke, but I could've handled a few drags right about then. Instead, I gulped wine.

Those sunglasses fixed me again and I knew Curlix could see me, but I wondered if it was just me he was seeing. "I saw the city," he said.

"What city?" I was almost afraid to ask.

Smoke drifted from Curlix's nostrils. "The same city, I believe, that the mad Arab Abdul Alhazred wrote of in the *Necronomicon*."

I had never heard of the man or the book, so Curlix filled me in. Alhazred was something of a mystic and wizard, some said, and was known as the mad poet of Damascus. The *Necronomicon* or *Book of Dead Names, Al Azif,* was a notorious and blasphemous book. One of those volumes banned by Rome, put to the flame during the witch persecutions. It was a "hell-book" or "witch book," filled with formulae and rites to call down demons from beyond the stars. It also recorded Alhazred's investigations into certain dark and nameless subjects, his collected knowledge concerning cults dating back to antiquity who supposedly worshipped entities and beings from outside this world and their attempts to invoke them. Of interesting note, Alhazred died in 738 AD, supposedly devoured by an invisible monster in a Damascus marketplace.

Curlix said there was a fifteenth-century Latin translation of the *Necronomicon* in the British Museum, as well as seventeenth-century editions at the Widener Library and Miskatonic University in Arkham...not that the latter surprised me. That old pest-hole with its witch-legends and pagan superstitions had been the source of more than one story for the *Examiner...* location changed, of course.

Curlix had a friend who was in charge of the Special Collections at Miskatonic (the stuff they don't let the public see), a guy who he'd gone to school with. This scholar—name deleted—had confessed to Curlix once of the awful secrets he had culled from that book. When Curlix first saw this city of his, he remembered his friend telling him of Alhazred's pilgrimages to certain shunned and shadow-haunted ruins in the desert. During one of his sabbaticals, Alhazred had taken some sort of drug and dreamed in detail of a city in another dimension. Curlix contacted his friend and was able to glimpse a copy of the 1228 Olaus Wormius translation of the dreaded book. This not from Miskatonic, but from the library of an elderly, reclusive folklorist in Providence who claimed to be in possession of many such books...as well as the unpublished stories and letters from a certain Providence author and antiquarian who had died under suspicious circumstances in 1938—though the official version gave quite a different story.

Curlix sat there, looking, it seemed, over my left shoulder. Something about that was making my skin crawl. "That city...

that unnamable, deserted city," he said, his voice wavering. "How I wish I had died like Shepard. How much easier things would have been. I didn't even know *what* I was seeing at first. Up until then, I saw nothing but greenish, darting blotches and sparkling vistas...then I saw the city. It was late and I was tired. I shut my eyes for just a moment. When I opened them, instead of my darkened bedroom wall, I was looking at the submerged landscape of an ocean or sea that was obviously neither. It was not water, but something gelatinous and rippling, an endless plasma sea, I thought. It was blurry at first, but soon enough I saw it in more detail...as much detail as you could make out in that opaque, runny emulsion. Yes, soon enough, I saw the city."

I had to prod him to go on. I wish to God I'd left it alone. I wish I'd just called him a liar and walked away. But I didn't.

Curlix said, "At first I thought I was seeing the bones of some immense saurians half-buried in the slime and bubbling mud, but it was a city...the ruins of some impossible cyclopean city. I saw skeletal rungs and gleaming white knobs, cages of yellowed uprights and pitted cylinders, hollow-socketed domes like skulls and great rising arches I took at first to be the vertebrae of sea monsters. Not so, not so. Yes, it was dead, that city, covered in clustered things like barnacles and knotted sea grasses that flowed like kelp in deep-sea currents. Most of the city had fallen, it seemed. I saw the shattered remains of walls and honeycombed towers, plates and disks, pyramidal shapes and cylindrical shafts...all gone to ruin, encrusted in webs of marine life. And everywhere—as my eyesight seemed to pull back and pan—I could see the litter and debris of that necropolis, mostly just irregular shapes blanketed in moss and creeping ooze. I knew what I was seeing was incredibly ancient, just as I knew it was not on earth or sunken beneath earth's oceans."

I sat there, breathing a little hard myself by that point. My palms were damp and I was having trouble wetting my lips. "Are you sure...sure you just didn't hallucinate it or dream it?"

He didn't seem offended by that. "No, it was there all right and though I had no point of reference, my instinct was telling me it was gigantic. A megalopolis that stretched across those bleak, fungoid sea beds for miles and miles. I could see parts of it climbing up a mountain in the distance, stretching down into valleys. A city like that...incredible, so very ancient and instead of being overwhelmed with scientific curiosity, I was simply *appalled*."

"Appalled?" I said. "Why? Why would you be appalled?"

His fingers were interlaced on the table and the knuckles were white and straining as if the bones beneath were about to pop from sheer stress. "I was more than appalled. Horrified, sickened, disgusted even. On some primary level...I was offended by it all. Yes, it had been dead maybe millions of years, of unwholesome antiquity to be sure, yet it was wicked and depraved, a tumorous growth on that sea bed. An evil, enshrouded nightmare that made me want to slit my wrists. The geometry of the place was positively perverted, the angles all wrong, completely impossible, frightening...it could not exist, yet it did. It reminded me of a heap of broken, moldering bones in the lair of some flesh-eating ogre. And that touched something in me, made me want to smash it, stomp it. Made something in me recoil and hate, simply hate. Whatever had built something like that, had brains sufficiently demented to erect a graveyard like that, they were obscenities, things so utterly loathsome I was picturing them as malefic, bloated spiders that filled their webs with the leeched carcasses of infants."

"Take it easy, Doc," I said, almost believing it myself now. "It can't touch you, it can't get at you—"

He laughed at me. A cold and bitter laughter that was deranged and shrill. "It scared me to death, Kramer. I was shaking just looking at it. Like some sprawling, surreal haunted house sunken in that mire. Globs of silt were drifting around it and from it as if it were decomposing like a waterlogged corpse. All those high, distorted buildings, leaning and falling and refusing to fall, trapped in some bastard form of gravity we can only guess at. It was a cemetery, a malignant alien cemetery and those structures were crypts and tombstones and narrow monuments, barrows and cairns and skeletal, haunted monoliths staring out like stripped skulls...and everywhere, odd, angular shadows and darting, contorted forms reaching out..."

I poured him a glass of wine. He was getting to me now, too.

The chills were going right up my spine and I had to actually tell myself the man was crazy, that none of it could possibly be. But I just couldn't make myself believe that. Something in me had shrunk down, was cowering like a kid beneath the covers of his bed, certain something macabre and monstrously malevolent was even then slinking out of the closet, claws held high.

And that was pretty apt, you'll see.

Curlix drank, using both hands to steady the glass. I asked him what else he'd seen, more for my nerves than his. The image of the drowned burial ground was burned inside my brain, festering. I needed diversion.

"Well, there were certainly wonders," he told me, seeming to relax incrementally. "For that primordial soup was alive with an amazing proliferation of life. Things that reminded me of bathypelagic horrors. I saw creatures like huge, ghastly white tube worms with sucking mouths at both ends. Some were smooth, others segmented. They inched along like caterpillars in that living jelly. There were plated things like albino crabs picking through the organic slime. Swimming, suctioning bladders fitted with yellow eyes. Growths of huge, tentacular anemones grabbing at anything that swam too near. Protoplasmic bubbles that absorbed tiny translucent creatures. When they were attacked by something else, they exploded into clouds of hundreds of individual bubbles. There were fish—I don't know what else to call them. Armored, swimming mouths with snaking tails. Serpentine eel-like things with gigantic, gaping jaws that snapped at all and everything. Multi-headed, shrimp-like crustaceans you could see through. Weird, oar-shaped fish whose skeletons were luminous and shined through their leathery skins. I saw huge things like black umbrellas with circles of brilliant red eyes at their apexes. They would propel themselves around, then open up and ingest some unwary swimmer, then sink into the mud with their prey. There were other fish-like creatures with pink thrashing filaments in place of their heads.

"Too much to recall, Kramer. But I do remember the spider. It was colossal, I knew that much. I saw it go walking through that organic stew, spiny and albino, more like the exoskeleton of a dead spider than a living one, something you see dried up in a web. A living exoskeleton. Just the sight of that freakish horror made me cringe. But it was fascinating stuff, seeing things any biologist would have cut off their left hand to view just once. If it hadn't been for the city—"

I was really hoping we were done with that boneyard, but we were far from done. Because there were things bottled up inside Curlix. Like pissed-off bees in a jar, they wanted out...so Curlix unscrewed the lid.

"I was watching them, Kramer, those creatures...but they were no more aware of me, really, than microbes are aware that a gigantic eye studies them through a microscope," he explained and that was somewhat comforting. "But, on the other hand, thinking of that place as being vast, unreachable distances from us is both true and false. For it is very close, in a different space, but right around us all the time, separated by a thin, ethereal veil. To explain myself let me fall back on the old physics crutch. Two dots on opposite ends of the paper. Very far apart, but if you fold the paper you can make them touch each other, right? Things like wormholes and the like can be explained only by the wildest, most theoretical branches of Einsteinian physics, yet such things are mathematically possible. Much more possible than anyone has ever guessed and I should know, because I can see into that alien space as easily as I can see you. No, those things cannot see us, yet they can sense our movements when the conditions are right. Haven't you yourself seen things move out of the corners of your eyes? Things that are not there? I know what it is we see when we catch glimpses like that...it must be some peculiar condition of peripheral vision."

I swallowed, tried to, anyway. "Are you seeing them now?"

"Yes. They're swimming all about us. That waitress near the bar, an immense jellyfish just passed through her...see her shake herself with a chill? Yes, a jellyfish whose bell is prismatic like gasoline in a puddle. But it can't see her. Only the wraiths can do that."

"*Wraiths?*" I said. I'd had enough. I wanted to leave. There was plenty stewing in my brain now to give me years' worth of nightmares, I didn't need to hear about these *wraiths*. But hear I did.

When Curlix started talking, it was hard for him. Sweat started trickling down his temples and his face was mottled, corded like maybe he was about to have a nasty coronary. "The wraiths. That night...I sensed movement in the ruined city. I focused past the swimming creatures and my vision panned in, showing me what I wish I had never seen. They were slithering out of the holes and hollows and low places of that alien graveyard, things that looked at first like drifting rags. But as they got closer, I saw they were more like gaseous fluxes of tissue that were eroding and rotting, ropes and streamers floating around them. They had faces of a sort—white, bloodless faces like narrow, exaggerated skulls, but not made of bone or papery flesh, but of thousands and thousands of tiny hairs or filaments braided into the shape of an alien skull and something like streaming orange kelp for hair. Their eyes were huge black holes, their nares upturned, their jaws not lined with teeth as such, but triangular protrusions that were jagged and sharp-looking." Curlix was leaning forward now and his voice went high and desperate, almost child-like. "No, Kramer, those others things—just dumb animals—they couldn't see me, but the wraiths? Yes, they saw me watching them. They *sensed* me or smelled me and that's what made them come up out of their holes and tombs. They saw me and followed me, felt my eyes on them and came out after me. I...I pulled back, but they kept coming, closer and closer, only stopping when they hit that veil that separates us and then they stuck there like snails on aquarium glass, searching, Kramer, searching for a way through. I...I saw them up close, pulsing and inflating, ribbons of their decayed bodies floating about in writhing clouds of tissue and those eyes, oh dear God, those eyes..."

"Doc, listen you don't have to—"

He cut me off: "Abdul Alhazred spoke of them in the *Necronomicon*. He said they walk 'not in the spaces we know, but *between* them, they walk serene and primal, undimensioned and to us unseen.' Do you see what he was getting at, Kramer?"

"That's enough," I told him. "You can't expect me to believe this kind of nonsense."

"Shut up," he snapped, as near a nervous breakdown as any

man I'd ever seen. "The city was their city, Kramer. A dead city and they were its *ghosts.* Ghosts, elementals, revenants of what had once lived in that degenerate place. For in that diabolic dimension, ghosts are not like they are here…they aren't wisps of smoke or cold drafts, but tangible, palpable entities. Ravenous, hideous things. And unlike the denizens of that plasma sea, Kramer, they alone are intelligent, they alone felt me watching them, and they alone…being neither entirely phantasmal nor corporeal…can stride between their world and ours. Don't you see what I'm saying…*they've found a way through!* Things more obscene and destructive than anything you can imagine—"

"Stop it!" I said. People were staring at us, but I didn't give a good goddamn. I'd heard enough. Something had snapped in my brain and I could not bear to hear any more of that man's polluted, infectious thinking. It was making something in me go white and brittle. "I don't want any more of this, do you hear?"

But he didn't hear. "They watch me now, Kramer. They've breached the threshold. At first, I only caught frozen images of them on window panes or saw ghostly, misty reflections in mirrors…but now they move about in *our* space, hunting me, searching for me and, dear Christ, maybe for you, too, now that you know."

But that was it. I shut out the rest of what he said for the sake of my own sanity. But I wish to God I'd listened, because I think old mad Curlix was trying to warn me, trying to help me, but I was terrified and I couldn't handle any more of it. Maybe it was my imagination, but there was a coldness at our table, a frigid blowing coldness like air from a meat locker and I was scared, really scared.

No, I did not listen to him rambling and shrieking about the wraiths and Azathoth at the center of cosmic, nuclear chaos. I couldn't. I just couldn't listen. But Curlix was intent on making me a believer, maybe before it was too late for him, me, and the world at large.

So, he took off his glasses.

About that time, one of the waitresses picked the worse possible moment to throw us out of there. She saw what I saw. She saw Curlix without his glasses on and screamed. For his eyes were green and crystalline like emeralds, winking and shining and flickering with spectral light.

I ran off then.

I had trouble sleeping after that. I was always seeing things out of the corners of my eyes, creeping things, amorphous bodies slinking between this reality and the next. Only with drugs and whiskey could I close my eyes and when I did, I saw them, those hideous skullish faces and leering black sockets watching me, studying me with morbid sentience.

One note on Howard Curlix.

I never saw him again. Two weeks after our meeting, he jumped from the fifth story of his flat on Benefit Street. That's the official version. But I found out something a little more unusual from one of my police contacts. He told me that the coroner said that it looked like Curlix was turned inside out and *thrown* from his window. And that the poor man's eyes were ripped from his skull by the stalks…along with his brain. In his apartment, they found something decomposing on the floor in a pool of putrescent jelly. It looked like a gigantic eel with bunches of quivering yellow feelers and a huge, gaping bony mouth that could have bitten a man clean in half. My cop friend said it stunk like a truckload of rotting fish with a strange, after-odor of raw ammonia.

Thirty minutes after the police got there, the eel-thing had dissolved into a puddle. The cops never even got a photo of it, just a large, sticky stain on the carpeting.

I guess we can surmise that something innocently swam through the hole the wraiths had sheared into the veil.

So ends Howard Curlix.

But what of me? Despite trying to block out what Curlix said right before we got thrown out of the pizzeria, my mind recorded his words. *Kramer, don't you see what's happened? I am their portal, their beacon, the unwinking, gleaming lighthouse eye they follow from their world to our own. They have marked me and…oh, Jesus, Kramer…they're coming, I can feel them! Run! For the love of Christ, run before they get your scent…*

But it's too late for that.

They know about me, just as I know about them. I've seen them looking through my windows at night and heard them scratching at my door. They got my dog…I found him frozen stiff as if he'd been drawn through glacial, unknown heights. My neighbors are complaining about the nauseous stenches surrounding my house, the weird drifting patches of mist, the freak electrical activity dancing over my roof. Flashing, arcing electrical activity with shape, intent, and wrath. People are scared to be around me because I am never truly alone. There are tangles of shadows in my wake, the sound of chattering teeth, a weird stink of eldritch decay. The wraiths have encircled me now, but like true sadists, they'll take their time as they did with Curlix for it's much more amusing to them to frighten me to death.

I had a dream last night that was not a dream, but a vision, a glimpse of some hellish, pestiferous dimension beyond time and space. I saw the city. I saw the wraiths. I saw them dragging Curlix down into their yawning holes beneath those alien tombs.

Physically, Curlix is dead. But what of his soul, his essence? What twisted, lunatic games do they play with it?

They won't get me. I have a gun and I'm going to use it. On myself. Maybe I'm the beacon now, as Curlix was. Maybe they'll lose their footing here when I kill myself. I only know one thing: I will not let them have me. I will not let them drag who and what I am down into noisome, tenebrous gulfs of insanity. They will not pull me screaming into some black, nebulous dimension of the unspeakable, the undead, and the unseen.

THE CHATTERING OF TINY TEETH

(Warfear, 2002)

"...there were worse things than rats and maggots
crawling in the unhallowed earth..."
—Henry Kuttner

1

It was a bad place and fear was something you choked down
with your daily rum ration. You lived with corpses and rats and
severed limbs, the shattered anatomies of your fellow soldiers.
There was always blood in your mouth and steel in your belly.
And, of course, there were always plenty of stories. Tales about
things that prowled No-Man's Land. Nightmare shapes that
hunted battlefields from time immemorial. Things that dragged
off cadavers and not all of them walked on four feet. But they
were just stories and you tried not to listen.

2

When Corporal Stubbs saw old Brass Balls making his way
through the hip-deep slime of muck and water that passed for
the forward trench—or at least their minute corner of it—he
knew there was going to be trouble.

"Here comes the frigging shit himself," he muttered to Piggy, who was licking the grease from a dented tin of sausages.

Piggy tossed the tin into the water, licked his lips and put a cigarette between them. "Lovely man, that one. Reminds me of me dear old dad," he said, blowing smoke through the slats of yellow-brown teeth. "If I but had the strength, I'd kiss him right on the arse."

Stubbs took the cigarette and pulled hard off it, spitting tobacco. "Glad you could join us, Sergeant-Major Bowes. Pull up a seat, why don't you? Would you like a cup of tea? Biscuits with jam? Do speak up, man."

Bowes was not amused. He stood there, the great flat spades of his hands on those broad child-rearing hips. Rain dripped from the lip of his steel helmet. "Lollygagging and running your mouth won't win us this war, Stubbs. The quicker we pull together and set things right, the quicker you'll be home to your whore of a mother and your nightly bottle of gin."

"Did you hear that, Piggy? He called me mum a whore of all things." Stubbs shrugged and flicked his ash, leaned against the parapet. "Guess he knows the old bitch, all right. God bless you, sir."

Piggy uttered a short laugh.

"Shut your pisshole, Stubbs. You, too, Pigget," Bowes said. He cleared his throat. The anger ran from his face then, like hot wax down the stem of a candle. A corrupt grin slit his features. "You lads look like you need a change of scenery. Right. I've just the thing for you." He cleared his throat again. "As you well know, things haven't been going well—"

"Haven't they, Sarge? Didn't notice meself," Piggy said.

Stubbs shook his head and sucked in a deep lungful of air that was rich with the stench of putrescence. "Can't believe you said that, sir. Why, take a look around. If this ain't Heaven, me boy, then just point the way."

Despite himself, old Brass Balls did look around.

And what he saw was Flanders. And more precisely, the famous sea of Flanders' mud. It was a colossal bowl of viscous sludge that stank and ran and fouled everything it touched. The rain kept coming down in blinding sheets and the trenches were filled with stagnant water that was flavored with blood, urine, and feces. Bodies floated in it. Parts of bodies. Countless rats that had tried in vain to reach the bodies and had drowned. And the rain kept coming and the mud kept flowing and the men kept dying. It was a gray world, gray and wet and stinking.

And that's what the sergeant major saw.

Had he any humanity left after three years of the Great War, he would've wretched and then quietly lost his mind.

But he was right about one thing: things hadn't been going real well. Nearly a week before, some nit back at battalion got a real prince of an idea for an offensive. Troops were mustered and ammunition passed out. It began with a thirty-six-hour artillery barrage of the German lines. Battalion figured that would soften the Hun up nicely. The smoke had barely cleared when some five thousand men of the British Expeditionary Force went up and over the wire and charged through No-Man's Land, hell-for-leather. Or maybe not so hell-for-leather, being that the terrain was riddled with chains of shell holes and great valleys from collapsing tunnel networks, all of which were separate bogs of mud. It looked like the dark side of the moon. The water was so deep in those polluted, filth-scummed pools that a man could drown in them carrying full fighting kit. They threw ladders and duckboards over them and if nothing else, those mires became good places to die.

As it turned out, the Germans hadn't been softened at all.

The majority of the shelling had been concentrated on what was thought to be the German forward trench system, but was in actuality a series of dummy trenches dug by the Germans in hope they'd have the very effect they indeed had.

Ultimately, when the infantry reached the high ground that bordered the German lines, hell conveniently broke lose. Hun flares filled the skies. Shells came screaming in. Bullets whipping. Machine guns clattering. All in all, the Brits lost over 2300 men in a few hours of fighting.

Minor, of course, in comparison with what had happened at the Somme the year before. But costly all the same.

The Germans hammered the BEF all the way across No-Man's Land, forcing the survivors—most of them weighted down with the wounded and dead—to retreat through a vicious artillery barrage. Those boggy crater holes sucked down most of the bodies and as for the rest, who could say? It wasn't even remotely realistic to send out stretcher-bearers into that hell-zone. For the next eight, ten hours all that could be heard were the screams and moans of the dying and dismembered as they succumbed to ghastly, agonizing deaths. Which came not only in the form of their wounds, but from the armies of rats that prowled No-Man's Land.

And it was only the night before that the Germans had ceased their bombardment.

Stubbs and Piggy were two of the survivors.

And now they sat in the muck smoking and listening to the rain fall around them and rattle against the wire up yonder, thud against the sandbags, run in rivers down into the trenches.

"So what sort of job have you for us, Sergeant Major?" Piggy asked.

Sergeant Major Bowes grinned like a cat with a mouse in its belly.

3

Vermin.

A constant of any war.

Anywhere there was garbage and human waste and bodies heaped like cordwood there would be vermin. Flanders was no different. Vermin came in the form of wild dog packs that prowled No-Man's Land and dragged off bodies or parts of them. They came in the form of rats that devoured the dead and dying (they rarely went after healthy adults, but there were occasions). Rat bites were common as dysentery. And then there were the lice. Entire companies were crawling with them. The soldiers would spend hours killing them, crushing them between thumb and forefinger. But the next day a new batch would replace them.

"Aye," Piggy said as they crawled on their bellies through the mud and debris, "I had the nits so bad one time, I tossed me shirt to the floor and watched it try to crawl away."

Stubbs knew it wasn't exaggeration; he'd seen it himself and more than once.

There were three others with them—Privates Benner, Sourton, and Pence—all green as summer grass to a man. Stubbs could hear them back there, trembling like saplings in a high wind. One of them was whimpering. No matter. Soon enough he'd have his heart ripped out and tears would be beyond him.

Piggy froze up and lay stock-still like a mannequin waiting to be dressed. He gave the others a hand signal to stay put. It was maybe thirty minutes until sunset, but it didn't matter with the drizzling rain and heavy ground fog. Dark and dreary is what it was.

Stubbs studied the terrain ahead and it was merely more of the same. Blasted, blackened, gray with spreading pools of muck and standing water. The ground was so saturated, absorption was out of the question. There were shell craters, big and small. Most filled with water and many large enough to hide more than one man. Rats skittered through ditches and paused atop blighted stumps. This place had once been a forest, but was now denuded of both leaf and branch. The trees themselves rose like burned masts from the sodden ground, many split in two and scorched by fire.

"Onward and upward," Piggy said and they began snaking their way forward again.

There were abandoned trenches full of heaped bodies. Collapsed tunnels and huge pits. Somewhere in the distance a dog howled. Piggy and the others could hear the Hun out there, joking in German, out on patrol or formed into burial parties attempting to steal some food from the rats and dogs. There were bootless feet jutting up from the mud, some stripped right down to the bone. Dozens upon dozens of bodies cast about in every possible stage of decomposition. Stubbs saw a skull leering from the top of a leaning tree and three Hun skeletons in dingy gray rags peering over the lip of a bomb crater.

"What's this then?" Piggy whispered to them.

There was a shallow depression in the swampy ground and, in it, the form of a man face-down in the mud. He wore the long tunic of an officer and a Sam Browne belt that was riddled with tiny puncture marks made by rat's teeth. He was bloated and noisome, but the real crazy thing was that his body was *moving*. In slow, boneless undulations it squirmed and shuddered. Piggy flipped him over and he had been eaten down to the bone, his eye sockets thick with feasting maggots and his body cavity housing five or six hungry, busy rats. Piggy shook his head at the sight and shoved the officer away, a great flap of flesh falling over the horror in the hollowed belly.

One of the new soldiers started vomiting.

"Do as you will," Stubbs told him, "but be quiet about it."

Just as the sun—what there was of it—faded behind the horizon, they found the set of abandoned trenches where they were to set up the listening post. Piggy directed the newbies in first. They slid into the water with silent cries. Dead Hun floated in the murk. It took some time to clear them out—they were so waterlogged and rotten they came apart like boiled chicken—and drag them off. But the stench remained. Stubbs had the newbies use their entrenching tools to help drain the place out, but after two, then three spongy putrescent corpses were unearthed, he gave up on the idea. Flanders was one huge and muddy burial ground. And the earth could only swallow so many bodies before spitting a few back up.

With the mist blowing down from the black hills to the east, it was hard to know where they were exactly. All Piggy could tell them for sure was that the Germans were just ahead and their own lines a few miles back.

It was a dark and shadowy spot brooded over by the skeletal remains of trees and singed rows of hedges that rode the squat and rolling hills. Like being trapped in a dead forest. The terrain was all craters and dips as before. The mud was heavier. There were bodies everywhere. Parts of them scattered in every conceivable direction and very often caught in the trees overhead. That and the wreckage of splintered coffins, headstones turned to rubble. Stubbs figured it was an actual graveyard they were in here, and an artillery barrage had blasted it flat and exhumed the dead in one form or another. The air stank of putrid decay. The mists smelled rank and evil. There was the husk of a church in the grainy distance, much of it reduced to crumbling masonry from the impact of shells.

Leave it to the Hun to dig trenches here.

"A churchyard," Stubbs said. "By all the saints."

He'd seen a lot in that war. He'd waded through corpses and death and disease on a daily basis, but, despite himself, something about this place made him uneasy. And it had nothing to do with the nearby Germans and even less to do with the obliterated dead. This place simply had a peculiar *feel* to it. The shadows seemed to creep, to prowl out of the corner of your eye...but when you looked, nothing.

Fucking Brass Balls, Stubbs thought. *A listening post out here. Damn.*

Piggy found a skull peering at him from the trench wall and dug it out. It was pitted with teeth marks. Large ones. No rat or dog ever born had dentition like that. It sent a chill worming through him.

He gave Stubbs a concerned look and then smiled at the dirt-spattered faces of the privates. "Well, if it ain't me old Uncle Dick. And thin as a rail he is," he joked, but his voice was low and cautious. "Don't worry, Unc, you and me will have ourselves a bite come first light. See if we don't."

The privates, all sadly numb now to war's atrocities and litter, giggled in the darkness.

But Piggy did not smile.

Like Stubbs, he studied the landscape with a wary eye. Knowing with complete certainty deep in the opaque depths of his soul that they were being watched, being studied. That something out there amongst the mud and bones and rubble was waiting for them. And it wasn't the Hun.

They were on higher ground here and the water was only two, three feet deep. Stubbs could see that the maze of waterlogged trenches fed into a huge and gaping pit just off a way. Probably the remains of a shelled bunker and its assorted tunnels.

Christ, tunneling through a boneyard of all things.

He wanted a cigarette, but there was no smoking out here. In the darkness, you could see the glow of a cigarette for a long way. Easy for a sniper to draw a bead on you. So, Stubbs waited in the heavy, rolling dusk and listened to the distant thunder of shelling, saw the yellow flashes of flares and the red glow of exploding rounds. Somebody was getting pounded good and part of him almost wished he was there rather than out here. At least an artillery barrage was a known quantity. You knew what you were afraid of…but out here in this Stygian, appalling netherworld you just couldn't put a finger on what scared you. What filled your belly with crawling worms and made your skin pebble with gooseflesh.

He waited.

He could hear the others breathing. He could hear skittering noises out in the gutted remains of the churchyard. He knew they were rats. Armies of bloated, gray-streaked rats big as cats. Their eyes shined like steel in the murk. You could hear them out there, chewing and rending and digging up half-buried things. The tear of flesh, the crunch of bone.

He figured it was rats, all right…at least most of it.

On around three as he drifted aimlessly at the edge of sleep knowing he had to stay awake, the drizzle stopped and the clouds parted like foam in the sky. A ragged crescent of moon washed down the pitted landscape in an eerie, ethereal glow. He could see the rats now, scattering at the intrusion of light. Blankets of mist clung to the earth, moving like wisps of smoke. He was studying the shadow-riven forest of stripped trees. He was tired, his eyes would barely stay open, but he was certain he could see shapes moving out there.

And that's when he heard the sound.

Out in that rat-infested blackness, the sound of teeth chattering. It rose up and died away. Something in his chest dropped. His breath was locked down in his lungs.

"You hear—" he stared to say, but Piggy's hand on his arm quieted him.

Through a burnt and ruined expanse of hedges he saw graves. Not old ones, but recent. Eight or ten graves in a row with mounds of earth piled atop them into which crude crosses were sunk. They were Hun graves, he figured. And as he watched, the crosses began to tremble and jerk, finally falling over as if what lay beneath was trying to claw its way out.

But that wasn't it at all.

Stubbs caught an odor. It wasn't the stink of decomposition or violated graves: he was used to that. This was different, a black and filthy smell, flyblown, yes, but sharp and acrid. Piggy's hand gripped his arm tightly. Over at the graves they could see small, slinking forms. Hunched over and lithe, they pawed at the mounds of dirt.

His throat full of dust, something tight squeezing in his chest, Stubbs brought up his Enfield rifle, sighted in on whatever it was he was seeing. Human-like forms. But small and vicious like rabid animals, shapes snipped from black cloth. They frantically dug at the graves, five or six of them, snorting and grunting and chattering their teeth and it was an awful sound. A sound to make your soul wither on the vine.

He had all he could do not to shoot.

"Don't, mate," Piggy said into his ear. "For the love of Mary and Jesus, don't draw attention to us."

And it seemed one of them heard, for it stood up and peered in their direction. It looked like a child…or something pretending to be one. A child with a mane of long, matted hair. The moon glowered down on its face and its skin was yellow as leprosy and corrugated, the eyes red and wet like fresh blood. Stubbs felt his insides melt. For it looked right at them and its mouth opened and closed rapidly, those horrible teeth chattering madly.

Stubbs didn't move for two, three minutes and neither did Piggy. The thing turned away and helped its kin exhume the Germans. In another five minutes, they had pulled two bodies from the rank earth. There was a thunder of small feet as they dragged the bodies off into the shadows.

It was some time before Stubbs allowed himself to breathe. His knuckles were white as he gripped the Enfield. "Good Christ…Piggy…what…what…"

"Don't know…those stories you hear about—"

There was a splashing sound just down the trench line where it widened into the water-filled gully. Privates Benning, Sourton, and Pence, who were farther down and closer to it, came awake with a start. Piggy had let them sleep, knowing they needed it. But now they were alert and frightened.

"What was that?" one of them said in a dry voice.

"Jesus, that stink..."

And then it rose up all around them, the sound of chattering teeth. Like skulls clattering their pearlies in the gloom. Stubbs, half out of his mind, scanned the darkness with his rifle. He had insane images of battalions of war-dead skeletons rising from the dank earth, chattering their teeth and rattling their bones. That grisly noise was in front of them, behind them. It was impossible to pinpoint. Piggy sloshed through the muck to the privates, trying to calm them. Stubbs saw shapes mulling about the trench. He started shooting and shooting. Something dove over his head and landed amongst the others. There was screaming and shouting and awful, inhuman slithering sounds. More shapes slipped into the trench.

Stubbs cried out and skewered one with his bayonet, its toxic stink in his face. He ran it through and still it fought and clawed just out of reach, attempting, it seemed, to force itself up the long blade at him. It was no child...it was a demonic thing from a grave.

More of those deranged faces rose from the gully of water and the things darted forward with spidery limbs and fell on the soldiers.

Piggy was slashing at them with his trench knife, but there were simply too many clawing, biting, malicious forms, all slavering and tearing. He started wailing as the writhing shapes buried him alive. *"Oh sweet Mother of Jesus...Stubbs...Stubbs...get 'em off me...get 'em off..."*

And the last sight Stubbs had of his old friend and comrade was of him being dragged down into the gully, his screaming face submerging in the stagnant water.

And then suddenly Stubbs was alone.

He bolted out of the trench and off into the darkness, moving in what he thought was the direction of the British lines. But, Christ, it was hard to be sure. He fought through tangles of barbwire and swam through inundated bomb craters and crawled through fields of bone. But he kept going, sure he could hear them creeping and hopping behind him. His face twisted in a continuous silent scream, he listened for the sound of chattering teeth.

4

Sergeant Major Bowes, who'd conceived of Stubbs's little adventure, didn't have it much better himself. Just as he'd had something unpleasant in mind for Stubbs and Piggy, battalion HQ had something unpleasant planned for him. Just before dawn as a light rain began to fall from the sky, he led a raiding party into No-Man's Land. Twenty men armed with Enfields and revolvers went over the parapet. Their faces were blackened beneath the rims of dented steel helmets. They carried hatchets and wire cutters and belts of grenades. The last four men carried ladders to breach shell craters and, most importantly, to lay over the German barbwire when they made their assault.

They'd been out maybe thirty minutes, making good time across the scarred and gutted landscape. At the Hun lines, they started cutting through tangles of barbed wire, making as little sound as possible.

Bowes was one of the first to go over the top and drop into the trenches and they were empty. Abandoned except for multitudes of rotting corpses floating in the muck. He landed right on one and it went to mush beneath his trench boots. And the smell...nothing new, but, Jesus, nauseating.

"We've been buggered," he told the others. "Goddamn if we haven't."

Gunfire rang out and a few of his men screamed and sank into the muddy water. The sky exploded with bursts of flame. Parachute flares drifted down in showers of white and green stars. The ravaged landscape was turned to glaring daylight as the raiding party tried to climb back out of the trench system and reach No-Man's Land and its relative safety. In the distance, German artillery guns thundered and trench mortars popped and suddenly the air was electric with high-velocity shells hissing and screeching and dropping amongst them with violent, earth-shattering eruptions of flame and debris.

Bowes called out for his soldiers to seek ground, and he

could see blackened taut faces and bulging white eyes in the flare lights, then there was a resounding explosion and three men not too far away were pulverized. Gore and bone shards slammed into the sergeant major and dumped him into the muck.

There were blinding flashes and screaming. Rending explosions and rifle-shots. Men trying to escape through water-filled trenches and the stink of blood and meat, voided bowels and dying…everywhere, there was dying.

Bowes pulled himself from the mud and shoved men before him up and over the sheared barbwire. He made it himself as more mortar rounds chewed into the trench system, detonating with plumes of fire and smoke and rains of dirt and tainted water. The concussion knocked Bowes face first into the moist, foul-tasting earth. A blasted tree took a round that threw it up into the sky where it shattered into fragments.

Somebody started moaning that they were blind, blind, blind.

Somebody else wanted to know where his legs were.

The sergeant major sucked down hard on the fear and despair and horror that is war. He was drenched with blood, muddy water, and powdered down with dirt and ash. But he had to rally these men together before it was too late, he had to—

But then the earth erupted before him and he was struck with clods of soil and water and wet things. More men were screaming and maybe he was, too. Maybe he even blacked out for a moment because he was on his ass and his arm was aching. A few shell splinters were lodged in his left bicep. Another flare illuminated the carnage of dismembered men. One of them stumbled back toward the German lines holding intestines that sprouted from the smoking chasm of his belly. Another was waving his own severed arm madly in the air.

And then a blood-maddened, insane voice shrieked, "*Gas… gassss…gasssss…*"

And whoever was still in one piece and not raving mad were clawing for gas masks as the shells burst with dull, echoing thuds. Bowes got his on and prayed everyone did as he thought of men he'd seen in the hospitals, gas victims, vomiting out bloody chunks of lung. He could hear a warning bell ringing shrilly at the German lines.

By then, the gas was everywhere in yellow, miasmic clouds clinging to the ground. Men were coughing and retching and some were giggling and sobbing.

Well behind them now, from the Hun's advance lines, there were shouts and cries and gunfire. And what in Christ was that about? A counterattack? The Germans were surely under attack unless they'd shelled their own trenches.

None of it made sense, not really.

Another parachute flare sputtered in the sky, drifting earthward like a burning meteor. Bowes saw that most of his men were dead. A few had gotten their masks on. Most were beyond hope. One soldier stumbled blindly forward and he seemed to be carrying something. Why...it looked like he was carrying two or three children. But he wasn't carrying them, they were *clinging* to him like leeches, gnawing and tearing at him.

About that time, the sergeant major heard the sound.

The chattering of teeth.

And then the real screaming began.

5

It was two days later, his arm in a sling, that Bowes found Stubbs. He found him away from the front in one of the myriad support trenches. He sat on a wooden bench, numbly filling damp moldering sacks with sand. Other men with glazed, staring eyes did the same.

He stared at the sergeant major, managed a morose and hateful grin. "Are you shell-shocked, too, love? That's what we all are here." A morbid laughter came from his throat. "All crazy. Too crazy to be at the front. Did they tell you what happened to us out there?"

Bowes only nodded grimly. "I heard."

"Piggy's dead, Brass Balls. You bastard."

"I'm sorry," was all Bowes could say.

Command had told him everything. The captain was

concerned about it all. He was certain that Stubbs was shell-shocked; had to be with a wild story like that. But as the captain told Bowes about it, you could see the dread in his eyes. Because it wasn't the first time he'd heard about such things. He looked even worse after Bowes related what he'd seen near the Hun lines.

"Right," said the Captain. "Bloody ugly business that. Heard tales myself. Such things shouldn't be. This war is hard enough as is. I leave it to you to sort out, Sergeant Major. Right." Then he wandered out of the command bunker looking very much like a man who needed to shit badly and couldn't find the latrine.

For a time, nothing more was said between the sergeant major and Stubbs. They'd never liked each other. Stubbs, the volunteer. Bowes, the career soldier. But sometimes a kinship is formed by mutual experience, mutual suffering. Bowes lit cigarettes for the both of them and they were good cigarettes, too. American ones.

Exhaling a cloud of smoke, Bowes told Corporal Stubbs what had happened to the raiding party. He told it easily and with complete belief. "...I survived by crawling back toward the abandoned Hun trenches. I threw my grenades at the little horrors and ran. I spent the night under a heap of wormy Hun corpses. But I survived. And now the captain has laid it all in my lap. He wants nothing to do with any of it." Bowes left out certain parts, like the bit about the thing that leaped on him and how he slashed it to bloody ribbons with his trench knife. How he'd gripped it by its greasy clotted hair and slit the head free and how that decapitated head had looked at him, *stared at him*, the teeth snapping hungrily.

"They said it was battle fatigue," Stubbs said in a wounded voice. "Treated me like I was half out of me mind. And maybe I was. Maybe I still am. But I could see it, sir, I could see it in their eyes."

"What did you see?"

"The *belief*. They believed me and they were scared. Petrified at the idea of it."

The morning sun tried desperately to burn through the cloistral mists of fog and smoke which hung in the sky like congealed fat. There was a booming in the distance. The rattle of a machinegun. Despite the horror each had witnessed, the horror that made the atrocities of war seem positively trivial, the battles still raged. The war had not stopped. It had not even slowed down.

Bowes dragged off his cigarette, scratched at a nit that nipped at his neck. "I've heard it before, you know. Those chattering teeth. In the past year or so...I've heard it on still nights out in No-Man's Land. Chattering and chattering."

Stubbs didn't admit if he had. He pursed his lips into a tight white line as he remembered his last sight of Piggy. "What the hell are they, Sergeant Major?"

Bowes cleared his throat. "Ghouls. They are ghouls."

"Ghouls," Stubbs said, rolling the word off his tongue and not liking its taste much. "Ghouls."

Bowes nodded bleakly. "Yes, you see I was with Kitchener's regiment in the Northern Sudan back in '97 and '98. We fought the Mahdists tooth and nail at Omdurman and Khartoum. Egyptian forces were billeted to us. Good sort they were, but superstitious." Bowes licked his lips, spit bits of grit into the air. "Fine soldiers they were for the most part, but bogged down as it were by centuries of tradition. There were places in the hills they simply wouldn't go. We had a devil of a time with them. Old burial places they wouldn't set foot in by night, said they were cursed, haunted. *Ghuls*, they said.

"Yes, that's where I first learned of the ghouls. How they would come out of their black holes amongst the old, crumbling tombs. A young Egyptian fellow told me all about it. Said the ghouls haunted the ancient crypts, lived in the decay and bones, fed on them. That there were places in Iraq, Persia, even the Sudan and Egypt, shunned tracks of desert into which no sane man would venture. These were the places the ghouls dwelled. He said that if ever I was out in the desert, in some lonely and desolate spot, and a child came out of the night, out of the sands and wind and called me by name, that I should shoot it on sight. Yes, and run like hell. Because they were like rats, human rats. Where there was one, there were dozens."

Stubbs believed it. Every last demented word of it. Because

he had seen. *He had seen.* "I wonder why they're here? This isn't Persia or one of them places."

"But the bodies, lad, so many bodies lying about. So much... *food* for them." He shrugged. "Maybe they've always sought out wars. Sought out the litter it produces."

Neither man said anything for a time. They sat and smoked and listened to the buzz of war and smelled the stink of it and saw the wreckage of it, thinking of worse things. Things that creeped by night. Things that fed on flesh and bones. Little things like children that were not children, but a dark and twisted secret of antiquity.

"The captain, as I said, has laid it at my feet," Bowes reiterated.

"And?"

"I have a few ideas of where they might be hiding, of where their lair might be. But I need a few able men. Men not afraid to shoot things that pretend to be children. Do you know any men like that?"

Stubbs grinned.

6

What the sergeant major did was ask for volunteers.

For a special mission, he said. Those that he did get, he couldn't use at all, men maddened by war that volunteered for anything. And that left the raiding party at just Bowes and Stubbs, which wasn't quite enough.

The captain was aware of their operation and it was he who steered them toward the far trenches where the trench mortar battery was located in an abandoned maze of ditches. It was a dreary and forsaken location. Stubbs and Bowes slugged through the mud and found it after some time.

They saw a heavily sandbagged dugout and a few forlorn men crouched out front doing maintenance on the mortar tubes and plates. Two others manned a Lewis gun atop the parapet. They were a beaten, lean lot.

One soldier, a private, dressed in little more than rags, aimed an Enfield at them until he saw Bowes's stripes. Then he sprang to attention. "Sir! Sorry, sir!" he called out, his face covered with sores and dirt. His military bearing was almost laughable under the circumstances. "The lieutenant's inside, sir!"

Stubbs noticed there was a cross painted over the doorway but didn't comment on it. Wearily, he and the sergeant major descended the few creaking steps.

There was a small excavated room within, more sandbags lining the walls, a rough-timbered roof overhead. Seven or eight men lounged on the dirt floor or were splayed across ammunition boxes or heaps of mildewed blankets. It stunk of tobacco smoke, body odor, and rum in there. A few religious pictures were tacked up.

There was a small desk with a packing crate for a chair. A lieutenant with a bearded face and great gaping eyes like open wounds stared at them. He stood and returned the salutes of Bowes and Stubbs. "Gentlemen, glad you could come. Volunteers, eh? A special mission you say? Yes, the runner was here an hour ago and filled me in. Excellent, excellent." There was a rosary clutched in his left fist. A charred pipe hung from his colorless lips. He kept trying to light it, the idea that there was no tobacco in it was lost on him. "Men," he said, turning to those lounging about, "have we any volunteers today? No? Yes? What's it going to be lads, eh?"

The lounging soldiers stared blindly at Stubbs and Bowes, wanting no part of them. They smoked in silence, passed a bottle of gin, ate tinned biscuits. Their faces were dead and emotionless, colorless masks pressed out by the ravages of war. It was hard to tell whether they were nineteen or forty.

Finally, one man with a shrapnel-scarred face said, "What sort of mission we talking here? Something bleeding dangerous, I hope."

"We're…" Bowes sighed, then drew in a quick breath, unsure how to broach the subject. "There's been a group of…*individuals* scavenging the dead. We're going to track them down, sort them out."

"The chatterers," someone said.

The lieutenant, pacing back and forth, said, "Chatterers, eh? What's this then?" He turned away and started discoursing freely with his desk. "Hope they've got their own tobacco. Dreadful business…"

"Out there at night," another said. "You hear them."

Stubbs stepped forward. "The Jerries? *The Hun?* Is that what you're worried about, mate?" he said, with little conviction.

The man, slat-thin, scratched himself and stared into space. "There's worse things than the Hun…them that eat and chew. Them that chatter. Them that crawl and slink. Out there—" he said, stabbing one white finger toward the doorway "—them that crawls and creeps and chatters. Them out there. Them that's hungry, yes. At night…we hear 'em clawing at the sandbags. That's why we hide in here. They whisper your name…"

The lieutenant was still trying to light his pipe. "Confounded business," he said, shaking his head. "Tobacco that won't light. Damp I should say."

Stubbs knew the man was hopelessly mad and paid him no attention. "That's right. We're going to clean 'em out. Rat-catchers and exterminators. That's us, love. In for a penny or a pound? Or would you rather hide in here? Sooner or later, they'll get in, won't they? Hungry as all hell, too."

One of the men hugged himself. Another began to whimper.

The man with the scarred face got up and crushed his cigarette beneath his heel. "I've had enough of this shit. Name's Keegan, Sergeant. Time to clean this mess up." He looked over at two men leaning against the wall. "Chalmers? Crumbly? What you say, then?"

They stepped forward.

"Better to stand and die," the one called Chalmers said, "than to sit and weep."

Stubbs patted them on the shoulders each in turn and led them up and out of the bunker. Bowes turned toward the lieutenant, saluted despite himself. He wanted to say something to the man. Anything. But the words wouldn't come.

He turned and left.

Behind him he heard the lieutenant rambling: "I say, this pipe's a bit of a scoundrel, isn't it? Well, no matter. Taste of the flame will soon sort it out." He tried to light it again. "Yes? Better…no, still not lighting, you rascal? Right. Give my best to

the general. Tell him to stop by for a spot. Yes. Would it be impru-
dent of me to request more tobacco? Eh? What's that you say?"

By then Bowes couldn't hear him anymore. He was grateful
for the stink of war. The stink of lunacy in the dugout was far
worse.

7

Single file, they passed through yet another blackened and burnt
graveyard of trees.

They had Enfield rifles and Webley revolvers. Jackets of
bombs. Lanterns swung at their belts. Trench knives were sharpened and bayonets fixed. Keegan carried the Lewis machinegun,
his men loaded down with pan magazines for it.

"Aye, what we need is one those liquid-fire contraptions," he
was saying to Stubbs as they walked across the gouged landscape. "Have you seen them, mate? By Christ, what a bloody
show they put on! Saw the Jerries using one at Ypres. They strap
these tanks of petrol on their backs that are connected to these
hose-pipes. *Flammenwerfer*, they call 'em. Saw the Hun attack
one of our pillboxes, those hoses spitting out twenty-, thirty-foot
tongues of flame. Saturated our positions. Cooked every last
man to a bloody crisp. And, Christ, that stink in the air—like
roasting meat on a spit. Great oily clouds of smoke."

"What did you do?" Stubbs said.

"We aimed for those tanks. Boom! Cloud of fire and no more
Hun!"

The ground was hilly, torn, glistening like grease. A rain was
falling and mist seeped up from the ragged brown earth. There
were sloping treed bluffs that had been turned into huge dead-
falls from the shelling. And more bodies, of course, some wasted
right down to skeletons. Others quite fresh and bloated. Stubbs
saw a hand sticking up out of the mud like it was asking to be
pulled out. They saw a Hun corpse upon which two mangy,
filthy cats were feeding. They had stripped much of the meat
from the face, tearing it off in raw filets and gulping it down.

Crumbly said, "Request permission to shoot the bastards."

"Denied," Bowes said.

They had a job to do, he told them one and all. Rats? Cats? There were worse things out here. Last thing they needed was to bring a patrol of Germans down on them. "We might find nothing today, lads," he went on. "And maybe part of me hopes we won't. But if we do...*if we do,* then we must be ready, eh?" He stopped them purposely, sensing they were getting close now. He passed out cigarettes. A pint of rum made the rounds. "You might see things today, lads. And they might be crafty, smart things. They might look like people, maybe. They'll certainly look like children...but, dear Christ, *they're not human,* get me? These things...they're evil...you're just prey to them. Remember that. They're no more human than pieces of walking meat. No matter how they look, how they act. You see 'em, you shoot 'em on sight. Is that understood? Because if you don't, God help us. We'll never see home again."

And that was pretty clear, so on they went, trudging through the ravaged, blasted countryside.

Stubbs was thinking about the tunnels.

Both the allies and the Germans had dug miles and miles of tunnels through the Flanders mud. Many were abandoned. Many were not. Others had collapsed. The point being, the countryside was honeycombed with them. And what better system of conveyance for those little horrors than the endless passages? Those burrows could take them anywhere and everywhere. Out to the battlefields and graveyards and back to theirs lairs again. It was perfect. And he himself had seen them come up through the water to get Piggy. Apparently, they did just fine in the submerged, flooded blackness.

It was a thought.

About thirty minutes later, they struck on a disused, weed-choked road and followed it. The trees here were black and leafless, tangled with fingers of mist, but it was Autumn and that was no surprise. It was from seasonal change and not war. The wind blew dead leaves underfoot and tossed them into cyclones in vacant, brooding fields. There were occasional shell holes, but no bodies. They saw few bones and these were discolored, gnawed-looking.

But nobody dared comment on that.

Ten minutes later Keegan said, "Aye, look at this then."

They all did. A skeleton dressed in dirty rags was wedged between the trunk of a sprawling oak and a few enclosing limbs, fifteen feet off the ground. Its jaws were sprung open as if in a scream. Something had built a nest in the cage of ribs. From where they stood, they could see no injuries—no broken bones, no bullet holes or charring.

"What you suppose got him?" Chalmers asked.

But they all knew, somehow, it wasn't the war. "Maybe he starved," Stubbs offered. "Maybe he was hiding. Maybe he was so afraid of something, he never came down again."

They followed the road another twenty minutes and then there it was.

The abandoned village.

It was clustered over a series of yawning hills—little houses and crumbling brick shops, the grim finger of a church steeple lording above. A frost-heaved cobblestone thoroughfare snaked through it, but, like the road in, it had been reclaimed by weeds and wild grasses. It was a lot of things, that mist-choked place, but it wasn't quaint. An almost palpable pall of dread hung over the high-pitched roofs and leaning walls. Dark, empty windows looked down on the soldiers with a vacuous gaze and whatever lurked in the dusty silence did not show itself.

"What happened, then?" Crumbly wanted to know. "Did they just up and leave, I ask? Was it the war? Is that what?"

Chalmers shook his head. "The war hasn't come within a mile of this damned place. It's not that."

And it wasn't. They all knew that.

The village had a bad feeling to it. A sinister, blighted feel. A strange and mephitic rottenness hung in the stillborn air that the stink of the battlefield could never hope to touch. This was cancerous, pestilent, unwholesome. Even the shadows seemed wrong. Too many or not enough. And quiet...so very quiet. Not a bird sang, nothing scurried in the woods that pressed in blackly from all sides. It was a huge and deathly stillness, a breathing hush of waiting and watching. The atmosphere of mortuaries and crypts.

But it wasn't empty.

Maybe there were no people, but there was *something*. Grim, hateful, and malevolent. Just a whisper of it, but it was there.

Bowes cleared his throat. "There was a Belgian fellow, a priest, used to visit the lines. Used to give last rites when our chaplain was injured by shellfire. A good bloke name of Vanderhoogen. You remember him, eh, Stubbs? Anyway, he said this village was abandoned thirty-odd years ago. People just wouldn't stay here." Bowes paused, studying the village as he would any other military objective. His left arm was still in a sling from the shrapnel he'd taken during the abortive and nightmarish raid a few nights before. He couldn't handle a rifle, but he had two Webley pistols on his belt and now he sighted one in. "You know the bit—sounds and the like. Haunted, they said. Shapes moving about at night. Strange smells. No one was concerned until graves at the cemetery had been opened. They'd find bones in the morning scattered about, chewed-looking. Then a family vanished. Then another. Villagers fled. Said they saw hideous figures skulking about, small things like children but not children. Faces peering in windows at night. Red eyes watching from the shadows..."

Bowes went on, telling them he'd heard such stories other places and paid them no mind. Every empty town in every dark wood had some ghastly tale attached to it. But after what he'd seen in No-Man's Land, he started putting things together.

"And that's why we're here, lads. This place, I think, is where our problem originates. So, let's get to it then."

Crumbly said, "You sure bullets and bombs are the trick, sir? Maybe what's needed here is something more spiritual, eh?"

"They'll do," Bowes promised him. "We're hunting something flesh and blood. At least, I hope so."

8

The village.

The air was impossibly heavy as they made their way amongst the buildings, like some saturated envelope of menace. The rain fell and the mud sluiced and there was a chill here that had not been present earlier. Everything seemed to be decaying like flesh in a grave—collapsing roofs held together mainly by fingers of mold; walls punched with inexplicable holes through which oily darkness leered; shutters torn off, bricks going to powder, doorways warped and askew with unnatural angles. And everywhere, shadows pooling and flowing like rivers of absolute blackness.

"Can't say I like it," Keegan said, his face streaked with dirt and beaded with raindrops. "Can't say I like it one bit."

Building by house by shed, they checked out everything carefully. Even cobwebbed cellars and outbuildings. Places cut into the dank earth where the smell was of rank corruption, a high and oddly pestiferous stench of violated graveyards and plundered charnel houses. They didn't linger in such places long.

But the truly unpleasant fact was that nothing had been touched or rifled through. Furniture, glassware, tools, lumber. It all sat untouched. Closets were hung with rotting clothing and piled with mildewed shoes. There were even a few hunting rifles, bottles of dusty liquor. The inhabitants had left in a great hurry and none, not beggar nor thief nor recalcitrant boy, had *dared* come here to take anything. It was a shunned place. A haunted place. And this was more disturbing than just about anything.

The only thing any of the edifices had in common besides desolation were the series of jagged claw marks furrowed into everything, shredding wallpaper and slitting open chairs. Doors were scathed by them, bed mattresses cleaved open, banisters gouged. But the most terrible thing were the prints in the dust—the footprints of tiny feet.

They found what might have been a tavern once. And in the dusty confines of the kitchen, a place that stunk of ancient blood and pain, they found a litter pile of bones in one foul-smelling corner. The bones were yellowed and punctured with teeth marks. And worse, the bones were human. And worse yet, they were the tiny bones of infants and toddlers.

"Bastards," Stubbs said, barely able to control himself. "Dirty murdering bastards."

Then they left the town and climbed up to the church that overlooked the village.

It was weathered a soiled gray and the doors were missing. It brooded over both town and churchyard at the rear. The steeple was stripped and skeletal, the cross covered in something black and nameless. They went in and found it untenanted, save for the heaps of bones piled on the altar. And every last one methodically stripped of meat and sucked dry of marrow. It smelled dead and decayed in there like an exhumed coffin. The ambience was noxious and godless. Whatever worshipped at that altar of bones, did so in cloistered darkness. The soldiers mumbled prayers beneath their breath, begging for mercy and deliverance from that horrible place, from that festering and invidious atmosphere which seemed to crawl over their skins like grave worms.

Then they visited the churchyard.

Whatever had enveloped the town in dank, hellish sweetness, it was worse here. Far worse. The atmosphere was soured, clogged with the stink of carrion and age and a depraved odor of defilement and degeneration. A cauldron of sunless, eldritch horror.

Weapons at the ready, the soldiers followed a sunken road through the sucking, yellow mud. What they saw was a travesty. Headstones and funerary crosses had been tipped over. Stone angels had been smeared with excrement. Vaults were flung open and emptied. Coffins had been dragged from their berths and shattered to kindling. And everywhere, bones scattered and pitted. Skulls laughed from the mud, were balanced atop sepulchers, and stacked in concentric circles. The rain poured down and water ran from their empty eye sockets. Even the squat bushes and denuded trees were decorated with femurs and ribcages and ulnas, crowned by jawless skulls. A necropolis decorated lavishly with the raw materials of the grave.

"This is their place," Bowes said in a hopeless voice.

And no one disagreed with that. They patrolled on, sweat-greased fingers on triggers as they moved amongst the open graves and ruined crypts. Suddenly Crumbly let out a piercing cry. The ground had given way beneath him and he was up to his chest in a hole, pawing frantically to get out. The others pulled him free, content that nothing pulled him down from beneath.

Stubbs shielded himself from the falling rain and lit one of the lanterns. Down on his belly in the running mud, he lowered the lantern into the hole. A tunnel led off in either direction. A stench of hot, gaseous dissolution rose up from it. "Aye," he said. "What I suspected. Honeycombed with passages. They probably dug right into the graves originally. And now? I'd say these hills are full of 'em, a network that starts here and connects with our own tunnels, those of the Hun, too."

The other soldiers were pale, thinking of what burrowed beneath them. Rain ran off the brims of their helmets, past dour unblinking eyes.

"Right," Bowes said to them. "Makes perfect sense. Now I couldn't order one of you in there. Wouldn't even think of it—"

"I'll go," Stubbs said. "Somebody has to."

No one disagreed or tried to talk him out of it. He took a Webley pistol from Bowes and two belts of grenades.

"Good luck," the sergeant major said, shaking his hand as if in farewell.

Stubbs looked at the rainy faces of the others, knowing he'd never see them again. War was hell.

9

Lantern in tow, he lowered himself down into the wet earth as the rain pounded from above. The passage was small and he had to creep forward on his belly, grenades on his back and revolver and lantern held before him. He pushed through the claustrophobic murk, a nauseous stench of subterranean rot washing over him.

He expected rats, but never saw a one.

There were places, maybe, even they didn't go. Forbidding places contaminated by a tenebrous, vaporous evil so complete, so utterly vile and contagious they dared not tread. And the burrows beneath that accursed village were such a place.

Stubbs pushed himself along through the muck and slime

like a reptile, noticing with some unease that there was no possible way he could turn around. Whatever underground nightmare he was inching toward, he was going there to stay. But it didn't bother him too much because he kept thinking about Piggy. How he'd died.

The walls were narrow, sweating foul water and clumps of dirt. The blackness was thick and pungent, misting and hard to breathe. He had been squirming along maybe ten, fifteen minutes when he started to find fragments of bones and finally entire skeletons tucked away in the wet, earthen walls. Soon enough, the passage was studded with jutting leg bones and scapulas and skulls that protruded from the oozing mud. All of them were silt-gray and riddled by bite marks. It wasn't just bones, but the soles of trench boots, ragged bits of uniform, discolored strips of belt, even a helmet or two, badly worried. Finally, the gnawed mummies of soldiers who as yet had not been completely stripped of flesh. Pipe-stem arms and broomstick legs thwarted Stubbs's advance. He had to press them into the mud or snap them aside to continue.

Ossuary, is what he was thinking. Some great and dire litter, the remains of their feedings.

A skull hung from the dripping roof overhead. Stubbs dropped it a wink though he was thoroughly terrified. More than once he passed beneath the clawed, polished bottom of a casket that had yet to be plundered.

He heard strange echoes from time to time. The distant sounds of guttural voices or shrill cackling. And sometimes just the ominous and lunatic sound of breathing—like someone exhaling into an empty metal drum.

The farther he went the more the stink changed from being merely rich and cloying with fleshy decay to something far, far worse. This new stench was overwhelming and all-encompassing and it fell over him like a shroud. A film of it gathered over his skin and hung on him, polluted and noxious. It was the stink he'd noticed at the listening post that night with Piggy and the others—that immense black smell of utter putrefaction, not of dead things, but of living things so profane and debased they turned the very atmosphere to a tainted, baneful malignancy.

Yes, he was close now.

His flesh was creeping, crawling in shuddering waves and he had to clamp his jaws shut and tighten down his throat so as not to start vomiting. That great putrid, sour smell was *their* fouled milk and it was spilled everywhere. It bled from the air like diseased blood.

He swallowed hard, shivering, shaking, closer to madness than the war itself had ever been able to take him.

The tunnel was weaving drunkenly from side to side now. There were offshoots and burrows going in every possible direction. And more bones. Fresh corpses. Their death masks staring at him, warning him to get out. The passage began veering downward and down Stubbs went, sliding through the slime and mud and then into a smothering channel that he had to fight his way through. Then it widened and he fell suddenly into a gigantic cavern. It was dug from rock and soil, easily ten feet in height, three times that in width and length.

Pulling himself up, he held out the lantern. He was standing in two feet of accumulated muck that was equal parts excrement, bones, and filthy water. Hundreds of black beetles the size of cigar butts crawled and fed in the pooled waste. The walls and ceiling were honeycombed with tunnel mouths or cells like the chambers of a beehive. A dripping gray fungus hung down from them like Spanish moss.

He knew he wasn't alone.

He saw glittering eyes shining from those darkened recesses, saw stealthy forms sliding from their berths like eels. Heard the chattering of tiny teeth that were like roofing nails. And all around him, it seemed, chatterings and chitterings and squealings.

He was in their den.

Yes, they looked like children—small, but hunched-over, moving with odd loping, hopping motions. Their naked skins were scabrous and sickly-yellow, their hideous little faces skullish, the skin drawn taut over the alien architecture of bone beneath. Wild, tangled mats of hair fell to their shoulders and beyond, hanging in greasy strands over their graveyard faces.

"*Stubbs,*" they whispered in a single mechanical voice. "*Stuuubsss. Stubbs. Stubbs. Stubbs…*"

He shut them out, would not listen.

Some part of his brain that was still intellectually functional started wondering how many terrible stories these things had inspired—tales of bogies and dwarves and elves and forest devils. Because when he saw them, when he looked them directly in the face, he *recognized* them. They lived in the twilight of his psyche, images carried by all men as racial memory. These creatures, these ghouls, were ancient adversaries of mankind and had lived by night even as man had lived by day since the very dawn of the race.

When his voice came, it was dry, worn, but clear as crystal, "Yes, here I am, you disgusting little bastards. I've come for you, one and all."

And maybe he should've been afraid, but somehow, he wasn't.

He was a soldier and he was a man and these things were perverse, they didn't deserve to live. They began to advance en masse in his direction, calling his name, and Stubbs stepped forward, not because he wanted to get any closer to those chattering horrors, but because of what was *behind* them.

"Oh, dear Christ," he said.

In an elliptical depression carved from the far wall was another ghoul, but this one an adult. It sat on an altar, a throne of heaped human skins, bones and dismembered limbs. A huge and flabby female with pulsing flesh, dough-white and horribly blotched with something that might have been a creeping fungus. A double row of teats ran down her torso and from them, the squirming maggoty bodies of her progeny suckled. She held them there, formless things with twitching limbs and mouths like lamprey that would someday walk and feast on the dead. A bitch and her brood.

She saw Stubbs and glared at him with red, lidless eyes and there was such a raw and unflinching hatred in them it turned his insides literally to sauce. Everything seemed to run in him. His mind, too. Drawn down into some safe place where things like her could not possibly be.

She made a shrill squealing sound that pierced the air, echoed through the tunnels, and punched right through Stubbs like poison arrows. He could feel the fetid hot blast of her breath. But distorted as it was, he heard the words: *"STUUUBBBSSS..."*

She was an obscenity, yes, but that oblong face smeared with gore was not the worst thing. Nor were those greasy, twitching growths that fell from her bulbous skull like living hair. Nor was the black tongue licking over spiked teeth. Or even that hideous voice that he could remember calling to him in a childhood nightmare.

For, as he watched, she was giving birth.

With clawed and leprous fingers, she was pulling a slimed and bloated larval form from her birth canal. A squeaking, writhing thing that made bile rise into his throat.

The lantern slid from his fingers, landed in the muck, but did not go out. It cast lurching, grotesque shadows as leaping things waded in at him. With the Webley, he dropped six of them in as many seconds. Then he started throwing the grenades, one after the other. The chamber became a hive of howling and screeching and dying. Inundated in her children, his flesh coming off in ragged strips, teeth sunk in far too many hurting places, he dove at the mother. With his left hand, he drove his trench knife deep into her swollen, undulating belly. And with his right, as she took hold of him and he lost his mind in the folds of her loathsome, necrotic stink, he shoved his last grenade into her mouth and pulled the pin.

There was a resounding explosion as her head blew apart into reeking jelly and he was filled with shrapnel. The children kept at him, shrieking his name, and then the world erupted into flame and light and raining earth.

10

Bowes and the others checked all the crypts.

They found more burrows and passages, many cut straight through solid stone. There were no limitations to the ghouls' depraved determination. He and his men patrolled the cemetery, waited for some sign from Stubbs and it was a long time in coming.

"Here! Sir, over here!" Chalmers called out, motioning

toward the hole Stubbs had disappeared into.

Rain in his face, Bowes went over there and listened.

Yes, there and there and there.

Gunfire. Echoes of gunfire from some distant subterranean lair. And then the sound of grenades bursting one after the other. Bowes grinned, though he was certain Stubbs would not return. Grinned because the corporal was giving them hell. He'd taken the fight to them and now they were tasting the scorpion's sting, all right.

Keegan cried out and started pumping out rounds with the Lewis gun. Bullets sprayed wildly from the machinegun, tearing up dirt and pulverizing headstones. As Bowes watched in shock, little mottled hands dragged him down into the earth. And then Chalmers disappeared and Crumbly's face followed it beneath the rank soil. And then they were coming from the earth, the ghouls, blind in the light of day. Coming for Bowes.

He heard his name whispered from the hole, echoing and echoing.

And then there was a sudden enormous concussion from below like the roll of an earthquake and the cemetery exploded into a rain of mud and bones and bodies and gravestones. And before blackness swallowed him, he thought, from some faraway place, of all those gases of decay built up in the tunnels below. And of the grenades igniting them.

And then the graveyard fell into a massive cavern beneath him.

11

It was dark when Bowes awoke.

Maybe he'd been awake for some time. Maybe drifting between dream and reality with surreal ease. His eyes flickered open and he saw the stars overhead. The rains had finally lifted. The air smelled clean, fresh and pure. He was thankful to smell it one last time. His body was knitted with pain. His left leg was a mangled stalk twisted beneath him. His left arm was free of the sling but reduced to raw and bleeding meat. He was cut and gashed and bled profusely.

Tim Curran

He knew he would not survive.

But he was a soldier and a soldier's life often demanded sacrifice. Seven generations of Bowes had sacrificed willingly for Queen and country. And he would ask for no more and no less. He was a professional soldier, a career man, and as such, pride, duty, and dedication to cause were the only things that truly mattered in his life. As he laid there, he remembered India and South Africa, Burma and the Sudan. He'd given a good account of himself as a soldier and he was content in death. A few lines from "The Young British Soldier" by Kipling visited him in his final hour:

"When you're wounded and left on Afghanistan's plains,
And the women come out to cut up what remains,
Jest roll to your rifle and blow out your brains,
An' go to your Gawd like a soldier."

Beautiful, Bowes thought. Simply beautiful. What more could a soldier ask for than a quick and painless death? Why—

The air went rank suddenly, smelled of foul things and foul deeds. He heard the chattering of teeth. He tried vainly to crawl through the slick mud up and out of the cavern, but it was hopeless. Quite hopeless.

Limned by moonlight, he saw a single ghoul. It came on with dragging, wet sounds, stinking of spoiled meat. An adult male judging by the distended phallus that swung between its legs like a pendulum. It was raw-boned and skeletal, ladders and knobs of bone gaping under the slack and fungous flesh. He could hear its clotted, phlegmy breathing.

"Bowes," it said in a hissing voice.

With his right hand, Bowes dug the Webley from his belt and fired three rounds into it. He could see the holes in its hide, glistening. Could see the dire beams of moonlight shining through them.

Still it crept forward, cold and remorseless, dappled with mud and gore. Its lurid skull-face was grinning with a glaring appetite.

Bowes laughed. "You won't have me, you filthy bugger," he said.

With his right hand, he placed the muzzle of the Webley to his temple. As those knobby fingers reached for him, he pulled the trigger and, gladly, happily, went to his God like a soldier.

NOT SUGAR SPICE OR ANYTHING NICE

(Dark Corners #2, 2004)

"I know something you don't know."

Roger Sachek started, nearly dropping his torque wrench. He was under the hood of his '76 Ford pickup, replacing the fuel pump, his face wet with perspiration, his hands grubby, his fingers aching from working those rusted bolts. He'd been thinking that the old ones were good to work on. No microchips or brainboxes or computerized gizmos, just the basics. A man could get his hands on those old engines and make things happen.

But now there was the girl.

She was grinning, not shy, not even remotely so. She wore a yellow dress with lavender flowers embroidered at the cuffs and collar. Her shoes were white and her hair was a nest of blonde curls. She looked, if anything, like she had just come back from Sunday school. But it was Wednesday. Wednesday afternoon.

"What did you say, honey?" Roger asked.

"I know something you don't know," she said again.

He was staring at her now, really seeing for the first time just how huge her eyes were, how violet they were and how they did not blink. Like painted-on doll's eyes, they stared and stared.

"Honey," he managed, feeling uneasy and not knowing why, "go on and play, I have work to do."

"But I have a secret for you."

"Sure, sure. But you should go play in your own yard."

"You don't want to know what I know?"

Who was this kid? He had never seen her in the neighborhood and the way she was dressed...little girls didn't dress like that much anymore. He figured she was only seven or eight, but there was something in those eyes that disturbed him. Was he losing it or did they seem almost...*sensual?* Filled with a glaring carnal appetite that had no business being there?

He told her to go and play, but she did not move.

He was looking around, hoping nobody saw him talking to this kid. People started getting ideas if they saw you talking to little girls. And that just showed you how fucked-up the world was. You couldn't even talk to a kid without feeling like some sort of criminal.

"Honey," Roger said. "You shouldn't go around talking to people you don't know. Run along now."

She was still grinning, those huge eyes on him and *in* him like boring bits. "But I *do* know you. And I know something you don't."

Roger sighed. A game. Just a game. "Okay...what do you know?"

"I know something about your wife."

That stopped him. He looked at the girl long and hard now and could feel something in those eyes reaching out to him, getting down deep inside him, crawling through him. "Tell me," he said.

The little girl giggled. "Your wife and Mr. Hayden. Sometimes they kiss when you're at work. And sometimes, sometimes they—"

"Really?"

Because he had been thinking it all along. George Hayden and Lisa. Sure. He'd suspected it for months but had not allowed himself to think it because he was jealous by nature and you had to keep the green-eyed monster behind lock and key. If you let it out...

"You've...you've seen them?"

She nodded. "Yes, I've watched them. Lots."

And why did her voice make him cringe? And why did those eyes of hers, those huge violet pools, seem to suck him down to some primal level? And worse, why did he only see graveyards and gallows in them?

Without really thinking, he pushed past the little girl—noticing with some unease that she was very cold—and went into the house. Lisa was wearing tight cut-offs and a sports bra. Her nipples were hard against the fabric. She hung up the phone as he came through the door.

"How long have you been fucking Hayden?" Roger put to her, wanting her to deny it, to lie, to dare try and play him.

But she froze up like something chopped from ice.

Looking into his eyes, she could only say in a numb voice, "Once, just the once. I swear to God it was just the once." And she seemed surprised that her lips had betrayed her. She shook her head from side to side as if she hadn't meant to say that at all.

And then Roger was on her, feeling it boiling out of him like some toxic waste, like venom spraying from the mouth of a cobra, and he did not realize he still had the torque wrench in his hand until he had brought it down on Lisa's skull about ten times. But there it was, in his hand. The end was bloody and clotted with flesh and hair, globs of gore dripping to the carpeting.

Lisa's head was ruined, her beauty erased, her skull collapsed.

Behind him, in the doorway, the little girl was grinning like a skull in a basket, her huge and hollow eyes practically luminous with delight.

He began to wail a high, piercing scream.

"I know something you don't know."

George Hayden was clipping the hedges. He stopped, crushed out his cigarette in the driveway. Just some kid, some little girl standing there. Cute, maybe, all dolled-up. Kind of pretty and George was thinking, *Come see me when you're eighteen, honey, and I'll show you where the bear sleeps.*

"What do you know, kid? I'm all ears."

The little girl smiled and licked her lips and that made something hot bubble inside of him.

"It's about Lisa Sachek," the girl said. "She wants to show you something."

George was smiling now, too. *Sent a kid to get me, eh? Well, here I come, baby.*

"You better take the shears, too," the girl said.

And then they were walking together and George was feeling funny inside as they went up the Sacheks' little path to the front door. And the real funny thing was the girl. Though it was broad daylight out, she cast no shadow.

PIT CREW

(Bare Bone #5, 2004)

Rivas had been at the prison farm for three months when he got his chance.

Three months. You would've thought it was some special honor, all the guys that volunteered for it. Like maybe they were going to a whorehouse or a frat party or some shit instead of just getting picked for the road crew. But after you'd been in-stir awhile, any opportunity to visit the World, to smell free air and taste it on your tongue, that was a big thing. First day on the farm, the other cons started telling Rivas about it.

"How long you in for, cherry?" they said.

"A year."

"Shit, do it standing on your head. What you gotta do is get on a road crew, man. That's what you gotta do."

Rivas didn't pay much mind to that.

He was there to do his time. All he wanted was for it to pass. To be over with. He didn't want any trouble, any involvement with the others, just do his bit and get back to the World. He was sitting on a year for possession. Narcs kicked his door in on a tip, found nearly a pound of black hash. Judge didn't believe him when he told His Honor it was for personal use. But it was the truth. Ever since Rivas got his first taste of the wicked leaf when he was twelve, he never could get enough. So, a year it was, farm time. Possession with intent to distribute.

Goddamn.

The judge acted like Rivas was some shit-crazy drug runner, some badass cancer on society. Bullshit. Rivas used, he didn't sell. When His Honor said prison farm, Rivas didn't really think it was an *actual* farm, but that's what it was. It had cows, produce, hay, you name it. The work was hard, like nothing he'd ever seen. Up at dawn, at it until dusk. But they fed you good, gave you breaks. If it wasn't for some of the hacks—mean, crazy ones—it wouldn't have been bad, just tedious. It wasn't like real prison; nobody was trying to get in your asshole or stick a homemade knife in your back. The cons were pretty mellow. Small-timers, mostly, like Rivas. A few hardcores, cons who'd started in maximum security and worked their way to minimum, and finally the farm. But even these guys, some of them real psycho-looking pricks, didn't bother anyone. They knew if they fucked up, it was back to real time. So they were good. Kind of friendly, most of them.

Yeah, it was all right.

Thing was, after three weeks of it, Rivas needed a change.

That's when he signed up for the road crew. Almost three months later, bang, he got his chance. Traynor, the sergeant hack—miserable, illiterate redneck who busted guys with his stick if they so much as yawned funny—walked over to Rivas at roll call.

"You fancy some outside work, boy?"

"Yes, sir."

Traynor eyeballed him, wrinkled his nose like maybe Rivas was molded from dog shit. "You think you can handle it?"

"Sure."

Traynor jabbed him in the belly with his stick. "Don't make me regret this, boy," he said, his mottled face like old cheese.

Rivas knew he'd pull his weight.

There wasn't much to him when he got to the farm, flab and bones, but he'd been hardening up just fine. Not much they could throw at him now he couldn't take.

About three in the afternoon, a bus pulled up in the compound.

Rivas and ten others were shuffled aboard. The sergeant hack came along, of course. There was one bastard you couldn't shake; he hung on like herpes. Before they pulled out, Traynor gave them the speech in which he informed each and every one of them what happened to guys—goddamn fuck-worthless cons—who tried to run once they were in the great outdoors. He said he buried them.

Rivas believed it.

He believed everything Traynor and the other hacks told him. When Traynor told him he wasn't nothing but a goat-humping pedophile, he agreed with him. When Traynor said he was a waste of his daddy's seed, he nodded happily. And when Traynor said his mommy sucked sweaty trucker dick in roadside shitters, he said that, yes, it was all too true. That's how you did it. If they didn't get a rise out of you, they moved on.

There was a black guy name of Willy Short that Rivas was friendly with.

When they got to the site—pretty much a big, deep hole about thirty feet long out in the sticks—Rivas and Willy were given shovels and picks along with the rest and told the hole had to be an easy fifty feet come sunset.

Yessir, yessir.

Except Willy didn't say yessir fast enough for Traynor.

"You got an attitude problem there, boy?"

Willy shook his head. "No, sir. Not at all." And then in a hushed voice: "And I ain't your boy."

Traynor clapped him upside the head with his stick. "WHAT THE FUCK YOU SAY, *BOOOYYY?*"

Willy's knees wanted to give out something fierce, but he stayed up. "Nothing, sir."

Traynor just shook his head. He walked over to one of the black hacks, mean sonofabitch name of Riles. He had a chip on his shoulder like a cinder block. "He's one of yours, Riles, so I'll let you take him."

Riles stormed over, barely five feet of him...but seven feet in attitude. "Ain't one of mine," Riles said, spitting in Willy's face. "Ain't nothing but a wanna-be toughboy nigger." Riles turned away, but then came back hard with his stick. Sank it right into Willy's belly. Willy fell apart like a house of cards, dropping into a moaning ball with a great whoosh of air from his lungs. Riles kicked him three, four times. Then he jabbed the tip of his stick in Willy's privates. "You got a problem with being called 'boy,' nigger? Because if you do, motherfucker, I'm gonna play me some miniature golf with your pathetic little gonads. Get me, BOY?"

The hacks stalked off, laughing, and Rivas helped Willy up.

Poor guy was hurting something awful, but he knew he'd brought it on himself. He filled his belly with hatred for Riles and hobbled down into the hole. Rivas did the shoveling, let Willy take an occasional swing with the pick. It was the best he could do for him. Fifteen, twenty minutes later, Willy was standing pretty much upright.

So, the hours passed.

Before long, both Willy and Rivas were shirtless, painted with beaded sweat. It was hard work, but it was *different* work. Beat the holy shit out of playing Farmer Brown back at the camp. Yessir. The road crew worked in the trench, shoveling out black earth, chopping at tree roots, tossing out stones, all matter of debris. The hacks stood above, slapping their sticks into their hands. With about five, six feet left to go, they got a break. Rivas, Willy, and three or four others sprawled under a big oak, nice and shady, drank water and smoked cigarettes.

"Got me a special cigarette here," a biker named Hoyle said. He held it up for all to see. Looked like your standard coffin nail. He fired it up, smoke was sweet and heavy. Hacks were off a way, not paying attention. "Imbibe, gentlemen."

Rivas took a hit, forgot how good the magic herb was. He held it in his lungs a long time. Already, he could feel that creeping, carefree warmth. "Oh, man, that's so good, that's so good," he said, like a horny sailor sinking his meat into some fine, tight stuff after eight months at sea.

They finished the cigarette, enjoying every moment.

"All right," Traynor said, "get your useless asses back in that hole."

It didn't take them much more than twenty minutes to chop through the rest. After that, they squared it off and were ordered out, one by one.

"This must be it," Willy said, "end of our little vacation."

Traynor lined them up in a tight little row and told them to wait. They chatted and smoked and giggled. There wasn't shit else to do. They had maybe an hour until the sun called her quits. Rivas was pretty stoned. His body was sore, he smelled like a leper's underwear, but he was happy. He felt smooth, easy, like polished glass.

Twenty minutes later, a dump truck pulled up, a big ugly Mack belching blue smoke. No insignia. Nothing. A hack jumped out, guided the truck up near the pit and motioned the driver to empty.

Rivas just watched, a silly grin cut into his features, his brain full of soft fuzz.

The truck dumped its load, pulled forward.

Rivas just stared.

There were maybe a hundred, two hundred bodies in various stages of decomposition. Men, women, and children. All slat-thin, wasted. Flesh-covered skeletons, bags of knobby bones. They looked like death-camp refuse. A litter pile from Bergen-Belsen or Mauthausen or one of those quaint little places you see on the old newsreels. The stink was green and thick, like dog roadkill to the tenth power.

Rivas was so wasted—he seemed to be getting off more and more by the moment—that he thought maybe he was imagining this shit. It couldn't be real, all those stiffs. He looked over at Willy. Willy was grinning, a black mirror image of himself. So was Hoyle. Bone-heap like that? Yessir, most natural thing in the world.

"You faggots just gonna stand there dreamin' of pumping your mamas or are you gonna plant this here crop?" Traynor said.

Pretty soon, everyone was in motion.

Rivas went at it, too. He grabbed an old lady, bag of putrescent sticks, and dragged her gray ass down into the pit. Pretty soon, all the cons got over the sight, the feel, the smell of it. They made a game out of it. Like old-time firemen passing buckets of sand or water, they formed a chain, several in fact, passing the bodies down the line. Some of the stiffs were so ripe they came apart like wet newspaper, but everyone leant a hand.

Hoyle was an old pro. He was down in the pit with a hook knife. He jumped around, slitting open bellies. "Lets the gas out," he told Rivas, winking. "Wouldn't want 'em popping up out of the ground, you know."

When they were done burying the hole up, Traynor pulled Rivas aside.

"You got a problem with this sort of work, boy?"

Rivas shook his head. "No, sir. Fine by me." His eyes were glazed, shiny. Good shit, that stuff Hoyle had. Dulled you away just fine.

"Good." Traynor seemed happy with this. "You did good, boy. Hard-worker, goddamn. Just don't get any funny ideas."

"Funny ideas, sir?"

Traynor nodded. "Yeah. Had cons so pent-up, so horny, you understand, they hopped in the pit and started humping that stuff. And that's simply disrespectful." Traynor kicked a child's head into the hole. "Don't care for that sort of business."

Rivas assured the sergeant hack that would never happen.

Thirty minutes later, the cons were spreading topsoil and grass seed. It was all done.

Rivas piled back into the bus with the others who all smelled flyblown and black. Nasty. It was hard work, but it was good work. Being outdoors. In the sun, the free air. It was okay. Especially with that weed Hoyle had.

Rivas signed up every week after that. It made the time go by.

You just didn't think about it, was all.

LONG IN THE TOOTH

"There is race-memory involved here. We
repel them and they repel us."
—Gerald Kersh

First off, the road was narrow and meandering, a crooked
and curling strip of pavement like some snake winding its
way across the misty fenlands. Then there were those yew trees
which lined it to each side, green and drooping. And whenever
there was a break for a farming road or a culvert, there was
nothing beyond but the fens themselves.

"Next holiday, I do the planning," Donny told his wife as he
struggled to keep the Land Rover on the road that seemed intent
to throw them like a mechanical bull. "I'm thinking somewhere
civilized, somewhere dry. How does that strike you?"

Colleen was laughing. "Oh, Duck, you are a dramatic thing."

The night was black as poured tar, the headlights of the
Land Rover like knives slitting open the darkness and all that
lay beyond. Which was, basically, the road and the fens themselves. They were ancient and lonely beneath the pale moonlight, crisscrossed by drains and dikes, clotted with high coarse
grasses and sedge, a few low hills and an occasional rotting
farmhouse or thatched cottage.

"I know now why I married you, darling," Donny said,
maybe just to hear himself talk, for out there the fens were
immense and dark and, somehow threatening...though he
wasn't exactly sure why. He navigated yet another turn, slowed
down, sped up, felt the yawning ditches reaching out for him.

"I married you because you're British and I knew one day you'd drag me from my cozy house in Chicago and bring me to Lincolnshire. You'd make me eat stuffed chine and haslet and fight my way through bogs."

Colleen laughed again. "Oh, now we've had a wonderful time even if you won't admit it."

"And I won't. I'd kill for a tree."

"There's plenty of trees, yews to the left and right."

"I mean a real tree. Yew trees creep me out." Donny slowed then, thinking he saw something coming out of the spidery tangle of yews, but there was nothing. "When I was a kid, dear heart, my old man decided we had to see the prairie as a family. So we drove west from Milwaukee, found an old dirt road and followed it for like a hundred miles until we were there, smack dab in the middle of the prairie."

"And did you like it, Duck?"

"No, I hated it. It was wide and empty and lonesome just like the fens. I knew if I had stayed there I would have slit my wrists. It was depressing. Darling, no offense, but your home county? It's depressing, too..."

Colleen opened her mouth, no doubt to comment on the banality of the American Midwest, but then she saw what came hobbling across the road and screamed. Screamed because there was no way Donny could avoid it.

And he didn't.

The Land Rover hit it, tossing it aside or under the wheels. He hit the brakes and the Land Rover fishtailed, nearly going into the ditch in a screech of burning rubber. Then it came to a stop, conked out. There was only silence and darkness and Donny's hands gripping the wheel like they never wanted to let go.

Colleen had gone the color of the moon, eyes wide and staring, lower jaw working up and down like a baby bird needing something in its belly. But she didn't need anything in her belly; it was already full of a thick, greasy sludge that was bubbling up the back of her throat.

Donny licked his lips. "I couldn't...it was just there...I mean..."

Colleen's hand found his own and hers was clammy. "We...I suppose we should go look..."

He let go of her hand and she pressed a flashlight into it from the glove box, because out there it was blacker than the inside of a leather bag now that the moon had sunk into a pond of clouds. Donny left the headlights on, clicked the emergency flashers, and stepped into the night. Quiet. God, it was quiet. Just the leaves murmuring on the yews. He could smell the fens, dark and rich and heady.

The front end of the Land Rover had a good ding in it and the radiator grill was smashed in, but nothing was leaking. It would survive. But what they'd hit...well, there was a smear of blood on the bumper, but nothing else.

Donny told himself it was probably a roe deer he hit, not a child. Because what would a child be doing out here in the middle of the night?

But he was having trouble swallowing that. He hadn't had any time to react, but what he'd seen was burned into his memory: something small and hunched and naked, frozen there as if transfixed by the headlights. And whatever it had been, it walked on two legs, not four.

A kid, dammit, it must have been a kid.

Okay, okay, just take it easy now.

He followed the skid marks back maybe forty feet, the fens bunching up to either side of the road, a scant breeze skirting them and producing an eerie sound like sighing.

"Do you...see anything?" Colleen called out, her voice loud and cutting in the uncanny stillness.

Donny started, swallowed. His arms, he realized, were pebbled with gooseflesh. "No, not yet—" then his voice sinking like a brick in a mire "—yes, yes, I think I found something..."

He heard her door open, heard her coming, but slowly, maybe hoping he'd tell her it was just an animal. But he couldn't tell her that because he wasn't entirely sure what he was looking at. "Just...just stay back, baby," he told her. "It's...it's pretty bad."

"Oh God," she said, nearly sobbing.

Donny's stomach sluiced with warm jelly, his knees

trembled. It was a child…it had to be a child but mangled from the impact…twisted and knotted-up, yellow-skinned and long-armed, more like an ape than a kid. It couldn't have been much over three feet in height with scraggly, streaming hair that was clotted with sticks and leaves, eyes like dirty opals, and flaking, scabrous flesh.

And it was spattered and slicked with gouts of blood that were black in the flashlight beam.

It was also naked.

If it was indeed a child (and Donny could not seem to convince himself of that) then it had been walking wild for some time, living like an animal.

Colleen said, "Is it…is it dead?"

"Yes. Yes, I think so."

He realized that he should have been trying to render some first-aid or comfort to the poor thing, instead of inspecting it like something in a sideshow jar. Yet…*yet*, the idea of touching it was offensive. Maybe it was the gore from the accident and maybe it was something about the child—*yes, say it, use the word*—but he could not bring himself to go anywhere near it.

Colleen refused to look. One of her hands shielded her eyes from an accidental glimpse. "Was it…was it a boy…or a girl…"

Donny was crouching near to it, but not too near.

He had the flashlight beam full in its leering face. It was loathsome up close, horribly distorted, its teeth narrow and sharp. He tried to tell himself that this was from the impact, too, but that was reaching. This *child* had been revolting before the Land Rover hit it, there was no doubt of that. It was unnatural as was the stink rising off it…a filthy, flyblown odor of spoiled meat and crevices stuffed with graying bones.

It laid there, the breeze ruffling its hair, blood still oozing thickly from its collapsed chest, a clear bile dripping from its flabby lips.

"Donny!" Colleen said sternly. "Was it a boy or a girl—?"

And, quite honestly, he said: "I don't know."

Arm in arm they made it back to the Land Rover. Colleen told him she'd tried the cell, but it was out of range. Way out here, on the backside of nowhere, it wasn't too surprising.

"Look," she said. "I see a light...I think..."

He did, too. You could just make it out, off the road. A cottage on high ground out in the fens.

"We better get help," Donny said.

"Should...should one of us stay?"

But he took her hand, pulled her along. "No, no I don't think that would be a good idea at all." And he didn't. Because he couldn't explain it, but the sight of that *child* had done something to him. What he was feeling was not pity or guilt, but absolute revulsion.

The fen astir with muted, secretive sounds, they began to run for the cottage.

Something was following them.

Long before Donny heard it, he *felt* it. Again, he could not explain this other than to think that the excitement and frenzy of the accident had shifted his mind into high gear, unlocked some elemental drive of instinct within him. His hearing was keen, his eyesight clear, his mind working with a frightening lucidity. It seemed to know exactly what to do, as if it had been through this before. And what it was telling him was to find shelter, and when he found it, to get a weapon in his hand.

Ridiculous.

Yet, he had felt something following them long before his ears conformed it. Colleen's hand was tight and damp in his own, he could almost feel her blood flowing beneath the skin. Everything was that acute. He was experiencing a supercharged intuitive sense that was alarming.

They found a twisting, built-up dirt road that led off the main artery and through the sleeping fens. There was a cottage out there, warm yellow light in its windows.

He stopped.

"What is it, Duck?" Colleen wanted to know, but it was obvious from her breathless voice that she was feeling it, too.

Donny heard sounds that his mind told him were tiny feet moving stealthily through scrub brush and grass. Rustling noises. The sound of guarded, careful motion. The fens were cut with long drainage canals that fed into distant leechfields and the wash itself. If it wasn't for this elaborate system of dykes and ditches, the fens would have been flooded. And out there in that sodden, grassy wasteland, he distinctly heard the sound of splashing as if something—and more than *one* something—were jumping into the ditches. His mind filled with an unpleasant image of huge, mutant frogs diving into the slough and he shuddered.

"Duck," Colleen said to him, almost too calmly, "there's something...something with us."

He brought the flashlight around in a slow, easy arc, illuminating the rippling sedge and slopping drainage ditches, shrubs and whip-like reeds. Yes, something was out there and he could clearly imagine it was holding its breath. Waiting.

"Who's there?" he called out.

There was a brief rustling along a low, grassy hill. He put the light in that direction and saw...or thought he saw...a fleeting glimpse of several grotesque, dwarfish forms melting into shadow.

He tightened his grip on Colleen's hand and they ran down the road, the flashlight beam jiggling and throwing jumping shadows and leaping shapes around them. The cottage was low and sprawling, roofed with willow and sedge, a brick stack chimney rising above. A traditional Lincolnshire mud and stud structure. And nothing had ever looked so good.

They came around an old truck with a tarped bed and began pounding furiously on a huge, oaken door. They beat on it so hard it rattled in its frame.

Behind them, more sounds, furtive shapes that were there and then gone when the flashlight beam sought them out.

"Donny..." Colleen began to say and then the door opened and two huge hands took hold of them and yanked them inside, so quickly and so powerfully that there was no time to do anything but gasp.

The door slammed shut behind them.

"Jesus, but you two scared the life from me poor bones," the owner of the hands said to them. "It is not common and rarer still that I receive callers out here, but I had a feeling—as me mother would say—I took a notion there would be callers after the terror of them screeching brakes. Why, and here you are. But you'll excuse me, surely, for the lack of proper introductions. I would be Sean Burrows. And yourself?"

Donny and Colleen looked at him and then at each other. Inside, it was warm and safe and cozy as only country cottages had a right to be. And the owner? Well, Mr. Sean Burrows couldn't have been much over five feet tall, but he was round like a tub, thick in the neck and strong in the arm. He sported a heavy, fanning red beard like a mop and nappy hair of the same color, though touched with snow. No not a young man, surely, but just how old it was really hard to say.

"I'm Donny Wester and this is my wife, Colleen. I'm American, but Colleen is from Lincolnshire. We…we had an accident."

"Did you? Well, no fear, you're safe as toast now and my croft is certainly yours," Burrows said, extending his arms to either side. He steered the both of them to the open hearth and the fire blazing away in there. "I'm thinking the two of you could use a wee drop of something strong enough to prop, but not strong enough to wilt—"

"No," Donny told him. "I mean, not right now. We…we hit something out on the road…"

Burrow's sparkling gray eyes narrowed a stitch. "And would that be animal, vegetable, or mineral?"

"It was a…a…" But Donny couldn't seem to bring himself to say the word, try as he might.

So Colleen said it, mouthed it really. "We hit a child. We hit a child out there and…I think we killed it."

"A child? A child? And out here?" Burrows studied them as if looking for the joke he thought he might find there. "Dear Christ, what would a little sprog be doing jogging out on the fen-road?"

"We hit it," Colleen maintained.

Burrow raised a shaggy eyebrow, found his whiskey and tossed back a swallow. "A child, you say?" He put his inquiry to Donny. Maybe the glazed, hurting look in his eyes was making him suspect something. Something other than a child. "You're certain it was a child?"

"A naked child," Colleen said pointedly.

Burrows waited, something hard around his mouth and eyes now. "Well, this is a clarted mess, ain't it?" He sighed. "Well...well, I suppose we'll have to have a look, throw our eyes on it and see what we see. Let me grab a torch."

He pulled a worn denim coat on over his red-and-black checked flannel shirt. Took up his torch and his double-barreled shotgun, too, an antique twenty-bore Parker. Neither Donny nor Colleen questioned the necessity of this. They followed him outside as he played his light around, maybe looking for something and maybe just being cautious in the way of fen-folk.

"It would be shorter, maybe, if we cut through the fen," Donny suggested and was overjoyed when Burrows nixed the idea.

"The fen at night?" he said. "No disrespect, Mr. Wester, none at all implied nor intended...but you're daft as a boiled owl. Nobody goes out on the fen by night, not round heres, not a safe idea at that. No, we'll take the lorry and be happy with that. It's best to stay on roads and such after dark."

As they climbed into the truck, Colleen asked: "Why don't people go out on the fen?"

"Well, dove, there's many reasons, ain't there? Some good and some not so good, I figure. Folks say and rightly so that it's a dangerous place...bogs and ditches and sinkholes...and more than one person has disappeared out there. And others have superstitious reasoning for staying far and away."

"Which are..."

Burrows laughed but seemed uneasy. "You say you're from these climes, pet, and you ask me that?"

"I'm from Barton," Colleen explained, studying the road in the gleam of the headlights, maybe looking for small, skulking shapes.

"Ah! From the North, are you? Barton...up above the chalk wolds, well that's settles it then." He let out a brief, nervous chuckle, saying, "Well, love, didn't you know? The fens are haunted..."

In the glare of the truck headlights, the fractured little carcass looked no more appealing lying in its viscous puddle at the side of the road. If anything, it seemed more skeletal, more distorted, even less like a child and more like some nightmare that had crawled out of a moldering well in a fairy tale. It had shriveled or dried out, the blood and fluids going to a dark crust, its lengthy, hooked fingers curled into gnarled fists. And the face... certainly no better, still leering and malformed, the eyes still glaring with poison, the lips pulled away from teeth that looked like they were made for rending meat from bone.

Colleen looked at it this time and had to turn away, the blood draining from her face, replaced by something mottled and sickly. Donny put his arm around her but felt not one degree better.

When Burrows saw it, it stopped him dead. He pushed the torch into Colleen's hand, took up his shotgun. He broke it open, then snapped it back. Carefully, as if approaching a wounded leopard, he gave it a prod with the barrels of his Parker. The little corpse shifted with a sticky, wet sound, but it was certainly dead.

"I'll be damned," he said, eyes wide and mouth trembling. "I'll be damned and then damned again. You surely hit no child, Mr. Wester, you surely did not."

"What...what is it then?"

But Burrows ignored him, his face mirroring a mixture of fascination and repulsion. "Aye, you got one, all right. After all these years, you bagged one of the little bastards."

"What?"

"A Yarthkin, laddy, a bloody Yarthkin! Dear Christ and Heaven if it ain't one of them little creeping devils in the flesh!"

Colleen would not look at it. What she did look at was Burrows. "Oh, come now, Mr. Burrows...a Yarthkin? Do you hear what you're saying to us?"

"I do, love, God, but I do."

"But it's a load of kilter and rammel! A story, a folktale, and this—"

"Is the inspiration for many a boggle story passed down and then down again."

"What the hell are you two talking about?" Donny wanted to know.

But Burrows silenced him with a finger to his lips, cocked his head and listened. Out in the fen there were noises like they'd heard coming up the road to the cottage. Stealthy sounds. Rustling sounds. The sounds of forms moving quietly through the tangled grasses. They were all hearing it.

Burrows ran back to the bed of his truck and pulled the tarp off. He carried it over to the carcass. "We'll wrap the little bugger in this," he said, spreading it out.

Donny just stood there.

"C'mon, man, can't you hear? Can't you hear what's coming through the fen?" His face was corded and his eyes bulging. "Lend a hand here! Quick with you now!"

The sounds were getting closer.

"Donny..." Colleen began.

Donny crouched down but couldn't bring himself to touch it. The idea was unthinkable, like handling leeches or grave-worms. Clenching his teeth, he took hold of the muscular, bowed ankles. They were greasy and cold like congealed wax. He twitched at the feel of them, then took hold again and helped Burrows dump the creature onto the tarp. Its face was fully revealed to him, that streaming oily hair fallen away now. No, it was certainly no child. More like a mutant half-breed ape or the skull of one, a sneering evil face, horribly wizened by diverging ruts and lines, the nose flattened with upturned nostrils much like the nares of a skull. He was glad when Burrows wrapped it up in the old green tarp, when he no longer had to look on its crooked body with its alien muscularity and the fine down of pale hair at its chest and throat, those hooked fingers.

They dumped it unceremoniously in the back of the truck and then Burrows shooed them into the cab, the sounds out in the fen getting louder and nearer, and beginning to sound like garbled, hissing voices.

Burrows didn't bother bringing the truck around, he just put it in reverse and backed them quickly down the pot-holed round to his own turnoff.

"The Land Rover, I should pull it off the road," Donny said, Colleen clinging to him.

But Burrows shook his head. He stopped at the turnoff and

flicked on his high beams. They illuminated the black lick of road for some distance, turning the fens to daylight. The Land Rover was a good distance off, but they saw what Burrows wanted them to see. A throng of shadowy, misshapen little forms thronging around the Land Rover, a few climbing atop of it. At the intrusion of light, they slipped away.

"Aye," Burrows said, "the little buggers are casting for your scent…"

They put the tarp and its contents in a lean-to structure at the rear of the cottage. Donny didn't know what they were called in England, but in America you'd see such rooms at the back of old farmhouses. Skinning rooms or butchering rooms. A place to hang your kills and gut them when the time came. The room was much like that with straw on the floor and hooks set into the rough-hewn beams overhead.

Colleen was a strong, decisive woman in his experience. She had the strength of her bloodline, but this had shaken her. She was pacing back and forth, breathing hard, her lips pulled into a tight, pale line. Her eyes were staring and hysterical-looking. "This cannot be, this cannot be, this cannot bloody fucking well be." In the strain of it all, her carefully polished, generic-sounding British accent had slipped a few notches, echoing the accent of her birthplace: "*This canna be, this canna be…*"

Donny tried to go to her and she slapped his hands away. "Don't you dare lay yer hands upon me, Donald Wester. Yarthkins, oh the bloody dirty things."

Shrugging, he watched Burrows unwrap the creature with shaking fingers like a kid on Christmas morning. He was excited and shuddering and completely beyond himself.

"All right," Donny said. "I've had enough of this shit. What the hell are you two going on about? What in Christ is a 'Yarthkin'?"

Burrows took a deep breath. "It's…well, sonny, it's a sort of goblin or elf that folks hereabouts believed in at one time."

"An elf?" If this was a joke, it wasn't very funny.

Burrows peeled the tarp away from the ghastly little face. "Sure and enough, it's a Yarthkin. Your woman knows of them and why should she not? What boy and girl of this place has not listened to stories of them around the fire? Has been sent off to bed before the Yarthkins got them."

"It can't be…it can't be a Yarthkin," Colleen said, coming around now.

"Oh, but it is, missy. And I should know, for these little horrors have haunted generations of me family. Oh, yes and yes." He pulled out a little lock-blade knife, snapped it open. Using the tip of the blade he pushed graying, rubbery lips away from the teeth. They were even worse under the amber glow of the oil lamps…discolored, yellowish, sharp as peg nails, the canines and lower lateral incisors long and sharp like the fangs of a cobra.

"Jesus," Donny said.

In the back of his mind, he couldn't imagine this little horror being related in any way to the elves of fairy tales or TV shows. The idea of it dancing around and singing, *we represent the lollypop guild, the lollypop guild,* was ludicrous and disturbing. It made his skull echo with shrieking, deranged laughter.

I ran over an elf, he thought mindlessly. *The mind boggles.*

And here he thought the most unusual thing he could tell people back home was that he had eaten a faggot. "Faggot" being Lincolnshire slang for something akin to Haggis.

Burrows covered the awful face back up and saw to it the door was bolted and chained. He slapped a Master Lock on the chain just to be sure. The door had to be about three inches thick and could have stopped a charging bull, but he obviously had reasons for security.

And Donny could pretty much figure what they were.

"All right," Burrows said. "Off with us, up into the croft proper. We'll be needing a hot fire and a drop or two."

And outside, the wind began to blow.

At least, they hoped it was the wind.

Sitting at the hearth with a mug of whiskey in his hand, Donny said, "But elves for chrissake…c'mon, that little monster doesn't look like an elf. Elves and leprechauns and all that nonsense, those are myths. Little fellows smoking pipes and wearing curly-toed shoes and little hats. Tolkien and that nonsense. Aren't they supposed to clean people's houses when they're out?"

Burrows chuckled under his voice. "What you're referencing there, son, is the result of hundreds of years of romanticizing about those little buggers. Sheer fantasy. What we have in there is no wee fairy nor pixie, no charming fairy nor brownie nor amusing Hobbit, but a savage. Nothing more, nothing less. A survivor from a race that should have gone extinct a thousand years ago if not ten or fifty, for that matter."

Burrows explained to him that the British Isles, like most of the world, were rife with wild yarns of bogies and imps, wood spirits and hell hounds. In England, there were tales every child once knew—Bucca Boo and the Fetch, Gindylow and the Brag, Spriggans and Silkies and Wrynecks. But most of those had been relegated to folktale and local legend over the years, and others were known only to folklorists as the days of the grand storytellers waned.

"Aye," he said, gazing into the fire, his face flickering with orange and yellow light, "when I was but a wee nip, my grandmammy would tell us little sprogs fearsome tales of bogarts and hags and Old Bloody Bones himself. Scary, they was, but like such tales, they was intended to instruct, to teach little ones. You stayed out of the dark forest and glens for fear that the hags or wood bogarts would devour you. You stayed out of lonely places and cellars for Old Bloody Bones would spirit you away to the old barrows. And you stayed off the fen at night, for the Yarthkins were a-prowl and they craved, so it was said, the flesh and blood of children…"

Certainly England, he told them, was filled with tales of the little people. Some were quaint, lovely tales and others were sheer nightmares. In Wales, there were hills called fairy mounds and in Lincolnshire they had similar earthen structures. The little people were thought to live in subterranean burrows beneath the mounds.

"What I'm saying to you fine people is that all these tales have a single, ancient origin: what we have back of the croft, that little devil there. God, and here I thought those things had died and years past." He downed his whiskey and lit a cigarette. "Well, these parts have been haunted by the Yarthkins since before the Celts came. The Romans knew of them, aye, as did the Saxons, who were my people, family history claims."

The Yarthkins superstition was very old and very deep-rooted. At one time, he explained, the Yarthkins were the very terror of the fens. They raided farms and took down lone travelers and devoured livestock and made every stripe of mischief. But after the 17th and 18th centuries, when wholescale draining of the fens began in earnest, the stories dried up, too, and the Yarthkins became things of hearthside clop and old wives' tales. And the reason for that was that the Yarthkins last stronghold in England, perhaps in the world, was being decimated.

"Scientists and that ilk would say habitat destruction and I agree with them. When the fens were drained—and only a finger of true fen remains today—the Yarthkins died out. Or, so it seemed. But a few relict bands have survived and even to this very day."

Donny kept looking at Colleen, knowing that in things natural and biological she knew a great deal.

"So, you think our Yarthkins were not elves as such, but merely the inspiration of such?" she said.

Burrows pulled off his cigarette. "Certainly. What the Yarthkins are, my dear, is a survival of a Neolithic race of pygmies. It's hardly a new theory, that one, but it's surely a sound one. I read once where it was thought that tales of bogarts and trolls could have been inspired by historical encounters with remaining tribes of Neanderthals and that stories of giants may have been like inspired by our ancestors encountering giant evolved apes. I am not an educated man as such, but it makes perfect sense to me. And through the centuries all these fine yarns have sprung up about these creatures.

"So. Our Yarthkins, like those other creatures, were hunted to near extinction by man as we know him today and a few of his ancestors. Driven into mountain and fen and the inaccessible wastes, there living a skulking existence and becoming the things of legend with an occasional chance meeting with man to keep the tales rolling. All those lovely fairy tales and book fantasies concerning little people are just that, for the reality is quite a bit grimmer, I would say. For these pygmies, our Yarthkins, are not a fine and wise fairy folk, but a band of little prehistoric men. Monsters, yes, and my family has had a hand in bringing these little devils an inch or two closer to extinction through the years."

Donny and Colleen were quiet. They took it all in, both supposing what the man said was at least a logical explanation for such phenomena and one that fit tight with their modern, scientific rationale. Maybe in the Middle Ages people could have swallowed supernatural explanations for such things, but not anymore. The modern mind demanded physical proof and a system of evidentiary reasoning by which such things could be classified and organized within the natural order of things.

Burrows said, "Aye, me people were Saxons and they came to the fens, fighting the Romans and all manner of adversaries, but when the Romans returned home to battle for their own country...around the fourth century AD...well, the Saxons saw no reason to cross back yonder over the North Sea. They decided to stay here in England. And why not? History has it they settled around the river Lud, in what would one day become Louth. And family tradition says me ancestors were amongst them." Burrows finished his cigarette and tossed it in the fire. "Aye, them were hard times, you can be right and sure of that. I've done a morsel or two of studying the Saxon way, so I can be fairly sure of certain things. Theirs was a hard, unforgiving existence amongst the fens and wild wolds of this land. They would have lived in dirty, smelling little wattle huts with sunken, muddy floors, reed roofs, and walls slapped together quite crudely of straw and mud and cow dung. Daub, they would have called it. The Saxons, taking their spark from the old Celts, would have become agricultural, fashioning what they needed from what nature offered and raising a few crops like barley and oats. Maybe keeping a few animals. Well, as I say, it was no grand existence, theirs. When the crops failed, entire villages would have starved."

But there were other desperations, Burrows explained, beyond hardship, disease, and suffering. For just as the Picts had overcome the aborigine pygmy tribes, they themselves were overcome by Celtic invaders and Roman Legions later on. Then came the Anglo-Saxons, first as mercenaries against the Romans, then as conquerors of these lands, fighting tooth and nail with the Danes for possession of Britain. This, he explained, was known as cultural or ethnic succession. That through it all, even well after the Norman incursions of the 10th century, there had been a constant: the little people. Though nearly decimated, they clung to existence as was their way being the direct ancestors of a fierce stone-age tribe.

The Picts, so said Roman scholars, had their tales of the little people, as did the Celts. The Romans themselves, according to written tracts, encountered a band of the little people in a great forest that was considered taboo by the Celts. During a midnight raid through the forest in search of Celtic strongholds, the Legions were assaulted by a band of "foul dark little men" who killed a great many Romans with stone arrows dipped in poison. The Romans managed to escape and kill a great many of the savages, but after that they no longer doubted the reality of Britain's savage little men. The Saxons, too, Burrows said, had fought against the pygmy tribes, considering them to be vile and sub-human.

But the invading armies through the centuries had managed to reduce the population of the pygmies to barely viable levels. One of their last strongholds beyond the wilds of Ireland and Wales and the Highlands of Scotland, would have been Lincolnshire and its primordial fens. Long after the little people had been vanquished to legend in those other places, they lived on in the fens. The draining of the fens probably destroyed most of them and now there could be scarce but a handful.

Colleen had listened and now she spoke. "But how could they survive? Through all these years and in secret?"

"Ah, the nature of the fens, love. The fenland is huge and sprawling, nothing but a few scattered market towns marring its surface. Miles and miles of lonely tracts and for a race which history tells us is solely nocturnal? Well, it makes a certain sense...now don't it?"

She had to admit that it did.

Maybe it was a good thing, she told them, that they had run down one of the tribe before its kind disappeared forever into the annals of folktale.

Burrows lit another cigarette. "When I was but a boy, there were stories of the Yarthkins, but we figured they was so much lark. We paid them little mind. Some of the old folks, they were believers, but not us which were young and spry. It was quite common back then for cottages around here to have stone bowls out front, things which looked much like frog ponds. But what they was, you see, were offering bowls for the Yarthkins. Folks would dump rotting fruit and vegetables, bad meat in 'em for it was well known the Yarthkins favored gamy, evil-smelling things. Scavengers, I suspect. But that was the custom, feed the little buggers—and particularly on May Day when they were said to be randy and active—and this would keep 'em from despoiling your livestock and fields. It was a very old practice, God could only say how long such a clotty thing might date back."

"So you never believed in them?" Donny put to him.

"Not so as you would notice, laddy. But then...well, just shy of me sixteenth birthday, something happened that changed me young mind."

"And what was that?"

Burrows exhaled smoke through his nostrils, smiling. "Why, I saw one and in the flesh..."

Burrows' story.

It was a true thing when he told them that when he was young and spry that few believed in the Yarthkins. The old folk told their stories and filled their offering bowls with spoiled goods and now and again, some chickens would turn up missing or a pig or two, perhaps the refuse bins were rummaged through during the dark of the moon, but beyond that life on the fens was slow and measured. There was always work to be done and tales of little men seemed to have little place. The farmers worked their fields of potatoes, wheat, and sugar beets. Men still cut sedge and dug peat, labored in the old clay pits and harvested reed.

Burrows himself, a robust lad of fifteen, cut peat with his brothers and uncles. Digging it from the fen with a becket in blocks that were sun-dried and used like clay bricks to fortify homes and cottages. Burrows' father, Thomas Burrows, had been injured gravely in the war and so was unable to earn his bread from traditional fen activities. But being of sound mind and ready ambition that marked his clan, the elder Burrows manufactured paraffin and wicks, ran a hatchery for geese, duck, and turkey eggs.

A week before his sixteenth birthday, Burrows returned from school one day, ready to dig peat with the others, only there was no digging to be done that day. A local girl—Elizabeth Godwin, a lass of but twelve summers—had turned up missing. She had failed to return the night before from her auntie's croft and her family feared she had crossed the fen rather than staying to the road.

A search party was organized.

Burrows was there with his brothers and uncles that gloomy, misty evening when they began to search the fen. Not a dyke nor ditch or lode went uninvestigated. The group rambled through tall fen and litter, sedge field and hay meadow. They poked in the old flooded brick pits, excavated meres, and sloshed through carr, fighting through sallows and buckthorn. But not a trace of the girl was to be had. Dogs were brought in the next day, but they lost the scent out in the dead water and morass, turning back upon their own trails.

Beaten, sore, and waterlogged, the search was broken off after three fruitless days. It did not go unnoticed by Sean Burrows that each time the name Elizabeth Godwin was mentioned, his old grandmammy crossed herself over at the hearth. And that night, while he was thought to be sleeping, he heard his father and grandmammy having one of their rare animated conversations.

"The poor child," said his father, "gotten herself lost. Is a shame. A terrible, terrible shame."

"Ah, Thomas Burrows, now did I raise ye to be daft as an old woman full of buttermilk?" said grandmammy. "Hear yerself on this now! Ye know plain as I what happened to that poor girl, do ye not?"

"Enough, enough, I won't listen to that rot!"

"Won't ye?" Grandmammy was angry. "Aye, ye might indeed by thick as six planks, but ye know full well enough what's out on them fens by night, ye know well as I."

But the elder Burrows refused to discuss it and through the coming days, grandmammy remained quite somber and sharp of tongue. Then one afternoon, Mr. Inskip stopped by. He was a friend of the elder Burrows and many was the night they shared a cup and gazed over a chessboard. Mr. Inskip spoke with Thomas Burrows in private and both men came away looking quite grim indeed.

It was two days later that Sean Burrows, his brothers, and uncles were taken away to Mr. Inskip's land. Inskip was a mink farmer. He raised minks and slaughtered them for their fur, making quite a handsome profit at it. Such a profit that he was one of the largest landowners south of Louth. And that day they were taken out to his gut-fields. After harvesting, the skinned carcasses of the minks—upward of two or three thousand, sometimes as many five or six—were taken out to a wide, grassy meadow a mile or two out in the fens. By special license from the ministry, Inskip was allowed to dump the skinned animals here where nature took its course.

Sean Burrows could well remember the putrescent, evil smell of that place, the thousands of rotting mink corpses heaped in piles. Left for scavengers, flies, and worms. Whatever fancied a taste. Even on that rainy afternoon, the buzzing of vermin was nearly deafening.

"Within a week," Inskip said. "There's not a scrap to be had."

Sean still did not understand why it was they had come here and his father would not elaborate. They came with shotguns and rifles and battery-powered search lamps. Sean's uncles seemed to know and so did his older brothers. As they waited, just within the fringe of the scrub, Mr. Inskip said how he'd always assumed that rats and weasels had been devouring the carcasses. But finding the skeletons of minks high in trees miles distant had made him question this.

"Could be birds," Thomas Burrows said. "Would not surprise me. A harrier would do such a thing."

"Yes, certainly," said Mr. Inskip. "As would owls and vultures...but that doesn't go a pinch to explaining those...ah, those terrible little footprints yonder in the field."

"What footprints would those be?" Sean asked.

"You never mind, Sean," his father snapped. "You just never mind."

And then darkness came and the men spread out, formed killing perimeters as if they were on a hunt. It was a dark night and Mr. Inskip said that "they were most active in the dark of the moon." So, yes, it was dark and windless, the air noisome and wormy, a light rain falling. The mud was cold and sluicing, swallowing their boots as they waited, waited in that dread, pregnant silence.

Then—

Sean's brother Henry had his hand on his arm, telling him it would be soon now, quite soon. And Sean didn't know what was going on, but a strange, inexplicable sense of foreboding was sinking into his marrow and churning his empty belly. He was shivering, but it was not from the cold.

A few feet away, Mr. Inskip whispered, "You stand ready with the light, Sean, and when I give the word, put it full on those gut-fields. And whatever you see, do not waver that light, put it on those you see, put it on them, boy."

Sean was too scared by that point to bother asking what he might see and the idea of Yarthkins was light-years from his mind, though his brain was even then fermenting with terrible imagery. Silence was drawn out, unbearable, and then...out in the gut-fields, movement, sound. You could feel the tension going down the line of men and Sean had all he could do not to break and run.

But they had allowed him along because they thought he was man enough. He could not let them down.

Soon, out there in that riven darkness, he could hear the sounds of something pawing through the heaps of carcasses. Yes, just pawing at first, bringing a high, repulsive stench with them. He could hear hissing sounds and slithering sounds that reminded him of something quite near speech, yet low and bestial. The very sound of it roiled his guts and filled his head with

reaching, long-armed shadows. Then came the sound of chewing and grinding, sucking and biting. Bones splintering. Meat
being rent. Hideous sounds. Impossible sounds. Whatever was
out there—and there were many—were feeding on the carrion.

Not foxes.

Not wild dogs.

But something…something unspeakable.

And Mr. Inskip's voice said, "Hold now, boys, just hold. Let
them eat their fill, let them get fat and lazy and then we'll have
our time."

Five minutes.

Ten minutes.

Twenty—

"Now, on with those lights!"

Three other men had search lamps beyond Sean. They were
arranged so that when they turned the lights on, the gut-fields
would be inundated in an ocean of brilliance.

Sean was the last to click his on and that's when he saw.
Little men. Dozens of little men out there. They were no more
than three feet in height, the largest well under four. But men?
No, this was some twisted aberration of the same. Some nameless mutation. These things were vulgar and debased, a grisly
race of dwarves with yellow, scaly skin and wild, knotted manes
of hair. Their legs were short and bowed, their arms long and
sinewy.

When the light hit them, some began to screech with an
awful, shrill wailing like that of wraiths bursting from crypts.
Others just waited, transfixed. There was gore dripping from
their mouths, ribbons of entrails in their hands. One of them was
feeding bowels down its throat like linked sausages. Another
had the putrefied, skinned body of a mink dangling from its
jaws like a cat with a mouse. Showing no true fear, its powerful
jaws crushed the mink's head to a pulp and, taking huge rending bites, crunched and chewed the little carcass, finally swallowing it. The heaps of dead animals were four- and five-feet
deep…and *moving*. Moving with an undulating, roiling motion,
and that was because the little men had tunneled into those
rancid depths, were swimming in that viscid, noxious sea of

putrefaction. And now…now they were emerging like worms from the green and black remains.

Emerging with full bellies and gnashing teeth, some sucking marrow from tiny cleaved bones and others with the feet of minks dangling from their serrated jaws.

This is where things got murky in Sean's memory.

He thought maybe he screamed. Or maybe they all did. But in the blinding glare of those lights, the little men shrieking and hissing and snarling, Mr. Inskip's little posse opened up with shotguns and rifles. A dozen little men died in the first volley, half that many in the next few seconds.

The air was acrid with the reek of death and gunpowder. Shells were chambered and fired and the little, horrible men died in great numbers, blinded by the glaring lights. Many others ran off into the night. And that was Sean's most vivid memory…one of them running off. A female with a gruesome, fissured face like an old storybook hag and a set of pendulous teats. And suckered to one of them, a pale and bloated larval form clutched in the crook of one skeletal arm. Her young. A wriggling, squirming thing like a maggot.

Within ten minutes it was done.

The little men were either killed or dispersed.

And that was how it ended for Sean. The men drove off in their trucks, guns at the ready. In the morning, they returned. Sean was not among them. Overtaken by a fever, he was laid low in bed. But his brother Henry told him that the little men were burned in great fires, that their ashes were scattered and their bones and skulls shattered with hammers and dumped into the fen ditches.

Sweating and shaking and near-hallucinatory, Sean asked: "What…what *were* they?"

Henry held his hand, gripped it. "Yarthkins, Sean," he said. "Them were Yarthkins."

There was silence for a time after that.

Colleen and Donny watched the flames and cast curious looks at one another from time to time. Burrows smoked, his eyes moist with remembrance and sorrow. They did not doubt that what he had told them was the truth. His face was aged, ravaged by the birth pains of that tale.

"I've told no one of that in all these years," he admitted to them, pulling off his whiskey. "Dear God...I don't suppose I believed it had even happened, not until tonight. But now? Yes, now I know better, curse my soul."

"But that was a long time ago," Donny said. "Surely, I mean, their numbers must have thinned by now."

"They were thin then, son. A starving and dying lot. And I would guess they fare no better today. Maybe they're too wicked to die properly and maybe within a generation, there will be no more Yarthkins."

Colleen said, "We...we really should be on our way."

Burrows stared at her. "Do you think, love, that would be wise? They're out there. They don't give up their dead easy and not to our kind, their traditional enemies. No, I would say stay put until first light."

That seemed to make sense.

Burrows served more whiskey and brought a blanket for Colleen now that the chill damp of the fen was invading the cottage. She did not like the idea of remaining there and being the sort of woman she was, there was absolutely no hiding it. Just as there was no hiding the fact that she couldn't honestly make up her mind whether Burrows was their savior or an out-and-out madman.

Maybe Burrows knew it, too. "Aye, this is an awful truck of dung to swallow in one sitting," he said to them. "What happened at the gut-field...it stayed on me brain all these long years, and after a time I couldn't be sure if it had happened or I'd gone a wee bit clotty with age. I moved up to Scotland after me mother died, never to come back. This croft, well, it was willed to me brother Henry, and when he passed, to me. So, I came back five years ago, came back and had an evil time of it those first few weeks. The memories of me family, certainly. But more than that...maybe the fact that certain of those memories might be true, that I hadn't imagined a scrap of it."

Donny said, "After the gut-field incident...did your father or brothers ever mention that night other than to say how they destroyed the remains of those Yarthkins?"

Burrows shook his head. "Nary a word, son. I had the fevers for a week, knackered out I was. The old man, why he'd get in a right wicked mood if you so much as hinted at such things as little men on the fen." He stood up, stretched his back. "Well, after I returned I found something that was willed to me besides this croft. Me poor brother Henry, why he left me a letter explaining that there was something passed down as it were from generation to generation by the Burrows' men."

He walked across the room, past the staircase leading to the loft above and into a back room. Fishing a key from his shirt pocket, he opened the door and fired up a kerosene lantern. It was a storeroom for the most part. Wooden crates and cardboard boxes, a couple of antique steamer trunks. Against the wall there was a mahogany cabinet that looked quite old.

"Take a gander at the secret of the Burrows," he told them, opening the cabinet doors.

The secret was a skeleton.

It was hung together with baling wire but seemed anatomically correct as far as Donny could tell...at least, all the parts seemed to belong. It was maybe three feet long, the bones yellow and gray and pitted with age. Stripped of flesh, you could see the degenerate architecture of the Yarthkin in all its aberrant, primal glory. You could see how much it was like a man and how very different at the same time. The cranium was low and sloping, the maxilla pulled in and the mandible pushed out. The teeth were sharp, though worn to nubs in spots as if from the wear and tear of great age. Many were missing. The ribcage jutted like a birdcage, the spinal vertebrae shorter and more compact than a man's. The legs were undersized, yet the femurs and tibias thick and angular. It didn't seem that in life the creature would have had a neck and its arms must have trailed nearly to its knees. The finger-bones were very long and hooked like scythes, the tarsals and metatarsals of the feet broad and splayed.

Donny knew he was seeing something very few men ever had. And something, no doubt, a thousand paleoanthropologists and comparative anatomists would have sold their souls for.

His rational mind told him this was the sort of thing you found hanging in carnival tents, something pasted together out of dog, ape, and crocodile bones. But he didn't believe that. For he'd seen a dead Yarthkin and knew without question that this was what one looked like divorced of meat and skin.

What he couldn't stop looking at was its skull. It was inhuman, savage, lewd. The nasal openings were elongated, elliptical, and nearly horizontal rather than vertical as in a human skull. The orbitals were huge and shaped like inverted crescent moons giving the creature a frightening, demonic look like a jack-o'-lantern carved to scare the kiddies.

"I have no way of knowing how old this thing is," Burrows admitted to him. "But my guess is quite old. Perhaps it's sort of a trophy from the days of my Saxon ancestors when they were trying to wrestle this land from its Neolithic masters. Aye, perhaps a trophy and perhaps a warning."

Colleen was crouched down examining the left foot. "Look at these metatarsals," she said. "They're irregular, twisted-up… the foot faces inward. Maybe a birth defect. I'll bet this one was a cripple of a sort."

Good old Colleen. Now Donny was certain it was authentic. No fake would have such attention to detail.

He finally turned away.

He couldn't bear to look upon it. It woke something in him that made his skin crawl, made him absolutely sick to his stomach. Just like the one out on the road. There was something in him, some primeval imperative that told him these little men were unclean, polluted, had to be exterminated at any cost. The feeling was physical and overwhelming. It made him clench his fists and grind his teeth.

"You feel it, too, don't you, son?" Burrows said. "The loathing for them Yarthkins. Aye, it runs deep. A race memory, perhaps. An inbred hatred of their kind."

They went back by the fire and Burrows announced it wouldn't be dawn for another four hours. It was only a matter of waiting the night out. When the sun came up, things would look better. Perversions of nature such as the Yarthkins were hard to believe in the light of day. And maybe that was for the best.

So they sat and fed the fire and Burrows drank his whiskey and smoked his cigarettes while the night drew out long and dark and uneasy. They did not speak. They listened to the wind outside…heard it speak as perhaps their ancestors once had, gathered around a smoky turf fire waiting for the wind to tell them if the Yarthkins were coming.

So they waited.

And true to form, the wind told them.

"Aye, they're coming," Burrows said. "And in numbers."

It began with a few sounds that could be overlooked—the creaking of a loose board or a rattling rain gutter, the sound of movement outside the walls. Things easily explainable in the context of the blowing wind. But then the sounds became more concentrated and more organized—little feet pounding outside the cottage. Scrapings and thuddings and hammering sounds… as if someone wanted to get in and bad.

Colleen was standing now, shocked to attention. Her face was colorless, rubbery. "They…they can't get in, though," she said, wanting to believe it.

But she knew the answer to that. If the Yarthkins wanted in, they'd find a way. Creatures like that always found a way. It was their nature.

Burrows took up his shotgun and handed Donny a pistol. "That was me father's, he carried it during the war. A Webley Mark 4. It's a revolver, .38, just aim and shoot. But don't shoot, unless there's no other choice."

"This is insane," Colleen said, so Burrows shoved a hatchet into her hand.

He handed out flashlights.

And then there was nothing to do but wait as the storm outside the cottage picked up intensity and the little men began their siege. For siege it was and no one there doubted that this was a systematic assault. Like any raiding party, they had sent out scouts, now the main force had arrived.

They could hear them circling the cottage, laying waste to Burrows' truck outside. They heard the windshield shatter, things like clubs pummeling it. But those outside didn't waste

much time on the old truck. For as Burrows had said, they did
not give up their dead without a fight. And particularly to their
ancestral enemies—the tall pale men who had swept over their
lands and slaughtered their people.

Maybe the Yarthkins weren't much more than savages, organized on a rudimentary tribal level, but they had long memories and they knew who their age-old adversaries were. And as
in the days of yore, when they had your scent, they would find
you. For certain animalistic traits had not abandoned them.

Donny was thinking these things, feeling like he knew the
little men and not for the first time that night. His gut instinct
told him those things had sniffed them out, just as they'd sniffed
out the cadaver of their fallen brethren.

Even Burrows had said it: *The little buggers are casting for your
scent.*

They were stealthy after destroying the truck…at least for
a time, moving around out there, investigating doors and running their fingernails along windowpanes with unpleasant
scratching sounds.

Then:

"Listen," Burrows said. "Aye…they're climbing up the
croft…I can hear them…"

They all heard them. Quietly, but with telltale clawing and
dragging sounds, they were climbing the walls. Many of them.
Then they were moving overhead with scampering sounds.
Creaking sounds. The sound of fingers digging and tearing
away chunks of sod from the roof.

"This is insane," Colleen said in a sharp, girlish voice. "What
do they want? What the hell do they want from us?"

"The dead one," Burrows told her.

"Then give it to them!"

Burrows was about to say something, but then there came
a shattering of glass from the kitchen and a thundering of fists
upon the door leading into the anteroom that held the dead
Yarthkin. This is where their attack commenced. More rocks hit
the other windows, slammed against the walls of the cottage.
But at the outer door was where they were, banging and clawing and kicking and hammering. It was a stout old door, but

it could only take so much. They heard it groan. Heard wood splintering. It finally gave in with a resounding crash.

And the Yarthkins came storming in, making low, guttural hissing noises that must have been some depraved form of speech. They brought an overpowering stink with them, a black, festering odor of rotting meat and dank places.

Donny's skin was crawling in prickly waves and his belly was filled with a sour blackness that made him want to vomit. Colleen clung to him, fingers digging into his arms and cutting trenches...but he was oblivious to the pain.

The cottage was now being hit by a barrage of stones, like hailstones the size of baseballs sent crashing into the walls. The din was crushing and maybe it had been planned that way...for those inside could not hear what was happening on the roof or in the anteroom.

Donny thought: *They'll take the dead one and then crawl back into their holes.*

But he didn't believe it. Not for a minute.

About that time Colleen screamed.

She was gesturing madly at the stairwell that led up to the loft above. They all saw it—a yellowish, abominable visage staring out at them from between the rungs of the banister. The head was cocked, almost curious, hair tangled over its primitive face. The eyes were shining, luminous by firelight.

Donny swallowed.

Burrows brought up his shotgun. "Well, well, me lovely, just hold still, hold still..."

He pulled both triggers.

The twelve-gauge buckshot blasted away the rungs and splashed that malign face from the bone beneath. The Yarthkin was thrown backward, crying out with a pathetic trilling sound that died out instantly.

But the others heard it.

Three more came down the stairs with a loping motion and the door leading to the anteroom groaned in its frame. It was vibrating madly as they threw themselves at it. The wood began to splinter and crack, paint chips spraying into the air.

Burrows brought up his shotgun and put a hole through it

the size of a dinner plate. Some of the things screamed as the buckshot tore through them, but the chasm in the door only weakened it and it split right down the middle and fell into the room.

Burrows didn't have time to reload.

He snatched up an oil lantern and tossed it at the doorway as they began to slink through, hissing and croaking and gnashing their long teeth. The lantern shattered and fire licked up the walls, spilled into the other room, and engulfed a pair of Yarthkins that went shrieking into the night. The others let out a resounding screech that was one of defeat and cheated hatred. But the flames had the desired effect and the little men were driven off.

Donny had followed Burrows' example and grabbed a flaming log out of the hearth and heaved it at the Yarthkins surging down the stairwell. It hit the banister with a shower of sparks and the little monsters howled and dragged the corpse of their brother with them.

"The light'll drive 'em into darkness!" Burrows called out, wild with glee.

Problem was, the burning oil from the lamp had found the straw in the anteroom and it was going up. The cottage was old and tinder-dry. Burrows and Donny and Colleen ran about madly using blankets to smother the flames, but the blaze was already hot and well-established. The air was acrid and hot and filled with smoke. Donny and Colleen sought the floor. Burrows went near a shattered window and a dozen tawny, rawboned arms exploded in at him, tearing out handfuls of his hair and raking his face with claw marks. He beat them away with the butt of the shotgun, reloaded, and put a salvo of buckshot through the window.

But it was hopeless.

The fire was spreading and there was no way to contain it.

There was no choice: they had to go outside.

The night.

Black and curdled and moist, the fen illuminated now with the flickering glow of the burning cottage. Burrows and his guests fell out into grass, gagging and coughing, crawling free of the blazing croft. The flames were licking free of windows, igniting the ancient interlocked willow twigs of the roof. The fire drove the moisture from the sedge and turf in gushing plumes of steam. Black, rolling clouds of smoke blew from the windows and doorways.

Colleen was screaming and Donny was shouting something for he could see revolting little faces hiding in the fen grasses, keeping in shadow, but waiting, inching closer. Burrows made a mad run for his truck. He took hold of the door and began yanking on it, trying to pull it free, but it was buckled and caved inward from the onslaught of the little men.

Donny saw what was about to happen, but Burrows in his frenzy to pull open the door did not hear his warning.

The Yarthkins had been lying in wait under the truck and now they came creeping out, moving quickly and efficiently, ringing Burrows in, encircling him, jumping and leaping and hopping like a swarm of locusts. They were darting in, biting him and clawing him and dancing out of range of his swinging fists with a feline grace.

One of them turned toward Donny and Colleen, its face demented and primordial, a thing of rage and appetite, completely appalling. Down on all fours like a stalking cat, it opened its contorted mouth and screeched at them.

Donny shot it point blank, drilling a hole through its left eye and dropping it dead in a shuddering mass of bicycling limbs.

Colleen pulled him back toward the burning cottage. So close, in fact, the heat singed the hair on their arms and blistered their skin.

But it was too late for Burrows.

There were dozens of the little beasts on him, nipping and tearing. They were like sharks, swimming in and drawing blood and moving away just as quick. Donny saw it all too well and knew this was a ritualistic mode of hunting, sharpened to lethal perfection through countless millennia. He supposed it was how they brought down larger game, much like primitive man must have.

Burrows was slicked with blood, yet still on his feet and

fighting. But he was overwhelmed, completely overwhelmed, and began to sink slowly under their numbers. Now the Yarthkins were not attacking and fleeing, they were hanging on with teeth and claws. Burrows began to scream. It was a high, demented sound of a soul emptying itself into the beyond. A piercing cry of pain and torment and utter horror: *"Get 'em off me! Get 'em offa me! Oh JESUS CHRIST—"*

A stone-headed spear plunged through his throat, one of the Yarthkins clinging to the shaft and pushing it around in an arc so that the spear nearly tore Burrows' head off. And then he went down and they began to rend him, opening him up and yanking out what they found inside and the stink of blood and death was raw and savage in the night.

One of the cottage walls fell in with an explosion of flame, the roof careening forward, glowing and orange like a burning haystack.

Donny took hold of Colleen and did what instinct demanded of him.

He ran.

They both had flashlights.

Donny had the Webley.

Colleen had the hatchet and a steak knife she'd grabbed off the floor.

They dashed away behind the cottage which was collapsing into itself, spilling gouts of flame and smudging the night sky with greasy plumes of smoke. They switched their flashlights on as they saw a narrow trail cutting through the tall fen grasses at the rear of the cottage. The flashlight beams created amorphous, jumping shadows as they followed the winding path, splashing through water and stumbling through mud, the sedge so high in spots they could barely see over it. And when it shrank back down, they could see the eyes of the Yarthkins reflected from low, boggy hollows and clumps of scrub.

They were following them.

They would not let them escape.

The trail meandered wildly, ended at a ditch of black, stand-ing water. Donny, holding Colleen's hand, dove right in. The water was cold and stagnant, full of weeds and logs and half-submerged things. They swam across, fighting their way to the bank and up through rank, dripping vegetation. Tripping and bumbling their way ever forward, slopping through hollows and stiff banks of reed grasses and rushes. Chilled and terrified, they kept moving, thankful they had not lost their flashlights or weapons. There was no time for rational thought, no time for anything but flight. The oldest of mankind's drives had set into them coldly, darkly...the will to survive.

And that was enough.

Ditch and dike, coarse grasses and low shrubs, fields of wild hay and mossy dips, wild splashing runs through peat bogs. The pattern repeated itself endlessly until they were exhausted and disoriented and totally lost. They slipped into a marshy stand of high, straw-like reeds that reached above their heads and here they waited, listening with ears attuned for the sound of the hunt.

"We can't...wait too long," Donny panted. "I don't hear... them but..."

There was no need to finish.

Maybe he did not hear them as such, but his mind, his primitive brain, told him that the Yarthkins could not have existed this long without being masters of stealth and concealment. They were near. They were very near.

Colleen said nothing.

She tried to speak, but something wouldn't let her. Silence was important now, dreadfully important. Maybe she, like Donny, was incrementally remembering things, memories, images impressed on her genes hundreds and thousands of years before. And this is what stilled her tongue. Told her that night was the time of the little men, the time they wormed out of their holes and hunted the sons and daughters of man.

Reduced to this primary, aged level, there was no need for speech between herself and her husband, her mate, for they both knew the little men would never stop coming. Not unless they were killed or burned out of their barrows.

So they would find a defensible position and fight them.

Kill them if they could, but never let those wicked, vicious things have them.

They ran again, finding new reserves of strength and will, drawing from untapped resources at the very ancient well of the race. Armed and fanning their lights, they burst through the scrub and found—

At first, they were not sure.

Maybe the primitive drives had confused them, but their modern brains then woke up sufficiently to understand what is was they were seeing. It was a church. A very, very old and deserted church in the center of a bogged-out clearing. It almost looked to be sinking, drowning in the black mire of standing water and sloughing mud. Its stone foundation was crumbling away to rubble, the steeple canting severely. Just a sagging, weathered structure with no windows, scarcely any walls, the shingles stripped free of the roof.

Leaning there, dark and sullen and somehow haunted out in the bog, Donny thought it looked like a gutted tomb.

But there really was no choice.

Moving low and cautious, they slipped into the turgid, oozing waters and made for the cavernous hole where an arched doorway had once stood. The church then was open to them, like the confines of a wormy, black casket.

And inside, it was a nest of snaking shadows.

Donny had an unconventional, complete superstitious thought when they breached that disintegrating, stygian doorway: that the Yarthkins could not enter the church, that it was holy ground and they were devils. Yes, devils cast into the wild, inhospitable places by man long ago much like devils cast out of paradise by God.

It was ludicrous, of course.

Particularly coming from a man who'd been a card-carrying atheist most of his life. For he knew without question that the Yarthkins pre-dated Christianity by countless grim ages. And if those low, terrible pygmies had a god, then it was something equally as low and equally as blasphemous. A pagan nightmare that demanded infants as sacrifice.

It was insane, of course, that he would be thinking these things.

Whatever mankind's relationship traditionally had been with the little people—and he knew it was horrible and antagonistic—it had left such a lasting, deep-hewn impression on the race that it was all coming back to Colleen and him as a race memory. But with it had come the instinct for survival, for adaptation, for battle. And more than that, an unspoken telepathic awareness between his wife and he. It had brought back to them a latent hive mentality, the sort of thing their prehistoric ancestors must have known and used with great efficiency in those barbarous days long gone now. Surviving, fighting, killing and hunting. And doing these things without thought, fingers of the same hand working for the greater good and the ultimate survival of the tribe. It was this very capacity that had kept those early peoples alive through ice ages and floods, starvation and disease, inter-clan warfare and the nocturnal predations of the little men.

His mind was sucked so deeply into the morass of primary instinct, that his modern, deductive mind coming back to him now and explaining these things to him was shocking.

He giggled at the intersection of primordial fear and advanced reasoning.

He giggled out loud and he could feel Colleen's eyes on him, narrowed and vapid, willing him to be silent or she would silence him herself.

The floor of the church had long ago rotted away to a grid of mildewed joists. Donny and Colleen followed them, crawling down them over to where the altar would be. Water had seeped up to the bottoms of the joists, creating dozens of pools of lapping blackness.

Finally, they reached the altar.

It was gone, but the stone and mortar framework still existed. They crawled up onto it, seeing stars through innumerable holes in the roof and great gaping openings in the walls themselves. Behind them, then, it was solid...but the Yarthkins could come from every other direction.

They turned off their flashlights and tried to accustom themselves to the darkness, to see through the murk by pale moonlight and nothing more.

Donny could hear Colleen breathing next to him, but she did not speak. He was able, he thought, to slip in and out of the instinctual fugue, but Colleen had gone under and he wondered what it would take to bring her back.

They waited and darkness enclosed the ruined church.

The Yarthkins came an hour later.

It was Colleen who noticed them. They did not come slipping through the doorway or sliding through holes in the walls. They were creatures of the fen and they used this to their advantage.

Colleen gripped Donny's arms and he smelled them before he saw them. That same decayed, gassy stench of filth and buried things. It came off the water in a nauseous fume.

Donny clicked on his light and Colleen followed suit.

He saw a gruesome, malformed face slip silently beneath the water. Then another and another. He tensed and Colleen did the same. They were on their haunches in battle mode, ready to take on the little men, but whatever humanity was left in them, sank away at that point. Or much of it.

The seconds passed, the shadows bulged and crawled. There were subtle splashing noises, rippling sounds, bubbles expanding and popping.

Then the Yarthkins came up out of the water.

They were dripping wet, stringy hair plastered to their faces. They were naked and lean, skinned with a saffron, scabrous flesh that looked oddly reptilian. Their eyes were wide and glassy and voracious, the eyes of spiders. They came on, hissing and slithering, lips pulled back from sharp yellow teeth.

In that moment of revelation, seeing them in the flashlight beams, Donny was struck by how they moved. Not like men moved at all. They propelled themselves along the joists with obscene, repellent gyrations and convolutions of their muscles like jungle snakes pulling themselves onto riverbanks.

It was enough.

Donny emptied the gun. He killed five of them and five more came up out of the water, then a dozen, sliding and slinking forward toward him. And it was there, as it had been all along, that instinctual revulsion to their kind. They were contaminated, unclean, impure. Vile things that did not deserve to live. They existed only to be stomped and rent and crushed to smears of cold slime.

Looking upon them, what remained of his thinking, cognizant mind told him that this was racial memory coming back full and strong. They filled him with hatred and a shuddering atavistic aversion. These things, these little men were the very seed of mankind's universal loathing for small people. They were the inspiration, something all men had carried within them from the dawn of the race.

And with that, Donny's mind reverted completely.

He took the hatchet away from Colleen who was sneering and shouting at the Yarthkins, brandishing her knife and flashlight. He took it in his hand and liked its weight and knew he must protect her at all costs. Shrieking out some forgotten dirge, he dove at them, opening the throat of one and then splitting open the head of another. It fell against him, slithering bonelessly like a headless snake. It sickened him...yet fascinated him.

The other Yarthkins pulled back, remembering something too, now. Remembering the violence and savagery of the tall men.

Donny dove amongst them, slashing and hacking, chopping and slaying, drenching himself with their foul-smelling blood. But they did not die as lambs, for they were warriors themselves. Their teeth sank into his arms and throat, their nails laying open his back and belly. He fought and they fought, but they had him in numbers and overwhelmed him, tearing and ripping.

Yes, this was how they did it in the old days...dropping from midnight trees and surging en masse from fen grass like soldier ants with a communal bloodlust, a hereditary need to kill the tall, pale giants. To revenge their race for the wholescale genocide afflicted on the tribes by men who shot down the old with arrows and clubbed the young to pulp and set the tribal warrens aflame.

They hated man as man hated them.

And this is why they devoured the children of the tall, pale warriors and brutalized their maidens, ripped their progeny from the pregnant bellies of their woman, built subterranean altars from the bones of the tall ones…all to stem the tide of the invading scourge who had driven them into hiding, into the wilds and pathless wastes of mountain and fen.

Colleen threw the flashlight at them, charged through them as they pulled Donny apart, yanking out his viscera in gleaming coils and divorcing his limbs from joints and chewing on his salty, hot meat.

She charged through them, slashing with her knife, escaping the church, vaulting through the bog and into the grass and sedge beyond, running and running, knowing she must never, ever stop. Because she had her own race memories and they told her implicitly what the little men did to women of the tall, pale warriors.

She came through the grasses, spotting a series of low mounds that reminded her of anthills. Her mind told her to seek high ground even as it told her that the mounds were taboo places, places of danger. But she went anyway, scrambling up over the top of one and rolling down and circling another…and then the ground gave way beneath her.

Yes, like the trapdoor of a spider's den, a rectangle of earth at the base of a mound fell away beneath her and she plunged headlong into darkness. The trapdoor swung shut above her. She landed in a seething, invidious blackness, feeling things under her and around her and recognizing the shapes of skulls and femurs and ribcages. A litter pile of ancient, gnawed bones.

She could hear the Yarthkins coming.

She was in one of their burrows that were dug beneath the mounds and hidden from view via trapdoors constructed in the ways of the ancients. This was why the tall, pale men never exterminated the last of the little men. They went underground and concealed their lairs expertly, lived and hunted by night.

Colleen was not frightened.

But she would not let them have her.

They came on, hissing and squirming, picking their way toward her through the ebon ossuary, the bone pit they called home.

"Not have me," Colleen said under her breath. "I'll never let them foul things have me..."

She began to sing a high, wailing dirge that was the ancient, forgotten death-song of her tribe. And as she did this, she slid the knife into her throat, sawing until the artery was severed and hot blood coursed down over her in a primeval baptismal.

She died amongst the bones, that song still bubbling from her lips, and once again, the sons and daughters of the tall ones had bested the little men.

THE RESURRECTION MAN

In Paris, they tell stories of the walking dead, of lovers living, lovers dead. Of heavy metal zombies haunting the Metro with their dead immigrant faces, funeral pyre eyes, and yawning skull grins. They whisper in lurid tones of the deadboy youth that throng about the decaying neon flesh shops and meat markets of Pigalle. They speak, too, of the mass grave artisans of death culture. Maggot-brained, bloodless, electric-fingered, they squat in Mexican mummy heaps along the Rue des Martyr, ghoul impressionists, painting cemeteries and embalming parlors on human skin canvas to sell to garish tourists. All in all, when the living dead society within a society are mentioned, one name inexorably trembles, froths on the lips of despair: Louis Crillon.

Louis Crillon.

"Life is to the dead what the sting is to the scorpion," Crillon has said mystically more than once, his words like autumn leaves on the wind.

No one knows death better than Louis Crillon. And no one is better at kissing away cold sepulchral eternity than he, the Resurrection Man, last-minute chemical reprieve of creaking gibbets, wind-howling gallows, and frost-licked graves. He has been referred to as Backstreet Lazarus, the White Pagan, and Doctor to the Dead. But these are mere myths, dark fantasies, as any good Parisian knows, urban folktale cut from the black fabric of the grotesque and morbid. The dead cannot walk; Louis Crillon does not exist.

Horror story smoke ghost, Louis laughs at them all with

the cold caw of desert hyenas. Exterminator of ravaging death, Louis walks the city of love with a faded leather bag of grave drugs and corpse orgasm looking for the truly worthy. No soul is too rotted, no intelligence too far decayed, no flesh too noisome that he cannot inject life's little addiction into the cold marble of cadaver aspiration. From crematory to bone pit to tomb altar he wanders, an oven heat in his damp alabaster eyes.

Prisoner of the shroud? Remorse no more! Cell by cell Louis Crillon will imbue you with sex-fire and life-flame and shambling beauty.

On this day, gray pretender of loathsome October, Louis makes his way through the screaming wind of the Boulevard de Belleville to his favorite workshop, the frost monument world of tourists, vandals, gravediggers, and the evil dead—Pere Lachaise. This is the world's boneyard, great garish mass grave of royalty, poets, artists, writers, and even salt-of-the-earth bone trash. Grim maze of tomb, vault, sepulcher, mausoleum, crypt, and pauper grave, Pere Lachaise is a still-life in white marble, necropolis of the ages.

"Ah, sweet surrender of death," says Louis, whistling a nameless tune of interment.

All things exist here—life, death, time, lack of it, dream, light and shade, fate, fortune, reality and dream. Here a storm is brewing, a crack in the universe, a shift, a crevice. An electricity of forever. It smells of dank earth and danker shadow. Mortuary perfume of dead October roses, withered funerary bouquet, cold stone, colder flesh, rusting iron and rotting pine. Salts, spices, embalming fluid, tears, dry laughter. Yes, here the gray freezing wind is moistened by rain and has the texture of bone dust. Blown from dire charnel house, dissection room, and crematory, it is like no other.

Louis breathes in, breathes out.

"You're late," says the gravedigger, brushing dirt and grief from his callused hands. His eyes are filmed silver, his flesh woven burlap. "And whom shall it be today?"

The resurrectionist pats his bulging bag of biochemical tricks, alchemical treats. "Someone special, Pierre. Someone deserving."

"Oui, M'sieur, someone special."

They walk now together, silence and time, resurrection and burial. Bottles and instruments knock together in Louis's bag; shovel and pick clang over the gravedigger's weary shoulder. The ossuary stillness is ominous.

"The nasties lie alongside the goodies, Louis. The righteous shake hands with sinners and saints alike," the gravedigger says. "Eh? And what a beautiful world it is the dead share! No strife, no war, no hatred! They lie side by side in harmony and bless each and all!"

"There is beauty in death," admits Louis. "Yes, beauty and peace and serenity."

The gravedigger spits over his shoulder. "Hallowed be the name of Death."

Dead leaves skitter and prance and play, carpet the peaked roofs of vaults and cling to dreaming white stone. Louis feels now the pressure and fizz and need of creation. It is a blizzard of glass shards in his head, raw and ripping. There is steel in his boiling blood, gray mirrored calm in his soul. Keeper of the elixir, turnkey of the concrete Golgotha jail, Louis is ready to knit and sew ice into warmth. Knotted branches like the blackened fingers of dead witches scrape the gunmetal sky.

Louis sights a grand and gaudy altar. His fingers tremble as a cigarette, burning bright, is fed into the smoke hole of his mouth. "The balls of Lazarus," he sighs, "what have we here?"

This particular grave is a circus of disrespect. A flat slab of marble heaped with withered and blossoming flowers, vandalized by graffiti and garbage and cans and bottles and mourning verse scribbled on wet tissues. The bust lording above it all is modest. The face all but chipped away, weather-worn, and finger-smoothed.

"The grave of Christ?" Louis wonders aloud.

"The American poet," the gravedigger informs him. "Morrison."

Louis grins like murder. "The Lizard King. Still adored after all these seasons of blush and blanche."

A syndicate of fans and faithful descend on this spot by fever moonlight, Louis knows. They cackle the words of their fallen master, bear the stigmas of the bottle, the shared needle, lost in a dead sea of what is memory.

"This one, I think," says Louis conspiratorially.

"Good as the next." The gravedigger sets to work. "What rhymes has the grave taught this one, Louis? What sonnets of despair? What odes of black earth and ballads of destruction?"

Louis's lips flex in a knowing smile. "Ah, you should have been a poet, Pierre. Your mind is a lyrical, romantic thing turning upon itself."

The gravedigger laughs. "Yes, a grave worm feeding off itself." Carefully, he pries the slab free with the cold hook of a crowbar, exposing the bounties of sleeping earth. "I am but a common man, Louis," he informs the resurrectionist. "But, yes, sometimes I feel touched, brushed, *kissed* by greatness. It is my work here, I believe. Spending so much time in this grand burial ground, the souls of the literary elite whispering by me in their ghost trains of beauty. Still, I wield no pen, merely a shovel!"

As the gravedigger loosens the teeth of his spade, lets it eat dank soil, Louis casts a shadow of harsh brooding authority. He is a tall masculine figure described by flapping coats and waving scarves. Cider-ruddy face of apple house, trailing black wax mustache, and deep cerulean summer twilight eyes. Yet something about him seems to moan discontent, looking too deep or not deep enough, seeing all and seeing nothing. There is curiosity painted in him. Science and superstition are brushed velvet on his soul. He is all parts black magic, pagan delight, snake charmer's lore, cover of drifting dirt, newborn wet cry. This and maybe the still breath of the Dark Ages and dust from a mummy's urn.

"Quickly, Pierre."

Louis grins now, and is there not more than biological machination there? But the murmur of worse things, graves and gallows, weeping death and pale trembling horror? The cemetery stands quiet now, stone gargoyle sentinel of other worlds and lost souls. The dead stand ready. In mythic, cryptic undercover channels and silent uncanny springs of catacomb rivers. Undead mob, they stand ready for human sacrifice wearing rags of time and silt, sporting ruined faces of crag fissure, green moss lips, and limestone eyes. Insects on the greased metal carpet of limbo, slipping, sliding, but going neither hither nor thither nor yon, they wait and watch.

Butchers of eternity, zombie poets of godless black holes.

Stranded in the Sargasso Sea of sour patience, Louis's heart finds a new rhythm as the spade kisses a casket with a hollow smack. Dirt, sod, and subsoil are brushed free. The coffin itself, pine vessel of squelched dream, is crusted with damp mildew, mineral deposits that smell of dead men's bowels. The shroud is gray crepe, sandy rotted gauze that crumbles into nitrous dust. And beneath, the Lizard King, molested by time and worm. A broomstick skeleton sheathed in cheesecloth flesh, ripped, abraded, sagging, acrid. The great and grand poet of lost generations and hallucinogenic clarity is all jutting bone, dark hollow, and stripped Autumn bush. He wears a parched winding crown of dead serpents and grins like funeral satin.

Louis, breathless, opens his bag of tricks and extracts a corked bottle of ruby liquid. The rotting pumpkin brain is spiked, fed, renewed.

"Your fire is lit," Louis whispers. "Break on through, my friend."

The Lizard King wakes, virus eyes of silent scream swim into tangled focus, cry tears of dust, leer from a gray fog of death. But there is more here, much more. God of the pit, the cadaver zombie stretches like a cat waking from a dark dream, the black holes of his eyes are catalogs of hunger. Snakeskin cerements weep and bleed from him as he rises.

"Louis," says the gravedigger in an uneven voice, "this is not right...this one is..."

But Louis has no voice. He sees the Lizard King move. Face like a livid bruise, scanning dead eyes are soulless voids of cosmic neon. He is yellowed film, dark mud, rank clotted soil, dry moonlight. Pillar of dead ice and black grave stench, he slithers, stalks, a pool of spreading midnight.

Predatory smile stitched to old leather, the Lizard King speaks. "Birth is beautiful," the marble angel voice coos. "And birth is painful."

Pierre is the first to know his gnawing, eager hunger. His skull comes apart in the King's greedy fingers and there is a pulpy wet snapping of shattered bones and a fleshy weeping, a howling, screaming, and thrashing. Louis is next, and sometime later the King wipes what remains of him from his chiseled chin. Sleeping lord of grisly appetite, the Lizard King sleeps no more. Tapestries of skin and jumbles of white-licked bones are dumped in the grave. His skin the color of vaults and headstones, the King waits with a glacial smile.

"Louis Crillon is a folktale," he says to the tombstones, the whistling dead wind. "He is a myth. And I am no longer just that."

So the grave poet, the Lizard King, studies the wounded sky with nebulous eyes of primordial need and living death. He dreams of mortuaries and morgues, cold suppers and sweet marrow sipped from bones. Jackal-toothed, ivory-skinned, beautiful white funeral orchid, he waits, scratching dumbly at a carpet of ants at his spine.

He doesn't wait long.

Soon, they come, worshippers of the casket poet, cold meat sacrifices boiling in honey stews of hot and hotter blood. They carry bottles of sloshing wine, hemp cigarettes, and cans of paint.

The first one is a girl. She smells of dewy strawberries and morning mist, red meat and vanilla skin.

"Dear God," she whimpers at the sight of him. "It's you."

"Yes," the ghoul purrs, moving with a pale sweep of snakes. "It is. I doth love you madly. Gather in my name and bleed for me."

LITTLE MISS WICKED

(Dark Animus #6, 2004)

The floor was an ocean of red and the swimmer had drowned. At least that's what Detective-Sergeant Martin Tallman thought as he gazed down at the body sprawled on the barroom floor. It belonged to a Hispanic man named Luis Merin. He had taken seven rounds from a 9mm Beretta at close range. The contact burns had actually lit his shirt on fire. After eating the bullets, of course, he hadn't been too concerned.

"You thinking this is gang-related?" the uniform first on the scene asked, pulling off a cigarette. His name was Donovan. He was a big Irishman with a square-hewn head of flaming red bristles, a flattened nose, and the sort of girth one normally associated with draft horses. He towered over Tallman, towered over just about everything and everyone. "Wouldn't surprise me none. You break up one crew of these pukes, ten more take their place."

Tallman nodded. "Could be."

They were standing at a yellow-taped crime scene in Bollo's Bar and Grill on South 8th and West National Avenue, Milwaukee Southside, turf hotly contested by half-a-dozen Hispanic gangs since the Latin Kings were broken up and tossed away on a federal RICO conviction.

Tallman was watching the crime scene technicians pick up expended brass cartridges with forceps and drop them into carefully-labeled plastic baggies. Reif, a ghoul from the medical examiner's office, was crouching next to the body in his rubber boots, shaking his head. He was inserting a little metal probe into the bullet holes and whispering things. Sometimes to his little digital recorder. Sometimes to the stiff. And sometimes just to himself. He was funny like that.

Tallman turned to the uniform. "Give it to me again."

Donovan shrugged, flicked his ash away from the taped-off area. "Well, it was like I said. Friday night. Pay day for a lot of these people. The bar was crowded. People eating and drinking, watching the game on the tube—soccer match from one of those Spanish channels. Suddenly the little guy...Tony Panjos... pulls his piece and starts shooting Merin. Busted seven caps into him and then just sat back down on his stool, finished his Corona. Go figure."

Tallman sighed.

He didn't like it, but then, he never liked it.

Ten years on homicide and it still sickened him, still disturbed him how quickly life could be taken and how damn foolish the reasons could be. When there *were* reasons. The witnesses—bartender, waitress, a half a dozen regulars who hadn't bolted when the caps were busted—all told the same story. No argument between the men. Just boom, boom, down goes the victim. See ya, bro.

"Nobody said shit about that teenage girl, though?"

Donovan shook his head. "Not a thing. Nobody remembers a girl that age in here." He shrugged. "Maybe a hooker...who knows? Bartender, it's his place. He wouldn't admit to some kid hanging around here."

Tallman figured that, too.

But something about the girl...it didn't sit with him right.

It left a hollow feeling in his belly that he just couldn't seem to get rid of. That hollow feeling usually told him something was wrong, something just didn't wash.

He had already been through the witnesses a dozen times, saw no point in hammering on them further. "Take their names and addresses, tell 'em they can leave," he said to the uniform.

With that, he went back out to the patrol car where Panjos was being held. Two uniforms were leaning against it, watching traffic, keeping an eye out for the reporters that would be descending any moment now like buzzards on roadkill.

Tallman slid into the back seat next to Panjos.

He was a little guy, barely five-foot-six, couldn't have weighed more than 150 with his boots on. His hands were cuffed behind his back and his eyes were bloodshot, set in puffy sockets the color of raw liver.

"You want to tell me why?" Tallman put to him.

Panjos licked his lips. His face was sallow and loose. "I…I just kill him, that Merin, that motherfucker, I just kill him. I already admitted that, hey? So why don't you lock my ass up, Kojak? Throw me away."

Tallman sighed. "Something don't figure here. Tell me about it again."

Panjos laughed with a bleak, bitter sound, but he did.

He was at the bar, drinking. Merin was in there. He knew Merin would be in there. Merin had knocked up his sister, Louisa, and Panjos brought the gun to scare him. He hadn't gone in there to kill him. Just to scare him. Took him a dozen beers before he had the nerve to pull the Beretta.

"Where'd you get the gun?"

"Bought it from some banger I know."

Tallman nodded. "Now tell me about that girl you saw."

The blood seemed to drain from Panjos's face. He began to shake, to squirm against the cuffs that held him. "She…she was just there. I'm drinking and suddenly she's there. Fifteen, sixteen, hey? She's standing there and looking at me with those big dark eyes and…and, shit, I feel all weird inside, hot and cold, I don't know…then she says something and the gun is in my hand and I'm putting that motherfucker Merin down and…and, shit, I don't even know why…"

He was sobbing and Tallman watched him carefully. "Did you know her?"

Panjos shook his head. "No, never seen her."

"What did she say to you?"

Panjos started to tremble badly. "I don't remember, but…"

"But what?"

He was grinning now, his eyes bulging. "But whatever she say, man, that's what made me start shooting…"

Tallman was at a coffee house on South 58th, thinking.

The place was called Maxie's Bean House and its owner, Maxie Loman, was an inner-city success story. Back in the '70s, Maxie ran with a black drug gang known as the Glendale Boys' Club, a pretty innocent name for a group of black street toughs who pushed heroin and murdered rivals with shocking regularity. The Club had been broken up, its members put in prison. When Maxie got out, he won nearly a hundred-thousand dollars in a numbers game. Instead of blowing it on whores or putting it in his arm, he bought a coffee shop. And made it a success.

Whenever Tallman stopped by, Maxie sweetened his coffee with whiskey.

Tallman sat there, thinking, sipping his coffee, knowing nobody in that place—not even Maxie himself—knew what it was like for him. When you were a fifty-year-old cop and your wife had left you for a younger man. Or how people had warned you when you married her that she was fifteen years younger than you and pretty and it was only a matter of time. And how you fretted over it for ten years until it happened and who could you blame but yourself? You were a cop and you worked homicide and you were gone a lot and you didn't make the kind of money a woman like Maria wanted. You knew she was unhappy, didn't like you working the streets, but you didn't know anything else. And when you added all that up, it was only a matter of *when* and not *why* she'd leave you. Shack up with some hotshot orthodontist who made more in a month than you saw in a good year.

This is what Tallman was thinking.

Because as bad as it was, it was better than thinking about Panjos.

Panjos and that crawling terror in his eyes.

Two nights later, that feeling still lying in his gut like nesting snakes, Tallman was on the Northside in Metcalfe Park, 34th Street and West Center. He stood before a row of tenements, checking out the graffiti and the garbage. Some of it was spilling from overturned cans, the rest was gathered on the sidewalk watching the crime scene. This time, the crime scene was a black Dodge Intrepid pulled up to the curb.

Though it wasn't his district, Tallman went up there when he heard it come over the radio, particularly when they mentioned a Jane Doe at the scene, possibly Caucasian or Hispanic. That's what brought him.

Tallman knew the neighborhood.

It was a bad area: gangs, prostitution, drugs, random violence. The people there were predominately black and poor. Mothers turned tricks and fathers did time, sons joined gangs and daughters sold their flesh. It was a deadly cycle of ignorance and intolerance that ended for most well before their twentieth birthday.

There was a ring of cops around the car led by Detective-Lieutenant Jeremy Holmes of homicide, a rotund man with flat gray eyes. "These four dudes, Martin," he said to Tallman. "They're all members of the Gangster Disciples street gang…see the colors, black and blue? The tattoos? But this was no drive-by, no hit, this was murder-suicide I'm thinking, and the damnedest case of it I've ever seen."

Holmes went on to tell him that mostly what you had up here was gangland-style executions, crimes of passion, wars that broke out between the Disciples and the Vice Lords, one pimp offing another to get his stable. That kind of thing. "Now and then you get something weird—something like this. People decide to kill themselves…but, Jesus, this one…I don't know…"

Tallman was looking in the car now.

Four black boys—two in front, two in back, none of which had yet seen eighteen—had bullet holes in their faces. In fact, they'd all taken their rounds right through their left eye socket. They were all still sitting up, guns in their hands, brains and skull fragments splashed in every which direction.

"Here's how I'm figuring it," Holmes said. "These four…I don't know, some sort of pact, I guess…they're each carrying Glock nines. At some particular moment, they turn to each other, put the barrels of their guns in each other's eyes and pull the triggers. Craziest shit I've ever seen, but nothing else explains it."

Tallman agreed: It *was* crazy.

Holmes waltzed over to a thin, hard-looking black guy sitting on the steps of a tenement. The sleeves of his sweatshirt had been pulled up so his tattoos could be seen. The Gangster Disciple logo was very evident.

"This is Archie Beacon, but around here he's called Lippy. I figure he's got a story to tell," Holmes said pointedly. "But he's not telling it."

"I don't know shit," Lippy said.

Holmes told Tallman that Lippy claimed to have quit the Disciples and didn't bang with them anymore. But Tallman knew that these gangs were like the Mafia—only death set you free.

"I told what I knew," Lippy said and seemed to mean it. "I'm just kicking, right? This car pulls up, four brothers in there, just talking. They neighborhood...I see 'em around. Then all of a sudden, this bitch comes out of nowhere. White or Mex or some such shit. Weird-looking eyes, right? Stare holes right through you. She walks straight up to that car, puts her hands on the hood, stares down them motherfuckers what's sitting in that ride."

"Then what?" Tallman asked, something caught in his throat.

"Shit and shit, boom boom, bang bang. I threw my ass down...when I look up, she's gone and they dead..."

Tallman had the feeling Lippy knew more, too, but there was no way he was going to tell them. Not here, anyway. Not with all the people watching. He gave Tallman a strange look, something passed between them. Something that said, *maybe later.*

A couple uniforms and an EMT had an old black woman in the back of the ambulance. She was shaking and crying, ready to come apart in all directions.

"What's her thing?" Tallman asked.

But Holmes shook his head. "Out of her mind or something. Said she saw the whole thing. Saw the girl, saw the shootings in the car, and then..."

"Then what?"

Holmes was grinning. "She said this girl...she turned and

headed for that alley right there. And when she got there—get
this—she walked right through that brick wall like a ghost…"

"It's my job, what the hell was I supposed to do?"

But Maria wasn't buying it. "I asked you to give it up. I asked
you a dozen times. I couldn't live with the stress of it anymore,
you know that. The idea that you might not come home some
night…I couldn't take it."

"Sure," Tallman said. "It must've been rough, baby. That's
why you started banging Dan the Dentist."

"That's not fair."

"Is any of this?"

"Goodbye, Martin. Don't call here again."

Click.

Tallman didn't learn too much from Holmes or that Northside
murder scene. Just one little gem—that the girl, witnesses
claimed, had tattooed fingers. More, that she was a Latino girl
associated with the Latin Kings street gang from the Southside.
A member of the Latin Queens, the female auxiliary which
were every bit as dangerous as their male counterparts.

At the county morgue the next day, he told Frank Shockley
all about it. Shockley was a lab tech that had joined the medical
examiner's office about the time Tallman had joined the force—
middle Neolithic, they joked.

Shockley was weighing a human liver that was pitted from
cirrhosis. "This girl…about fourteen? Maybe fifteen?"

Tallman, leaning up against the green-tiled wall, his nose
filled with the acrid stench of disinfectants, said, "Yeah, about."

"Small, dark, pretty?"

"That's her."

Shockley forgot about his liver now, pulled the plastic sheet
up over his cadaver. "Tattoos on her fingers?"

"That's what they say."

"We got her."

Tallman stared. *"You got her?"*

Shockley dropped his rubber gloves into a biohazard bin,
motioned for Tallman to follow him. They maneuvered around

the stainless-steel tables, walked across the corridor and into the freezers. Shockley opened the cold steel door and stepped into a room that stank of chemicals and defrosted meat.

He slid open a drawer, unzipped the black vinyl bag resting inside, exposing the Hispanic girl within from head to toe. She was a small thing, maybe five feet tall, just over a hundred pounds. Her body was tight and sleek, her breasts smallish. There were two clean, antiseptic-looking bullets holes in her—one in her chest, the other in her belly.

But what struck Tallman, what hit him hard and left him dizzy, was not only how pretty she had been—long dark hair, full lips, high cheekbones—but how she easily matched the descriptions he'd gotten at the two crime scenes.

"She's been here about three weeks now," Shockley explained.

"Three weeks?"

"Sure. Her and a couple other players got themselves greased over on the Southside three weeks back."

Tallman had to step away.

Sure, she looked like the girl...but she could *not* be the girl. That hollow feeling in his belly came back, only now it was filling up with something cold. He almost expected her eyes to snap open.

His guts crawling, Tallman took hold of her left hand and it was cold, stiff. But there it was—ALKN. A letter on each finger, just below the knuckle. Almighty Latin King Nation.

"You got a picture of this one?" he managed.

Shockley slid the drawer closed and Tallman found he could breathe again. Out in the office, Shockley pulled her file.

"Lorita Vega," he said, "fifteen years old..."

Tallman stared at her picture and thought that she hadn't looked quite so dead when they took it. In fact, she looked oddly alive, sleeping, waiting, something.

He didn't know why he wanted the picture.

But something told him it was important.

Three days later, his wife was murdered.

Good old Dan the Dentist had driven down to Chicago for

a tooth-picker's convention and while the cat was away, Maria had been murdered. Someone had slipped into the orthodontist's high-end Tudor down in Hale's Corners—swimming pool out back, Jag in the garage—and stabbed her thirty-six times with a carving knife.

Jack Alembra was the one who broke it to Tallman.

He tracked him down to his ratty, cluttered apartment in Parklawn and, tears in his eyes, told him all about it. Tallman took three days' leave and did a lot of drinking. When he was alone at night, he did some crying, too. But the pain hadn't really purged itself. It had been sucked down somewhere dead-center in his chest, hanging there in a black ball of dormancy like something waiting to be born.

On the third day of boozing and self-pity, Alembra called.

"Martin...I know this isn't the time," he said, very carefully. "But, I don't know, I figured you'd want to know that—"

"What did you find? You got a perp?"

Alembra sighed. "Yes and no. We were able to pull a set of prints off that knife."

"And?"

"Well, they matched those of a Southside girl gangster named Lorita Vega, but..."

And Almebra went on about it, saying there must have been a colossal fuck-up somewhere, her being dead and all.

But Tallman wasn't so sure anymore.

The only thing that Alembra didn't tell Tallman—couldn't bring himself to—was that, although the Latino girl's prints were on the knife, the coroner said that from the angle of the wounds and the way Maria had been clutching the blade...it looked very much like the wounds were self-inflicted.

But he couldn't tell Tallman that.

Back up in Metcalfe Park, Tallman found Lippy.

He picked him up and took him for a drive far away from the neighborhood. They stopped in one of the sprawling lots over at Miller Park, the Milwaukee Brewers' stadium. The lots were empty, blown with dead leaves.

"You wanna tell me about it?" Tallman said to him now that

the niceties were out of the way. "Because I know you got a story and I need to hear it."

Lippy dragged off his cigarette. "Question being here, you gonna believe what I say?"

Tallman told him he would. As proof of that, he pulled out the morgue photo of Lorita Vega.

Lippy took one quick look at it, shook his head. "Put it away, put the motherfucker away, I ain't looking at that fucking spook."

And there was Lippy, tough inner-city gangsta, looking pale as black could be, eyes flicking this way and that, hands balling into fists, lips pressed in a tight white line. And all over, shaking and trembling, making choking sounds in his throat.

After a few drags off his cigarette, he gathered himself, breathed in, breathed out, watching the traffic winging by on 94. "What I say stays between us?"

"Yes, you have my word."

Lippy laughed. "Hee, the word of a white man. What the fuck...suppose I have to tell someone."

So he did.

In general, Hispanic and black gangs would rather kill each other than look each other in the eye. Rival posses. But now and then they came together for business. A drug deal was set up on the Southside. A cocaine buy. Three keys primo stuff. The Latin Kings had it, the Gangster Disciples from the Northside wanted it. Their connections had dried up after a major bust by the DEA, so in the parking lot of a deserted factory down on South 9th, the buy came down. It was set up by a Hispanic gangster named Luis Merin, who had connections with the Kings. The Disciples came down to get the stuff with Merin.

"Sounds sweet, eh?" Lippy laughed. "Weren't sweet at all. See, Merin set the Kings up. There were four of 'em. One of 'em was a Latin Queen name of Lorita Vega. Little thing, but dirt mean, see? So, out come those keys of blow and out comes that case of green what to buy it with. Business concluded? Hardly. Dope burn. Here come the gats and down go the Kings. Then shit starts getting interesting, you dig? One by one, them what had ripped off the Kings starts dying. You saw Merin? And you saw the four Disciples? Then you know. Now there's only one left and I ain't about to say who that might be."

But Tallman knew, all right.

There was only one left and he was scared shitless as he sat in a detective's car out at Miller Park, telling stories. But he wasn't done talking, there was more and it was even more entertaining.

"You know what Macumba is?" Lippy asked him.

"Voodoo or something, isn't it?"

Lippy shrugged. "More or less. But a real nasty sort, black magic, you know? They practice it on the Southside, sacrifice animals and that sort of shit. There's this Macumba witch down there, name of Vega. Seems her niece got offed by some bad playas, so she decided to get revenge for the family. She cuts her chickens and shakes her rattles and sprinkles her bone dust, says her mumbo jumbo voodoo bullshit words…and you know what? She calls up some devil out of hell, except this devil, it looks like her niece and it likes to eat souls. In fact, that's what folks call it: a Soul-Eater."

Tallman sat there.

Bullshit was right. Had this been a week ago, he would have laughed Lippy straight out of the car…but now? It just made him feel queasy and nauseous, that hollow in his belly filling with poison and his nerves jangling like wind chimes.

Worms were crawling up his throat and he swallowed them back down. "Where would you find this crazy old witch?"

"She has a crib on West National…you ask for Mama Vega, they'll point you in her direction."

"And what about you?" Tallman said.

"Oh, don't worry about me. I just wanna go home, see? Last night I get this phone call. I answer it and this bitch on the other end is just laughing and laughing, except it sounds like her throat is full of dirt. I wanna get back home, wait for her…"

Just like Lippy said, it was easy to find Mama Vega.

She had rooms above a bodega on South 9th and West National Avenue. Tallman had gotten a lot of funny looks—some of them not so funny—but those he had asked steered him in the right direction. He went up a set of stairs in the back that smelled of spices and cat piss and old booze. When he got to the door at the top, it was opened.

"*Boa vinda, Sr. Tallman, boa vinda,*" a small old woman said. "Welcome to my home. I have been expecting you."

Tallman stood in the doorway. "How could that be?"

"Ah, I have my ways, Mr. Tallman."

He followed her inside, into a series of interconnecting rooms that were set with candles and incense burners and cheap prints of Catholic saints. There were jars and wooden bowls of dried leaves and twigs and what might have been dehydrated insects. There was something like an altar with a carving of Jesus on the cross and some pagan devil made of coiling snakes.

Mama Vega made him a strong drink of fruit juice and sugarcane liquor that was very tasty, hit him hard right away.

"Mama," Tallman said, "they tell me you practice Macumba."

She laughed, a wizened old thing dressed in scarves and shawls of turquoise and red silk. Her face was like old pine bark. "They say many things, many things they should not be saying, yes? *Povos loucos, loucos.*"

Tallman figured that was a dead end. "You had a niece..."

Her eyes became shiny and wet at the memory. "You speak of my Lorita, my darling Lorita." She crossed herself. "I told her to stay away from those bad boys and bad girls, those *criminosos,* to stay off the streets...but she did not listen. And now she is gone."

"Is she?"

Mama laughed again. "Oh, Mr. Tallman, you are a policeman...you do not believe in Macumba, do you? Man like you don't believe in those witch-stories, do you?"

"Maybe not. But I wonder about something called a Soul-Eater."

Mama crossed herself again. She took a pinch of powder from an urn and threw it up into the air, let it drift down around her. "*Alma-Comedor? O comedor das almas?*" She kept laughing, but there was no humor now. "Mr. Tallman, that is an old wives' tale from Brazil. You believe that? Oh, let me tell you. You like this one. The Soul-Eater, it takes the form of a wronged person, a dead person, destroys their enemies, eats their souls."

"And sometimes it just kills innocent people, doesn't it?"

"It runs its course like a storm or a drought, no more, no less."

Tallman set his drink down. "It murdered my wife."

"Perhaps you interfered."

But maybe she could sense the rage and grief twisting in him, for she began to soften. Tears ran from her eyes. "Suffering begets more suffering, yes? Sometimes an old woman is overcome by grief and does a bad thing. But she is old and foolish. Maybe a policeman like yourself, he would like to stop this?"

"Tell me," he said, his voice hard as hammered iron now.

So she did.

The Soul-Eater was attached to the corpse it was called up to avenge, much as a limb was attached to a tree. In the old country, Mama told him, when such a thing was called up the body was hidden away so it could not be pierced. A metal rod had to pierce the body to its grave and thus, the Soul-Eater would be held in the grave for eternity.

If you could find the body, that was.

Lorita Vega's body was interred in a simple grave out at Holy Cross Cemetery.

And this is where Tallman went.

He was mad by that point and was fully aware of the fact. His eyes were fixed and glassy, his face corded and tight. Maybe it was the grief, maybe his brain had just gotten soft, but he *believed*. He honestly believed in what Mama Vega said. So, he came to the graveyard after dark with a shovel and pick. Out there in that charnel world of stones and markers and leaning crypts, he did what he had to do. What his madness demanded of him.

He opened the girl's grave.

He figured it was only a matter of time before someone saw the lantern light out there and came to stop him. But he wouldn't be stopped. And luckily for them, they never came.

The moon was out and autumn leaves were drifting from

the trees, blowing around the graves and mossy vaults in little whirlwinds. The earth was loose, being that the Vega girl had only been buried a few days before, the city washing its hands of her finally.

Tallman dug.

While the wind blew and the moon grinned, he dug out moist clots of earth, tossing them from his excavation. While the tombs around him sighed and the shadows slithered and shifted, he kept digging. He counted the shovelfuls he threw from the grave, only stopping when he couldn't recall if he was in the two- or three-hundreds. Four feet down, he was black and soiled, wet with sour-smelling sweat and grubby with grave dirt. He kept going, panting and gasping, a shrill noise in his head, chopping and scooping and squaring off the grave as he went. Thirty minutes later, he struck what he thought was the coffin, but being a cop, he should have known it was either a vault or a grave liner.

It was a law to enclose the coffin in something.

They didn't really keep out the bugs, but they kept the cemetery looking nice and even, with no unsightly depressions when a coffin collapsed inward from the weight of all that earth.

If it was a vault, he was screwed.

But they were expensive and the city opted for a simple grave liner, one made of fiberglass. Tallman scraped the dirt away from it, took hold of the metal loops, yanked the lid up and pushed it out of the grave.

The coffin.

It was a cheap outfit and he easily snapped the latches with his shovel. Then he got his fingers under the lip while a demented, screeching voice in his brain cried, *Are you sure, are you sure you want to do this?* But he was and with his breath frosting in the chill night and his teeth chattering, he pulled the lid up and aside.

The stink pushed him against the wall of the grave, against that black wormy earth. Of course, the body stank. Water had gotten into the coffin from all the rain lately, seeped through the earth and pooled on the body, and it had begun to decay very quickly. But that stink…Jesus, black and dirty and putrescent.

Breathing through his teeth, Tallman forced himself to look upon the girl. He held the lantern out and the flickering, uneven light cast wild shadows that were slinking forms and curling snakes. Lorita's pretty face was covered in a caul of mold. Fingers of mildew reached across the back of her folded hands.

Tallman felt a maddening urge to start cackling.

He wondered if maybe he was actually under sedation somewhere, but no, no, he was here and rooted by the noisome organic stench of corruption. He knew what he had to do, but as he looked at the body, staring at that shrunken, cadaverous form, he started remembering who and what he was, how he had been sworn to uphold the law.

Then he thought about Maria.

His flesh greasy and dirty, he crawled from the grave, and came back with a sharpened fourteen-inch iron stake that was used to support concrete forms. It was the best he could do.

Iron, it must iron, Mr. Tallman. For iron represents earth, and only with iron can you pin the Soul-Eater in the grave.

Then Tallman was down there again.

But the grave was filling. Not with water, but with a shifting, nebulous blackness that was viscid and alive. It was crawling and oozing, moving over him and under his clothes like wriggling maggots that he tried to brush off him, but it was no good. He could feel grave worms under his skin, in his eyes, feasting inside his skull. Oh dear God that insane biting, tickling feel—

Lorita was sitting up in her grave, eyes wide like charnel pits.

But no, the body was still in the casket.

It was just the Soul-Eater come to stop him. It had wormed up from the black soil beneath the grave, was creeping and crawling and now it was a woman that stared at him with glistening black eyes and a mouth that grinned with too many teeth.

It reached out for him, its body hideously alive with the motion of the larva that was feeding on it.

Tallman brought the stake up over his head and...something happened.

She had him and he could not move. Her dead face was swimming in for a kiss and a black, worming tongue played over his lips, forced itself into his mouth and it tasted...tasted of metal.

Then Tallman came back to himself in the damp grave in that lonely cemetery and realized he had his service revolver out and was pushing it in his mouth, finger stroking the trigger.

He tossed it aside.

Grabbing up the stake, the Soul-Eater fell on him, moving like some living, malefic shroud made of cobwebs and ecto-plasm. Not truly physical, but not ethereal either. A fleshy ghost. It fought and clawed and cried out obscenities while Tallman slashed and cut at it with the stake until it fell around him like writhing confetti, a collection of undulating, gaseous tissue.

Then he brought up the stake.

Thought about Maria. How he'd really loved her.

The Soul-Eater screamed with the breath of hell and thunder.

He rammed the stake into Lorita. It went right through her belly and stabbed into the coffin wood below, catching fast. There was a great heaving, whispering, tormented sigh as if from miles away and then...nothing.

The lantern went out.

He was alone with a desecrated corpse and nothing more.

He laid there a long time while the dementia bled from him in tangles and ribbons of darkness. Then he filled the grave in, made it back to his car. When he got home, he said a prayer for his wife's soul, then called Lippy and told him it was over, told him what he had done.

Then he went to bed.

He slept nearly fourteen hours. When he woke, he told him-self it was all some crazy nightmare. It was easier that way.

THE ARCHITECT OF PESTILENCE

(Vicious Shivers, 2004)

Beneath the looming shroud of the high Southern Appalachians, there was a medicine wagon pulled into a rustling field of bodies. It was garishly painted the color of spilled blood with fancy gold piping and parade lettering. From it and its companion wagons, banners and tarps flapped like freshly-stripped pelts. The sun was a burning coin above, and far below, there was Dr. Leon J. Lighthorse, disciple of the healing arts and a shimmering star in his own right. A tall, gaunt man with a face sharp enough to slice vellum, he dipped and gesticulated, prayed and prophesied. The crowd was his and he worked them in his hands, molded and pressed them like clay effigies.

The words that flowed from his silver-gilt tongue were velvet and cream, rare silks spun by rarer spiders. "Why have I turned my back on conventional medicine and scientific theorem?" he asked his audience, nodding his head, thumbs hooked in the pockets of his double-breasted brocade vest. "Why indeed, you may well ask. Why would I, Leon J. Lighthorse, who hold medical degrees from Leipzig, Vienna, and London University...why would I be so inclined to shun my very vocation and advocate what some may deem...a *heathen curative?*"

He timed it all carefully, expertly, knowing when to cast,

when to bait, and when to start reeling. When he felt their enthusiasm wane, he gave them what they wanted, the answer they sought.

He told them of his three years spent among the Piegan Blackfoot in Montana, of his association with the esteemed and esoteric medicine man, He-Who-Walks-On-The-Wind. And how that old Indian taught him the carefully guarded secrets of his people, of the sacred black root and spirit herb, echinacea and the holy wolf's leaf.

And as he spoke, the crowd became a great and bustling sea of angry ripples, shifting eddies, and secret tides. Dirty, desperate, and forlorn, these were the faces of the human moles that chiseled and chipped the subterranean coal seams in these West Virginia highlands. They grew to manhood in a cult of ignorance and intolerance so that their sons might have the same privilege and their daughters could marry hopeless, abusive men much like themselves.

It was their life and they knew no other.

They strode off to the mines each dawn, lunch buckets bumping at their hips. And there they were crushed by falls of slate and asphyxiated by toxic gases, entombed beneath mountains of rubble and laid low by the creeping black damp. At their sides were their wives, a raggedly grim and hollow-cheeked lot whose own lives were pregnant with despair and drudgery. And it was they—and the children they brought forth out of duty—who would cry over the miner's graves or lack of the same.

Lighthorse knew these people; he gave them what they wanted.

The crowd was slack-jawed and wide-eyed as he rambled eloquently. They watched and blinked and mumbled, knotted grubby hands into fists and nodded with morphic assent. They were hungry and Lighthorse fed them, preaching the gospel of medicinal absolution. Their lives were tight, dark, and harsh. Had he fed them swill, they would have swallowed it greedily, happily. Anything, anything to escape the drab monotony of a company town existence, to fill their bellies with something spicy, something exotic, something exhilarating. For the daily fare was mundane and restrictive beyond reason.

So, Lighthorse set the table and it was a feast.

"...ladies and gentlemen, I was a convert, an instant convert. And it was through this apprenticeship and years of diligent research that I produced what surely may be the world's finest specific, the veritable philosopher's stone of medicaments." Like a stage magician producing a dove from thin air, he brought forth a cobalt-blue patent medicine bottle from behind his back. "Ladies and gentlemen, young and old, it is with great pleasure I offer to you...Dr. Lighthorse's Marvelous Medical Metabolizer!"

He studied the faces of the faithful, the saved, and the curious. They had stepped into his carefully baited trap and now he sprung it.

"Now what can this magnificent Metabolizer do for you?" he put to them. "Better ask, what *can't* it do for you? For I have here in my hand not a mere nostrum or remedy, but a regenerator and rejuvenator, a restorative and reactivator! Lighthorse's Marvelous Medical Metabolizer cures the sick and invigorates the weak, it activates the bowels and accentuates the kidneys! It electrifies the liver and animates the heart! It stimulates the brain and energizes the muscles! It cleanses the blood and purifies the tissues...yes, oh yes, friends and neighbors, it treats the whole man, the whole woman, the whole child! It dissipates cholera and evaporates pneumonia, obliterates consumption and invalidates the grippe! The insufferably barren blossom with fertility and sexual potency! But it is no mere liver regulator or physic, friends, but a magical elixir that remedies the entire metabolism! Three tablespoons a day and you will walk taller and feel stronger, spit farther and jump higher! Remember the bounce in your step when you were a child? When life was a fine, uncorked wine? You can discover it again with this amazing serum..."

He had them. He held them tight in his hands, stroking and caressing them, knowing their desperation as they knew he was the keeper of the keys to a better life.

Crossing his arms, he pulled them in, webbed them, prepared to suck them dry. "Now...you would no doubt expect to pay a king's ransom for a mere taste of this sensational tonic.

And who wouldn't? If—and I say *if*, kind friends—this miraculous cordial were available in high-dollar eastern salons and spas, one would fully expect to pay twenty or thirty dollars a bottle. But, fortunately, as I am a humanitarian and devoted to the betterment of mankind and the alleviation of universal suffering, I can offer you a bottle of this stupendous serum for the paltry price of two dollars per bottle..."

By dusk, Lighthorse's show idled in dormancy in that whisper-grassed meadow. Lanterns were strung from canopies, sighing out shadowy tissues of light that flickered in the breeze. Crickets chirped and frogs lamented the dying day. Everywhere it was the hum of summer twilight and green silence. The whip-cracking and trick-roping were done, the gun-spinning and knife-throwing locked in steamer trunks. And the cases of Marvelous Medical Metabolizer were stored in padlocked chests.

And Lighthorse himself, in his wagon, counted the night's take and decided even he had outdone himself. What might have been wood alcohol, sugar, and pine sap to others, was the fountain of youth when he hawked it. Though his medical training was limited to a few dusty manuals, his verbal acumen and stagemanship were boundless.

He slapped the lid shut on the little metal cashbox as the back of the wagon creaked like a ruined house. The door breezed open. Madame Vorina, the show's fortune teller and tea-leaf reader, was standing there.

"So how was it tonight?" she said with acid in her voice. "How many dope fiends did you create this time?"

But Lighthorse would not look upon that black mirror which was Madame Vorina. She was all rough edges and contusions. Her limbs were pipe cleaners, her throat corded like a noose. When old age visited her, it would find her already a mummy, wizened by sharp-toothed survival. She was no more a clairvoyant than Lighthorse was a medico, but she played the part with conviction.

His smile was thin as a paper cut. "You speak in riddles, my dear," he told her, stroking the beard stubble at his narrow chin. "Dope fiends? Unthinkable. I am a medicine man and I cure the sick. It is my God-given duty."

Madame Vorina—whose real name was Peggy Lee Wilkes—laughed, and it was a bitter, cheated sound inspired by alcohol and anguish. "I know what you put in there, you quack. I know you lace every bottle with laudanum. You're creating a legion of opium addicts...my God, have you no decency? Even the children..."

Lighthorse kept smiling. "It keeps them coming back for more, my dove. And can you honestly say that the Metabolizer does not open heaven's doors for them?"

But she couldn't say that. She'd been addicted to laudanum herself and knew of its pleasures, its mystical promise. The first taste was luxury. But after a time, horror, when you ran out. And she told him so, nightly she told him...but then as now, he did not hear. He was a parasitic worm feeding on the oozing slag of mass appeal. He required nothing more.

Vorina stood there, the corn whiskey sloshing in her belly like pickle juice in a barrel. Nightly, gravity pulled at her, pressed her into a jar of alcohol like a medical anomaly and snapped the lid shut. She drifted and bobbed and felt the cool glass against her face. "You think you're some kind of healer, do you?"

"That," Lighthorse said, arranging his chemicals and flasks on the shelves like missing years, "is a proven fact."

Vorina nodded. "Then have I got something for you."

What she had, walked into the wagon under its own power and sat at the end of Lighthorse's cot. It wore a straw hat discolored by sweat and toil, a soiled jean cloth coat and trousers dyed blue-gray with sweetgum bark. Its face was bearded and its complexion jaundiced yellow. And it claimed its name was Starke, just Starke from "the high crossing, up past the wallers, right smack dab in Old Widder Holler."

"And how may I be of service?" Lighthorse inquired, not exactly taken with the man's smell or look, for he was a skeleton fleshed in cellophane and carried the morbidly distinct aura of shallow graves and mortuary slabs.

Stark fixed him with eyes black as sinkholes. "Ye have to save m' life, Doc, ye have to preserve it fer mebbe a week, mebbe two, then all will be put right. Can ye do that? Can ye?"

Lighthorse's left eyebrow arched like the back of an inch-worm. "Perhaps, dear sir, you should explain…"

Starke was breathing hard, droplets of sweat beading his brow. "It's on account of m' talent, that's what. A blessing and a curse. But it runs in m' family, see? We Starkes, well, we've been romancin' these hills for near on eighty year now. We been workin' the seams and drift mouths, yankin' coal from the belly of the mountain and plantin' our crops come spring same ever' year. Lots of us has gone over the fence what from flooded shafts and firedamps, from the lung and the gas, surely. Been born and died in these hills and reborn, and at least one of my kin—Old Mamy Darlin'—she were resurrected same as Jesus. Came just a-walkin' out of the tomb up in Graveyard Holler yonder on a windy, black night scarin' Christ and the saints outta jus' about ever'one. And it's from her, ye understand, that we gets our talent…"

"And what talent is that?" Lighthorse inquired.

Starke's eyes narrowed. "The etin' of the sin, ye fool, what else? My kin, least most, are sin-eaters. That's our talent."

Lighthorse had heard of it, of course. A curious, macabre Welsh custom of absorbing sin from the dead by feasting from cadavers piled with food. When the Welsh came to work the drifts, they brought it with them.

Lighthorse shook his head. "I'm afraid I don't understand."

"Why, who in hell ever learned ye to be a doctor? Right plain ignorant is what ye are." Starke sighed and placed a spidery hand over his chest. "Was over at the Hangtree Mine, afterdamp suffocated twenty miners in a cave-in while they was a-workin' their tonnage. I had to gorge for three days straight to take the sins off 'em…never carried so much before. And now…" Starke looked over toward the door, still holding his chest.

"Ye hear somethin', Doc?"

"No."

"A scratchin'?"

"No."

"A buzzin'?"

Lighthorse assured him that he had not.

Starke calmed a bit, but his hands were shaking and his face was rubbery like a spook-show mask. "Now, all them sins upon me...well, last few nights *He* been sniffin' around m' shack. I can hear Him...chatterin' his teeth and lickin' at the planks, whisperin' things I won't not listen to. Ye see, he wants them souls, wants to et 'em, fill his black belly with 'em. He knows I'm a-dyin', knows he can get 'em if I expire. See, He put the mark on me. The mark. Y'all know what that means..."

Lighthorse cleared his throat. "And who, dear sir, is this mysterious other?"

Starke fixed him with those eyes again, made something warm run inside him. "The Architect, ye fool, what else? Him that slithers down from them high, forbidden hollers...up there them from the old country set the bone altars to Him and sacrificed their firstborn and the like so as to keep Him full and fat, ye see? Stave off disease. He gets lean, gets a-hungry, he crawls down and brings the disease winds with Him. The Architect, the Architect of Pestilence."

Lighthorse found it all very amusing but was outwardly somber. "Yes, well, we can't have that, can we?"

"No, sir, no how." Both of Starke's hands were at his chest now, clutching and trembling like mating spiders. "See, I can't let Him get these souls which I carry. But m' heart...not so good, hear? Got me pains deep in the chest, right down m' left arm. Seen it happen to m' old man, heart jus' stops. In a week or two, m' cousin Hawley Caine will be here and he'll take the sins offa me...but until then, ye got to keep me alive, hear?"

Lighthorse nodded grimly, understanding completely. He brought out a bottle of the Metabolizer. "As my supply runs short, I must ask a contribution of five dollars for this medicinal wonder which—"

"Yeah, yeah...will it animate m' heart as ye say?"

"Oh, without a doubt, sir, without a doubt."

Starke grabbed the bottle, tossed a few bills in the air, and left the wagon. Lighthorse, on his hands and knees, madly grabbed up the cash.

The next few days brought a stifling hot wind down from the high peaks and ridges. It blew with the suffocating breath of blast furnaces and coke ovens, funeral pyres and ash pits. The breeze withered before it and the grass turned yellow, flowers wilted and trees drooped. Dogs were pushed under porches and livestock broiled in their own hides. Men sweated and grew angry, swatting at flies and children alike.

Lighthorse watched the crowds thin and sales drop, for not even the Marvelous Medical Metabolizer could turn back the cremating breath of hell.

The second day of the heat wave, he sat in his wagon in the insufferable humidity, fanning himself with a leaf torn from a book. He had decided that he would make one more night of it, then move the show to pastures that were greener and folding.

He killed a pesky bluebottle fly that seemed insistent on investigating his ear and saw a man standing at the open door. "Come in, friend, come in," he said graciously, always ready for a sale. "Get out of that burning sun before I have to turn you with a fork. Yes...how may I be of service to you?"

The man was a heavy fellow with a neck thick as a chopping block and large, hairy hands. "Name's Stoddard," he said in an even, hard voice. "I'm the law around here."

Lighthorse sat up and took notice now, ignoring the fly treading his sweaty throat. "Ah, yes, yes, Sheriff, a pleasure, a pleasure. I hope I have not violated some trifling town ordinance or statute. If so, we can rectify—"

"I'm not the sheriff, just a town constable," Stoddard said dully, his voice flat and gray as metal shavings. "I collect taxes and uphold the law, break up fights between the miners and pull 'em off their wives before they kill 'em when they've had too much."

"An honorable profession, surely—"

"Ain't nothing honorable about it, Lighthorse. Just necessary, is all. I didn't stop by to chat," he said sharply. "I stopped by to tell you that Sean Starke passed yesterday. I know you sold him a bottle of your rattlesnake oil and I thought you'd like to know, is all."

Lighthorse coughed lightly into his hand. "I...that is...did he take the Metabolizer as directed?"

"I found the bottle empty in his shack," Stoddard explained.

"I'm not saying you had anything to do with it. Starke had a bad heart and everyone knew it. That swill you sell can't kill any more than it can cure. Sugar water, vinegar, and a taste of grain alcohol never killed anyone."

"Um…yes…*uh!* These flies," Lighthorse said, swatting at them. "Please give my heartfelt condolences to the widow."

"Save that shit for your show, Lighthorse." Stoddard waited in the doorway, heavy and powerful and blown full with hostility. "There's no regulation against selling patent medicine off a wagon, so I can't run you out much as I'd like to. But I will give you a word of warning. These people here…they've got peculiar beliefs. Starke was a sin-eater. They think he carries them souls with him."

"Do you believe that?"

"What I believe is not important, Lighthorse. They do and that's enough. They believe in lots of things. Like this wind we've been getting, haven't seen it in years…but when it comes, it's always bad. Folks around here call it a 'Cholera Wind'. They believe it brings disease and pestilence. And I'm not the one to say they're wrong."

Lighthorse was admittedly no physician, but he knew about cholera and it was not brought by wind. It was passed through food and water, the result of inadequate sanitation. "Ah, yes, these hill folk are often wise beyond their ways."

"Mmm-hmm. What I'm saying is that if people start getting sick, they might blame you. Some of 'em already do for Starke and the souls of their loved ones which they believe are in the belly of some mountain devil by now. It might be a good idea to push on."

Lighthorse tried to keep his composure, but it was flaking away like cake soap. "I'll…I'll certainly take that under advisement." There seemed to be more flies in the wagon by the moment. They circled him like moths at a lamp. "Damnable pests, they're everywhere."

"They're drawn to refuse," Stoddard said pointedly. "And dead things."

"Well, I'm certainly not dead," Lighthorse proclaimed proudly.

But Stoddard only nodded. "Maybe they know something you don't."

That night.

Madame Vorina's tent.

A black seething oven of stillborn air that hung in moist cerements and winding sheets, it dripped and steamed and mildewed. Everything was wet, hot, and rotting like a misting, miasmic jungle swamp.

Madame Vorina was on her cot, bunched painfully in damp sheets. Her flesh was pale and blotchy, beaded with perspiration. Her eyes languished in puffy blood-red depressions. From time to time her blistered lips shuddered, released a moan or a dry racking cough and she went still again, still as the warm darkness outside the tent.

Lighthorse held her hand and it had the feel of dank meat, limp and boneless. He let it drop at her side, sucking in a soggy breath of green growth and rancid heat.

"The fever," a voice behind him said. It belonged to the Gunpowder Kid, the show's pistol trickster. "She's burning up...she won't make it long like this."

Lighthorse wetted his lips. "She...I saw her this morning. She was fine, just fine. How could it..."

"You're the doctor, aren't you?" the Kid said. "Give her some of that remedy of yours, it'll fix her right up."

The Kid left the tent, but his sarcasm lingered.

The canvas walls and peaked roof of the tent were a crawling stucco of mosquitoes and gnats, meat flies rubbing tiny forelegs together. But the former did not light off Madame Vorina, as if they sensed that while her flesh was searing, her blood grew cold. Only the flies took notice.

Lighthorse slapped them away from her.

The Kid was right: she was done in. Even had Lighthorse any true medical training, he doubted he could fight something that consumed and wasted so quickly, so completely. It was not cholera, surely, but it was no less virulent. The only thing left to do was to find a preacher and dig a grave.

Lighthorse wetted a rag with rubbing alcohol. Brushed it

across her flesh to cool her. Her skin was a map of some diseased wasteland, a graphic relief of sores and contusions and
swollen lumps. His fingers roamed them, reading them like
Braille, searching for significance and finding only enigma. He
began to notice, as his hands freely roamed the sweaty draws
and hollows of Madame Vorina, that the bumps he navigated
seemed to be…well, *moving* beneath his fingertips.

And not just moving, but wriggling.

Yes, thumb pressed to a reddened bulge at her throat, he
could feel the busy, squirming life beneath…a seething, undulating nest of *something*. Taking out a penknife and sterilizing
the blade over a candle, he carefully slit the bump, spread the
incision open so he could see, see, *yes*, that knot of viscid profusion, of coiling and writhing white worms interlocking and
wrestling like pale fingers.

With a cry, Lighthorse fell back.

A single, investigative worm inched its way out, followed by
another and another and another. Madame Vorina shuddered
and shook, suddenly sitting bolt upright in the cot. Her face was
a bloodless and hideous mask, her eyes glassy yellow pools
ringed by red half-moons. She stared unblinking, but did not
see. Her lips peeled away from swollen gums, her teeth chattering madly and a single thread of black festering blood slid from
the corner of her lips.

She coughed with a ragged sound…and a fly crawled out of
her mouth.

Lighthorse stood there, his bare arms and neck shingled
with mosquitoes. But he did not feel them. He watched Madame
Vorina hack out more flies. There were dozens on her lips, dozens more in her mouth. A particularly bloated one slid from her
left nostril and lighted in the air.

Infested, Lighthorse thought, *infested*.

Though he wanted to pull his show from that despicable place
the morning after Madame Vorina's death, Constable Stoddard
would not allow it. There were questions that might need to
be asked by the county coroner, he said. He told Lighthorse,
chances were, he could pull out that afternoon.

So Lighthorse waited in that simmering yellow heat, sweating and worrying and wondering what was happening and what his part could possibly be in it. The other performers were irate and afraid, arguments inflaming themselves into out and out brawls. Around noon word reached the little encampment that there was some kind of plague sweeping the town. That three people had died and dozens of others were gravely ill.

Shortly thereafter, Lighthorse was summoned into town to do some doctoring. He refused, of course, until money was mentioned.

He followed a woman named Fiske up into the town.

It was, he knew, called Hook Creek.

There were fifty or so company houses rising like scabs on that scarred landscape of dead trees and gouged hillsides. Each was identical to its neighbor—dirty frame houses on dirty roads peopled by dirty children. Everything was blown black with coal dust. The homes and company store, porches and side yards, even the people themselves. Smudged and sooty. The hills were stripped of timber, barren knobs set with looming headframes and hoist shacks. Plague or no, the mines churned away like perpetual motion machines, sucking coal from the drifts below.

Lighthorse was led into a house that leaned precariously toward its neighbor. It seemed to sway and shake like an unmoored ship as he mounted the steps. He was directed through a grimy door and into a grimy interior. Inside, the heat was heavy and turgid, roiling like gelatin. He could smell body odor and boiled vegetables, black earth and garbage. But there was another stink, too, one of sick wards, feces, and soiled dressings.

A ring of children with dirt-streaked faces sat at a scathed table eating fried apples, cornbread, and ramps with their fingers. They stared at Lighthorse, eyes wide and white, standing out in sharp contrast to the filthy faces that housed them.

"Good afternoon, children," Lighthorse said with a courtly bow that made one of them giggle. "I am Dr. Lighthorse, late of London University."

Mrs. Fiske said to them, "Ye just et and never ye mind."

In another room, a little girl was sprawled on a daybed with dingy, fouled sheets. She was unconscious, sweating and shaking, her legs and arms twitching with occasional spasms. Her flesh was oddly shiny like oiled rubber.

"She got the cramps in her legs and arms and belly something terrible," Mrs. Fiske told him, running a hand through the child's greasy locks. "And awful diarrhea. Everything runs right through her...she can't seem to swallow good."

"Yes, a malady of the lower regions, no doubt," Lighthorse said, making a perfunctory examination of the same.

He was no doctor, of course, but what he saw was something he had seen once in an Indian camp up in Dakota Territory: cholera. An outbreak due to improper sanitation had wasted most of the tribe. And that's what he was seeing now and had no doubt of it. He reached in his little leather bag for a bottle of the Metabolizer, but something stayed his hand, told him that once, maybe just once he should do the right thing.

"My dear lady, I believe your child has cholera," he said.

Mrs. Fiske gasped, swooned, but controlled herself.

"Now listen to me. Bodily secretions must be disposed of immediately—they spread the disease. Boil your water. Give the child sugar water and hot green tea. Bicarbonate of soda, salts of tartar, oil of annis mixed in water," he said, feeling very good about it all. "You must keep the fluids up. The sugars and salts are very important. As much as she can take. She should be better in a few days...but boil all water! No exceptions."

"Oh, thank you, Doctor, thank you!"

"I am only too happy to be of service, madam. I—"

But then the door opened and a man dusted black from head to foot entered. He was big and burly, his white eyes jutting from the blackened skull. "Git out m' house, ye quack! Ye git out with that snake oil!"

"John," Mrs. Fiske implored, "he was trying to help us."

But all that got her was a swat from a large, callused paw that left a black streak down one cheek.

"Git out, I say! He ain't of no help! Lookit him! Lookit him!" the man cried. "He got the *mark* upon him, the mark like that fortune teller!"

Lighthorse quickly excused himself and made it out to the

road when one of the children came running after him with his bag.

"Here, mister!" the boy said. "Ye forgot this! Daddy don't want it in the house, being that you and yourn are marked by Him That Walks Above! The Architect..."

Lighthorse felt a queasiness in his belly. Something in there shifted, turned over upon itself. "Who, child, is this Architect?"

The boy looked about fearfully. "They say he lives up in the old burial ground yonder, up in that holler where the sun never touches! They say folks brung Him here from the old country, brung him in a casket of rotten meat and slimy bones to protect 'em from the pestilence..."

"That's ridiculous, son."

"Oh no, sir! Is not! They say when that hot disease wind blows like it is, that it's His breath. That he's a-coming down, yessum! I heard daddy say He lives in the bottom of the flooded Number 13 Hangtree Company mine, down there in that black water and fungus and bones."

"Nonsense. Utter nonsense."

But the boy kept shaking his head. "Ye'll see soon enough, on account ye got the mark. Ye'll believe, mister, ye'll believe when ye hear him slithering and hissing, feel him coming through the stalks..."

But Lighthorse would listen no more.

He went back down to the encampment and it was no easy trek. He was chased by stone-throwing children, threatened by old ladies with sticks, and had his pant leg torn by dogs. A knot of men outside a saloon said loud enough for him to hear that witches should be burned.

When Lighthorse finally reached the meadow, there was only one wagon left.

His own.

The other performers had bolted.

The shadows were lengthening by the time Lighthorse got the horses hitched to his wagon and climbed up into the leather seat. Something was crawling in his belly. Something, maybe, telling him it was too late, too late, that you could run, but you could never hide. That when your apple dropped from the tree of life and went to soft rot in the grass no drooping limb could hope to scoop it back up again.

Lighthorse was thinking this, deciding his mind had taken a decidedly poetic, unpleasant turn and that it disturbed him greatly. And maybe it was because the mark was upon him. Of all the superstitious nonsense.

He would not think such things.

The reigns were snakes in his hands as he tried to get the horses under control: they slithered and looped, went taut, coiled and snapped. He had a hell of a time with them. He did not wait for Stoddard to tell him he could leave Hook Creek; he just left. Left, perhaps, before the townsfolk strung him up or burned him...like a witch.

He would not come back to West Virginia.

So he rode down the twisting, narrow road that was rutted clay and black blood vomited from the deep shafts. The town rose above with its shanties and shacks and company houses. And above it, the mines and high spruce forests. The sun was sinking, impaling itself on craggy peaks.

The horses were nickering and shaking their flanks, not liking any of it. And then the town was gone and to either side were the poplar forests and thickets of spice bush, hemlocks brooding in deep-cut ravines which were cool and misty. Already Lighthorse could feel that hot wind dissipating, the twisting and turning road canceling it out. The spluttering team of black geldings carried him away through bottoms and up hills and down vales.

Suddenly, the air began to simmer and drip and then the forests went from poplar to scrub pine and he saw the town up on the ridge, looking down at him.

Lighthorse stopped the team.

He blinked. He stared, but he could not be seeing the town because he had left it behind. A wrong turn, an unforeseen fork? He could remember none. When the show had originally come into Hook Creek, it had come in on this road. He himself had led the wagons on horseback.

So...how could he have been turned back around?

He refused to think of it.

Hook Creek brooded above like some industrialized cemetery and he felt its blackness, its malignance and, yes, pestilence
and, God, they seemed to feel him, too.

He brought the team around and this time he did not coo
or coax but gave them the sharp kiss of the whip that sent them
pounding up and out of town. Forests. Brakes. Bottoms. Ravines.
Then poplar, scrub pine…and Hook Creek.

Ridiculous, impossible.

But there it was.

Lighthorse began to sweat and tremble, and despite the heat,
chills raced up his spine and flooded over the back of his neck.
Again, he brought the horses around and this time he did it carefully, eyes studying the road and looking for what had turned
him around. The countryside was exactly the same. Only, it was
darker now. The forests were oozing with shadow, ebon tangles
of it spilled across the road with the slow undulations of desert
serpents. He urged the team ever forward, through murky pockets and draws and he had to give them the whip again to get them
to move and then—

Then they reared up, nearly throwing him from the seat. The
hitch groaned and the wagon rolled.

"Whoa!" Lighthorse cried out. "Here, here now!"

But they would not move…for standing just above on the rise
of a hill, a black and towering form with eyes like burning red
embers.

Lighthorse felt something compress painfully in his chest.
"You…you there…"

But the figure did not respond.

It waited, an incinerating wind blowing off it, a hot and tainted
stink of funeral pyres and boiling mass graves. Lighthorse could
hear a muted, busy hive of phobic buzzing which grew louder
and louder becoming a droning whine. Then he saw it, yes, he
saw that the figure was not wearing black but *was* black, a cloud
of black insectile motion. Flies. Thousands and thousands of flies
caught in a dire, buzzing whirlwind of storm that mimicked a tall
human form.

"Who…who are you?" Lighthorse asked, but he knew, oh
how he knew.

The tall form seemed to drift closer or maybe Lighthorse drifted closer to it, there was no way to know. For it was all hallucinogenic and distorted and he couldn't be sure of anything.

The form laughed with a mephitic roar...and that laughter was not laughter but the wail of children suffocating in a deep well and the wet scream of eviscerated pigs. In his head, Lighthorse saw carrion birds plucking at eyeballs and sterile deserts strewn with the bones of infants.

The Architect of Pestilence inched closer and closer, a honeycombed thing of flies and chittering deathwatch beetles. A tanned and abraded sack was slung from one shoulder and it was fashioned of human skin. More so, a hide sack of dozens of agonized faces stitched together into a mass of weeping eyes and chattering teeth. And the Architect himself—a faceless nightmare of holes and hollows, wormy meat and flyblown shrouds. His eyes were red pearls veined with black.

As flies lit from him, seeking out Lighthorse, the medicine man turned the wagon back toward town or maybe the horses turned it. Regardless, the team was suddenly racing back to Hook Creek and finding it with no trouble as a tornado of flies blew and blustered behind them.

The first thing Lighthorse saw was Stoddard on horseback.

He reigned in the team and was telling the constable what he had seen and how it was after him and that he needed protection, protection. "Jesus, Stoddard, you haven't seen, you don't know—"

"I know all I want to know about that business," Stoddard said. "Only reason I came to see you was to tell you that the coroner says the fortune teller died of asphyxiation."

"Asphyxiation?" Lighthorse panted.

"Yes. Her lungs were filled with hundreds of carrion flies... can you imagine such a thing?" Stoddard chuckled grimly. "Yes, I think you can."

Lighthorse shed his coat of showmanship now. He was just a thin, frightened man whose flashy clothes were too large for the frame beneath. "Stoddard, please...you know about that thing, that Architect...there's gotta be some way, some way to call it off, call it off..."

"I don't know what you mean," he said, checking his pocket watch in the gathering twilight. "The Architect...that's just a story. Educated man like you...London University and all...you should know better."

"Dammit, man, don't play with me here!" Lighthorse said frantically. "What do you want? Money? Is that it? I got money, lots of money."

"There's some things you just can't buy off, mister. What's been promised has been promised."

"But there's gotta be something that can be done, somebody who can pull it off me, some old witch woman up in the hills—"

"I wouldn't know about that, I'm just the law here." Stoddard slid his watch back in his shirt pocket. "None of this is my doing, you understand. And what's after you, well, it's just a force of nature like the wind or a storm blowing. It'll just have to run its course, that's all. If I was you, I'd lock myself up in that wagon and pray for sunrise..."

So that's what Lighthorse did.

He locked himself in the wagon and prayed and whimpered and kept listening, because he could really do little else. From time to time he heard that slithering sound around the wagon, that hissing and buzzing, the sound of teeth chattering. Sometimes a scratching, a clawing, the sound of something like roofing nails dragged along the length of the wagon.

That's how he spent the night.

Thinking about the old Welsh bringing the Architect of Pestilence from the old country in a casket of meat and bones so it would protect them from disease. How they made sacrifice to it. And how, either by accident or purpose, it had gone dormant until it heard about Starke and all those souls and woke back up, yawned, stretched, decided it was time to play a few games.

By morning, there was acceptance for Lighthorse.

Acceptance because there are just some things a man can't hide from. Things like death and the grave. So the sun rose like a shimmering slice of lemon and the hot diseased wind blew and the cholera spread and the Architect stuffed himself full. Lighthorse scratched and itched and could not get comfortable.

By noon, he was giggling and feverish and drooling. And it wasn't so bad going mad. Wasn't so bad being full of grave worms as he was. In fact, it didn't get really bad, truly hideous, until all those maggots started hatching into flies...

NIGHT AND FOG

The fog crept in over the sea, lonely and cold and ancient, something born of darkness and stark depths. First in threads and tangles, then finally in great knots and twisting banks that wove themselves into a blanket that shut us off from the world. What had steadily been growing obscure for the past twenty minutes was suddenly gone. The lights of the shoreline a mile distant winked out like cigarettes dropped in a puddle. Then it was just the two of us trapped in that shroud of billowing fog and you couldn't see more than fifteen feet in any direction.

"Where the hell are they?" Jenna kept saying to me like maybe I had all the answers.

"I don't know. They should have been up by now."

"Well they're not up, Rog. In case you haven't noticed."

I wanted badly to smart off to her, something I did a lot when she started crawling under my skin like that, but I kept my mouth shut. Now was not the time. She was scared and I knew it. I think I was getting a little scared, too. Mick and Andy were still down there and night had fallen, the mist swallowing us alive and winding us up tight. Jenna and I sat there in our wetsuits, not saying a damn thing, the small waves lapping up against the side of the Zodiac inflatable.

During the daytime, Monterey Bay seems pleasant and inviting...but after dark, it was something else again.

"When you came up the anchor line," Jenna asked me for about the tenth time, "were they behind you?"

"Yes...at least, I think so."

"Which, Rog?"

"Mick gave the signal and I went up the line. I thought for sure they were right behind me."

Jenna shook her head.

Mick, Andy, and I had dove on the wreck of the *Ambergris,* an eighty-foot collier that had burst into flame on Christmas Eve, 1933, and went to the bottom with all hands. Mick knew where it was so we dropped anchor and, sure enough, all we had to do was follow the anchor line. The first sight of her in our dive lights was enough to take your breath away...immense and ghostly, laying on her side down there on the sandy bottom, encrusted with marine growths and haunted by schools of fish. We were down there for about forty-five minutes when Mick gave me the signal to ascend.

Which I did.

Alone, apparently.

I kept staring at the water which had gone black as ink now, praying for a few telltale bubbles that would tell me the others were on their way up. But I saw nothing. Just the ripple of waves, the reflection of my light in the water, the fog blowing around the raft. Way I had it figured, Mick and Andy had maybe fifteen minutes left in their tanks. If they didn't come up soon, they never would.

"Well?" Jenna said.

"Well, what?"

"Are you going down after them for godsake?"

I knew I had to, but I didn't like the idea. Not in the least. The *Ambergris* was down fifty feet. In the broad daylight, when the sun was overhead, the light would reach down far enough so that you could see the vague shape of the wreck. But it was night now. The water was black and ominous. I didn't like the idea of following the line down there. At least not alone. I had about twenty dives under my belt by that point, but none of them had been night dives. That's something strictly for pros... or fools. Mick had been on plenty of them and Andy was an ex-Coast Guard Rescue Swimmer, one of those guys that drop from search-and-rescue helicopters into thirty-foot seas and drag shipwreck victims into baskets so they can be winched to safety. Those two were experienced in things like that, but not me.

And that's what had me spooked, I suppose.

They were vets. There wasn't much the sea could throw at them they could not handle. And I could understand something happening to one of them...but *both?* What kind of trouble could have kept both of them down there? Of course, with night having fallen and that damn fog enclosing us, my mind was coming up with all kinds of crazy reasons. I imagined they had been ravaged by sharks or big squid or any number of pelagic nightmares. We were, essentially, in the shallows, but farther out Monterey Bay submarine canyon dropped down a good two miles. And because of this, various deep-sea creatures were known to show up—basking sharks and killer whales, blue whales and humpbacks, white sharks and giant squid. Just about anything could—and had—come into the shallows out of curiosity. And in the past, some pretty weird and monstrous things had washed up that still had the marine scientists scratching their collective heads.

So, those were the kind of things I was imagining.

The dive on the *Ambergris* had been my sixth dive in Monterey Bay. I'd seen sharks before, plenty of them—mostly blues and makos, none of them particularly large—but they generally darted off when we neared them. But that was with the sunlight streaming down into the water. Who the hell knew what might come into the shallows by night to feed?

"I think we should both go," I told Jenna, knowing she would not like the idea. The only reason she had started diving at all was because Mick had talked her into it. I suppose, as her boyfriend, he could talk her into all kinds of things. But the truth of the matter was that she was terrified of the water and what lived in it. She honestly thought there were sharks like that one in *Jaws*. Not great white sharks, I mean, but monsters that lived to eat people.

But it just wasn't true.

Yet, staring down into that black water, I was beginning to think the same things.

"I'm not going down there," Jenna said. "Are you nuts?"

"It's not safe to dive alone at night," I told her.

"Why don't you grow a set already, Rog."

"Fuck you, Jenna," I said. "How about, just for once, you forget that you're a natural-born bitch."

I should point out that we hadn't always disliked each other. There had been a time when Jenna wouldn't have said a word against me. But that was when I was dating her sister. After we broke up, Jenna hated me. I was only around her because I was Mick's friend. She sat in the stern of the raft, pouting. She probably figured that would work wonders on me, but she was sadly mistaken. Jenna was a very attractive girl…long red hair, model pretty, she filled out her wetsuit in a way that made a guy want to unzip it if it was the last thing he ever did. She was used to getting her way with guys. But even had she whipped out her impressive breasts—Andy like to joke that with a set of lungs like that, she didn't need an air tank—I still wouldn't have felt sorry for her. A cute little girl pout even from a tall, leggy redhead could not erase months of her insults.

But there I was pulling on my tanks and swim fins.

Yes, I was going down there, but I was doing it for my friends, not for Jenna.

"I don't know what happened to them," I told her as I grabbed my dive light and speargun, "but I'm betting it's not good. So get on your cell and call the Coast Guard."

Jenna looked up at me. "Mick would kill me. He told me never to do that unless the shit really hit the fan."

"Well, it has, so make the call."

That's when bubbles began to break the surface just starboard of the raft. A few at first, then a flurry, and something inside me tensed. I knew it was one of the guys coming up, but I was thinking it might be something else. But it wasn't. It was Mick. He rose up, splashing, yanking the mouthpiece of his regulator out.

"Did Andy make it up?" he shouted at us, gasping and swimming to the raft. "Did Andy make it back up?"

I told him that he hadn't.

Mick handed me his speargun and face mask. In the lights from the raft, he looked bloodless. His face pinched and his eyes wide and shocked. "Haul me aboard for chrissake," he told us and we did, yanking him up the dive step and into the raft, helping him peel out of his tanks and gear. I noticed that he had lost his dive light.

He looked over at me. "What're you doing? What're you suiting up for?"

"I was coming down after you," I said.

"Bullshit...not down there, not fucking down there," he said, breathing real fast and trying to catch his breath.

"Where's Andy?" Jenna asked him.

Mick rubbed his face with his hands. "I'd like to know that myself." He shook his head back and forth. "Something happened. Jesus, I don't even know what."

Mick did not spook easy.

I want you to understand that. This guy swam with whales and manta rays and had more than one underwater photo of himself with sharks. For a time, he had even been part of a team that was exploring underwater caves off the Sea of Cortez. And that takes balls. But right then? He was scared. He was pale and panicky, looking around in the fog like he expected something to come swooping out of it and take a bite out of him. And because he was scared, I was, too. Ever since night fell and the mist came rolling in, I'd had a bad feeling. Don't ask me to explain it to you. Just a funny feeling in the pit of my guts like you get when you're expecting bad news. Anxiety, agitation, something like that.

"What happened, baby?" Jenna said, trying to put her hands on him as he swatted them aside, definitely in no mood to play house.

He looked over at me and I saw his Adam's apple bobbing up and down as he swallowed. "There was something down there, man," he said in a voice as brittle as white ice. "Something fucking big."

"A shark?" Jenna said.

You could almost see images from killer shark movies parading through her little mind.

But Mick shook his head. "No, it wasn't any shark and it wasn't a whale either. It was just big and...weird."

Well, that didn't go over so well. It hit me with all the sub-
tlety of a severed limb. Something sank inside me. *It was just
big and...weird.* Maybe Jenna was thinking man-eating sharks,
but I didn't know what I was thinking. Mick had been diving
Monterey Bay since he was fourteen and he was nearly forty
now. He knew the things that lived in it, even the bizarre, sel-
dom-seen creatures like the oarfish. And for him to be admitting to us that there was something down there he could not
identify and that it was big and weird...well, that wasn't so
good. Not so good at all. Whatever it was, it had scared him.
And that in combination with Andy never coming up, well, it
really got my mind rolling. I wished all I was afraid of were big
monster sharks like Jenna, but what Mick claimed to have seen
was large and unknown. And there's something about those
words in connection with an unidentified sea animal that can
really scare the shit out of you. And particularly when you're
sitting in a twelve-foot open raft at night with the fog drifting
around you like phantoms.

"We better call the Coast Guard," I said.

Mick calmed himself, took Jenna's phone and did just that.
The conversation lasted about five minutes. They were coming
and hopefully it wouldn't take them long. The part I didn't like
was that we had to wait until they got there.

The night was getting cold and I was starting to see my
breath. The fog was knitting itself thicker all the time, yellow
and white and enveloping, swirling around like it was being
stirred with a big spoon. I could hear the channel buoy dinging
in the distance with a hollow, lonesome sound. Jenna was hugging herself and Mick kept looking around like he was waiting
for something. And God help me, I didn't think it was the Coast
Guard patrol. A foghorn sounded from the lighthouse down
the beach and I jumped. I don't know what I thought it was.

"Tell me what happened down there," I finally said when I
couldn't take that drawn-out silence any longer.

After a moment, he did.

He said he'd given me the signal to ascend. I remembered
that much. I remembered being almost glad to be getting out
of there. The *Ambergris* had looked like some malefic ghost

ship rising from the sand. The sea had been murky and clotted with sediment that rose from the wreck like it was flaking away. Other than a few small schools of fish, there had been no life down there. That had struck me as being unusual. It had disturbed me somehow like maybe we had dove on a haunted house or something. I started following the anchor rope up and I was certain Andy and Mick had been only a dozen feet behind me.

"No," Mick said, "we weren't. We started after you, but Andy grabbed my arm. He found something and wanted me to have a quick look at it."

"What?" I said, imagining a rotting treasure chest with a pirate skeleton or two wrapped around it. Too many old pirate movies as a kid, I guess.

"A rocking horse."

I looked at Jenna and she looked at me. "A rocking horse?"

"Yeah. We didn't know that at first. Andy found something poking out of the sea bed near the ship. It took us about fifteen minutes to pull it free. It was a rocking horse. An antique rocking horse, a kid's toy. It was in rough shape, lots of holes in it from burrowing worms and the like."

Jenna said. "What was a rocking horse doing down there?"

"It was Christmas Eve when the *Ambergris* went down, Jenna. I figured it was a toy one of the sailors was bringing home for his kid. Maybe from San Fran. You know, there's still a lot of people around here who remember the night that ship went down and lost family members on it. I thought if I could bring that old rocking horse up, it might mean something to one of them."

I smiled. Good old Mick. He came off as a tough guy, but inside he was all warm and fuzzy and I knew it. He was thinking that some guy had been bringing his little son or daughter a Christmas present and that that son or daughter might still be alive and the rocking horse would finally, ultimately bring them full circle with the death of their father. A heartfelt connection would be made seventy-odd years later, father to child. Despite the way he sometimes acted, things like that meant a lot to him because his own father had been such an asshole.

Mick always volunteered to help the needy during Christmas. He loved seeing the kids' faces light up.

"So you risked your life for a dumb rocking horse?" Jenna said.

"Yes, I did," Mick told her, proud of the fact. "And I'd fucking do it again. That toy means something to someone. I just felt it."

She rolled her eyes with all the requisite exaggerated drama.

I patted his arm. "You're a good guy, Mick."

He smiled for a moment, then frowned. What he told us next was not so heartwarming or sweet. They'd just gotten the rocking horse out of the sand when something big passed over them. They didn't really see it, they just felt the incredible vacuum of a very large object pass maybe ten feet above. And fast. So fast that when they looked up they saw a massive black shape but nothing else. But it was enough to make them stop thinking about rocking horses and start thinking about getting the hell out of there. I told you before that it was creepy around that wreck and I could just imagine what it must have been like when that object passed over them.

"We were shining our lights around," Mick said, "but with the goddamn sediment and the clouds of sand we kicked up, you couldn't see shit. We both had our spearguns, but the size of that thing…well, they were precious little comfort."

Mick said he tapped Andy on the tanks and they both decided, wordlessly, to get the hell out of Dodge. Like I said, Mick did not scare easily and that went double for Andy, being an ex-Rescue Swimmer. But Mick said he saw Andy's face in the dive lights just fine. Behind his face mask, Andy's tanned and wind-burned face was sallow and sickly-looking. They made their way over to the wreck and the anchor line and it happened again. Something big passed right behind them. Again, it was moving so fast it was nothing but a blur.

"We were freaking out," Mick said. "Shit, I've been diving long enough to know that you don't panic down there. But, believe me, we were both were. Whatever that thing was, it kept swimming past us. This side, then that side, above us…it seemed like it was everywhere. But then I was at the anchor line and Andy was right behind me. I swear to Christ he was right behind me. I started up...I started up and that thing passed by me, close, real fucking close. So close that its backwash almost pulled me right off the rope. I hung on for dear life, and when I calmed enough to look down...Andy wasn't there. He just wasn't there."

You could read stories about what Mick was telling us in skin-diving magazines or books about weird encounters with sea life. If you're like me, you read them in the can or out on the back porch, then you toss the magazine aside and you don't give much more thought to encounters with octopuses or sharks or what not. But out in that night and fog with the idea of something immense and frightening swimming just below us, I couldn't put it out of my mind. Our anchor line was still leading straight down to the wreck. If that thing wanted to get us, all it had to do was follow the yellow brick road.

I'd had enough, but Mick wasn't done yet. "I saw Andy's light. It was about fifteen or twenty feet below me. That's all I could see. I went back down. Christ, I didn't want to...but what choice did I have? What goddamn choice did I have?"

"Just take it easy, man," I told him.

He kept looking around in the fog and at the water and it was positively infectious, because I started doing the same damn thing.

"I got down there and it was only his light lying in the sand. Andy was nowhere. I looked around the wreck, looked around much as I could, but I knew he was gone. He was gone and that thing had gotten him." Mick looked like he needed to cry, to scream, to vent somehow. But every time Jenna touched him, he shrugged her off. "I just came up the line...but it kept swimming around me. It wouldn't fucking leave me alone. It finally went away maybe twenty feet down."

"Did you see anything?" I said.

He took his time answering that one. "Just that shape...that big shape. But the way it moved, I knew it wasn't a whale or a shark."

"Anything else?"

"Eyes."

"What?"

He swallowed. "I passed my light beneath me once and I thought I saw big eyes looking up at me...I'm not sure."

Jenna said, "You know you're really scaring the shit out of me with this, Mick. Can we just get out of here please? I can't stand it any longer."

I thought Mick would slap her. I really did. Andy was our friend and he was down there and I could not imagine a more cowardly or irresponsible course of action than abandoning him. Mick gave her a hard look, but only briefly. Then it actually looked as if he was considering it. I guess, if nothing else, that was the gauge of how shaken up he was. Because Mick would never have left a friend, left any diver, had he been in his right state of mind.

"We have to wait for the Coasties," I said. "We can't go anywhere."

"Yes," Mick said.

But I wondered how long that would take. The Coast Guard station was probably three of four miles away. So, we sat there in that moving yellow fog, the beams of our dive lights like white pencils scraping against its mass. I don't think I've ever felt so alone or so damn helpless in my life. With that mist around us and the darkness pressing in we might as well have been on another world or in another dimension. Everything was surreal and nightmarish.

I kept shining my light around, listening to the lap of the water and the dinging of the distant buoy, maybe expecting to see a set of huge eyes looking back at me.

"I heard something," Jenna said.

We all listened. I thought I'd heard something, too. Something moving through the water. Our lights, of course, showed us nothing but the mist. Visibility was maybe twenty feet at best. Our lights hit the fog, penetrated a few feet, and were reflected back at us. The night air was chill and I was shivering. The seas were slight. For a long time, I'd been smelling the dankness of the fog and the brine of the sea, but now there was another odor, something pungent and sickening and pervasive: the stink of rotting fish. As if maybe there was a fishing boat nearby with a hold filled with rotten, wormy tuna and halibut. Or maybe the sea had vomited up something large and decayed. It was too strong and it did not belong.

"God, what's that smell?" Jenna said.

"Shut up," Mick told her. "Just shut up."

I knew what he was thinking. I knew exactly what he was thinking: we were not alone now. There was something else out there in the fog. We were smelling it and hearing it sliding through the surf. But even without those tangible clues, I think I would have known. I would have felt it out there—immense and hungry and evil. Because I *was* feeling it. Sensing it.

The question was: did it know where we were?

Was it casting about for our scent? Moving around us in the fog, zeroing in on our position? And what in the hell *was* it? I had no reason to think so, other than what Mick had said, but I was sensing its *bigness*. I knew it was large and dangerous. I could almost feel its girth pushing the air around, making the fog swirl and billow like steam coming off a pot.

"Can't we just go?" Jenna said like a little girl who'd had enough of the neighborhood haunted house for the night.

"Shut up," Mick told her again. He had his dive knife out. I think he was considering cutting the anchor rope.

We were only a mile out. If we cranked up the Johnson outboard in the stern, we could make shore in ten minutes. But we weren't doing anything. Just sitting there, waiting. The sea had gone flat as glass now, tendrils of fog blowing over the raft. The air was heavy and moist. Jenna was clinging to Mick and he wasn't fighting against it, he was holding her tight. And I didn't blame him. I wanted to hold onto both of them as that rotting stink seemed to be getting closer like somebody was holding a dead salmon under my nose. I kept moving my light around, scanning for any sign of the thing.

Jenna let out a cry. "I saw something."

I thought I had, too, but out of the corner of my eye. I couldn't be sure. But I did hear the motion of it out there in the water, getting closer, swimming around us. There was no denying its reality; it was creating a series of lazy, rolling waves.

"What did you see?" Mick whispered, like maybe he was afraid the thing would hear them.

Jenna shook her head. "A shape...something big moving in the fog."

I heard a great splash in the distance and then another much farther away. I had a sudden ray of hope that the creature had given up on us and was simply going away as such things always did in the stories you heard at bars when the old salts were half in the bag and the alcohol let the skeletons out of their closets. My rational mind, despite evidence to the contrary, was still fishing for a logical explanation—a whale or a big shark or maybe a couple of bull sea lions out frolicking.

But what we heard next canceled all that out.

It was a cry—a primordial roaring that was cacophonous and booming. The sound of some primal beast howling from a steaming, oozing swamp. It echoed off into the fog and my entire body went tight as a wire from the sound of it. When I was a kid, we went to a zoo where they had this big lion in an iron cage. You could only get within ten feet of it. The lion just laid there and swatted at flies with its tail. We looked at it for a while and walked off. We were maybe fifty yards away when it roared, just like you hear them on TV. Except, it hadn't been TV. That roar was so loud and savage that little kids started screaming and people started running. You could hear something like that on the late show all you wanted, but in person it was the most frightening thing imaginable. I went stiff as a board at the sound of it. I was feeling like that again...except, whatever was out there was like maybe *ten* lions roaring. A guttural and prehistoric sound that just made me want to scream. Although I didn't say it, I was thinking that that sort of cry had not been heard much in the past seventy, eighty million years.

It came again, only it was closer.

I couldn't say how close, maybe a quarter mile at most, but probably much nearer. The sound of it locked something tight in me. The nerve ganglia of my spine were alive and electric with dread. If you were inland and heard that sound on a foggy night, you might mistake it for the bellowing of a foghorn. I wondered how many times I had heard that cry as I lay in my bed over in Seaside, thinking it was just the horn sounding.

Jenna was sobbing.

That's when I said it. It just came out. "Sea monster," I said.

"Ain't no such fucking thing," Mick said, but it didn't sound as if he believed it.

Jenna's sobbing picked up volume. She was too weak for this. She hated the sea in general and what lived in it and this was all just confirmation that she'd been right about it all and we'd been wrong. She was not the girl you would have wanted out there that night. You would have wanted somebody tough and resourceful, but Jenna was none of those things. But I didn't blame her, I was scared, too.

Sea monster.

It was something you heard about if you spent much time at Monterey Bay. The place had a history of sightings of weird marine animals and unidentifiable carcasses thrown up on beaches. Back in 1925 something had washed up about two miles north of Santa Cruz. Something with a streamlined body, flippers, and a long neck. Some scientists said it was a rare beaked whale, so rare, in fact, that it didn't even have a scientific name. Other naturalists that examined it claimed it was plesiosaur, a long-extinct marine reptile right out of the Mesozoic. One biologist even postulated that the corpse of such a creature could have been trapped in a glacier and been released by gradually melting ice, drifting on the currents into warmer water to be finally stranded on a beach of Monterey Bay. Eventually, the rotting carcass began to stink so bad that it was towed out to sea. It was said you could smell it for a mile and the odor was nothing like that of a whale. Regardless, in appearance the beast was very much like the flurry of sea monster sightings in the Bay that went straight back from present day to the Portuguese explorers of the 16th century. There were plenty of fishermen that had claimed to have seen such creatures.

I had always opted for the unknown species of beaked whale.

Now I was thinking differently.

The stench of rotting fish started to grow stronger again. It had dissipated for a few moments there, but now it was back and it was strong enough to make me want to throw my guts over the side of the raft. There was another big splash, this one very close. So close that the waves from it hit the Zodiac and made it bob up and down in the water for a time.

"That's it," Mick said, taking hold of the nylon anchor rope, preparing to cut it, "we're getting the fuck out of here."

"Quiet," I said.

The thing was close, it was practically on top of us. It splashed off in the fog just behind the raft and I put my light over there and I saw something. We all saw it. Something long and sinuous and glistening with a huge narrow head on top of it. Then it dove under. I only saw it for maybe two or three seconds, and this behind a curtain of fog. It was all so fast I couldn't even be sure that I *had* seen anything. Whatever it was—and I, like you, had already reached my conclusion—it was gone. It left that same stink of dead fish behind it and something more, a weird and musky, violent odor that made my guts flip over.

"Oh my God," Jenna started to say over and over.

"Get us out of here," I said to Mick.

He kept shaking his head. "Maybe…maybe it was the buoy tower."

But the buoy was still dinging far off to our left and this thing had been right behind us. Regardless, Mick took hold of the anchor line and put the knife to it…and it snapped right out of his hands. It jumped and lashed about, skidding along the side of the raft's gray neoprene. Nobody said anything. We just watched the rope straining at its d-ring as something beneath us took hold of it and yanked it around, and us with it. The raft spun in a circle, went this way and that, the sea around it agitated and foaming, water spraying up and over us. It nearly flipped over and then it righted itself. I fell over and crashed into the others. Something hit us from below and lifted the entire raft three feet into the air.

Jenna screamed.

I think I did, too.

Then the raft was hit again and again. The motion almost threw me overboard. I clung to the port gunwale, the water thrashing around and splashing in all directions. And for just a moment as my face was pressed to the cool rubber of the Zodiac, I saw a black shape in the water not two feet from me.

Something big and dark moving just beneath the raft. And then whatever it was hit the boat with enough force to lift it five feet in the air and flip it right over, dumping us into the cool, roiling water.

I came up fighting, breaking the surface and seeing the raft ten feet away, floating upside down. Jenna made it to the surface and then Mick about five feet from her. Something passed beneath me and the undertow almost dragged me down. I shouted to the others and it passed beneath me again, knocking my legs out of the way and pitching me backward into the water. I went under again and this time I felt the thing. My hand brushed against it. It was no whale and it was no shark. The skin of a shark is somewhat rough, but this was smooth-skinned, glossy. I likened it to the flesh of a snake. Lots of people think snakes are scaly and dry, but they're actually very smooth. This thing was like that.

But it was no snake.

Maybe a relative from the ancestral closet, but certainly no snake.

The thing passed right beneath Jenna and I saw her lifted up and dropped back down. Then the sea went flat again. I paddled over to her and she grabbed hold of me. Mick swam over, too. He had managed to grab one of the dive lights that was floating around along with most of our equipment. He panned it about in the fog, but there was no sign of the beast. It must have dived deep again or lost interest. I know I was hoping for the latter. We all had our buoyancy vests on, so we were in no danger of drowning. We could have floated around until morning if we wanted to.

But we did not want to.

We waited for maybe five minutes and then we started to relax a bit, started to breathe again. I kept listening for the drone of a Coast Guard boat, but there was absolutely nothing. Just the sound of that buoy dinging and us in the water. Nothing else. The fog thickened around us and left a wet sheen on our faces.

"I'm going to get the raft," Mick said. "Stay here. I'll tow it back and then we'll right it, get our asses out of here."

Jenna didn't like it and neither did I. But there really was no choice in the matter; we couldn't just wait out there. Whether we liked the idea of moving or not, we had to do something. Nobody else was going to do it for us and those goddamn Coasties had yet to show. Mick paddled off. The raft was about fifteen feet away by then, slowly being sucked into the fog. He caught hold of it and flashed us a thumbs up. I kept the light on him the whole time. I swear that I did. Have you ever been in a fog bank out at sea? Even at night, the fog has its own odd luminosity. Something to do with the refraction or absorption of light, I imagine. Even without the dive light on Mick, we could see him just fine.

"Hurry," Jenna called out to him.

But he couldn't have hurried fast enough.

For the beast rose up on the other side of the raft. The sight of it took my breath away. The water rippled and then bubbled and a head like that of a crocodile rose up on a long, muscular serpentine neck. I could see the teeth overlapping the jaws like those of a big croc. Water and slime dripped from its mouth. The neck had to have been twenty feet in length or more, the head four or five feet, elongated and set with bony hollows, cruel yellow reptilian slit-eyes looking down at Mick.

It looked much like the paintings you see in books on fossil marine life or on those prehistoric shows on the Discovery Channel. But those were feeble attempts at capturing the raw splendor and hideous magnificence of the thing. It was a deep-green, shiny mass of muscle and bad attitude that probably went in at two tons, if not three. A predator built for speed and strength and savagery. It towered right over Mick and there wasn't a damn thing he could do.

He played possum for a few moments, but it knew he was there.

It began to crane that huge head down toward him and the raft, moving very slowly like a snake getting in position to strike at a mouse. Slowly, slowly, the head came down and as it did so, the jaws yawned open. They were set with gleaming, backward-slanting teeth that looked to be about the size of steak knives. A low growling/grunting came from its throat. Ribbons of mucus hung from its mouth.

Mick shoved himself away from the raft, paddling furiously in our direction.

And the beast had him.

It moved with incredible speed like a rattlesnake striking. The jaws were big enough to bite a man in half and they closed right around him. And as they did so, the beast vaulted up out of the water and dove with Mick. He never had a chance. He never even screamed. But as it vaulted up, I got a good look at that lethal, streamlined body. It must have been bigger around than a full-sized pickup truck and twice the length. I saw a single flipper break water and it was easily five feet long and scythe-like. And then it dove and the sea exploded, casting rolling waves in every direction.

It was gone.

But so was Mick.

It had taken the raft down, too, but it rocketed back up to the surface about ten feet away. Jenna was screaming and fighting against me, but finally I took hold of her and we started swimming away as fast as we could. It's hard to describe how I felt, the terror that was inside me, how it tore me open and wounded me, and at the same time made me forget I *was* scared as sheer adrenaline and survival instinct took over. I imagined Jenna was feeling much the same. We swam and kept swimming. The instinct, the fight-or-flight drive, pushed us on. There was no way we could fight that horror, so we tucked our tails between our legs and swam our asses off. Thing was, we were so amped up and freaked out, we swam blindly, just trying to distance ourselves. After about five minutes when our limbs started to feel heavy and fatigue started to settle in, I stopped and made Jenna stop, too.

"We have to swim, we have to swim, we have to swim!" she kept saying.

She was beyond simple panic now, treading water in that dead zone roughly between hysteria and out-and-out shock. If I'd have had any energy to spare, maybe I would have slapped her across the face like they did in the movies. Instead I just took hold of her as she fought against me and screamed in my face. Finally, the tenseness left her and she went limp in my arms.

We floated there, clinging to each other.

The sea was still pretty flat. The mist was thick and drifting, the water growing colder all the time. We had to get out of it and I knew it. Either we made a wild dash for shore, whatever direction that might be, or we made for the buoy. Either way, I knew we had to think. We had to reason. It was the only true edge we had over the beast: we could reason, we could plot and scheme, and it couldn't. It knew only hunger and violence, and nature, unfortunately, had engineered it perfectly to those ends. Had we been on land and that thing crawled out of the surf, we could have easily run from it or shot it down with enough firepower; but out here, we were in its environment, one it was perfectly adapted to and one that was essentially alien to us.

So, we floated there, listening and feeling and holding onto one another, our minds locked into the atavistic zones of prey. Our senses were heightened. Our eyes were seeing better in the gloom than they would have under normal circumstances. Our ears were alert, our skin taking in every minute change in water temperature, vibration, and hint of movement. The thing was not near us. I could not smell it. And I could not feel its volume in the water. That may sound crazy, but if it was there, my sensory mechanisms were so highly-tuned I would have known it.

Jenna and I held onto each other. We were pressed so close we were practically one. And as absurd as it sounds under the circumstances, her nearness, her body heat, her firm and clinging body was actually turning me on. I was feeling aroused. Yes, Jenna was very attractive, but I think it was more than just that. The adrenaline, the primal awareness, the cat-and-mouse intrigue between man and beast was the sort of thing our ancestors had lived with on a daily basis. I could almost feel their blood rushing through me. And like them, I felt a maddening sexual excitement over it all. I felt alive and free and full-blooded. I think Jenna did, too. She pressed herself tight against me, her hips rotating against my own in a delicious rhythm. It was ridiculous. Absolutely ridiculous. But I couldn't help it and neither could she. We were in constant danger of being munched by a monster from the Cretaceous seas and all we wanted to do was screw. She pressed her lips against my neck and then against my mouth and I knew, without a doubt, that she would have slipped off her wetsuit pants if I had asked her to, let me enter her. Was that how it was for our prehistoric ancestors? Did a man and his mate, after fighting off a cave bear or a sabretooth tiger, go back to the cave and fuck like rabbits before the fire pit?

It was so absurd I almost started laughing.

I pulled my lips off of Jenna's, trying to clear my head so I could think.

In the night and fog, it would have been very difficult to gauge exactly where the shoreline was. The channel buoy was dinging far to our left, so that meant shore should be straight ahead. But that depended entirely on our position. If we had been turned around completely and were facing *out* to sea rather than in, the buoy would still technically be on our left. Judging by the small, almost nonexistent waves and what I could feel of the sluggish current below, I thought that shore was directly ahead. But there was no way to be absolutely sure, not with calm seas like that.

The buoy was our only hope.

"C'mon," I told Jenna. "Let's make for that buoy and get out of the water."

We started swimming again. And we didn't swim out of fear this time, blindly paddling off. We swam in tandem, doing the crawl toward the constant dinging. We had to adjust our course several times, but finally the buoy loomed above us. I saw the blinking red light set atop it first. It made the fog look like a mist of pink blood. We followed the light to the buoy itself. It had a round base tangled with seaweed and barnacles, an iron framework tower rising twenty feet above. There would be room for us to stand on it, cling to the tower, even climb it if we had to, but little else. I let Jenna go up first. I pushed her up and then she took my hand and I was up out of the water, too.

"We made it," she said. "We honestly made it."

I held onto her and she held onto me. I think if there had been more room, we would have started screwing right there out of joy and primal glee. But there wasn't enough room. We hung onto the tower and the buoy moved slowly side to side in the gentle, building waves. The dinging was right on top of us and I figured it would have driven me mad if I had to stay there all night.

Ding...ding...ding.

"We're going to make it," I said.

"Oh, Jesus, Rog," she said. "Mick...and Andy."

"Don't think about that now."

We waited there, listening for the sound of the Coast Guard boat. I thought I heard an engine, but it sounded like it was a mile away. The fog moved and shifted, flashing red with the buoy light. The air was chilly, but being out of the water would save us from hypothermia, I figured. About ten minutes into it, I was actually starting to relax. And then I smelled the odor of rotting fish again.

"Rog..."

"Quiet!" I said.

There was a big splash out in the fog followed by another and another as if the beast were at play, jumping and diving, jumping and diving. Rollers from the disturbance hit the buoy and it began to bob wildly from side to side. We held on even tighter. The stink grew worse and I smelled that revolting musky odor again that I acquainted with a reptile house at a zoo...thick and oily and nauseating. If our beast was the same kind of thing that had washed up in 1925 and it smelled this bad when it was alive, I could well imagine what it might have smelled like dead.

We could hear it out there, circling like a shark.

I wondered if it was looking for us or merely doing what its species did, splashing around and diving for fish, searching for sea lions or small sharks to feast on, taking advantage of what-ever happened by. Be that some big tuna or a couple of people out in the water.

For a time, there was silence broken only by the dinging. Everything inside me was drawn up tight, my guts filled with knotted wires and bedsprings. It was coming and I knew it. I just didn't know from what direction. The buoy bobbed up and down, from side to side and the fog was thick and roiling. Jenna was trembling, mumbling what I thought were prayers under her breath. Out in the fog, I saw the beast for just a moment, that long, elegant neck dipped out of the water and slid back down again.

But the stink...Jesus, it was like having a net of decaying fish waving in your face.

Five minutes, then ten. I saw nothing and heard nothing.

The smell began to fade.

"It ate Mick, didn't it?" Jenna suddenly said.

"Yes."

She kept shaking her head back and forth. "Why did it eat him?"

Her tone and her questions were silly, almost childlike. But I had to answer them because she was not in a good way. "It's just an animal, Jenna. It's just a creature that eats other things. It doesn't want people, really, it's just taking advantage of us being here."

"I think it's evil."

"It's not. It's just a sea monster."

She sighed. "There's not supposed to be any. That's what they say. That's what they always say."

"Well, they have to say something, don't they?"

But I had been thinking about that. How could such a thing be? I had seen the books and TV shows and heard some of the tales that floated around the bars on Monterey Bay. The name *plesiosaur* always came up. And the people who mentioned it talked about it the way they might beaked whales or giant squids...rare, but certainly not extinct. But the plesiosaur was a Cretaceous marine reptile, not a dinosaur like some people thought. And the Cretaceous had ended 65 million years ago. I found it hard to believe that this sonofabitch was hardy enough to survive *that* long. Which meant that there had to be more, a small population somewhere. It stood to reason. I wasn't a biologist, but even I knew that if anything existed, it existed because it was supported by a viable breeding population. Plesiosaurs were predators, so there wouldn't be many. Predator populations are always very small in comparison to the prey populations they feed off.

Regardless, if there was one, there were more unless this

just happened to be the very last one, which I doubted. So there was a population out there somewhere, small and secretive and nocturnal, but there all the same. That was, unless our beast fell through a time warp or something (and who could say such a thing was impossible?).

The beast roared again and it split open the night. The sound was horrifying and deafening. It made my ears ring and the hairs stand up on the back of my neck. It cried out and then dove again out in the fog.

I remember thinking: *Just go away, you fucking monster, just go away! Find yourself a nice school of porpoises or yellowfin to eat or better yet, swim down to L.A. and audition for a fucking B-movie already! Just go away, go away...*

About fifteen feet from the buoy, the water thrashed and boiled and the beast raised its head. It raised it very silently and you could hear the water dripping from it even with the ding-ing of the buoy. My heart pounded.

We waited there, Jenna and I, absolutely still. I didn't have to tell her not to move any more than I had to remind myself. I went stiff and motionless and she with me. It was instinct. Same way a rabbit knows to freeze up and become inanimate in a field when a hawk flies over or a desert rodent knows not to move when a snake is nearby. We were trying to fool it with one of the oldest ploys in the book.

The beast raised its head up straight on its neck like a tele-phone pole, then slowly arched it back down until it was eye level with us. It was looking right at us. I can't say there was intelligence in those huge, yellow eyes. Bigger than softballs, they shined and glistened. Their upturning sockets gave them a malefic look. No, not intelligence, but certainly awareness. It just watched us, weeds draped over its neck, a rancid heat blow-ing off of it. Then it opened its mouth and I could smell the vile hotness of its breath, see a great black tongue washing over spiked teeth. Its head canted this way, then that, like a dog hear-ing a sound it could not identify. But there was nothing cute about this thing. It opened its mouth wider so that we could see our oncoming death and a low, rumbling growl came from its throat.

Propelled by its flippers, it moved closer to the buoy.

Maybe it was not sure. Maybe its eyesight wasn't that good. I don't know, but its snout was twitching as if maybe it smelled us.

It moved closer.

So close that I could see the beaded flesh, the individual sea-green scales and the water that ran from them. Its breath was hot and sickening. Jenna and I were shaking. We couldn't help it with that huge mouth moving in closer and closer. I remember very clearly the warmth of piss running down my legs, the abject terror that filled my belly with needles, the sense that I had but a few moments to live. And I also remember the thoughts that went through my brain: *Take her! Take the girl! Oh God, oh dear Jesus, take the girl! Take her! I won't fight you, just take her and let me live LET ME LIVE—*

I'm not naïve enough to think it could read my mind or that somehow my own thoughts touched those of that massive, voracious nightmare, but what happened next, in my feverish and hysterical frame of mind, made me almost certain that something like that had happened.

The beast took her.

It opened its mouth all the way, roared at us, blasting us with its searing, rotten breath that stank like poisoned tidal pools and carrion thrown up on a beach. Its eyes blazed yellow like steaming cauldrons.

Then it struck.

Just as fast as before, it struck out and its jaws closed around Jenna. Its snout scraped against my arm and its teeth slit right through my wet suit, but those jaws firmly closed around Jenna with a snap. She made a grunting, gurgling noise and I clearly heard her bones go with a wet snapping. The jaws crushed her, impaling her on jagged teeth, and she was squeezed nearly flat from the immense pressure as if she was caught in a ram. A spray of hot gore splashed my face.

It began to pull her away, chewing and tearing at her, and I grabbed her arm, yanking with everything I had, crying and screaming and out of my mind, "*No, no, no, no, you sonofabitch! I didn't mean it! I didn't fucking mean it...*"

Then the beast submerged with her in a bloody foam and I stood there, panting and whimpering and shaking. It took me some time to realize that I was still holding her hand in mine. Her arm had been bitten off just above the elbow.

Things get blurry then.

I remember screaming, crying out into the night for help, just insane with the reality of the situation. Maybe it hadn't hit me with full force before that, but then it did. The weight and impact hit me and squeezed the juice right out of me by sheer, unspeakable force. I climbed inside the framework of the tower which is exactly where Jenna and I had should have hid if we had had any sense. It would have been a tight squeeze for two, but we could have managed. I climbed inside there and scrambled up the inside of the tower as far as I could go. The tower kept narrowing until it reached the bell and light at the top, but I got up as far as I could.

And the beast came back.

It launched itself out of the water and hit the buoy, making it swing wildly back and forth, filling me with a crazy sense of vertigo. The beast fell back in the water and its head kept striking again and again, trying to get me, but the teeth only rang off the intersecting bars of the tower framework. They scraped against the metal like carving knives, peeling paint free and gouging the surface.

The beast went crazy because it couldn't get at me.

And the more it couldn't get at me, the more I laughed at it, and the more I taunted it. It would slide back into the sea for a few minutes and then lunge out again, from the front, the back, either side. It hit the tower like a monster shark hitting a submerged cage. It banged against the welded bars so hard, it bent and buckled several in, almost pinning me in there. It kept roaring and crying out into the night and I knew that anyone on shore had to have heard that enraged primeval baying.

It sank into the sea again.

The minutes passed.

Then it came again, leaping right out of the sea and straddling the buoy for a moment or two, that snakelike neck whipping around, jaws snapping and teeth tearing into the metal.

The buoy tipped under the creature's incredible weight, going right over and hitting the water, sinking me under in my cage of metal. But the beast's flippers were not meant for anything but swimming. They were not meant for climbing or gripping and it soon fell back into the ocean with a roaring growl and the buoy flipped back up, swinging from side to side with careening strokes with me hanging on for dear life.

The water boiled and steamed and finally settled down and I started waiting again while the buoy found its gentle bobbing roll and quit trying to throw me like a mechanical bull. The sea was calm again, not so much as a ripple. I waited there like that I don't know how long. An hour. Maybe two. The beast did not return. I did not hear it splashing out there or see it moving in the mist or roaring.

There was only silence and waiting.

A few times there, I almost wished it would attack. I wished it would just show itself already. The tension of waiting was maybe the worse thing about that night. The unknown. Wondering where it was and when it would come leaping out of the water at me. There were a lot of bad, ugly times that night, but the waiting is the thing I remember most. The dinging of the buoy. The fog. The night. The gentle lap of water. The sound of sea birds calling out in the distance or a stray fish jumping.

From time to time, I thought I heard a boat motoring through the fog. It was probably the Coast Guard out looking for us. I even saw a few lights one time. But every time I thought the boat was getting closer, it would veer away, leaving me marooned and shivering, my back aching and my legs cramped from crouching up inside the tower frame.

After a while, I just couldn't take it.

The fog horn kept sounding from the lighthouse and I figured I knew which way shore was. Maybe it was stupid and downright suicidal, but I couldn't wait there any longer. I slipped into the water and began to swim in what I thought was the direction of shore. Each stroke I waited for the teeth that would bite me clean in half. But they never came. Things bumped into me—big fish and even a sea turtle once that made me scream—but no sea monsters. The water was colder than the air, but even so it felt good to be doing something, to be exercising the kinks and cramps out of my legs. The fog was still thick and soupy, but I began to *feel* the shore getting closer.

And then something gray and shiny came drifting out of the mist and my heart skipped a beat.

I thought it was the beast playing possum, drawing me in.

But it was the raft. It was the goddamn Zodiac raft. And somewhere during the commotion, it had righted itself. I took hold of the grab strap and dragged myself on board. A couple of the chambers were deflated, probably from being punctured by the teeth of the beast, but other than that it was in good shape. The motor was still attached to the stern and the oars were still fixed to their locks.

Panting and shaking and soaking wet, I tried to start the motor a dozen times, yanking on the pull cord with everything I had. But it was a no go. Later on, I realized that the gas valve was probably shut off, but I was too wired up to do any constructive thinking. I popped out the oars and started rowing. In the flat seas, the Zodiac skimmed right through the water.

It seemed too good to be true.

And it was.

Because just as I could feel the land reaching out for me and see the scanning beam of the lighthouse, something hit the raft. And then hit it again. I think I would have happily embraced a shark or whale if either of them had been behind it, but it was just my old friend. He came up right near the raft, breaking the surface on his side so I saw two huge flippers and nothing more.

Then the raft began to lurch and jump, yanked this way and then that. Right away I knew what was going on. Earlier, the beast had bitten our anchor line in half and now he had taken hold of the frayed end down there, was playing with it like a dog pulling on a rope. I could imagine that monster jerking his head back and forth with the line in his mouth.

But I tricked him: I took my dive knife from its sheath on my calf and slit the line right at the d-ring.

Then I started pulling on the oars again.

What an optimist I was. I made it maybe ten feet and the beast hit the raft with everything he had. It went airborne and me with it. I went down into the wet darkness and popped up maybe five yards from the raft. It was overturned, slowly rotating in a lazy circle. I started swimming again. I swam like hell as hard and fast as I could. The beast had surfaced again and I could hear it growling and snapping its teeth. I took one look behind me and I saw it back there. A gigantic, long-necked silhouette with gleaming yellow eyes in the drifting fog that I knew I would see forever in my nightmares...if I survived. It had lost momentary interest in me. It had the raft in its mouth and it was shaking it from side to side like a puppy with a shoe. I could hear air chambers popping, the raft folding in half.

But then I was swimming for dear life.

My heart was hammering and my lungs were rasping, my legs and arms sore and rubbery-feeling. Like I said before, I could just feel land getting closer. It must have been the water. Its buoyancy and pressure changes drastically the shallower it becomes and the closer the shoreline is.

The worst thing I did was look back.

The beast tossed the raft and vaulted from the water in my direction, coming down with a mammoth explosion of water. Then it was swimming right at me, just under the surface, its back breaking the surf and its head at water-level. Propelled by those flippers, its neck was extended to full length and its jaws wide open, seawater spraying up and foaming from its mouth.

It was coming fast.

Too fast to be believed.

But I swam with everything I had, preparing to die, but not giving up without one last gargantuan effort on my part. The crazy thing was the beast saved me. The huge swell it created in the water hit me and carried me forward like a surfer riding the crest of a breaker. When I came down, my feet brushed weeds, then sand, and I knew I was going to make it. I fought through water up to my chest, then waist, then down near my knees and fell onto the shore.

The beast had given up.

It turned away and I saw it break water one last time, rising up and extending its head skyward and letting out a careening, shrill cry of defeat. A cheated and angry sound. Then it disappeared into the fog and I pulled myself up onto the cold sand, crawling on my belly like a commando until I was completely out of the water and the beam of the lighthouse swept over me.

I heard the beast out in the mist, roaring with an odd bellowing howl that echoed across the water. It sounded almost lonesome, hollow and reverberating, but lonesome. A sound of blown mist and crashing waves and foghorns groaning. The sound of depths and steaming prehistoric seas. It came again, echoing and echoing from the boiling fog and it made me shiver and convulse. And then, from much farther out, another roar answered it. But this one was bigger, thundering, rolling out of the fog with teeth and hunger and attitude. The beast that made it was much larger and I had the craziest feeling it was calling to the other, to my sea monster.

It went on like that for a time between the two of them until it just faded away. Then I guess I passed out cold.

The Coast Guard found me. A shore patrol got me to the hospital. I spent three days there for shock, hypothermia, and exposure. I slept most of the first day and was not really coherent until the evening of the second. The next morning, a guy from the Coast Guard came to see me. He was a petty officer named DeWitts. He was okay. I told him a severely truncated version of events. Something, maybe a whale or a shark, had hit the raft after we called him and we were flipped into the sea. We lost each other in the fog. He told me flat out that they had not located the bodies of my friends. But a fragment of the raft washed up about five miles down the shore. He said it looked like somebody had taken a sword after it.

"It could have gotten caught in a prop, I guess."

"Yeah, maybe."

He kept watching me and I knew he didn't believe a word of what I said. But at the same time, he seemed to understand. "It was a bad night last night. A weird night. A fifteen-foot boat with some fishermen in it was overturned about a mile south of where you were. Two of 'em were lost, but we picked up the other guy. He's upstairs right now."

"What happened?" I said.

DeWitt shook his head. "Who knows? Guy was in shock, had a nervous breakdown after we got him to the hospital. He was saying some crazy business about sea monsters. You believe that?"

I swallowed. "Of all things."

"Yeah. We get our fill of sea monster sightings, I tell you. I got a file thick as a telephone book back at my office. Whenever the fog is thick, they pick up. People claim to see things and hear things."

"Yeah, the night and fog can make your imagination run wild."

He nodded. "Sure can. Even my boys get spooked some-times. The Coasties out looking for you that night said they heard sounds out in the fog, roaring sounds like something a tiger might make...or a dozen of them. You didn't hear any-thing like that, did you?"

"No. Nothing like...tigers."

He sat there by my bed looking at me a long time. "The channel buoy got pretty beat up. The tower is all bent and smashed-up like a whale hit it real hard. Can't figure it. Full of scratches and gouges. Funny business. I wonder what could do something like that?" He let that lay a minute, then he said. "Son? Is there something you want to tell me about? Something you might have seen or something that happened to your friends?"

"Would you believe me if I did?"

He shrugged. "Maybe. You'd be surprised what I'd believe. What I've seen out there and heard at night. Regardless, I'd log it because it's my job."

I opened my mouth, then shook my head. "No, I guess not. If I started talking about sea monsters, I'd end up upstairs with that other guy in the psych ward."

"Sure," he said. "That's how it works. People don't believe in sea monsters and I can't blame 'em. Such things make it hard to sleep at night. It's easier to just laugh and walk away."

He left after that and I never saw him again.

He knew and I knew, but neither of us was admitting to a thing and I suppose that was for the best. Last thing I wanted was for people to be asking me about any of that once word got around.

That was all fifteen years ago. It comes back to haunt me in my dreams just as I knew it would. For a time, I tried to forget, but then I tried to make sense of it. If there is a small population of plesiosaurs out in Monterey Bay—and I absolutely believe that there is—then why is it they're only seen at night and particularly in the fog? Because my research into the matter showed that foggy nights have an unusually high percentage of...occurrences. From what I understand, plesiosaurs were air-breathers. How often they had to come up for a breath is anybody's guess, but they did come up. I can understand them being nocturnal feeders and only coming in when the fog is thick, but where are they the rest of the time? Do they dive deep into caverns or go out deeper into the Pacific? Or did my beast and the one that called out to it get sucked through some time warp or something?

I don't have any answers and neither does anyone else.

All I know for sure is that I have not set foot in the water since. No swimming, no diving, not even any wading. The sight of large bodies of water makes my knees weak. And when the foghorn sounds in the night, I get so worked up I have to swallow half a bottle of Jack Daniel's just to calm down. I suppose I should have left Seaside and Monterey Bay for good, but I just can't.

Because as much as it terrifies me, I want to hear the cry of the beast one more time before I die. I need to hear it. I need to prove to myself that I didn't go insane out there that night.

Tonight, the fog is moving in and I think the beast will come. I just feel that it will. The sound of it roaring out there will either cure me or kill me. And I figure I know which.

QUEEN OF SPADES

(Flesh & Blood #11, 2003)

Clothed in somber grief, the children of the ditch climb, hop, and prance in the gutter ruin of shattered concrete and twisted metal. This is their reality, home away from home. A labyrinth of iron mesh, jagged tier, spiral of destruction, bombed-out cadaver of civilization. They live on the blasted, broken back of the urban war widow. They have toys to play with here: rusted cables, snapped beams, shattered glass. Places to run and hide in: the skulls of collapsed buildings, burnt fields of dead wood, jutting Ferris wheel skeletons of denuded trees. This is the graveyard they have inherited. Suffer the children in their rusted houses, be they sugar and spice, snails or puppy dog tails. No more rules. No more loud voices.

They have not seen an adult in two weeks now.

Long ago the soldiers came and carted away their parents, brothers, sisters, uncles, aunts, neighbors, everyone. The children who hadn't been wise enough to hide had been taken, too. Maybe to the ghettos. Maybe straight to the camps, it doesn't matter. Not really. Nobody returns from the camps. As the soldiers liked to joke, the only way out is up the chimney.

Three days later the city was bombed—by the allies, the enemy, again, it doesn't matter. All that's left are the children.

They share their playhouses of crumbling night with slat-thin cats, mad dogs, buzzing insects, and fat frogs clustered in the ponds of bomb craters.

The children have now gathered on a charred platform.

"Maria," says the child called Georgi, "last night I dreamed and dreamed and dreamed. I dreamed I had a bag of candy as big as a potato sack and you know what? You know what? No matter how much I ate, and I kept on eating and eating, the bag was never empty!"

Katya's grin is clear and cold. "You're silly, Georgi. There is no candy left and there never will be. Quit thinking about it."

"Oh, let him. It does no harm," Maria says.

"It does no harm? I think it does a lot of harm to sit around dreaming about things you can't have," Katya tells them, rubbing black cotton eyes with fingers of dirt. "I miss candy, too. But there's none left. No one who knows how to make it. No stores left to sell it in. It's gone. Like everything else, it's gone."

"Oh, stop it." Maria turns to Georgi. "Go collect some wood, Georgi. We'll need a fire tonight."

Reluctantly, the boy turns away, shrugs, then skips off through the wreckage, vaulting blackened girders and shattered concrete pilings.

"You have to watch what you say around the younger ones, Katya. It's hard enough on them as it is."

"It isn't any easier on me. I miss everything, too. I miss candy and temple and mama and papa and—"

"Stop it, Katya. You'll only make yourself miserable."

"I am miserable."

"Enough, I said," Maria maintains in a low steel tone that implies there will be no argument on the matter. "I have to go get the others. Keep an eye on Georgi. Help him with the wood or there'll be no supper tonight."

Katya sits by herself for some time, not moving, just thinking and missing and hating. When she does move, it is with no haste. She shambles off alone, dressed in dusty rags. Her gait is almost narcotic. All she can hear are the screams of the damned, remembering the night the world died. Fire, smoke, burning metal, scorched flesh, death. Awful smells of flaming hair and cremated bones. Schoolyard faces blasted to singed jackstraw waste. Big houses and bigger buildings razed to rubble. Exposure and sputtering flames and funeral pyres of smoldering bodies. Construction into destruction. Weird nameless stinks like burnt coffee, sharp ozone, moldy dark cupboards, sweat, bile, blackness, death. Clicking bones in burning shrouds. It is always in her mind, these memories, these smells, sounds, and sights. A symptom of the evil that has leeched the world. A braying song in her brain.

Although the adults and most of the young were carted off like cattle, there were still other children who had hidden from the soldiers and had been hidden. Some were as old as fifteen or sixteen. But the bombing had killed all but a handful. Disease had taken a few more. Still others, she knew, just disappeared. Maybe they wandered off. Maybe the dogs got them. Maybe they were dragged off in the night by—

Katya would not allow such thinking. It was dangerous.

She thinks of the bombing again. The aftermath. Maria scouring the wreckage, dragging out bodies and bits of them, burying them with little or no help from the others. Seventeen years old going on forty.

"I don't want to be here," Katya says to herself, picking her way through the maze of white bleached stone and black earth. "I don't want any of this anymore. I just want things the way they were."

The city is the broken body of a needle-ridden junkie before her, all sores and decay and ragged contusions. She listens for Georgi and hears nothing. Siren call of stillness.

"Georgi?" she calls. "Georgi? Where are you?"

After thirty minutes of searching, she comes upon a shattered ruin of monuments, headstones, littered tombs, and craggy black trees. She knows what this once was. Does not like it. She waits outside the sagging black iron gates.

"Georgi?" she calls again.

There is a wind here. A yellow wind of machinery steam. An embalming wind. A razor wind of dank earth, dark heart, cold stone, and rusting iron. Mortuary wind. Resurrection wind. As she feels these things like too many ants tickling her spine, she sees Georgi come running. Leaping, hopping, skipping through this new necropolis wonderland of charnel weep and ossuary grim silence.

"Look! Look! Look!" he cries, stuffing something into Katya's hand.

There are three of them. Greasy, dog-eared, faded. All the same. Three cards. Queen of Spades.

"Where did you get these?" Katya asks.

"I found them. One stuck to a tree. One pasted to a rock. Another here on the gates." He produces a fourth Queen of Spades. "And this one on a slab! A big funny white slab with old letters. It's a game. Someone left them for me to find!"

Katya looks down at him with eyes that are glistening stones polished by a creek bed. His pink face, grimy fingers. The baggy clothes. The funny soap smell about him. To her, he is summer suspended, owls hooting in lonely churchyards, marbles played in sunny back yards. All things a boy should be, a child should be. Things that she cannot be any longer. Youth died in her tenth summer. This summer.

"It's a game," he says again. "Someone left them."

And Katya's brain thinks, moves with a metallic grind: Yes, someone left them. But who? And why?

"C'mon," Georgi says, a rabbit sprinting through the burial ground.

Katya follows hesitantly, knowing she shouldn't. Knowing Maria wouldn't approve of this. The cemetery fills her with cold ladders of serpents. It is dead space and subterranean cries, crawly things, mildew, and dissolution. Cold gravestone, white faces, rotting flowers.

"Look!" Georgi's voice sounds out with an echoing drum sound. "I found another!"

Katya goes to him, stepping over fractured slabs, splintered markers dressed out in clotted mud, and coiling, withered vegetation. In the grim, gray shadow of a leaning marble cross festooned with crepuscular fungus, squats Georgi, card in hand.

A sickness of dark evil places falls over Katya. "We should go from here, Georgi."

"Why?"

"This isn't a good place. Those cards...they..."

But she does not answer, cannot answer, for she does not know why this marble world, orchard of frozen stone, is bad. It just feels bad. Like broken mirrors and black cats and fevers. Maybe it smells bad. Like starving shadows if they had a smell.

For one trembling moment, she can feel staring concrete eyes on her.

This place is an urban ghostland, she thinks. Brush of fallen angel hair, sweet rot of baby's breath. And the cards. Left by who? By what? Some black mausoleum guardian? Some piper of dead bones? Yes, progeny of dank tombs, its kiss, disease.

Katya stands there, Georgi staring at her with faded eyes. Caught in this yellow dream of crypts, she cannot speak. Her flesh is borrowed from jellyfish, her lungs popping with bubbles. She feels the acid caress of eternity.

"Katya!" Georgi chants. "Katya! What's wrong with you? You look green."

"I'm all right," Katya reassures him in a pale voice, but she *is* green.

Before she can stop him, Georgi leaps away again. "I am the soldier of doom! I am the soldier of doom! I show no mercy!" He stalks and whirls and hunts the enemy in this deadland with an invisible weapon made of pointing fingers, his machinegun lips spray saliva bullets. "Soldier of doom! Beware! Beware!"

Feeling sullen and strange and hopeless, Katya goes after him. There will be no discussion this time. The soldier of doom is coming away with her by brute force. She trails him with heavy feet, heavier heart, through sepulture shadow and charnel waste, over marker and shattered urn. She finds him at the crumbling stone steps of a leaning vault. It is all mortuary darkness, brooding death, splintered gray marble. Something flutters in her belly—coiled serpents, withered vines, desiccated flowers.

Georgi trots up the steps, slashing dry-rot vegetation away from rusting iron gates.

"Stop!" Katya cries out, but her voice is distant, gagging.

He pulls the nitrous gates open and then falls back, tumbling down the steps, a naked scream shivering his lips. A form sweeps out from the vault, a shadow-shape cut from black with a child's scissors. Katya wants to run, but cannot. The form is a woman in a winding gown ragged and trailing like ancient moldering tapestries, blotched by creeping blights of fungi. Her skin is a gray windblown awning—soft, rotting, hanging from yellowed bone, flapping with holes. Her eyes are phosphorescent lanterns in a sunless catacomb. She bears a mephitic perfume which spoils the air. Like dirty rain on iron streets, sick wards, worms eating at a shroud.

"Do not be frightened, children," she says in a voice like creaking ice and shattered glass. "I am your friend."

Katya, caught between shrill laughter and echoing scream, looks and looks again. Wasn't this woman a bone-thing, a tomb horror of frost earth seconds ago? But now...like a black-and-white photo colorized by twinkling sunlight, she blossoms into soft warmth—a garden of dewy roses, ripe spring berries, thick enveloping quilt on an old woman's lap, inviting, inviting.

"Come to me, my children," she says now in a shining voice of bright August days. "I've missed you so. Show me your smiling faces, your plump bellies."

Georgi goes to her as does Katya. There is music in that voice—nightingale soprano, mother's sweet lullaby, children singing hand in hand. With the velvet touch of an illusionist, the woman enfolds them in her flower-smelling shifts and says, "Use your noses, my children. Close your eyes and no peeking. What do your noses tell you?"

"Chocolate!" Georgi calls out.

And he is right, Katya realizes then. It has been so long that she has forgotten the honeyed fragrance. Chocolate. Milk chocolate. And fudge. Now vanilla, now sweet cherries in thick syrup, mints, licorice, orange taffy, lemon creams.

"Candy!" Katya sings. "*I smell candy!*"

And then eyes are peeled open and into greedy, smudged fingers chocolate bars are inserted. The children, laughing and laughing, begin to eat. The chocolate melts in their mouths like rivers of the sweetest flowing cream, luscious, warming, dreams to be devoured.

"And more!" the candy lady promises and delivers without delay.

Ropes of licorice unwind from her fingers, from secret spinning wheels. She is a sweet factory, her eyes are golden, her touch that of a candy maker. Chocolates, jawbreakers, taffy, bubble gum, candy canes, caramels, cinnamon sticks—they rain from her in sugared confusion as she spins round and round, the children in tow. And everything is laughter, innocent piping voices, giggling. At their feet, dear God, candy store nirvana. The children squeal and shout, diving into a saccharine ocean of lollipops, bonbons, toffee, peppermint disks, chocolate kisses, and butterscotch fantasies. They swim in a candied sea. Backstroke, sidestroke, dog paddle, crawl. And these waters are confectionary tides, sugarplum pools, nougat depths, cane sugar, ice cream, and custard. The children eat and eat and eat until their bellies are bursting. Georgi collapses in a bed of cellophane and wax paper debris. Lost in sugar dementia, he sleeps and snores. Following his lead, Katya does the same.

The sun is drifting lazily in the western sky when she wakes. Georgi is gone. The candy lady is gone. She looks and looks and finds neither. Perhaps Georgi has gone back to the others. Her throat hoarse from calling his name, Katya leaves, her pockets stuffed with goodies. Her belly is a sack of nausea. She moves sickly through the wasteland of rubble buildings, kindling homes.

"Where is the wood?" Maria asks, falling upon her immediately. "And Georgi? Where is Georgi?"

"He came back...I thought he came back."

"You weren't with him?" Maria snaps.

"We were together and then..." Katya tells her tale, spins her web of trouble and daydream uneasily like a spider in a high, windy place. Before she has finished, the others have gathered, abandoning the fire and smoke and the meat smell of what is cooked over it. Their eyes widen at tales of sweets. Maria, forever suspicious, is not moved nor impressed.

"You were tricked," she says. "You left him there with that woman. God knows what will happen to him."

"I know where the graveyard is," says Joachim, steel determination and pearly eyes of destiny.

"Me, too," Silas says. "Joachim and I can be there in ten minutes!"

Maria, now refusing to look upon Katya, to admit her existence, sighs. "Go then. But be back by dark, Georgi or no Georgi. Be careful."

But by dark, no one has returned.

Maria sits in concrete silence, watching, waiting. No one disturbs her. No one dares.

Least of all Katya.

In secret, Katya unwraps her treats, but there are no treats here, only tricks. Inside cellophane shrouds and waxen cavities there are only black cinders and gray ash, clots of graveyard earth. A worm twists from a soiled wrapper. Katya pouts and finally cries, a fat fly escaping the black spider's den with pockets of dream, of nothingness. Her tears form a salty blanket that enwraps her and keeps her until morning.

And all night, all through the lonesome, long night, Maria keeps watch, studying the desolate gutter-land for shapes and shadows and warmth. She sees nothing. Toward dawn, a dog barks. Nothing more.

At full light with empty bellies, the search begins. Maria, Alex, Pol, Lydia, Kris, Gretta. Everyone goes. They are led by Katya who is now an outcast, daughter of alienation, sacrificial lamb. She wears her burdens well, plods heavy under skins of remorse and dread. And soon enough, the world of marble, of stone, of stillness and shadow.

"This is it?" Maria asks.

"Yes," Katya says, eyeing the ruined vault with unease, a cowering rabbit beneath an owl's searching wing.

"All right then," Maria announces, "everyone gather wood. We need to make a bonfire."

No one questions her. A fire is built, a pyre of deadwood. It burns and flickers, pops and crackles, consumes and hungers for something other than wood. Maria opens a sack and spills items to the ground. A knife. A bag of salt. A mirror. These things are mysteries to the others and no one asks, no one wants to know. She is trusted completely. Had the world not been kissed by flame and pestilence, she would be graduating high school this year. So to the children, her advanced age is an office of respect. She is a sage of wisdom.

Greasy rubbish smoke paints the noon sky black. Flames eat and are eaten. The air is cloying and motionless. The children and their sage wait in this dreaming dead zone of toothless marble skulls and fleshy decay. The soil is black, the grasses withered yellow. A gasoline perfume sweats. And all wait for the candy lady with charnel dimension eyes.

After a time, Maria, armed with a jagged knife and iron hate, descends into the vault alone. She sees a flash of metal eyes. Smells death and rotting flowers and centuried dust, cinerarium ash, worse things. There is a buzzing of countless meat flies. Georgi is there, throat slit, strung up by his feet, metal blood stink hovering about him on black insectile wings. There are others, wasted, wormy. The most rancid are partially devoured. All the others that have gone missing are here, including Joachim and Silas. Georgi is too fresh. Days and weeks will season him with the spices of dank putrefaction. Then he will be devoured, noisome meal spread over a crumbling noxious slab.

Maria sees the candy lady as she truly is.

Blossom of terror. Gray ropes of tumescent flesh, braided skin of crypt legions, leering blood-moon eyes. She rises from a bed of rot, moves toward the light through heaped bone and stinking carrion. A storm of squirming white rice rains from her yawning flyblown mouth.

With a shamble of bone gardens, the candy lady emerges, fire light winking off her hideous leather face. The children see her and scatter. But not Maria nor Katya. They see who and what she is. Stolen breath and haunted summers, graveyard winds and torn newspaper skin, iron talon fingers and cannibal teeth. Ghoul. Cemetery witch.

"You've come back, my children, have you?" she brays in a voice of suffocation and empty cribs. "Always plenty of sweets and yummy treats..."

She moves toward them, a mannequin draped in dead skins. Her face is a death-mask that crackles into a toothy grin like autumn leaves underfoot. Maria throws salt in her face, spears her with a flaming limb. The candy lady does not fall, but screams, howls, cackles with morgue breeze, stinks of rancid tidal flats and scrofulous carrion rats. A tower of boiling worms and peeled skin, snapping joints and shale eyes, she stalks ever forward.

Katya screams and seeks the ground.

Maria meets the candy lady, the Queen of Spades, the ghoul maiden, and, holding up the mirror, shows the dead its own reflection. Its own wasting appetites. The candy lady freezes, icicle dangling from a gambrel roof. Her maggoty stone flesh fans out with drought cracks, billows white steam and all that she was or could be comes apart in a shatter of candy glass and black ash. Heaped red, green, and yellow glass catches the sun, goes to slag and soil, becomes a twinkling heap of chocolates and stale sweets, yellowed bone and chattering teeth, miasma of crawling insects.

Sometime later, the children have been ushered home by gentle winds. Maria stays, tending a coal bed of cemetery ash, smelling the candy lady reek of sewer gas and cordite that is dispersed by the breeze. She sows the ground with salt. She thinks of Georgi, misses her brother, and, in distant realms of smoke, is missed by him.

She buries the victims of the ghoul. Salts the ground. She cannot bear to salt Georgi's grave. She runs off into the setting sun, seeking shadows, friends. Places to hide and forget.

Three days later, of course, Georgi comes out of his grave, bearing sweets.

THE WRECK OF THE GHOST

(High Seas Cthulhu, 2007)

No perceptible face or front did it have; no conceivable token of either sensation or instinct; but undulated there on the billows an unearthly, formless, chance-like apparition of life.
—Herman Melville

Of whales, there were precious few. We were north of Umnak Island with a latitude of 56° 15′N and a longitude of 169° 26′W, bearing north-northwest. In the past thirty-six hours, our luck had been practically nonexistent. We had sighted but a single pod of small Grays that weren't worth dropping the boats for or sinking iron into. And there had been one massive Fin Whale that dove out of sight long before we were in range. At high summer in the Bering Sea, you could expect large numbers of Grays making for their feeding areas up north, but our luck had brought us nary a one. We had 1200 barrels in the hold, only three hundred of which were full of whale oil.

Not a Humpback nor a Greenland Right to be seen.

Not alive, that was.

And that was perhaps the most disturbing thing. For these grounds were rich and, other than those mentioned, in the past eight hours we had encountered only two Greenland Rights and both were dead. Great floating carcasses like the hulls of overturned brigs, flocks of birds pecking away at them. Dead whales were no rarity in these waters. Often, they were harpooned and lanced by whalesmen, making their runs and dying miles away, never to be retrieved. But these bore no marks of the harpoon nor lance but were viciously mutilated as by some predator. Great slabs of blubber had been cleaved free, their flanks set with linear incisions and saw-toothed lacerations that cut right to the bone beneath. The second whale corpse had been stripped from rostrum to blowhole, its skull gleaming in the sun, its flukes ripped clean. Both were fresh, far as we could tell, great beasts slaughtered by a force unknown and inexplicable. Besides the usual slick of oil around the carcasses, we saw a great quantity of a pale coagulated slime floating about that looked very much like the spermaceti squeezed from the case of a sperm whale…though much more viscid. It carried a sharp, foul odor about it that sickened several crewmen. I likened it to the stench of a tannery: chemicals and rotting hides.

This was not the work of sharks nor killer whales, for neither had the equipment nor bite to produce such prodigious wounds. It was a strange business and not I or the other mates or even Captain Inglebritzen, that stern old Dutchman, could make sense of it.

But our business was not the post mortem of dead cetaceans, but the killing of whales.

The Dutchman, as our captain was wont to be called, summoned myself and the mates up onto the quarterdeck at seven bells. Silver-haired and mutton-chopped, he stared out over the restless sea.

"What say you?" he asked Clegg, the First Mate.

"We stay our course," Clegg said. "North-northwest. These grounds are rich. Our luck will turn."

"And you, my man? What sayeth you, Mr. Hollywell?" the Dutchman said to me.

"Aye, sir, I concur with Mr. Clegg."

Greer, the third mate, concurred as well.

Clegg said, "We have the word of the *Buxton*, sir, and that's fine by me."

Yesterday morning we had encountered the *Buxton*, a Yankee whaler out of Nantucket making her homeward run, barrels full. They had seen great numbers of Greenland Rights, so thick, said the chief mate, that "one could all but tiptoe over their backs."

"Make it so then," the Dutchman said. He cast a wary eye upon me. "And the log, sir?"

A couple hands and I had already ascertained our speed with line and sandglass. "We're making twelve knots, sir."

"Keep her so."

I joined my harpooner, Shwayneeg, up at the fo'c'sle rail, feeling the spray of water in my face. Shwayneeg was a Carib Indian like all our harpooners, a man of very few words. But I could see right away, as he cast his tattooed face in my direction, that he had something to say.

"Out with it," I said to him.

"We see two dead whale, torn and ripped by a great mouth." He shrugged. "Soon, we see more. Then three dead whale and four. A trail, eh? Leading us somewhere."

"To the grounds," I said. "The grounds."

"Aye. But grounds of *what* me ask you?"

I didn't bother questioning Shwayneeg on this point, for very often much of what he said was nonsensical to white ears and if he did not wish to elaborate, no force on earth could make him do so. I was at the rail, the sharp bow of the *Ghost* slicing open the belly of the sea in a wash of white foam. The sky was clear and the wind crisp. A finger of smoke wafted from the try-works stack behind the foremast where blubber was rendered. The decks were white from salt spray and the constant scrubbing to keep them clean of blood and oil.

The *Ghost* was a three-master, square-rigged on the fore and main, fore-and-aft rigged on the mizzenmast. A finer bark had never sailed. She had a crew of thirty-five including harpooners, hands, mates, and shipkeepers, four fine whaleboats hanging from davits at her bulwarks ready to be lowered and give chase at a moment's notice. Her bow was high and sharp enough to cut a throat, her belly deep with whale oil casks. She handled the seas well and her master, the Dutchman, was an old hand at our business.

As I stood there, feeling her under me and knowing her as well as my own body, I looked astern and saw the path of foam she left in her wake. It twisted and surged atop the hilly landscape of the waves, finally dissolving in the crests of great rollers. Closing my eyes against the spray, I could hear the hissing of the foam and the distant thunder of the sea breaking before our bow. The wind roared aloft in the masts, spars creaking and chain-sheets grinding. It was the sound of motion and progress and pursuit.

At eight bells, I mustered the watch and put two new hands on the fo'c'sle and sent three men from steerage scrambling up the ratlines to the mastheads as standers. From the moment a whaling ship left port standers were up in the masts. We switched them every two hours. I was dearly hoping three new sets of eyes would bring us news of those elusive spouts we hunted.

I left Shwayneeg at the bow and made my way to the waist of the ship, sighting Clegg there at the main hatch. He was alone. His harpooner, Oddrog, another Carib, was absent. Usually, a mate's harpooner is constantly with him. They are inseparable. But something was brewing with our boys this day and I knew what it was. Clegg was watching the heavy seas boiling about us, the ship rolling from port to starboard and back again. He was studying the sea with his spyglass, giving with his legs to maintain his balance with the pitching of the decks. Without taking his eye from the glass, he said anon to me:

"Well, Holly, I see your man is chasing his own ghost like mine."

"It's the whale carcasses, sir. Shwayneeg is spooked over the business."

"As is Oddrog," he said. "I dare not even mention them around him for fear that he'll fall to the deck, cut himself red, and begin to sing his death-song. What do you make of it?"

I listened to creaking and groaning timbers overhead. "Thing is, sir, I don't know. We should be thick amidst our whales, but nothing but dead ones. It doesn't wash."

"Aye. Oddrog is of the impression we are sailing straight into some whale's graveyard of all things."

It was nonsense…but I could not repress a chill at the idea of it. I listened to the breeze rushing amongst the rigging overhead, the canvas blown full with a breath of wind. These sights and sounds had always filled me with an exhilaration and, by night, a calmness and sense of purpose. But today, they were lonely and forlorn sounds. I wanted nothing better than to dismiss the vagaries of our harpooners, but I couldn't. For I was beginning to feel something myself. Something stirring in the pit of my being, something cold and grim opening in me like the petals of a mortuary flower. I could not dismiss it. I could liken it to nothing but the sense that disaster was looming, something unknown but immense and even palpable with its grim weight.

"And you?" said I.

Clegg collapsed the draw-tubes of his telescope. "I wish to God I knew."

As he made his way to the quarterdeck and the Dutchman, I wondered if the whole crew wasn't feeling it. For hadn't they all been on edge these past few days? Somber, surly, nervous? Yes, arguments were common, camaraderie nearly nonexistent. The mates and I had broken up several altercations and the Dutchman, despite himself, had to punish more than one man.

And why was that? Because of something they sensed or merely the hard life they led?

Ours was not an easy life, granted. It was monotonous for days on end and often quite unprofitable, particularly for the hands that received but a sliver of the total lay. Life on a whaler meant long years at sea, fatigue, frustration, even danger. And when it ended, there was never any promise of profit. The work was of the most grueling and unpleasant variety. Once a whale was towed back to the ship, a cutting stage would be hung over its body. And it was from this that the captain and mates would flense the blubber from the whale's carcass in great five-foot sections using spades, flensing knives, and blubber pikes. Hooks were attached to these sections and they were hoisted aboard by the crew and sectioned. And then the real work began for the hands. On decks slick with blood and oil, they would work with cutting tools, slicing blubber while the ship pitched to and fro, a stench enveloping them that could not be washed off, but had to be worn away through days or weeks. With mincing knives, the blubber was cut down in the blubber room and pitched into great kettles in the try-works that bubbled in the brick furnaces there. The boiling oil was baled into copper tanks and drawn off into casks that were stored down in the hold.

The men were never idle. They were in constant motion with danger to all sides. Some were crushed on deck beneath slabs of blubber that might weigh an easy ton; some were gored by cutting blades; others fell into the churning shark-infested waters; and still others were scalded by boiling whale oil. And even when the last cask was filled and stowed, the men were put to work cleaning and scrubbing, the stink of smoked blubber clinging to them in a nauseous pall.

It was said that merchant vessels and men-of-war could smell a whaler coming and I had no doubt of it. I myself had noticed for days after returning to port that every time I sweated, I could smell the blubber and oil and blood. And I could only imagine the stink emanating from them that processed our kills.

No, ours was no easy life, not for mate nor hand. But the hands had it worse and I never doubted it. They lived in a world of rotting fish and rancid whale oil, blood and grease and urine, shoulder-to-shoulder with the unwashed, reeking bodies of their shipmates crowded down in steerage or the fo'c'sle. They lived the hardships of voyages lasting some three and four years and at the conclusion of which, the pay was often poor or nonexistent. They had their reasons to be unhappy, I knew.

But I wondered if that's what was bothering them, if it wasn't perhaps something more. Some impending sense of doom and tragedy that they could feel and was stitching each and every one of them up into their own shrouds. Because, I swear, I was beginning to feel it myself.

A few hours later, after a dinner of sea bread, salt beef, and cracker hash, I stepped out on deck at four bells to take charge of the starboard watch. The seas, I soon saw, were not running as high which I saw as a good, hopeful sign. Our head was still pointing north-northwest and Mr. Clegg was on the poop with the Dutchman, apparently involved in some heated discussion which was absolutely none of my business. What the skipper and the chief mate discuss is of no consequence to the second. Men were scraping rust and peeling paint. The breeze was fresh, but not bitterly so for the Bering at summer. The seas breaking before our stem were uniformly gray and frothy. The sun was out, gleaming off brassworks and skylights. I felt uniformly cheerful after my brief nap and a bite.

But it was not destined to last.

Up on the foremast, one of the standers began to shout: "Oi! There's something up ahead! I see three of 'em…carcasses maybe!"

Everyone started shouting questions at him up on the masthead, but our hearts had already sunk. If it had been a spout he sighted, the time-honored call of "THERE SHE BLOWS!" would have been cried out.

"What do you got, lad?" the Dutchman called up.

Aloft, the stander kept his eye to his spyglass. "Can't be sure!" he called down to us. "Three shapes…dead, maybe, I see no spout! But…but there's movement out there, by Christ!"

The captain did not look happy. "Where away?"

"Three points off the weather-bow!" called the stander.

Mr. Clegg was at the wheel by then, spinning the spokes, bringing our head around accordingly.

The stander called down that the mysterious shapes were maybe a mile and a half, perhaps two, from us. The Dutchman told him to keep his eye on them and to sing out when our head was true. Usually, aboard any whaler, this is an exciting time. But with no spouts espied, we were a glum and guarded lot, expecting the worst and knowing, somehow, that we would not be disappointed. The entire crew was on deck now, each man hoping against hope that a spout would be descried, for that meant more full barrels of whale oil and a richer lay for all. I stood up in the bow, waiting for those shapes to appear and almost dreading the moment when they would. The wind filled our canvas and our bow sliced through the onward rushing waves. The ship rose and fell, timbers groaning and rigging creaking as we glided forward.

Soon enough, the foremast stander called out, "Dead ahead! Just off the port bow!"

Standing by my side, Shwayneeg, whose eyesight was utterly amazing, tapped me on the shoulder. "There! Them shapes show themselves!"

I saw them now. Two great whale carcasses drifting on the

rolling sea, their mountainous bulks lifted to the crests of huge waves and then sunk down into the troughs between with a slow, easy motion which belied their immense weight. Both were Greenland Rights, massive females, glistening black and barnacled as their rounded backs broke the water. I estimated they both had fifty feet on them and a likewise amount of tonnage. There was enough blubber on whales that size to fill hundreds of barrels.

Or would have been had they not been mutilated.

For even at our distance, I could see that the poor creatures were not only dead, but horribly mauled. The carcasses looked as if they'd been hit by cannon shot, ripped and mangled and nearly exploded in places. Great chunks of blubber had been torn free, the water awash with oil and blood and what looked to be loops of entrails. I could see drifting mats of that pale, viscid slime. Both were off our leeward side. The closest was nearly torn in half; the other was gutted down to the skeleton on one side, while the other side appeared unscathed. They both rolled with a grisly, slopping motion and the stink of their blood and meat was overpowering.

"Another ahead!" cried the stander. "Something…there's something after it!"

"Now we see," Shwayneeg said to me. "Now we see."

"Hands!" called out the Dutchman. "Lay the main-yard aback! Let go the main-braces!"

Clegg, manning the wheel, luffed and soon the weather-leeches lay flat and the ship was no longer moving, just rolling with a gentle seesawing motion like the sea itself as the weather main-braces were let go.

The Dutchman was up at the bow, eye to his spyglass. "By God, what in the hell is that horror?"

We could see the third whale now, another Right, to our windward. I judged by the size—sixty-feet, I guessed—that it was a big female. A simply gigantic animal. Like the others, I could not imagine something that could attack such a creature. But something was. Even through my glass I could not be entirely sure. I saw…I saw something ghostly-white and undulant breaking the surf, tearing at the whale with great slicing motions. With each strike the whale shook, jerked like a piece of bread being struck by a fish in a pond. But this was no fish and I honestly could not say what it was, only that its motion and rolling form filled me with an avid repulsion. Each time the beast hit the carcass, the whale jerked and huge plumes of bloody spray shot up into the air.

"Mates! Harpooners! Crews! Stand by your boats and prepare to lower!" the Dutchman shouted out.

"We're...we're going after that thing, sir?" I said.

"Damn right we are, lad! We'll have this beast! This sea-monster and whale-killer! We'll sink iron into it and stuff it for a figurehead, this damn horror which eats away our livelihood!"

The idea of going after that nightmare seemed ridiculous to me and I knew the same was felt by the entire crew and you could see it in their pale faces. But the captain had given an order and we had to obey. As afraid as we all were to face that thing in open whaleboats, we were curious to get a look at it. To see such a thing in the flesh, that great behemoth and slaughterer of whales. The Dutchman told us not only to bring our usual weapons—harpoons and lances—but to arm ourselves well. And so we did. The men took axes and gaffs and pikes and the Dutchman gave each mate in command of a boat a fine Sharps .52-caliber carbine.

Clegg, Greer, and I mustered our crews to our respective boats. We climbed into our oilskins. Weapons were loaded and line tubs fixed. The cranes swung our boats out over the sea. The entire crew was watching us, steely, tense. Six men including mate and harpooner were assigned to each boat. The rest of the crew, known as shipkeepers, stayed on board the *Ghost* while we hunted our prey. Only the foremast stander was still up in his nest, the mizzen and main standers had come down to watch the proceedings. Never, ever had there been a such a tense moment aboard any whaler in my life.

The Dutchmen sucked in a lungful of air and called out, "Lower away! Lower away, my fine lads! Out ye go to give the devil his due! Lower away, I say!"

The whaleboats were lowered into the sea and we scrambled over the sides of the *Ghost* and jumped aboard our respective craft. After casting loose, I put my crew to the oars—Posun, DeKamp, White, and Shornby—and manned the rudder, while Shwayneeg stood in the prow, waiting for his chance to throw iron. He was singing some ancient dirge under his breath as he always did when a kill was in the offing, though today with much more vehemence than usual. His dark eyes smoldered in his bronze, tattooed face and he was no longer with us. The blood of his people ran hot and ancient in his veins as he sang and tied off the whale line from the tubs to the iron straps of his primary and secondary harpoons.

Our whaleboats were thirty-footers with six-foot beams. They were razor-sharp at stern and prow and cut through the rolling seas quickly. We came around the bow of the *Ghost*, Greer's boat making way behind us and Clegg's boat to port leading us away.

"Spread out!" Clegg called to us, his boat riding atop a breaking gray wave. "Spread out and scatter! We'll come to the beast from three directions! Mind now!"

"You heard the First!" I shouted at my boys. "Now, pull and pull and pull! That's it, lads! Pull for God and country! Pull for your mothers and wives and sons born and unborn! Pull, by Christ! Bring us to that ugly whale-killing monster so that we can put the iron into him and give him a taste! Pull, I say! Pull and pull and pull, damn you all!"

This was the most exciting part of the business; just ask any man who has stood his boots on the deck of a whaler while she pitches and yawns, throws the greenhorns to and fro and the mates stand solid as posts. This was the moment that ordinarily cancels out the weeks of boredom as you row at your quarry and bring him in range and the harpooner lets fly his iron. Then it's the sleigh ride and when the whale tires, the mate delivers the killing blow with his hand lance. "Chimney afire!" call the hands as the leviathan spouts a fountain of blood and the real work begins.

Ordinarily, I say. But this was no ordinary quarry and every man in the boats knew it. We were going up against the unknown and we felt it deep into our marrow. There was always tension and always fear, but the fear we knew at that moment was a much older fear, electric and primal and godless.

The dead whale was easily sighted now. Even the roll of the waves could not take that huge black form away from our eyes. Like the other carcasses, this one rolled and slopped and cast its death-smell into the air...blood and blubber and entrails. But this smell was overpowered by a much stronger stench. That same caustic, revolting odor of the tannery, the slaughterhouse, and the charnel. That odor had nothing to do with a dead leviathan, but something quite alive. This was the smell of the thing itself: its life-force, nauseating and malignant, stewing like medical waste in buckets.

"Dear God," said one of the hands. "That stink!"

Yes, it was enough to ream out your nose and turn your brain to mush. A more unnatural, polluted smell could not be imagined.

Thirty yards from the whale I could see her in great detail. A Greenland Right without a doubt. I could see her stacked nostrils and twin blowholes, the rounded glossy back and the ivory peduncle patch near her tail which told of her great age. Like the others, she had been savagely mutilated. Her shanks were nearly divorced of blubber, great gashes cut into her that were deep enough to lose a man in. Huge chunks of meat had been ripped free by some circular mouth that must have been easily ten feet in diameter. The sea was roiling with blood and oil, wormy pink loops of viscera drifted just beneath the surface. Macerated hunks of flesh and organ bobbed like the floats of jellyfish.

And slime.

That same greasy pale slime moved in waxy rivers and sluiced against our keel. Great gelatinous ribbons of it hung from oars like the phlegmy spawn of fish, steaming and rancid.

I had never, ever once felt pity for the leviathan. She was raw material to me. Something to be transformed into casks of oil that would themselves become coin in my pocket. But there, my stomach in my throat and a hatred burning in my brain, I pitied her. I honestly pitied that poor creature. I saw her beauty for the first time, recognized it for what it was, and knew I would never sink my lance into her braincase ever again. For there *was* beauty in the leviathan. Streamlined, symmetrical beauty in what I had once thought to be but a swimming tub of blubber to be harvested by harpoon and hook. The stroke of her flukes was poetry and the breeching of her spout was God's own song. And it was blasphemy to slay such a grand creature. With that in mind, my hatred became hot coals upon dry tinder, filling the whole of my being with rising flames. I hated the thing which had brutally killed this old girl and I lusted over its death.

"Pull! Pull! Pull!" I shrieked above the roaring seas and the complaints of my oarsmen. "Bring us to her! Bring us to her! Quick now, you bastards! Row steady and strong! Aye, the closer and the closer!"

And the closer we got and the more of that gore and slime we cut through, the stronger the stink became and the more we saw of the dead whale. It rose up like an island before us, a massive mound of bobbing flesh that was nearly as long as the *Ghost* herself, the rounded back rising up nearly to the height of the ship's bulwarks. She had been eviscerated, opened up like something from a dissection room, what was inside scattered in all directions. Great sections were scathed with slash marks, but untouched other than that. Still others were laid right down to muscle and base anatomy. I could see part of her bowed skull and the pitted holes drilled into the bone by teeth I could not conceive of. Through her flanks I saw the splintered rungs of her ribs and from her back rose the jutting blood-stained staves of her spinal vertebrae. She looked, in places, like a ship laid bare to keel and frame.

It was an atrocity.

As hypocritical as that may sound from a man who killed whales for a living, I say that now: it was an atrocity.

The smell of that unknown beast was so strong, Shornby retched over the side and several others gasped and choked. It was like breathing in the gagging methane stink of swamp vapors. The beast was nowhere to be seen, yet we all knew it was damnably close. Shwayneeg stood up in the prow with his harpoon, his iron, scanning the whale's carcass and the fouled sea all about it. I could hear the men in the other boats swearing and complaining, the fear so thick on them it sweated from their pores.

Then the sea around the carcass roiled in a maelstrom of whitewater and that huge cetacean cadaver began to move and bob as if it was coming to life. The stench was suddenly much stronger and my eyes watered, tears running down my wind-burned face.

"Him coming now," Shwayneeg said, utterly divorced from human terror as only one of his race could be. "Him coming."

Water whirlpooled and gushed around the carcass as if from some great turbulence or suction below. And then...then a single white tentacle rose up from behind the other side of the whale. It was white as corpse-flesh, set with irregular bumps and knobs and thick around as a hogshead. I cannot adequately judge its length, only that it could have easily wound itself around a fifty-ton whale and that what it was attached to was still submerged. It rose up and up, dripping and swaying in the air like a cobra rising from a basket. Its underside was set with puckering ovals much like mouths which were fixed with cir-cular fans of teeth that were easily the length of marlin spikes. They weren't teeth but claws, I reckoned, but they looked the part just as those puckering ovals they came from looked like mouths.

I heard someone in one of the other boats cry out.

In my boat, DeKamp said, "Oi...that's a great monster squid, it is! A bloody great ship-eater! The kraken!"

Shwayneeg made a grunting sound. "Him no squid. Him no nothing man ever saw before. Him something old, old, old. Old as the sea. Him should not be no more. Him should be long dead, him should—"

And that was as far as he got, for that great gigantic tentacle coiled itself and struck with a wild, blinding fury. It whipped out like a cat o' nine tails with a wet snapping sound and those teeth or claws on its underside hit the whale and gouged out a trench of blubber and meat that became a clotted spray of gore that rained over the boats. It hit us in a cold, meaty mist. A chunk of blubber struck Posun and laid him flat, knocking the oar from his hands. We were covered in slime and blood and atomized whale meat. It was on my oilskins and in my face. And as I brushed it away from my eyes with a shudder of disgust, the creature rose.

It rose up from behind the whale, dwarfing it.

I heard men scream. I may have screamed myself.

It was a great undulating, fleshy mass of jelly, mounded and humped and ribbed obscenely. The entire mass was gray-white and pulsating, veined with purple networks of throbbing arteries. It was something that was many things and nothing in particular. Twitching growths rose from its body, looping coils of tentacles and…eyes. Mammoth emerald-green eyes that were stupid with blind hatred, but perversely intelligent. There had to be six or seven that I could see.

"Row!" I heard Clegg call out. "Row the hell away!"

I wanted to give the same order, but I was frozen with horror. I heard a gunshot and saw a bullet drill into that pulsing mass and then another. It shocked me out of my paralysis. I remembered the gun in my own hands and brought it up, aiming quickly and firing. My bullet punched a hole in one of those emerald eyes and it irised shut with a bile of watery green tears.

The beast let out a thunderous roar, continuing to rise.

Its tremendous ill-shapen body set with hundreds of slithering tentacles, I saw it had not one mouth, but *three*. Three mouths oozing a pale slime. They were not the mouths of ordinary animals, but huge and oval and puckered like the mouths of old men. Any of them could have swallowed a whaleboat and its occupants in one bite. They shriveled down to the size of beer kegs and then opened back up to their full measure which must have been three or four fathoms in diameter. They did this again and again as if they were breathing. Inside those hideous blowholes were enormous yellow teeth like broadswords, unsheathed, sliding from the gums. And not just a single set, but three and four sets which moved independent of one another, chewing and thrashing up and down, side-to-side.

As we watched, a set of those teeth jutted from a mouth and took a great bite from the whale, tearing free a slab of blubber that must have weighed a ton. The jaws retreated with it and the blowhole mouth puckered close.

It was at this time that I saw something utterly appalling. There was a great cylindrical mass encased in a sac of membranous flesh floating near the whale. It was her calf. She'd been pregnant. And what was particularly gruesome was that there was movement within the birth sac; the fetus was still alive. But then several of those white tentacles wound it up and dragged it under and it was gone.

At this point, the beast sank back into the sea with a weird squealing/mewling sound. The water blew up in a great spray, hissing and frothing, and a shock wave ran through the sea, striking our whaleboat and nearly turning her turtle.

We were shocked, horrified, driven insane perhaps by what we had seen, what we had witnessed. I shouted no order, for my men knew what had to be done. They manned the oars and I worked the rudder bringing us back in line with the *Ghost*. She was there, rising and falling in the heavy seas. I could see men at the rails. I knew they shouted out to us, but there was nothing they could do. My men worked the oars and I saw Clegg's boat to our leeward side making for the ship. And it was then that I saw something that took the breath from me: the hull of Greer's overturned boat and not a soul in the water near it.

We all saw it, and seeing it, Shwayneeg began to slash himself with his knife, singing the low sepulchral tones of his death-song.

We made it nearly halfway to the ship when the waters began to roil around us. Something butted into our keel, nearly turning us over. Clegg's boat was in equal distress. Something hit it and pitched two men into the water. And then around us, that white slime filled the sea and the waters boiled and frothed and I saw a series of white humps break the surface. The beast was not done with us.

One of my men screamed.

Shwayneeg jumped to his feet, a shrill wailing coming from his mouth. He grabbed his harpoon and I my killing lance.

"That's him! That's him!" I cried as if this was some ordinary Sperm or Gray Whale. "Give it to him! Give it to him!"

A perfect balance of muscle, determination, and bravery, Shwayneeg tossed his iron and buried it in one of the humps.

He threw his other harpoon and sank it, too. Oddrog, Clegg's harpooner, had done likewise. The sea exploded around us and the creature ran. It darted away, dragging us with it, foaming waves breaking before our prow and nearly swamping us. It ran, towing both boats behind it, and then simply stopped, the sea surging and pitching. Peering over the gunwale, I caught sight of those eyes just below the surface staring up at me with a deranged, alien glee. I let out a cry and rammed my lance into one and the creature jerked, our whaleboat rising five or six feet out of the water and then crashing down, everyone thrown into her bottom.

I heard Clegg call out as his whaleboat was tossed into the air, men flung in all directions. The boat came down, hull up, and the men swam wildly for it. One of them was yanked beneath the surface and another was gripped below the waist by something and dragged off in a frothing spray at least a hundred feet before being pulled under. We rowed in the hull's direction. But it was no good. The beast kept bumping us, turning our head this way and that. I caught one last glimpse of Clegg, Oddrog, and two hands clinging to the hull and shouting out. Then a brace of white, slimy tentacles erupted from the sea and closed over them like a clenching fist. They went down and did not come back up.

We tried to row to the *Ghost*, but the sea boiled like a pot from the motions of the beast. Waves broke against us and fleshly appendages slapped against our keel. One of those tentacles rose up off our starboard side and White struck it with his oar. When that had no effect, he grabbed his axe and cleaved the thing nearly in two, a gushing mass of slime oozing from the wound...then it lashed out, encircled him, and yanked him under. And with such constricting pressure that blood flew from his mouth.

Back on the *Ghost*, the Dutchman must have been aware of our plight for the ship was in motion, sails filled and bow cutting. She was sailing top speed in our direction. At least, that's what I thought. But at that speed they would never have stopped in time for us. No, our captain had another idea. The sea around us was filled with the rising mounds of that gelatinous horror and the *Ghost* made right for one of them, ramming it, her keel cutting a trench right through it. The ship jerked with the impact, listing badly to port, then righting herself at the last moment and ghosting to a stop, hove to.

The beast was gone.

We had a chance and we knew it.

Shwayneeg took to the oars with the others, making for the ship. But we never made it. For the ocean around the *Ghost* was on fire. At least, that's how it looked. A great white phosphorescence erupted around her with bubbles and froth and plumes of steam. And out of the stagnant depths, the beast rose up like some slimy fetal nightmare expelled from a womb. I saw its heaving, nebulous form rising, pulsing and throbbing, the color of white fat and set with barnacles and fungal marine growths. From it grew eel-like ropes and pale coiling tentacles, things like the stinging tendrils of sea anemones and the whips of jellyfish, flanks pitted like coral and honeycombed like the flesh of bryozoans. An absolute monster. Hideous in all respects. Bloated and serpentine, a thing of slobbering blowhole mouths and wide gelid sea-green eyes, slimy and offensive and somehow primeval. It was composed of everything that haunted the sunken ravines and others things you could not imagine. As if life, all life, had sprouted from this chimeric, multiform monstrosity, a seething garden of organic profusion.

And this, then, is how it took the *Ghost* before our eyes:

It rose up and up in a tide of pustulant gray-white flesh, vibrating and slithering, coming right over the bulwarks as men screamed and ran to and fro. Writhing, steaming coils of the beast spilled over the decks and gargantuan tentacles and fleshy ropes hundreds of feet in length corkscrewed up the fore, main, and mizzenmasts like jungle serpents. It exuded a flood of that pale slime that overflowed the decks and drowned men in its snotty depths. The ship listed badly to port with that incredible weight, creaking and groaning. Spars and yards snapped like sticks, shrouds and rigging collapsing and decks buckling and still more of that colossal, creeping horror came aboard. Those translucent green eyes swept the decks with a raw, primeval hunger. Tentacles and tendrils and clasping crab claws swept men into the slobbering, mewling mouths.

I think all of us on the whaleboat screamed until tears came from our eyes.

But there was nothing to do except turn away or study the horror in detail. I saw as much of the beast as I would ever want to. It had a twisting, bloated worm-like body set with tentacles and spines and claspers and dozens of crawling convoluting appendages. Its flesh was not only extremely white as of corpses, but transparent in places so that you could view the workings of the arcane anatomy within. It was protoplasmic, yet chambered and rigid; a mollusk, a crustacean, a monstrous worm. From its sides, rawboned and segmented legs like those of a locust sprouted to assist in pulling its weight aboard the ship. It was, essentially, everything and nothing. Every horror and slimy monstrosity dreamed up by every sailor in his most feverish nightmares since men first plied the sea.

It broke up the *Ghost* like a toy ship thrown together out of sticks and odds and ends. Booms fell and stays snapped. The mizzenmast collapsed completely and then down came the main and foremast with their shrouds and canvas and lines. Her port bulwarks were staved in and the sea filled her holds. About that time, the beast yanked her right over to her chains, so that her bulwarks touched the waterline and I saw those tentacles sweep the decks clean like brooms sweeping debris into a dustbin: deckhouses, spars and masts, hatchways and lifeboats were shattered into wreckage and swept overboard. And then the decks completely fell in and the ship was literally broken in half and the sea rushed in. There was a rushing, roaring sound, an eruption of bubbles and effervescing foam and the *Ghost* went to her sunken grave in the grips of that monster. There was nothing left to mark her passing but a great whirlpooling vortex and floating debris cast in all directions.

I saw men try to swim away from her, only to be yanked down or crushed or ripped asunder by the beast. Two sailors swam madly for a floating yard and a mammoth set of spiked jaws rose up from beneath them and snapped shut like a bear trap, taking them down with a gurgling hiss.

And that is all there is to say on the matter.

There were no survivors and our ship was gone and we were cast far out in the Bering Sea. Our only chance was to row back the way we came, to make for the Aleutians. But after what we had just been through, no one dared move. We sat there in the boat, stock-still, sculpted things, figureheads incapable of motion. The whaleboat drifted, the sea bobbing with the remains of the *Ghost*. It was not until after sundown that we dared move. And it was then that Shwayneeg finally spoke.

He said, "It is said that in the beginning, them ones came from the sky and seeded this world with life. They created the beast to serve of them. And the name of the beast is forbidden; no man shall know of it. But we know of him for the beast, he is here. We have seen him."

That's all he said and all he needed to say. Just a myth-cycle of his people as my own people have their own creation myths. Except, perhaps, there was a germ of truth hidden away in that age-old story that was probably handed down father to son orally since the dawn of time.

No matter, we took silently to the oars, and the sound, the motion, brought the beast. It took Posun and DeKamp first. Then Shornby. Those tentacles slithered into the whaleboat and plucked them away. And then later, it got Shwayneeg. It was pitch black, but I heard him cry out. I heard the rubbery sound of that tentacle as it wound him up, heard it constrict him, his bones shattering like crockery. I felt his hot blood break against my face. That was how my only true friend met his end. Afterward, I lay stunned and shocked and mindless in the bottom of the boat, waiting for my turn, waiting for the tentacle that would smash me to a pulp and drag me down to that puckering oval mouth.

But it never came. I remember the long chill night, the sun coming out, but little else. I was feverish and delusional. My only clear memory is the sound of oars and men's voices, hands taking hold of me and how I fought when they touched me. I was rescued by a boat crew of the *Katherine H.*, a whaling brig out of San Francisco. When I was lucid, I told them my story, but they judged me mad and locked me away for the rest of the journey so the hands would not hear my ravings.

Yes, they thought me mad as you no doubt do now, too.

No matter. Only understand that when you ask me why it is I will never go to sea again that I have my reasons. And they are, I think, good ones. For there is something that haunts the dark graveyard depths, something from an age beyond time when an unknown race descended from the sky and brought all life into being on this desolate, barren world. And one of the primal things they created from the cold clay is still out there, deathless and ravening, still haunting the depthless stygian canyons and abyssal plains that are a cemetery of skeletal, sunken ships littered with the bones of drowned men. And so I will never go to sea again. I will not be the prey of something that should have died out black eons before. For the name of the beast is forbidden and no man shall know it. Ancient and evil, nameless and unnamable, it exists only to suck the sweet marrow from the world.

ONE DARK
SEPTEMBER NIGHT

(Dark Animus #4, 2003)

1

Thing was, Scratch almost missed out on account his old man was pissing a blue streak because he'd gotten into trouble again. Not big trouble like the time he'd stolen Pastor Fagan's new Chrysler, missed that turn, and firmly planted it into the side of the beauty salon. Or like the time he'd jumped that senior high chick, tried to cop a feel, and she'd beaten his ass. No, not big trouble like that or even medium-sized trouble like when he'd spray-painted old lady Tryan's poodle fluorescent green or when he'd removed all those STOP signs and replaced them with ones that said GO. No, this was small change, really. He'd been caught peeking into the girl's bathrooms at school. Nothing much, but his old man, shit, he was ready to have kittens.

And, you know, leave it to Scratch to fuck things up.

And here we were, all set. It was September and all our parents had okayed the sleep out and we were primed. It would probably be our last of the year. Just the four of us out in the field in our tent, carrying on all damn night long.

And then Scratch went and did something stupid.

It wasn't like we couldn't have done it without him…but he was one of us. One of the gang. Sleeping out without Scratch would have been like jerking off with your left hand...fun, but just not the same.

It was Thursday when we found out.

Joe and I went over to Scratch's after junior high let out—Joe was in eighth, I was in seventh—and he told us all about it. After we got done insulting him, we stood around and smoked a couple Winstons Scratch ripped off his old man.

About an hour later, Tommy showed up.

Tommy was fifteen. He had scraggly long hair the color of fresh hay and big biceps with tattoos on them. He was our leader; we worshipped him. The very fact that he wanted to hang out with punks like us, a high school guy, was just too much. When he wasn't kicking our asses, he was a great guy. Really cool.

Tommy stood there in Scratch's garage, a pack of Marlboros rolled up in his t-shirt sleeve. Fifteen years of hard attitude and experience. "You little peckerhead," he said to Scratch. "Fag-boy shit-for-brains. Peeking in the girl's bathroom? Fucking dildo. What the hell's wrong with you? Next, you'll be hanging around outside the day care, sniffing dirty diapers."

Me and Joe broke up. It was rich.

Scratch shook his head. "No, I ain't never done nothin' like that," he said, as if it were a possibility he had contemplated, but dismissed after due consideration. "No way."

Tommy passed out Marlboros to me and Joe, but not to Scratch. "You better get in there and lick the old man's hairy ass. If you ain't there Friday night, you're gonna miss a lot."

Scratch stared at us expectantly through his thick, duct-taped glasses. His eyes looked like goose eggs. "Well...well what are you guys gonna do?"

"Got some fuck books," Tommy told him. "Good ones. Show everything. Got a paperback about some stepfather guy screwing his stepdaughter. Good shit. Mike's gonna read it out loud, ain't ya, Mike?"

"Yeah," I said. "Yeah."

"Cool," Joe said.

Tommy shook his head. "Leave it to you to fuck up the works. More I think about it, more you piss me off. Question is: What's to be done about it? Hmm, hmm, hmm. Punishment.

It's the only answer. Yeah, I think you should be punished," he said, tossing his cigarette and grabbing hold of Scratch. "Yes, I do think so. Big Time Wrestling for you, little man."

Scratch squirmed away from him and ran outside.

By the time we got out there, Tommy already had him.

"No, no, no," Scratch whined. "Don't. C'mon, don't. Please, Tommy, no, Jesus, stop it..."

Tommy scythed his arm under Scratch's armpit, gripping his shoulder, and flipped him through the air to the ground. "Bail throw," he said and then pulled Scratch to his feet. "Headlock."

Tommy worked him over good: Atomic Drop, Sleeper, Mongolian Screw.

Scratch kept saying: "Ow. Jesus. C'mon, hey? Stop it. Yer breaking my neck. Yer killing me. Oh, my fucking head. I'm bleeding inside."

It didn't even slow down Tommy, though. "Yeah, Scratch, you're Al Costello and I'm Pampero Firpo. Time to pay the piper, my friend."

Me and Joe ate it up. *Big-Time Wrestling* was on every Saturday morning from ten until noon. We never missed it. The Mighty Igor. Ivan Koloff. Baron Von Raschke. Mr. X. The Sheik. And our particular favorite, Pampero Firpo, the Wild Man from Brazil. He was this big, beefy guy with a mop of hair like a cheap Halloween fright wig and a matching beard. Guy wasn't even human. While the announcer introduced him, Pampero would grunt and pick through the guy's hair, looking for nits to snack on. Pampero would pound on guys and bite them and shit. It was lucky they were even alive after the Wild Man finished. Hell, they had to lead that animal into the ring in chains. Sometimes he'd even hammer the refs. Cool.

"Forearm smash," Tommy said, slamming his elbow into Scratch's ribs.

"Backbreaker," he called out, hoisting Scratch up into the air and ramming him on his knee. Then, gripping Scratch's ankles, he pounded the ground with his head. "Piledriver." Finally, he finished with the much-dreaded scissors, squeezing Scratch on the ground with his legs in a vise-grip. "Ref, I think this boy's finished."

With that, Tommy rolled off of him.

Scratch laid there, gasping for breath, making a big show of it like he was mortally wounded. We knew better. Scratch was tough. His temper was legendary. If Tommy had hurt him, Scratch would have fought back. He was the sort of guy who'd swing at anybody. Even Tommy. Tommy always kicked the living piss right out of him, but old Scratch didn't care.

Tommy liked picking on Scratch best.

Probably because of this.

We all knew the only reason he had anything to do with Scratch—eleven years old and a sixth grader to boot—was that he was banging on Scratch's sister Wendy. We all knew that. Every now and then we all took a pounding from Tommy.

It was cool, though.

We were just punks, but we were *his* punks. He took care of us. Like that time that jock shitball (whose old man owned half the fucking town) was giving me shit, shoving me around and stuff. Tommy went right up to him and decked him. Dumbfuck knew better than to get up. Or the time we swiped some candy and smokes from the A & P and were feeling pretty proud of ourselves. We get out into the parking lot and Scratch decided to do one of those bullshit stupid things he does: He waltzes up to this hot-looking GTO and pisses all over the door. Well, the owner comes running out and before Scratch can get his snake back in the cave, guy grabs him, starts slamming him around. Tommy walks over there like nothing and pounds that prick right in the face two, three times. Quick, rock-hard punches, that muscular arm of his snapping like a piston. Guy goes down, blood fountaining from his nose like piss through a leaky drainpipe. Tommy kicked him a few times and he just laid there, moaning.

Tommy was like that; he took care of you.

And before you start thinking he was just some teenage thug, guess again. He was from a real bad family and everyone knew it. He walked the walk and talked the talk like all the tough kids from his neighborhood, but down deep, he had a heart of gold. He valued friendship and honor and trust above everything else. All he ever wanted to do was join the army and jump out of airplanes. And if you had to go to war, Tommy was the guy you wanted by your side. Because if the enemy got you, Tommy would go right through ten of them to get you back. And you know what? He'd could have done it, too.

Scratch finally got up. "Prick," he said. "Fucking prick faggot. I think you broke my goddamn ribs. I can't breathe. My lungs...I think you punctured 'em."

Tommy gave him a shove. "Maybe you want a cage match, queer-boy."

"No, no, no, I don't—"

But Tommy already had him down. He put his ass in Scratch's face and cut a loud, wheezing fart.

Me and Joe were on the ground laughing our asses off.

It was cool.

"Now get your ass in that house," Tommy instructed him. "Kiss up to daddy or I'll Pampero your ass but good."

As it turned out, Scratch did get to sleep out.

And, for him, that was the worst possible thing.

2

The Big Field is where we pitched our tent.

We called it the Big Field, proper noun, probably because we'd never heard it called anything else. It was out beyond Joe's house, just through the trees, right on the outskirts of town where city met country. A huge, winding expanse of meadows dotted by occasional stands of trees like whiskers on a teenager's face. In the summer, a sea of grasses baked hot, yellow, and straw-dry. In the winter, an Antarctic plain blown white. But in the fall, fleeting September and October, a wind-washed prairie of tumbling autumn leaves and football-playing boys.

We had the tent set up beneath the spreading, trembling branches of this big old oak. We had everything we needed— beef jerky, candy, chips, fuck books, smokes, and even two six-packs of Pabst Tommy had lifted off his brother. And, most importantly, we had ammunition: soft, over-ripe tomatoes and eggs. Essential tools of the trade for Ditch.

But that was later.

Me and Joe got there about an hour before sundown and rolled out our sleeping bags. We whiled away the time paging through screw mags like *Penthouse, Club,* and *Oui* (which we pronounced *Oooeee*). We discussed the merits of movies like *The Return of Count Yorga, Cleopatra Jones, Hells Angels on Wheels,* and *Countess Dracula.* The latter was one of those British horror movies and was real bloody and filthy with tit. We both gave it two thumbs up on the blood and boob scale. Then we started arguing about who'd be a better lay, Raquel Welch or that blond chick who was in *When Dinosaurs Ruled the Earth.* They both looked hot in animal-skin bikinis.

"You know," Joe finally said, when we couldn't decide, "I bet Black Belt Kelly would just kick ass on Billy Jack."

I didn't buy that one. Black Belt Kelly was just a jive-ass kung fu wannabe. Billy Jack was the real thing. So we started kung-fuing out there in the field, me and Joe. He was Black Belt Kelly and I was Billy Jack, back from the war and looking for a fight.

Scratch finally showed up, his hand down his pants itching at his balls like usual, hence the name. "Bruce Lee could kick both their asses."

"Yeah, maybe," I agreed, "but not Shaft's. Richard Roundtree would pound 'em all."

No one disagreed with that because Shaft was really cool. He was always slamming guys around and calling them niggers and honkies and shit. Wasn't a white guy or a black guy he couldn't handle. Dude was heavy. And the things he said, man, cool, lean things, made you think he talked like that in real life.

Yeah, he was the best...except for one man: The Mighty Igor.

"Sure," Joe said. "Goes without saying. The Mighty Igor could kick all their asses without breaking a sweat."

That got no arguments. The Mighty Igor was the toughest guy on *Big-Time Wrestling.* He had a chest like a keg of beer and arms thicker than willow stumps. He used to toss other wrestlers around with one arm and pull trucks around. But he was a good guy—always going around hugging people and handing out Polish sausage, laughing, always laughing. He was something, all right.

Anyway, me and Joe were always debating crazy things like that.

Joe was my best friend on Earth. I tolerated Scratch and I worshipped Tommy, but Joe was my real, true pal. He was something, that kid. Straight A's in school. Teachers all loved him. His parents thought he was some kind of saint. But let's get our facts straight here. Who was it who put the Icy Hot in all the boys' jocks in gym class? Who was the guy who pissed in Mr. Hebermann's coffee Thermos? And, yes, who was the demented little bastard who put ex-lax powder in the cocoa mix in the teacher's lounge and created a mass shit-a-thon that almost shut the school down? And just so we don't forget, who was the pervert who ran through the girls' locker room wearing a ski mask, their dick standing higher and harder than the pope's hat? You guessed it. Sure, to look at that innocent, cherubic face you'd think that kid couldn't do no wrong. But, trust me, the Devil was in old Joe.

Every time I went to his house to see him, his mother always managed to look concerned, disappointed even. Like I was some drooling deviant that was going to subvert her precious angel, soil him maybe, wipe my baboon ass on his shirt. Don't make me laugh. The first set of naked lady cards I ever saw came from Joe. He had a little hole cut in the wall so he could watch his teenage sister and her friends showering. This was the boy who explained to me exactly what "69" and "buggering" actually meant. I won't get into the Polaroids he had of his sister's drunken friends passed out with their tops off or the 8mm fuck movie he swiped from his uncle and showed us. Yeah, he was an angel, all right. Maximum-security prisons are full of angels like that.

You get the picture.

That evening, Tommy was the last to arrive.

When he got there, we were just laying around, waiting. Joe and I had given up trying to kung fu each other to death. Scratch had found a nest of carpenter ants and was pissing down the hole. That's the way it was with Scratch; most things, most forms of amusement for him centered around his genitals. Joe and I were ignoring him. We were talking about comic books like *Weird War Tales, Jonah Hex, Sgt. Rock,* and *Monster of Frankenstein* that we had read when we were kids. We were in junior high now and we didn't read comic books anymore. Those things were for kids...yet we sure liked to talk about them a lot. But only when Tommy wasn't there. He caught us doing it and he'd call us pussies and shit. Tommy thought comic books were for faggots. He always pointed out that Batman was giving it to Robin and grown men that wore fucking tights also sucked a lot of knob.

So we were careful talking comics. Just like we were careful about a lot of things. You had to be.

You hit seventh grade and the world rose up, groaned, flipped over, and stood up on its ass and you were expected to do the same. It was the demarcation line between childhood and teenage-dom. No adult would ever understand that— twelve years old is just a fucking kid, right? *Wrong.* You had to put away your toys and your comics and all the good, fun stuff no matter how much you loved those things. It was expected of you. Politics. You were big-time now and you had to act it. You weren't a kid. You maybe had some hair on your balls and a few zits on your face and these were symbols of office and that office came with certain responsibilities and, damn you and your kind, if you didn't respect those responsibilities and conventions. Because the future would be bleak for junior high kids who acted like *kids*, who still played with Creepy Crawlers and GI Joes, Aurora plastic monster models or the Johnny Seven toy machineguns all us boys absolutely adored.

You would be chastised, singled out, purged from the greater communal hive, banished. You would be a non-entity, an object of scorn and derision and, yes, laughter. There would be no dates or parties or the right friends or the wrong ones for that matter. Just forget about ever getting laid. You'd be thrown in with the other losers—the nerdy *Star Trek* boys who carried around stacks of books and the fat girls no one would talk to.

I wasn't about to be excluded from the herd, so I did the right things. I listened to the right music and talked the right way and acted the right way. The summer before when I turned twelve, I packaged up all my toys in boxes and took them up to the attic. It wasn't like *I* wanted them anymore, but I figured some other kid might...someday.

My old man caught me doing it. He waited there in the hall-way with a Camel straight hanging from his lower lip. "What you doing, son?" he said as if he didn't really know. "Putting away all your good stuff?"

"Yeah," I said. "Yeah."

"Those things broken?"

"No."

"You gonna sell 'em?"

"No."

He pulled slowly off his cigarette, looked worn like always, frayed around the edges. "Just outgrew that stuff, eh? Sure, I understand. I remember doing that, too." He flicked his ash into his palm. "Don't go growing up too fast, hear? Kids, they go running from their childhood right smack dab into the bullshit of adulthood. And it's not worth it, son. It's just not worth it. Overrated. You wanna play with that stuff sometimes, you go right ahead. I won't tell no one."

"I know, Dad."

But he wasn't finished yet. "Sometimes, sometimes I wish I was still a kid. Back in my room. Building all them balsa wood airplanes. Them were good times. I was happy then, I was really happy."

He walked away and I had the oddest, inescapable feel-ing that something had passed between us. That he had just imparted on me the wisdom of the ages. *Don't be in any hurry to grow up, son, because it'll come soon enough. Hold onto your child-hood, hold tight and don't let no one try to wrestle it away from you with their grubby paws. Because being grown up...it ain't worth a high, happy shit. One misery piled on another and the only payoff is the grave. You keep that in mind, because God help me, I wish I had never grown up...*

Those were the words I heard in my head that day.

I can still hear them now.

Thinking back on it all, I know only one thing for sure—my father was the most brilliant man who ever walked the face of the earth. Because he warned me, he tried to straighten me out before it was too late. But I didn't listen. I just didn't listen.

Anyway, Tommy finally showed.

"Christ," Scratch said when he got a look at him. "What happened?"

Tommy had a black eye and the left side of his face was starting to swell like rising bread. Joe and I didn't say a thing; we knew better. Tommy would tell, but in his own way and time. "The old man," he said after a time. "Got into it with my old man. Fucking prick sonofawhore goddamn drunk."

We understood perfectly. Tommy's old man was just a drunk. A useless old, dried-up welfare pissbag who liked to tie one on and beat up people. Problem being, most adults could kick his ass unless they were crippled and blind, so he went after his kids. But it was getting to the point now that Tommy was giving better than he was getting.

"Did you knock him good?" Scratch wanted to know.

Tommy stared at him. Stared at him good and long and hard the way maybe a snake stares at a toad before he eats it. "What the fuck is it to ya, four-eyes?"

"Nothing," Scratch said, but not apologetically. "He's just a fucking rummy, man. Hope you cock-knocked him good."

"Never mind, asswipe."

"I was just saying—"

"You were just running that shithole you call a mouth is all. My old man ain't none of your faggot business, hear?"

Tommy's face was red as September apples. Thick, tensing cords stuck out in his neck like high-tension wires snapping with juice. His arms were tight and corded with muscle. He was pissed, pissed like a Doberman who'd slammed his balls in the doggie door. Rule number one: Tommy's old man was a drunk, shit useless as a titless stripper, but you didn't tell Tommy that. You kept out of it. You minded your own business. You let him rant and rave and blow a nut over it and you agreed with him, sure, but you never, ever called his old man a drunk.

Scratch didn't back down. That crazy, irrational temper was surging in his veins like hot lava. "Fuck you," he said. "Fuck you and your shitfuck old man."

"Sonofabitch. *Sonofabitch*," Tommy said, looking from me and Joe to Scratch and back again. "You hear that shit? *You hear that?* Can you believe what this little dick-sucking assmite just said?" To emphasize this, he jabbed me in the chest with two fingers, nearly knocking me on my ass.

I shook my head like, no, I couldn't believe it.

"Like you should talk about families, cockbreath," Tommy snapped, "what with your old lady up at Newbury. Crazy old fucking whore went soft in the head from sucking too much root."

Scratch went white.

He literally went colorless. Whatever gives skin its pigment, be it blood or pink lemonade, it literally drained right out of him. He stood there, swaying uneasily, marble-white and trembling. When the color came back it came back in bright reds and brilliant purples. Like Tommy's old man, you didn't say shit about Scratch's mother. She'd had a nervous breakdown and was in the nuthouse, but you never mentioned it. Not if you were smart. Scratch was eleven, a sixth grader, but when he got pissed, really, truly mad-dog pissed, he was a killing machine. A real psycho. And he was like that now. Mad, deranged, coiled up and ready to explode.

And Tommy knew it.

He knew which buttons to press.

As Scratch lost control, Tommy waited, a knife-edged grin slit into his face. Enjoying himself. Enjoying how Scratch was nothing but putty in his hands, clay he could mold to his liking. And at that moment, Scratch was molded into something ugly and enraged.

"You, you, you, dirty fucking SONOFAFUCK BASTARD!" Scratch droned like a toy wound up too tight and turned loose. "Kill you, damn kill you—"

He launched himself at Tommy, but, of course, it was hopeless. Tommy had already kicked Scratch's ass half a dozen times. Scratch came up, all savage bloodlust and primal scream hatred, his fists swinging madly like threshing hooks. Tommy slapped him across the face and spun him around, punching him in the back of the head hard enough to drop him face-first into the grass. Scratch came right up like a Weeble. Tommy put him in a headlock and flipped him through the air like he was stuffed with rags. Scratch landed four feet away with a tremendous thud. But he came on yet again. This time, one of his fists nipped Tommy in the chin. And Tommy, who'd pretty much been toying with him up to that point, smashed Scratch in the face with his left. Scratch went down, screaming. Every time he tried to get up, Tommy kicked him in the ass and sent him back down again.

It was an ugly scene.

Made you just sick to watch.

But watch you did.

Finally, Scratch ran off and started hitting and kicking a tree out of frustration. It was the best he could hope for. The very best. After a while, he collapsed into a heap and moaned and sobbed and swore. We all knew it would pass. And when it did, he'd be back to normal.

So we just waited.

3

By sundown, things were back to normal.

Scratch finally got bored weeping and pulling out handfuls of grass and pounding the dirt. He came back over and just stood around silently, his head averted. Finally, Tommy went over to him.

"Gimme some skin, soul brother," he said and they slapped hands.

Before long they were doing the Al Costello/Pampero Firpo thing and laughing their asses off. Tommy went easy on him, though. He even let Scratch put him in a sleeper and finally pin him. When, we all knew, he could've swatted Scratch away sweet and easy as a pony's tail swats away a buzzing horsefly. But that's the way it was with those two. They'd get into it and get over it just as fast. And to Tommy's credit, he always went pretty careful with Scratch, never hammering him too badly, never giving him more than he could take. Just enough to knock the sense back into him.

In the tent, by flashlight, we ate chips and beef jerky and swigged beers and insulted each other and smoked cigarettes.

"Nothing like a good beer," Tommy said. "Fucking-A."

"You get it from Frank?" Scratch asked him.

He nodded.

Again, no more needed to be said. Tommy's older brother Frank had been in Vietnam, seen a lot of action. When he came home three years before, he wasn't the same guy who'd left. The old Frank gave us rides on his motorbike and taught us how to cuss and swim and how to knock blackbirds out of trees with slingshots and how to burptalk. That guy, that wonderful, funny guy we all looked up to, had died in the jungle. What came back was a delusional shell. Frank was on half a dozen medications and he couldn't remember your name for more than five minutes at a time and usually slept under his bed. His hair was long and wild and tangled like a thorny bush and he sported a Jesus beard that very often had bits of food lodged in it. His only pastimes other than smoking grass and going to the VA hospital every month were staring off into space and mumbling while thick loops of drool ran freely from his mouth. If he didn't get his medication on time, he would run away and hang around on Main Street or out by the freeway saluting cars as they sped past. More often than not, he would sit in his basement room surrounded by the trappings of a lost and forgotten life and alternately laugh, then cry. Sometimes both.

Nobody liked to talk about it.

It was a sore spot with us all.

After about an hour spent minutely examining our fuck books, Tommy brought out a little porno paperback called *Slaves of Leather*. The cover painting showed some slutty blonde in a motorcycle jacket—and nothing else—sticking her oiled ass up in the air like a tabby in heat.

About five pages into it, I had everyone's attention. Tommy even stopped pinching Scratch. It was the lurid saga of this guy and his nymphomaniac stepdaughter, Cassie. What it lacked in literary skill, subtext, and metaphor, it more than made up in tit, spanking, and blatant screwing.

"*...she knew pleasure; she was pleasure,*" I read to them, savoring every word. *"From the full, moist round of her lips to the heaving, erect cherry blossoms of her nipples to the taut, silken landscape of her thighs. Yes, Cassandra was pleasure—"*

"That's my kind of girl," Scratch interrupted. "I like 'em with tits like that."

"Only tit he ever saw was his mama's," Joe said.

"Both of you shut up," Tommy warned them.

I cleared my throat. *"Dirk watched her, devoured her with a fiery gaze. His eyes were embers, fires of need fed by flames of passion. He watched Cassandra, a woman of nineteen who would tomorrow be his stepdaughter. He watched her with a gnawing hunger as she dropped the robe to her feet and exposed every delicious inch of her vanilla flesh. From the blond, luxurious curls and limpid blue eyes to the full, muscled hips and triangular thatch of hair that was a signpost of desire.*

"'You should never dare me,' Cassandra said hotly. 'You never want to do that.'

"'I dare you. I dare you plenty.'

"Cassandra giggled girlishly, almost innocently. But they both knew better than that: this girl was not innocent. She was a machine and her fuel was loving; hot, hard loving—"

"I could feed a machine like that," Scratch said, giggling. "I could—"

But Tommy kicked him. "You couldn't feed a fucking a hamster with that dick. You're hung like a tick."

"A tick?" Scratch said. "Shheeeit! I'm hung like a horse. I gotta twelve-inch cock hung on me."

Me and Tommy burst out laughing.

Joe said, "No, no, no, you guys. What Scratch meant to say was that he's *had* a twelve-inch cock and more than once. Had it *inside* him."

"Now that I believe," Tommy said.

Scratch launched himself at Joe, trying not to laugh. "You goddamn faggot fairy fem sonofabitch!"

Tommy pulled them apart and motioned for me to continue.

I started yet again. *"'Oooohhhhh,' Dirk cried as she lowered her wet mouth over his throbbing cock, taking him inch by trembling inch.*

'Oooohhhh! Suck me! Suuuuck meeeeee!'

"Dirk could stand it no longer. After five minutes of her licking and sucking and nibbling his huge, straining penis, he threw Cassandra down on the bed and rammed his massive, swollen meat saber deep into the steamy prison of her cunt—"

"See?" Scratch said. "That could be me."

Tommy nodded. "Yeah, you're right. I could be ramming my massive, swollen cock deep into your steamy prison."

I laughed so hard at that I had tears welling from my eyes. I thought my sides would burst right open. Scratch was on a roll now. He was the center of attention and loving it. He would keep interrupting just so we would give him a ration of abuse.

"C'mon, Mike," Joe said. "Get on with it."

I cleared my throat, but I had the giggles bad by that point.

"'OOOOOOO!' Cassie moaned, her hips tensing and slamming against Dirk's thighs like a battering ram. 'Your cock is huge! OOOOOHHHHH!'

"Dirk fed off her desire. Gripping the shuddering globes of her ass, he positioned her for maximum penetration. Without mercy, he began riding her, slamming his cock into her like a speeding locomotive into a tunnel. He fucked her harder, faster, nearly throwing the both of them off the bed with his gargantuan thrusts.

"'You're getting what you need,' he grunted. 'What you want.'

"'Yesssss! Oh my God YES!' Cassandra moaned with a high, shrieking voice. 'YESSSS! DO IT TO ME! FUCK ME! FUUUUUUCK MEEEE! OH MY GOD! I'm COMING! COOOMMMIIINNNG!!! AAAAAHHHHHHOOOOOOAAAAA!'

"Cassandra collapsed on the bed. But Dirk was far from done. He massaged the ready iron lance of his manhood, and, none too gently, flipped her on her belly. Slowly, easily, he slid himself into her doggie-style. Cassandra cried out, but not from pain, but pleasure, need, and raw hunger. And Dirk started again, ramming his hot meat into her dripping love-hole...'"

Tommy took hold of Scratch and started dry-fucking his ass and we all burst out laughing again. Scratch fought and clawed.

"Get the fuck off me! Goddamn homo! Goddamn dick-sucking homo!" he cried.

"Hey, Tommy was just showing you the ready lance of his manhood," Joe said.

This time, I ignored them. *"Then, at that very moment, the bedroom door opened.*

"Nicole, Cassandra's mother, stood there, a shadow of authority, menacing the lovers. Explanations, apologies fell from their lips nonstop as they pulled apart.

"'Enough!' she cried out. 'I don't want your foolish words! I demand more! I will have more!'

"As the shocked lovers watched, Nicole stalked forward out of the shadows. She was dressed in thigh-high black leather boots with stiletto heels. And, other than the leather bondage mask she wore like a greased second skin and the riding crop she snapped in her fist, she wore nothing else.

"'Who's going to be first?' she purred...'"

"Fucking-A!" Scratch said, jumping up and down on his sleeping bag. "Her own mother! Shit!"

We all joked around about that and never once admitted to one another that we really didn't completely understand what was going on in the book. These were the days before the easy accessibility of hardcore pornography and we knew about as much about bondage as we knew about the dark side of the moon. In those days, *Playboy* showed very little beyond breasts. It had yet to become a slit and tit expose.

I was lying on my back, the paperback open on my belly. Just relaxing, thinking about Nicole and that bondage mask-thing and wondering what the hell a bondage mask was...but I wasn't about to ask.

"You see Mike when he was reading that book?" Scratch said. "He had it on his lap and that book just kept rising and rising..."

"Ah, piss off," I said.

He laughed. "Dipshit. You're such a dipshit."

"Least I don't dip mine in shit like you do."

That got everybody laughing real hard.

"Oh, oh, oh, har, har, har," Scratch said, laughing despite himself, his laughter turning into a snorting as it always did sooner or later. Finally, he stopped, said, "I gotta drain the old snake, gotta bleed the happy worm."

"Here that?" Tommy said as Scratch unzipped the door and crawled out into the night. "He's gotta go squat."

"Yeah," Joe laughed, "don't get your ass wet."

"Fuck off!" we heard his voice say in the night.

Tommy lit a cigarette, cracked another beer. "Either you guys got Mizzes Ollocutt for math this year?"

"Last year," Joe said.

"I got her," I told him. "A real ballbuster with those fractions."

"Nice tits, though," Tommy informed us. "Great tits. Good old Oily Cunt. Sucks as a teacher, but she's got those bitching melons. She still wear that black bra all the time?"

"Shit yeah!" Joe said. "Always bending over so you can look down her shirt."

I laughed. "Fucking right. Juggly City."

Joe punched me in the arm. "Yeah, Mike here, he's been staying after class, slipping her the bone."

"Lick me," I said.

"She like it up the snatch or in the back door best?" Tommy inquired, very serious and all, like it was really happening.

"Up the ass."

"I figured that." Tommy nodded, pressing his lips together so he wouldn't burst out laughing. "Just like Joe. He likes it up the poop shoot, too. The old tar hole."

"Piss up a rope."

"What? Piss down your throat? I cunt hear you, I got a hearing infucktion."

When Scratch got back we were all punching each other and rolling around and laughing so hard we had tears streaming down our faces. When I think back on those days, on my childhood, I like to remember those guys like that: laughing, living. Being kids and loving it.

I try not to remember what happened later that night.

After we calmed down and there was very little passing back and forth but a few mild insults, Joe said: "We oughta go down to the lake."

"Yeah, sure, what's the hurry?" Tommy said, lighting

another cigarette and funneling the smoke out through his nostrils. "What we need now is a story. Get us in the mood."

"A story?" Scratch said.

"Yeah, you know, douchebag, it's a thing with characters and places and some kind of shit happens."

"I know what a story is."

"Yeah, Joe, give us a story," I said. "A real good one. But not that one about the guy with a hook for a hand. I'm sick of that one."

Joe was good at telling stories. Maybe, had things been different, he could've been a writer or one of those people who read books-on-tape. He had the perfect voice, the perfect pitch. He knew how to use drama and suspense, tension, all that stuff. You add onto the fact that he had a pretty twisted imagination, well, he was the guy you wanted doing the storytelling. Whether you were sitting around a fire or squatting in a tent in a dark field, he was the man for the job. I was okay reading the sex books, but Joe had style.

Scratch said, "Yeah and not that one about the girl's boyfriend who's hung up outside the car and his fingernails are scratching the roof."

"That one scares Scratch," Tommy said.

"Does not...I just think it's dumb."

Poor Scratch. Joe's stories scared the shit out of him. He wouldn't admit it, of course, but he had a real low threshold for spooky stories. He was easy to scare.

One time, we were sleeping out in Scratch's back yard. Tommy decided to play a trick on old Scratch. Not the fingers in the warm water or the shaving cream in the hand or the matches between the toes—Tommy had done all those things to him too many times even by then. What he did was, he got one of those Styrofoam wig heads and put an old witch mask on it and this mop of ratty, gray hair. It was pretty spooky-looking. Then, when Scratch was sleeping, he slipped out of the tent, got the head, and stuck it on Scratch's pillow...about three inches from his face. Then on the count of three, we all let go with these bloodcurdling screams and Tommy lit the lantern. Not real bright...kind of dim so that the tent was crawling with shadows and the head would look like it was cut off some old corpse.

Which it did. Believe me, it made my skin crawl with all those shadows creeping over it.

Scratch opened his eyes, saying, *"What? What? What?"* And then he got a good look at what was on the pillow next to him. He must've jumped about two feet. Started thrashing and screeching, dove right through the mesh door on the tent—Tommy's tent, too—and started yelling and shouting, waking half the neighborhood up. It was great. My side ached the next day from laughing so hard. Scratch wouldn't speak to us for three days. And when he did, he said he *knew* it was all a gag, he was just playing along was all.

Anyway, Joe rubbed his hands together, getting ready.

I knew it would be a good one.

And it was.

4

"It was a dark and windy night," Joe began by saying, warming up to the subject matter as was his way. His face became a tight rubber mask and he pulled the night in, the darkness, the shadows. They were his tools, you see, and as we listened, we heard an artist at work, sculpting a nightmare. "Yeah, dark, windy, a soft rain falling from that cold sky. There was a car parked out in lover's lane. Out there in the trees and shadows and it was the only car around. Just that one. The wind whipped around it and the tree branches reaching over it were scraping together. They sounded like bones. Yeah, like bones scraping together in some tomb. And behind the fogged-up windows of that car in that dark lot of trees and wind, there was a guy named Johnny and his girlfriend Maggie.

"Well, she wasn't really his girlfriend. Not yet. It was their first date. He had taken her to the dance and they'd had a good time. He'd gotten a pint of vodka from his older brother and mixed it up in a plastic jug with orange juice, see? Johnny and Maggie, they drank some of it at the dance and they were kissing and getting pretty close and stuff. So by the time they got out to lover's lane, they weren't feeling any pain.

"Maggie, though, she was a little on edge and even the booze wasn't softening her as much as it should've. See, a week before over in Clarksdale—the next town over—a couple had been out parking and something horrible had happened. A psychotic killer had attacked them while they were making out. The cops found the car. It was full of blood. They found the bodies, too... all except the heads.

"So Johnny, now he's got a real thing for Maggie. He wants her real bad and all. Wants to make out and cop a feel maybe, thinking it might even lead to something better. So they're sitting there drinking, kissing with their tongues, and feeling each other up and things are going real well...then, Maggie freezes up.

"'What was that?' she says.

"'What?' Johnny asks her, his hand up her shirt now, feeling up her tits.

"Maggie knocks his hand away. 'I heard something...something outside.'

"Of course, the windows are so foggy they can't see anything. All that making out and fondling has raised the temperature in the car to like a hundred degrees, but outside, man, it's cold and windy and damp and that rain keeps falling, falling. Sounds like somebody stuck a big knife in the sky and it's bleeding all over the place. That's what it sounds like.

"But Johnny, he only cared about his dick. He wanted things to keep rolling, figured she'd give him a handjob or something or maybe he'd slip her the bone. Way things were going, could've happened. But Maggie wouldn't have none of it...not now. Johnny kept saying there was nothing to worry about.

"Maggie says, 'Maybe we should go home, Johnny. You know what happened over in Clarksdale.'

"Johnny knows all about that, but he don't care. 'Ah, that's just a bunch of crap people made up so kids won't go making out and shit.'

"But Maggie tells him it's not bullshit, it really happened. See, her aunt is a nurse up at the state hospital and this aunt told her a maniac escaped from the criminally insane ward. That they were keeping it real quiet so as not to scare people, but this maniac, he was in the asylum because he had been going around chopping off people's heads. Even chopped his own mother's off. They called him the Chopper. Anyway, this psycho escaped and was shot down by the state police and buried in a secret grave. Then one night, a few weeks later, the cemetery caretaker found that grave opened...like maybe the Chopper had crawled back out...

"Still, Johnny, thinking about his dick, isn't buying that business. Not any of it. But to keep Maggie happy, he keeps his hands to himself for a minute. Listens. The night is real quiet except for the wind that makes the car rock from time to time, that rain coming down, and leaves blowing around out there. For a second, just a second, he thought he could hear a scraping sound...like a tree branch on the roof or fingers or maybe a knife. *Scraaaape*, it goes.

"Maggie is going nuts though, says she can hear someone circling the car, walking through the wet leaves. Thinks she even hears someone breathing out there, real raspy and wet like his lungs are full of wet dirt. The windows, like I said, are all fogged, so they can't see nothing. Maggie rubs a little spot clean on her window, about the size of a teacup...and she screams. Screams bloody murder. Johnny keeps saying, what, what, what? It takes her a minute to calm down and when she does, she tells him. She had rubbed that spot clean on the window... and when she got it clear, *something was looking in at her*. A big, bloodshot eyeball, staring and wide and hungry.

"Just then...they hear something else. A scraping, scratching sound again, but this time it's loud and grinding like someone is dragging a knife along the outside of the car. Johnny's scared, too, but he's more mad than anything because it's his older brother's car and he'll get killed if anything happens to it. He goes to open the door, but Maggie stops him, no, no, no, she begs, he's out there...something is out there.

"Johnny says hell with it. He decides to get out of there. But when he turns the key...nothing happens. The lights won't even come on. Whoever or whatever is out there somehow got the hood open and pulled the cables off the battery. And now

Johnny and Maggie, they're stuck in that windy, dark field out in the trees and something, something evil is out there. Something that collects heads...

"Johnny's scared shitless, but he knows he has to be brave. So he rubs a circle on his window and when he looks through it...he sees nothing. Nothing at all. Just the rain coming down and the puddles, leaves blowing around out there. They have the doors locked...but how long can they just wait and wait like that? Wait for whoever or whatever is out there to bust through a window. Johnny is on the wrestling team and he's built like a brick shithouse, figures he can take on a psycho any day of the week.

"But he waits and waits and waits.

"After an hour, they haven't heard anything else. So Johnny decides to go out and hook up the battery. Maybe it was just some punks playing games on them. Maggie doesn't want him to go, but he does. He tells her to lock the doors after him. Which she does. The windows are all fogged up again and even when she wipes a spot clean, she can't see nothing with the raindrops all over everything.

"She hears Johnny lift the hood, fool around with something in there. And then there's this thudding sound...except it's not the hood being slammed because through her little circle on the window she can see it's still up.

"Time passes. A half-hour, an hour. Maggie is terrified. She bites down on her fist so she doesn't scream. Where is Johnny? Oh God, what's happened to him? She keeps hearing things out there...sounds like somebody walking, somebody breathing, brushing themselves up against the car. Then...*boom, boom, boom* something keeps hammering against the car. The hood. The trunk. Then the roof. It makes the whole car rattle and shake. Maggie starts screaming. Just then, on the driver's side window...she sees a big handprint pressed there. And then a face...but it's like no face she has ever seen before. It's all green and black and rotten-looking. The face is grinning with broken, yellow teeth.

"Maggie can't take anymore. She quickly unlocks her door, decides she's going to make a run for it. She throws open the door, the rain and wind pouring in on her. She jumps out and into a mud puddle. She slips and falls against the car and right away smells it...like something dead and putrid. Then *boom, boom, boom.*

"And then whatever it is, it's right behind her...tall and thin like a scarecrow wearing a long black coat that flaps in the wind. The Chopper. He begins to laugh, cackle like some old witch over her cauldron of kiddy bones and meat, laughing, laughing, and as he moves toward her, she sees he carries a meat cleaver in one hand. And in the other? The thing he was beating against the car.

"Johnny's head..."

5

Scratch was the first one to speak, "Oh shit, that's sick, that's sick..."

He was scared and we all knew it. The rest of us stayed silent to heighten the effect. You could hear the wind out there in the trees, shaking leaves loose and scattering them, pushing its way through the grass and making that green canvas tent tremble.

"You hear something out there?" Tommy said.

"Yeah," I said in this low, whispering voice. "I thought I heard a voice whispering...it was saying, *Scrrraaatttch, Scrrraaaatttch...*"

"Oh, suck the hairy root," Scratch said, but real quiet like maybe he thought there *might* be someone or something out there. Something that was listening, trying to find out where we were.

"I don't know," Joe said. "I thought...I thought I heard someone laughing out there. *Heh, heh, heh. Heh, heh, heh.*"

Tommy, practicing perfect timing, got his head up close to Scratch, shouted: "WHAT WAS THAT?"

Scratch jumped up, flopped over, rolled in a ball, came up swinging and cursing and calling our mothers every name he could think of, many of which made no sense at all—*Mother of a fucking Son Bitch, Dirty whore-sucking fuck mothers, cockfucking lick suckers.* Of course, we were all laughing our asses right off.

You could say what you wanted about Scratch, but, dammit, he was entertaining.

6

"I think we're ready for the lake now," I said. "Never know what you're gonna find down there."

"Sure," Joe said, that mischievous twinkle in his eye. "Things happen down there, they say. Awful things by night. One time, my brother said, they went down there and found a body washed up on the beach. They went and got the cops and the body was from some guy who had fallen through the ice the winter before. They had to use hooks and poles and things to drag him in because he was all rotted and soft and chewed-up by the fish...he kept falling apart, pieces of him bobbing in the water."

"Shut up," Scratch said. "That ain't true."

"Sure, it is," I said. "They say his ghost is still down there..."

"Listen, you two are scaring Scratch here," Tommy said to us. "I just changed his diaper and I don't want him pissing his pants again."

"Oh, kiss my ass, faggot."

"Bare it and we'll share it," Joe said.

"All right," Tommy said. "Let's go down to the lake. See if anybody's parking down there."

"Check out some ass!" Scratch howled, events finally shifting in a direction he could appreciate.

It was something we did when there wasn't shit better to do. We'd hike down to the lake and check out the lovers parked down there. See if we could catch a glimpse of anybody fucking. Sometimes, if we saw the back end of a car rocking, we'd bomb said car with eggs or rotten tomatoes. And, of course, now and then old Scratch would get some stupid idea like jumping on the hood or dashing up to one and shining a flashlight in the window to see if he could see any tail in motion. It was his way.

"Do you wanna, Mike?" Tommy said.

I wanted to say no. To this day I can remember very badly

wanting to say no, to weasel out of it any way I could. But all I said was: "Yeah. I guess."

It was the worst decision of my life.

The very worst.

7

"Looks like a car down there," Joe said. "By the pines. See it?"

There was something down there, all right, but beneath the dappled shadows of the pine boughs, it was really hard to tell. There was a full moon out. Just as big and naked and white as a dead man's glaring eyeball. It lit up the countryside, washed everything down with a surreal, glowing illumination. Nothing in that light looked real. More like an artist's interpretation than anything. *Lakeside by Moonlight*, it could've been called.

Like every other little pissant town in the Midwest, Brayton had its lover's lane. Mirror Lake was maybe a half a mile outside town. There wasn't much out there but some summer cottages and a small picnic ground. That and a lot of winding, flat fields and thick stands of pine to bust up the monotony. The lake itself was long and L-shaped. A good place for sunfish, perch, and crappie in June and a great place to swim in or catch a tan by in July. But in the middle of September it was just cold and lonely. Scary. A place to leave alone.

"Don't see any others down there," Tommy said, surveying it all from a little hillock we were standing on.

"Let's check that one out," Scratch said. "Probably some heavy-duty boning going on in there. Hoo yeah!"

I dragged on my cigarette. I still had that feeling. It made me uneasy. Like my belly was filled with warm Jell-O.

"All right, men," Tommy said. "You too, Scratch."

"Eat me."

"Let's go look."

We crept across the fields, real stealthy and silent, like commandos who'd just come ashore in France or some shit. Loons screamed out on the lake and nighthawks shrieked in the sky. We weren't saying a thing. Nobody was joking or whispering or even farting for comic relief. It was like we were crossing some old, creepy cemetery and we were afraid that if we made noise, somebody or something would hear us.

When we got to the pines, we moved from tree to tree until we were close enough to the car to get a good look at it. It was a big, butt-ugly Impala and looked to be painted flat black. The chrome grille caught the moonlight, winked and sparkled, and against that midnight black it looked like the grinning teeth of a shark. And that grin…it wasn't friendly. It was lethal. It was evil. It was hungry.

Out behind the car there was a guy. Not big, not small, just some average-looking guy in a cowboy hat. You couldn't make out any features. He looked to be snipped from black cloth. And he was digging a hole.

"What the hell is he doing?" Joe asked.

"Digging a fucking hole, cocksweat," Tommy said.

"But why? Why out here?"

"Because he's burying something," Scratch said mysteriously. "Something secret. Maybe…hey, I bet he's burying some money. Like a pirate or something. Money from a bank robbery or a kidnapping. I bet that's it."

Tommy chuckled. "When he's gone, it's ours."

Something had been lodged in my throat, it felt cold and greasy. I finally cleared it. "What…what if it's not money?"

"What else would it be?"

I couldn't answer that…or maybe I could and I just didn't want to.

He dug for maybe ten more minutes. Then he crouched down behind the car and heaved something into the hole. You could hear him brushing dirt from his hands. He waited for a while, a lone black shadow, all menace and mean. After a time, he lit up a cigarette and in the glow of a stick match we saw he was dressed in black. Even his hat and shitkicker boots were black. Like Jesse James or Doc Holiday or Death himself. He took a drag or two and then walked down to the lake, through the picnic grounds. We watched the orange of his cigarette until it disappeared in the dark.

"Let's check it out," Scratch said.

It was a stupid idea, yes. The sort of half-assed, poorly-conceived, brain-dead bullshit Scratch always seemed to come up with. And had we been older or wiser or just more sensible we would've told him he was out of his fucking mind, that the dried-up, flyblown piece of dogshit he used for a brain just wasn't firing in sequence again.

But we didn't.

We knew there was something wrong here. We knew, each and every one of us, that this entire thing smelled worse than an unemptied kitty box. We all knew in some deep, dark, shadowy realm of our souls that there was danger here. Danger like we'd never known before and probably wouldn't again. And horror? Yes, maybe that, too.

But we were curious. Like mangy dogs smelling some good piss on a tree trunk, we just couldn't pass it up.

"Be quiet," Tommy said and we were off.

When we got down to the car, Tommy told me to keep watch. He told Joe the same thing. I took my posting seriously. Unlike the others, I desperately wanted to know if this guy was coming back. If tall, dark, and gruesome showed up, I wanted to be the first one to know. So I kept watch. A perimeter guard wasn't any more alert. I swear it. I swear the only time I took my eyes off the surrounding night was to look at that car. To notice with a slow, creeping chill that, although the moonlight did indeed wash over it, the car and its mineshaft-black paintjob seemed to repel the light. I know how crazy that sounds, but it was true. The light could get near it, float around it, glimmer off the chrome, but it could not touch that black metal.

"Anything in there?" Scratch said to Tommy.

Tommy had his face pressed up to the driver's side window. "Can't see. Blacker than Toby's ass inside."

But by then, Scratch and Joe were at the hole. They stood there next to this enormous pile of dirt. Had to be past their hips.

Joe crouched over to look, he stuck his little penlight down into the hole. "Something...I think...Jesus—"

Right then, of course, with his usual good timing, Scratch planted his foot on Joe's ass and propelled him into that pit. Then he started giggling high and girly as was his habit. Tommy didn't find it funny, though. Not at all.

"You stupid fuck," Tommy said and slapped Scratch upside the head. His hand struck like a clap of thunder. Scratch went to his knees, swearing.

But we lost interest in him fast enough.

Joe was screaming.

Down in that black pit, he was wailing: "GOD OH GOD OH MY GOD A BODY," he cried out and we could hear him squirming and pawing around like someone had dumped ants down his shorts. *"A B-B-BODY DOWN HERE!"*

By the time we got to the edge of the hole to look, he came barreling out of there, clawing and squealing. His little light was down there, though. It lit up everything. We saw what he saw. What he had landed right plop on top of. It was the body of a woman, stone-dead. Her face was the bloodless color of the moon, but spattered with stains and streaks of red that looked black in the night. Her throat was slit open. In fact, she was slit from throat to crotch like a hog. Her eyes were open, glassy and sightless. A beetle was crawling down her nose.

I suppose we could've run.

But we didn't.

We hesitated and a voice as cold and malignant as cancer said: *"Well, what the fuck do we have here?"*

8

Even before we turned around, we knew it was him. Only *he* could have such a voice. We all stood stock-still and we would've run if it wasn't for what he carried in his right hand: a shotgun. It was long and lethal, the barrels pointed directly at us. I think somebody pissed their pants. I think it was me. Maybe all of us. Everything was tomb-silent. I was trembling so badly I thought I might come apart at the seams. But the world was trembling, too. Like maybe it had swallowed something grave-cold and decayed, something like fear, like terror. Something it couldn't digest, couldn't work back up, so instead it just shuddered with waves of nausea as the awful thing boiled and brewed in its belly.

Just like it brewed in ours.

"I said, what do you little fucks think you're doing?"

And my brains, nothing more than a dirty plate of scrambled eggs by that point, starting thinking: *That's not what you said the first time, mister. That's not what you said at all—*

"Were you boys planning on stealing my car?" he asked.

"No, no," Joe stammered. "We wouldn't do that, sir, we... ah...wouldn't do nothing like that."

"Oh no?"

"No."

He kept the shotgun on us. Moonlight gleamed off the twin barrels. He spat a stream of something dark at Joe's feet. Maybe tobacco juice, maybe blood. "Maybe you want to take a ride in my car, is that it?"

"No, sir."

The Dark Man was grinning, his teeth long and narrow like a rodent's. "Just me and you," he said to Joe in a breathless child molester voice. "We take a ride, slim. We go down some dark road...then I show you some things. Maybe I make you do some things. You wanna do that, boy? You like things like that?"

Joe's voice would barely come, but when it did it sounded like his throat was filled with vomit. "No...no...no, sir, please, no..."

"Shut the fuck up," the Dark Man said. And meant it.

He had us lined up in front of the grave whether on purpose or by plain accident. Beneath that black hat, his face was one big shadow, a shifting oil spill, the sort that asphyxiated fish and ducks. But we could see his eyes. Shining. Watching. Two evil stars in a dark, godless nebula.

"If you weren't gonna steal my car...then what?" He mulled that over, enjoying it all too much. Like some leech that fed on human pain, suffering. "Hmm...well, you boys...*now*, you boys weren't looking in that hole, were you?"

What hole? a Three Stooges voice said in my skull.

But it wasn't a funny voice. No, in fact it was very unfunny. Stooges on death row. Stooges OD'ing on sadistic black humor. Stooges from hell.

"What did you see in that hole?"

"Nothing," Scratch said.

"Then you're dumber than you look, monkeyfuck." You could see his narrow teeth. They were white as new headstones. "What do they call you? Monkeyfuck? Cockfuck? *Cocksuck?* C'mon, tell me. Won't hurt to tell, will it? Not now. I don't see how anything's gonna matter at this point. Greasy little shit-worm like you has to have a nickname, am I right?"

"Scratch," Joe said mechanically like a recording. "We call him Scratch."

"Scratch? Yeah, he looks like a Scratch. Tell me, Scratch: What kind of livestock did your mommy fuck to pump out an ugly little four-eyed freak like you?"

Scratch just stared at him. You could almost feel the anger welling in him. It blew off him in hot, rancid waves.

Not now, dumbass, not now, I thought.

"You no speekee English? No speekee, fuckface? Maybe you suckee-fuckee your friends? You like that, Scratchy?"

Scratch kept staring.

"I think this boy has an attitude. You think so, Slick?" he said to Tommy.

"Fuck you," Tommy said.

I almost went to my knees. If I had any piss left in my bladder it would've went right down my leg. The Dark Man giggled an awful wizened giggle. It struck me that a puppet might laugh like that if puppets laughed. Wooden, emotionless, dead.

"Well, well, well. It just might come to that, Slick. That might be next." He kept staring at Tommy, but Tommy would not flinch, would not avert his eyes even though that guy had eyes black as open graves. "Slick here is the tough guy, eh? Scratch is the dumbfuck. What about you? What are you?"

"Me?" I said.

"No, not you, shit-for-brains, the clown with the red nose and the glass pecker dry-humping your tight ass. Yeah, you. Who the fuck you think I'm talking to?"

"I'm just...I don't know..."

Next, he turned back to Joe. "And what about you, ass-munch? What's your story? And if you say you don't know like Ein-fucking-stein here, I'm gonna kill you. And when you're dead, I'm gonna do shit to your body that will make your mommy fucking puke."

"Shit...shit..." Joe said, breaking up, tears beginning to run. "Don't hurt us. Please. Just don't..."

"Mama's boy? Okay, I get it. Tough Guy. Dumbfuck. Einstein. And Mama's Boy. All present and accounted for."

He fished a cigarette out of his pocket with his left hand, keeping the shotgun on us steady and sure. He fired a stick match off his zipper and we all caught a look at his face. It was a craggy, bony expanse of scar tissue lorded over by two shining black balls. Not eyes, but black marbles.

"Well," he said, "we don't have all night, do we?"

And for a split second maybe we all wondered what the hell he meant by that, but then he leveled the shotgun at Scratch and pulled the trigger. There was a roar of thunder. An explosion like a dying sun. We all went on our asses...save Scratch. Split nearly in two, he tumbled into the grave. Tommy was wet with his blood, his tissue.

Nobody screamed, nobody shouted, nobody breathed. We were chiseled from ice. Anything beyond silent, rending shock was completely beyond us.

"Einstein," the Dark Man said. "There's a roll of duct tape in the backseat. Get it."

I did. No dome light came on in the Impala. It was black as the inside of a body bag in there and smelled like tears and blood. He made me tape Tommy's and Joe's hands behind their backs. Tape their ankles together, too. And they watched me while I did it. I'll never forget the way they were looking at me.

"Okay, Slick. You and Mama's Boy get in the hole. Get in there and lay down. Right on that sweet little cunt I planted nice and proper."

But Tommy wasn't moving and unless he did, Joe wasn't going anywhere. Even in a situation like this with hell knocking on the front door, that hadn't changed; we all took our cues from Tommy.

"You got shit in your ears, Slick?" the Dark Man wanted to know.

But Tommy stood his ground. Boy, he was something. The

Dark Man was a lean, mean grave-digging machine…but without that shotgun, I don't know, I think Tommy would have went right up one side of his ass and down the other.

The Dark Man laughed. It sounded like shattering glass and breaking bones. "Okay, Slick, okay. I get it. You need some motivation." He took hold of me, forced me to my knees, made me open my mouth. Then he slid the barrel of that shotgun so far down my throat I thought I would gag. "Wrap your lips around it, Einstein. Pretend your sucking my cock."

The barrel tasted of iron and flaking rust. I started to sob. The feeling of violation had come full circle now.

"Okay, Slick…get in that motherfucking hole or I'll shoot my load in this faggot's mouth and blow his fucking skull apart."

Tommy slid down into the hole, Joe stumbled in after him. Joe was crying, balling like a hungry baby. I think I was, too. But not Tommy. And not Scratch. He wasn't going to be doing anything anymore.

Whimpering, I waited for the Dark Man to pull out the barrel. He just grinned down at me, loving my humiliation, the fact that he had broken me. He slid the barrel in and out of my mouth, degrading me, ripping open wounds in my soul that to this day have not healed.

Finally, he pulled it out, examined the wet barrel like it was his dick and he liked what he saw.

"Okay, Einstein. Take up that shovel and fill it in."

I was shaking and crying and my nose was running and my head was filled with white noise. I tried to speak, but I couldn't. I couldn't say a thing.

"Pick. Up. The. Fucking. Shovel."

I did.

"Bury them," he said. "Bury that shit deep."

I could've swung the shovel at him, sure. I could've done a lot of things. But all I did was bury my friends alive. I shoveled the dirt in their faces and I did not listen to them crying, pleading. I did not feel their pain and horror. I felt absolutely nothing. My mind was gone. It had gone right to mush. It slopped in my skull and ran out my ears, dirty and black like the shit from a dying man. I did as I was told. I buried my friends alive. I did it.

When I was done, I said: "Kill me. Please kill me."

The Dark Man thought that was funny. He laughed and laughed and laughed and somewhere in all that horrible, echoing laughter, I made a move at him and he swatted me away. Then he gave me the shotgun butt to the temple.

I went to sleep.

When I woke up, I couldn't remember where I was or maybe I didn't want to. My head ached like somebody had kicked the winning field goal with it. There was blood on my neck. Sticky. Dry. The moon had nearly gone across the sky.

I looked over at the grave.

It was still filled in.

My friends had not clawed their way out.

"No," the Dark Man said. "They're planted, son. Sleeping with the worms now. Just as cozy as bones in a pit."

I stared at him. It was all too much for my twelve-year-old brain to process. So I just sat there, my head aching, my body numb. I kept wondering what my mom would make for breakfast. If my dad was up yet, getting ready for another day at the mill.

"I'm going to let you go, boy."

I swallowed. My mouth tasted like dirt. "Let...let me...go?"

"Yes. Now run off. Run away."

I got up dizzily, started staggering off. I thought he would shoot me in the back and I vaguely wondered what it would feel like to get hit by buckshot. Maybe like a kick from a draft horse, I decided. An explosion. Awful pain. Then darkness. I hoped he would shoot me. I prayed he would. I wanted death, God, how I wanted death.

With what I had done and what I had seen, well, the grave would have been a gift. But there would be no gifts. The Dark Man was not Santa Claus and I was no innocent, naïve kid who could believe in such things by that point. I believed in guilt. I believed in suffering. That was it.

"Keep going," he said. "Go back to your life. Go back and live with yourself. Live with what you've done."

9

I made it home.

Somehow, I did. I don't remember very much about how I got there. My mind had taken in too much, it had fed full and fat at the trough of atrocity and something in there had just shut down. I can only recall walking through the fields, stumbling through the woods, getting lost on trails I knew better than my own hands. My brain was buzzing. I do remember that with a godawful, nightmarish clarity. My brain was actually buzzing like there was a hive of hornets in my skull. I couldn't understand it then and I lacked the ability to reason, so it was beyond me. But now, yes, now I know what I was hearing: the sound of a mind whose gears had been stripped smooth and was humming, idling in some dead-end mental neutral.

I found our house by the time the sun came up.

I stripped my clothes off and stood in the shower for a long time, however long it takes for the hot water heater to empty itself. I stood there long after the spray had become as cold and unforgiving as the Dark Man himself. Shivering finally, my mind still spinning its wheels in a black pit of mud, I got out.

I walked into the kitchen completely naked.

My mom almost dropped her cup of Hills Brothers. Her mouth fell open, her eyes snapped wide. "Mike...Michael," she managed, not wanting to look, but looking all the same. "What in God's green earth do you think you're doing? Walking around the house barenaked! Dear Lord, put some clothes on before we all get arrested."

I just stared at her. It took me a few moments to remember who she was. "Mom?" I said. And then part of my mind, oh some pathetic, wonderful lost part of my mind reached out from my days of infancy and spoke. Spoke the way it must have from my crib when the world was huge and scary and my mother was the only buffer: "Mommy? *Mommy?*"

"Mike...oh dear God..."

She must've seen it on me or heard it in my voice, that shrill infantile voice that had not come from a twelve-year-old, but from a toddler.

I saw her coffee go one way and she came running toward

me, such a look of horror and love and concern on her face that even to this day it sucks the breath out of me. For whatever bullshit your parents hoist on you, remember this: they love you. They brought you into this world and down deep, whoever or whatever they might be or have done, they love you with every fiber of their being. And when they tell you not to grow up too fast, you better listen to what they say or God help you.

I saw my mother coming at me, only she was very far away and it was just like I was little again in my highchair and she was miles from me at the sink and I started to cry because I needed her. And then the room turned sideways and the ceiling came down and the floor came up and I kissed the tile hard.

Before I blacked out, I heard my dad coming in, smelled his after-shave lotion. "What in the name of Christ is going on in here?"

10

Go back to your life, the Devil said to me. *Go back and live with yourself. Live with what you've done.*

And for nearly thirty years, I've done just that.

They said I couldn't tell them who I was or what had happened to me. They put me in the hospital. I was in shock for two days, near coma. When it started to recede, when the gray fog of my brain lifted, I told everyone what they wanted to know.

They buried Tommy, Joe, and Scratch side by side out at the cemetery. Half the town turned out.

I didn't go. I was under heavy sedation by that point. I laid in my hospital bed, drugged like a sick animal, unable to sleep, but unable to wake up either. I watched TV. I studied the folds of my sheets. I drummed my fingers. But I could not cry.

They never found out who the Dark Man was. Just some transient serial killer passing through, they decided. The woman in the grave was a prostitute from Milwaukee. Nobody ever figured out why he'd taken her body two-hundred-odd miles north to bury her. She'd been dead for some time, apparently. It was rumored...*rumored* that he'd done things to her long after she was cold.

I've never married. I've never had a good relationship with a man or woman since. I am unable to. I work a lot, drink a lot, think a lot. But I never forget. Every day I think about that night, replay it through the rusty wheels of my brain. The ending is always the same. I can think of a hundred ways it could have been avoided, a hundred ways it could have turned out differently. Day after day after day I think about it.

For months after it happened, I expected that black car to pull in our driveway in the dead of night. At first, I was afraid. Then I started hoping he *would* come. Come and take me where my friends went.

I wanted to go to.

But I grew up. Moved away. I did that for my sanity as well as my soul. Then, eventually, I managed to finagle a job back in Brayton...it was the worst thing I could've done. See, while most of the particulars in this little nightmare were either dead or moved away, none of it was over. All those years it had been waiting for me like a tripwire in the grim darkness. I came home again and inadvertently tripped it and sprung the mantrap and those gleaming blades slashed me open, spilling out all that was left. All that had not been buried down by the lake that night. And it ran out of me in black, toxic rivers, emptying me like a bottle.

Every night now I drive down to Mirror Lake.

The picnic ground is still there. Many of the pines have been cleared for camping sites. The fields have been mostly taken over by subdivisions. But I know where the grave is. I like to stand there where I buried my friends, where I buried their souls and trust and, ultimately, my childhood. Sometimes I remember things when I'm there. I laugh. Then I cry. And then I get very, very angry. I try to keep away, but it's like some kind of demented magnetism. I'm a salmon drawn upriver to spawn by forces I do not or cannot understand.

One of these days *he'll* be down there, I figure.

If not, then maybe some punk kids. Kids up to no good. And if I find them down there, down there by the grave, well...

well I'm going to tell 'em the way it is. And they better listen if they know what's good for 'em. Because if they don't, things might get ugly.

I don't want to hurt anyone.

But, good God, I might not have a choice.

MIGRATION

(Dead Planets, Unhallowed Stars, 2003)

Like anything bad, it had been brewing for some time. But the first indication came that afternoon when they were out at the #6 substation shack and Isley was bitching about the heat.

"Gets much hotter, my dick's gonna melt," he told Holliman, scratching at the scraggly beard he wore that looked oddly like a nest of mating black worms on his chin. "It's gonna steam and melt right off."

Holliman was checking the pressure readout at the main coupler. "Well, won't be much of a puddle."

Isley ignored that, kept right on running down Cygni-5, saying how he could feel his nuts sizzling in his shorts like meatballs in a fry pan. How one of these days, those goddamn stuffed-shirt pricks from the Company were going to show up and he was going to drop his pants, let 'em get a good look at that burnt smoky link and the two charcoal briquettes which was all that was gonna be left of his manhood.

But, he had a point.

The heat on Cygni-5 was unbearable. Imagine a flat, burnt-yellow world of endless grasses that climbed up to your chest and sometimes right over your head and you had a good idea what the planet was like. It was hot and dry and monotonous. No hill, vale, or tree broke up the repetitious landscape—in every direction, from horizon to burning horizon, just that silent, burning sea of grasses. All of it washed down by the relentless heat which no breeze dared disturb.

It was called "the barrens" by those who called Cygni-5 home.

Isley stepped out of the shack and the sun hit him full and hard, sucking the moisture from his skin. It rode that misty, saffron-colored sky like a great blazing platter of hazy orange. Sweat ran down Isley's face and immediately evaporated. With the scraggly beard and seamed face, he looked like a prospector from old Earth.

"Jesus," he said. "I hate this goddamned place."

Holliman came out, slapped his bush hat on his hand. It was khaki in color like everything worn on Cygni-5, banded with ancient sweat stains. "Guess, we can head back to the compound."

But Isley wasn't paying attention. He had his head cocked to the side like a dog, listening intently. He held a finger to his lips when Holliman tried speak. Then he shook his head. "Damnedest thing," he said. "Damnedest thing."

"What?"

He licked his flaking lips, swallowed hard. "I heard something...a sound...I'm not sure what."

Holliman's red-rimmed eyes scanned the grassy desert, saw nothing. Just that infinite waste of yellow grasses, the ochre sky reaching down to touch it until they became one. Heat waves shimmered like the air from an oven. Nothing moved. Nothing stirred. Out there was a dead, arid world where the only sounds were the stalks of grass crisping and popping from time to time, but that was about it.

Holliman turned away, "I don't hear anything."

He refused to look or listen further, knowing that people had gone mad on Cygni-5, just staring out over that barren, scorched savanna. In the undulating waves of dry heat, you sometimes saw things, heard things that weren't there. Quite a few had lit out across those plains and had been swallowed by the grasses never to be seen again. Their bodies were still out there, hidden in that parched womb of sedge, bones bleached white by a sun that never set.

"Listen," Isley said and meant it.

Holliman did. He leaned up against the rover and the plastic shell was so hot he burned his hand. He snatched it away and heard a weird trilling sound that rose up to a whining like that of a locust and faded away.

"What the fuck?"

Strange. There was no animal life on Cygni-5, at least not on the surface.

He opened the rover, dove into the air-conditioned cab, and thumbed the radio. "Urmanski? This is Holliman out at six... are you there? Get your goddamn hand out of your shorts and answer."

"I'm here, I'm here," a tired, bored voice said from the speaker. "What's up your ass this time? Every time I sneak away to whack off over your wife's picture, you call me."

Holliman said, "Listen to me. You picking up anything weird out in the barrens?"

"No, not a thing. Why?" You could hear him tapping his peripherals back at the main compound. "No. Dead out there."

"No strange atmospheric shit?"

"Nope. I can give you the weather forecast, though. Tomorrow up to a hundred-twenty, dry as a spinster's twat. Next day, same. Next week, same. Next month—"

"All right, all right. We're hearing some sounds out here. Let us know if you pick up anything. We're making for Five."

Isley was still listening.

He heard it again, but farther away. He didn't know what it was or what it meant, but he did know that it made the flesh at the base of his spine crawl. Gave him a chill here on this blistering world where a cool day was ninety plus degrees.

Scared shitless, he climbed into the rover.

On Cygni-5 there were no roads as such.

Trails were cut through the grasses by huge automated mowers that worked daily to keep the network of roads open that led from the compound to the various substations. Currently, there were over two-hundred miles of these shorn paths. But if mining operations increased, there would be more. The grasses looked dead, but they were very much alive, fed by underground water and nutrients, constantly growing.

When the rover arrived at the #5 shack, right away Isley knew something was wrong.

Gillis or Olger always came out to meet them. At the very

least they heard from them on the radio. But today, nothing. They couldn't even raise them.

"Maybe we should head back to the compound," Isley suggested.

The rover rolled to a stop next to the shack and they climbed out hesitantly, Holliman in the lead. The shack looked much like a long, aluminum Quonset hut. Inside was machinery that pumped radioactive plasma from the pockets deep within the planet's crust. The reason for human presence on that hot, empty world. If you were to have flown over the mining operation, you would have seen what looked like a wagon wheel: the sprawling, central compound and dozens of substations connected to it by innumerable arteries cut through the grasslands.

While Holliman went into the shack itself, Isley circled around outside. He checked the maintenance sheds, the footpaths, saw nothing. Nothing at all. Twice he heard that weird, eerie sound out in the barrens. He did not like how it rose up, then died away just as quickly. He couldn't seem to convince himself that it had no meaning. A sound like that...

He hurried back around the front of the shed, popped the hatch and was expecting to feel the cool embrace of air conditioning...but what he got was a blast of hot, fetid air. Inside, everything was a mess. Cables were snapped, hoses ripped open. Pipes had burst. Electronic equipment had been shattered. It looked like some awesome, ravaging storm wind had blown through there, tearing and rending and smashing. Everywhere circuit boards and broken plastic and destroyed bits of equipment.

"What...the hell happened here?" he asked, glass crunching underfoot.

Holliman shook his head. He looked pale as cigar ash. "In there," he said.

Isley went through the archway into the crew's quarters, wished right away that he hadn't.

Gillis was in there...or what he thought was Gillis. His body was bloated-up like a barrel, his limbs swollen like sausages. He was nearly snapped in half, as if something incredibly strong had tried to make the back of his head touch the back of his ankles. He was bent in a lurid V, his eyes wide and staring, his mouth frozen open.

Isley, sucking in a sharp breath, kneeled down by him.

His flesh was the color of oatmeal, his glazed eyes full of blood as if every vessel and capillary in there had burst at the same time. The corners of his lips were ripped open right to his cheeks and his jaw appeared to be broken like maybe he'd had so much screaming to do, his mouth wouldn't open wide enough.

Isley left him. "What in Christ happened?"

Holliman shrugged. "You find Olger?"

Isley said he hadn't.

Outside, they stood by the rover, both thinking, thinking.

And out in the barrens, a huge and manic buzzing rose up like the lunatic drone of thousands if not millions of yellowjackets. It cut through the stagnant air and then fell to a weird shrill whistling that echoed away into silence.

Isley was trembling. It felt like there was something stuck in his throat, something he just couldn't swallow.

"Listen," Holliman said. "Are you hearing that?"

It was a secretive rustling out in the barrens, a stealthy motion plying through the dry stalks. A busy motion. Like there was something out there—maybe a lot of somethings— that were trying damned hard not to be heard. And the idea of that was worse than just about anything else. It filled Isley with a gnawing, dawning sense of horror that would not be ignored, would not be shut away by rationality. It rattled in his brain, cold and glaring and malefic.

He thought: *If something doesn't want to be heard, then that means it's intelligent. That means it's plotting and scheming and, oh Christ, God knows what else...*

"I think," Holliman said and his voice was just as dry as cinders in an ash bucket, "I think we better have a look...if it's Olger, well, he might need help."

Isley stared at him, unblinking. "Do you really think that's a good idea?"

Holliman nodded, licking his lips. He was a big man and fear did not come easy to him. Yet, he felt it now; that much was obvious. "Stay here. I don't come back right away...anything happens...you jump in the damn rover and get the fuck out. Got it?"

Isley tried to nod, but it seemed like everything in him had gone to ice, had locked up and shut down. Something was telling him to breathe shallow, to stay still, to keep his heart rate low. To not draw attention to his location. Some crazy vestigial instinct that was feeling suddenly very threatened.

Like a rabbit in a field, he told himself. *That's me. Just waiting for the owl.*

Holliman stalked off. All he had for a weapon was a torque wrench from his tool belt. A pretty good weapon if you were going after a man, but if it was something else, something else...

Isley watched him disappear around the side of the shack.

Through sheer force of will, he made himself move. He wanted to at least be able to see which way the man went. He saw Holliman's big, brutish form slip off into a footpath cut though the grass. He heard him walking, heard dry grasses crunching under his boots. Then the tall, yellow stalks enclosed him.

There was a short, high-pierced whirring sound. Then a clicking noise.

Silence.

Five minutes went by, then ten.

The sun—61-Cygni to astronomers—blazed down hot as a torch. Out in the barrens, the grass crisped and popped. The silence was huge. Isley edged toward the path Holliman had vanished into. He pulled a cable cutter from his belt—it had a ten-inch, hooked blade. He began to smell an odd sweet odor. Reminded him of honey, but pungent, sickening.

"Holliman?" he called out. "Answer me, dammit!"

He heard a thrashing, stumbling sound and knew without a doubt that Holliman had gone off the path. Although the grasses looked dead and dry, they were very much alive. The dominant form of life on Cygni-5. The root systems below were very active. If you wandered off into the grass and didn't bust all the stalks in your path, then within fifteen or twenty minutes, they'd stand back up, erasing your trail.

If Holliman had gone out into the barrens...

Isley ran down the path, to either side thick and bristling stems rose high above his head. He saw a path broken through that yellow, dusty wall. Christ. He moved into it, slowly, cautiously, calling out Holliman's name. Stalks brushed his face. All around him there was a weird piping. He clutched the cable cutter tightly.

Holliman came plowing through the barrens like a man through a cornfield, fighting and clawing his way. He came right at Isley with a crazed, desperate look about him. Isley got out of the way, dashing back to the main path.

Holliman made it there himself, screaming now.

That noisome stench of sweetness was thick as taffy.

There were six or seven little forms clinging to him. Isley thought at first they were wasps or ants grown to obscene proportions. And that's what they looked like, except they were eight to ten inches in length. They had bright orange-red bodies and dun-brown, eyeless heads, their jointed legs and whipping antennae and forceps-like jaws colored a brilliant, glaring yellow.

Isley uttered a cry at the sight of them. He had an instinctive revulsion of them. As Holliman fell, he could see there were five or six others on his back, buzzing and clicking, hanging on by their spurred legs and immense jaws.

They had Holliman and as Isley watched, feeling utterly helpless, they began to bob their asses up and down, inserting fire-red stingers into him like seamstresses threading needles.

The effect was immediate.

Holliman went stiff as a board and then instantly began to writhe and convulse, flopping over the ground, legs going one way, arms another, and body still another. A bloody froth vomited from his mouth and he jerked and twitched so violently, Isley could hear tissues tearing and bones dislocating. It all lasted about thirty seconds, until Holliman was a broken, bleeding mess.

Isley, his head full of Holliman's death stink and that awful honeyed stench, began stumbling back as the insects abandoned the body. Something brushed against his foot and he saw one of them poised at the tip of his boot, its antennae flexing and trembling.

Crying out, he stomped it.

It let out a maddening shrill cry. He tried to squash it again and again, but it was too well armored. Like trying to squish a tick. He remembered the cable cutter and brought the blade down in a vicious arc, the blade entering between two thorax plates and impaling it. Its death cry was a wild, weird fluting, black bile dripping from the wound.

The others moved in.

Isley turned and ran as they buzzed and clicked behind him.

Still holding the dead bug skewered on his blade, he got in the rover and made for the compound, the squeaking, humming sounds of the insects echoing in his skull.

They tried to sedate him, of course, but he wouldn't hear of it.

There was no way he was going to be drugged and helpless now. Not after what he'd seen. He had to be awake, he had to be ready.

They were in the infirmary at the compound and Isley, after they'd calmed him sufficiently, had just finished his story. They probably wouldn't have believed it except that they were still unable to make contact with substation #6. That and the fact that Isley had brought the dead bug back with him.

Walker, one of the drillers, was pacing back and forth, looking decidedly unfeminine with her greasy coveralls and oil-smudged face. "So you left him out there?" she said, incredulously. "You left him out there with...with those *things?*"

"I didn't have much of a choice," Isley said. "You know, like when nature made you a woman and you couldn't grow that penis you'd always wanted."

"Fuck you," Walker said, coming at him. "Goddamned stuck here in this fucking oven and I gotta listen to your sexist bullshit. I'm sick of it—"

Gavlek stepped between them. "Settle down, Walker." And then to Isley. "I have to ask this—did they seem, well, intelligent?"

Isley told him he couldn't say. "I was too busy trying to get my ass out of there." His face was pinched and pale, his eyes drifting in a bloodshot soup. "You want, you could send Walker out with an IQ test, hand out some fucking pencils, see how they do."

Walker glared at him, simmering away like a goose in a pot. "Goddamn asshole."

Isley blew her a kiss. "You just want me."

"Want you? You're hung like a pipe cleaner, Isley. You couldn't make a field mouse come."

Isley managed a laugh, feeling some of the tension drain out of him. "See that, Skip? Goddamn broads. They get pissed, right away they start making fun of your dick. But that's not sexist, no sir. But you or me? We say something about their saggy damn tits or how their hole's so big it flaps in the wind, right away we're sexist pigs."

"You are a sexist pig," Walker said. "If the sky is blue, you want me to call it green?"

"No, course not. Tell the truth. Like when I look at you, I don't see a woman. But more power to you, sister. Right on, butch."

Walker looked like she not only had one large, grade-A bug up her ass, but that it had just given birth and space was at a minimum up there. "You fucking—"

"Take it easy, both of you," Gavlek snapped at them. He pulled on his neck as he did at moments of stress. He shook his head. "This installation has been here...what? Eight, nine years now and in all that time, all I've ever seen is grass. No bugs, no animals, nothing. Where the hell did these things come from?"

It was a good question. Cygni-5 had originally been surveyed twenty years before by a robotic probe. Five years after that, an exploratory team dropped down. They found nothing but grass, some simple forms of life below the surface where the water was—microorganisms, fungi, primitive burrowing worms. Not a damn thing else. They even tried to colonize the planet thirteen years back. Gave up less than a year later when too many people kept getting lost in the barrens. Then the Company bought the planet to exploit the mineral wealth. It was a project that was just getting going. But one thing that had never been found on Cygni-5 were insects.

"I mean, have these things been here all along, hiding? But if they're so damn ornery, why haven't they attacked before this?"

There were no answers to that one.

"All right," Gavlek said, running a hand through his thinning white hair. "I gotta be wondering these things, people. We make contact with an EBE, there's a goddamn book I gotta fill out."

Two of the maintenance crew had shown up now, Jensen and Broeder. They didn't say a thing, they just listened.

Gavlek said, "Company's gonna be pissed. We're gonna have to shut down. The Agency's gonna want to send some egg-heads out here, check this all out. You know how that goes, too."

Walker stood up. "That's fine and dandy, Skip. But if you send word today, they're not going to be out here for six god-damn months and you know it. If we've got some nasty bugs out there killing people...well, shit, we can't just sit around with our thumbs up our asses in the name of science. I'm from Arkansas, boys. We got ourselves bugs there, we step on 'em."

Isley brightened. "Exactly. Trust me, Skip, these mothers are mean."

Jensen and Broeder grunted in agreement.

"Way I see it," Walker said. "We gotta save ourselves here. So let's find 'em, fix 'em, and fuck 'em."

Gavlek thought it over, knowing full well he was ham-strung by regulations but also knowing the company was very clear on things like this—protect the project and its workers at all costs. In other words, science was great and little green men were wonderful, but if they got in the way of making money, spill all the green blood you had to.

Gavlek cleared his throat. "Okay. Anybody know where we can get a big can of bug spray dirt cheap?"

The Agency had one rule when it came to commercial projects on alien worlds: each colony had to have a biologist. And the biologist had to be paid by whatever firm was running said colony.

So the mining operation on Cygni-5 had one. His name was Stemick and he spent most of his days digging in the soil, taking cuttings from the barrens, playing in his little lab just off the supply bunker. He was the sort of guy nobody noticed.

But, today, he was a celebrity.

Everyone, except the crews monitoring machinery, was there, crowded around like vultures over tasty roadkill. Except this offering was anything but tasty. Stemick had the insect in a dissection tray, its thorax split open. It was a hideous little creature and gave off an awful sewer smell now that it was beginning to decay. It swam in a glutinous stew of black fluid.

"What we have here is an unknown arthropod," Stemick told them. "Unknown because it's never been documented—or seen, far as I know—and arthropod, because that term takes in just about any invertebrate with a segmented body, jointed legs—insect, arachnid, crustacean etc. This thing seems to be composed of all of these and has a few things of its own going."

He went on to explain how it possessed rudimentary circulatory and digestive systems and—judging by its stomach contents—ate mainly the roots of the abundant grasses. It also had, interestingly enough, a very complex nervous system. And there was a good possibility that it was intelligent to some degree. Its DNA was very similar to that of the other organisms on the planet and this would suggest it was native to Cygni-5.

"Some of you have joked that this creature looks like an oversized ant or—what did you say, Walker?—a wingless wasp on steroids? That's good." Stemick tittered. "But, obviously, this is no ant or wasp as such. But there are similarities. These mandibles for example"—he forced the hooked appendages open—"are much like those of a tropical driver ant back on Earth. The jaws beneath are hinged and I believe they can be dislocated to hold enemies. It has no eyes. No evidence of nasal passages. But these antennae, they might be a generalized sensory organ. And these legs"—he pried them up from the black bile—"I've never seen an arrangement like this before."

The creature had what appeared to be four legs on each side, but there were in fact only two. Two thick limbs jutted from either side, but at the first joint they branched into two separate legs.

"Preliminary computer analysis would suggest that this creature—we'll call it a Cygnan—has something of a symbiotic relationship with the grasses. I might go so far as to say that our Cygnan here might be part of a social hive whose primary function is cultivation and pollination of the grasses. I've found pollen sacs on its legs, so I'd say that's not too far off the mark."

"How come we've never seen 'em before?" Walker said.

"Good question. They may be very good at concealing themselves. And if they spent their lives out in the savanna, we'd never see them anyway."

Gavlek nodded. "That's fine. But we've left them alone. Why are they attacking now?"

But Stemick had no answer for that. He told them he could only make a physical analysis, make extrapolations from what he'd discovered via anatomy, physiology, and biochemistry. Behavioral speculation would be premature and reckless.

"However, I can substantiate what Isley saw," he said. Using forceps, he took hold of the stinger which had now gone black. He held it up so they could all see it. "Holliman—and presumably the others—met their end with this little mechanism. It's hollow like the stinger of a hornet. It's connected to a gland with an extremely potent neurotoxin. Once its injected into the human body, it would have the same effect as nerve gas."

That brought silence to the room that was heavy, nearly suffocating. Bad enough these things gave human beings the creeps, but to possess a weapon like that which could bring about such an appalling, agonizing death...that was just too much.

Stemick said, warned really, "If anyone's thinking of fighting these things, think it over carefully. They are quite capable of defending themselves. If they're anything like other social insects we've encountered, they'll be ferocious fighters. Their own lives are probably meaningless to them. They'll live for the hive and die for it."

Again, that deadly silence.

It hung like that for maybe two, three minutes while Stemick began dropping tiny organs into transparent specimen envelopes. Everyone watched, amazed at how the biologist could manage to touch the thing. He used plastic gloves...but still.

Then Urmanski came flying through the door. "Substations seven and twelve," he gasped. "They're...they're under attack."

After Urmanski's announcement, the bio lab lost its appeal and the comm room was the place to be. The comm room was the nerve center. It was here that the AI programs that ran everything were located. It was also here that contained the interfaces for the transmitters that could beam a message home.

Gavlek decided not to risk more lives by sending crews out to assist the beleaguered workers at #7 and #12. It wasn't a very popular decision. But he was in command and the rules of engagement with a hostile enemy force were quite explicit.

It had been several hours now since anyone had heard from either substation.

Gavlek had used codes only he possessed that would lock down the compound so no one could get out short of blowing a hatch. There was one other work crew out, over at substation #3. But they were sitting tight. They had sealed themselves in and were following orders.

What was concerning everyone now were the odd series of sounds coming over the radio. Like a distant chiming, high-pitched chirruping and pinging. Urmanski assured them that these were no natural emissions, no reflections or echoes. They were artificial and they were being directed at the compound from deep in the barrens, a dozen miles away.

Isley said, "If that's how they talk, they better speak up."

He didn't care for the sounds. Like something weird and eerie you'd hear out in a black jungle in the dead of night. Shrill, insectile sounds. The noises beetles and spiders might make talking to one another.

Gavelek had been deep in thought for some time, just listening, listening. "All right," he said, "let's give 'em the benefit of the doubt. You got a lock on where this noise is coming from?"

"Approximately," Urmanski said.

"Send these sounds back at 'em."

Stemick made a low groaning sound in his throat. "Not advisable. First off, we don't know what they're trying to communicate or if they're even communicating at all. The computer has a translator, doesn't it?"

"Sure. But it's not telling us shit about this business."

Stemick nodded. "What I'm saying is, the translator is programmed with thousands upon thousands of languages both actual, figurative, symbolic, and variations thereof. Have it send, say, mathematical symbols at them in their own wavelength. Give that a try first. If they're intelligent, they'll understand we are, too."

"Yeah," Isley said. "Take it slow here. Don't be pissing 'em off."

Walker sneered. "You want my opinion? We arm ourselves and we go find 'em. Kick in the door and introduce ourselves proper."

Stemick tittered. "You have a decidedly militaristic, aggressive turn of mind."

"Quit talking like that," Isley warned him, "you're turning her on."

"Go fuck yourself," she said.

Urmanski started broadcasting and almost immediately the sounds stopped coming. Then they waited fifteen, twenty, thirty minutes for a response. The silence was heavy, tense. You could hear lungs sucking in air. Hearts pounding. Hair growing, cells dividing. The pitiless, unrelenting sun beat down on the roof of the compound, making the metal contract, uni-rivets creak.

Then...more sounds, more pinging and strident, drawn-out chittering noises, clackings and sharp ringing peals. The tone was definitely different this time around. Apparently, they had gotten the message. If anything, they seemed to be aroused.

"Well, let's see how smart they are," Gavlek said. "Send this out on their wavelength. Have the translator run it through every language it knows and some it doesn't."

Urmanski's fingers played over the touchpad. "Okay, let her rip."

"Greetings, Cygnans. I am Gavlek. I come from the planet Earth in the system of Sol. We mean you no harm. Our intentions are peaceful. Please respond."

"Take us to your leader," Isley said.

Urmanski sent it out.

The sounds stopped.

Walker threw up her hands. "What the fuck's with you people? We're talking *bugs* here," she raged, feeling like the last person afloat in the gene pool. "Let's spray 'em, let's step on 'em. You don't negotiate with crickets for chrissake."

But no one was paying her any attention.

Isley was about to say something smart-assed, had a come-back all set and ready to fly…but then a harsh, screeching static came over the wire. It was unpleasant, jangling, but not necessarily menacing. Everyone in that room felt it down into their bones. An awful, alien cacophony that sucked the blood from their faces and made their teeth grind together.

Then it ended.

Utter silence.

Stemick sat there, nodding. "We can deduce that either they are intelligent or they're merely responding to the sounds you're sending. That noise…it really proves nothing."

But Walker wasn't so sure. "It proves they've got a transmitter, doesn't it? Can't you lock onto it, Urmanski?"

He shook his head. "It's not coming from any one place… from lots of places. I can't get an exact fix." He sighed. "I'm not even picking up any energy pulses out there. If they've got a transmitter, I have no idea how they're creating that signal, boosting it, or directing it."

Walker turned away. "Well, what fucking good are you."

"Any thoughts, Stemick?" Gavlek asked.

He smiled thinly. "A few. We should look at the possibility of an organic technology."

All eyes were on him.

"By that, I mean a technology unlike anything we have. A technology that doesn't require mechanical or electronic gadgetry. A *living* technology. I've seen it on other planets. Some of you probably have, too. Let me simplify that." He stood up, looked out the bank of windows at the burning plains beyond. "Some of you mentioned ants. Okay, let's go with that. On Earth, driver ants use a primitive form of this. They have no true nest. When the colony rests, the soldiers make bivouacs of themselves by interlocking their mandibles and leg spurs. They make living structures that protect and house the others. Their bodies are their tools, their houses, their everything. What I'm saying is the Cygnans might be like that. These transmissions we're getting might be originating from their bodies. A communal shortwave sent to us."

There was something sobering about that, something unnatural. Though it was anything but, realistically.

"Sure, fine," Gavlek said. "But are they really intelligent? Are they actually communicating or just sending out noise?"

"Good question. These sounds might be attempts to discover who and what we are or just their method of calling out to us in some base Cygnan language that any good bug would understand."

The static rose up again. It was not a single noise, but hundreds if not thousands of them—high, low, sharp, dull, flat, piercing. A chaotic sound. But then the individual sounds rose up into a single, uniform, electronic sort of humming that made everyone cover their ears.

"Turn if off!" Walker cried out. "Turn it off! It's...it's driving me crazy! I can't take that fucking noise—"

But then it stopped and her voice was loud and echoing. She looked at the others sheepishly, knowing she'd made a fool of herself. Or thinking so at any rate. Truth was, they all felt it jangling in their heads, rubbing their nerves raw, making them want to shut it out or crush it in any way possible.

"Interesting," Stemick noted, evidently enjoying it all. "Like hundreds of voices calling out at the same time, a hundred minds. A hundred minds that suddenly coalesced into a single shrieking thought. A hive brain composed of thousands, but in reality, a single brain. A single dominating, irresistible consciousness. Incredible."

Isley found Stemick interesting before, but now he was just being a goddamn pain in the ass. Interesting? Incredible? Goddamn egghead. Only someone like that would get a hard-on over something like this. Maybe it would have been a little different if he'd seen them all over Holliman, seen them using their stingers.

Urmanski was pulling up screens on the interface now, nervously fingering the touchpad. "Something's happening out there...Christ, Skip, they're on the move. I got a fix on 'em now." His face was tight, pressed white like a flower in a book. "The numbers...gotta be thousands of them and they're coming this way."

Urmanski was right about one thing, the Cygnans *were* on the move.

But he was wrong about the numbers. Not thousands, but millions. The entire Cygnan hive was on the march. A crawling, buzzing perpetual motion machine with millions of moving parts. It came out of the barrens, destroying and devouring everything, leaving destruction in its wake.

And the compound was directly in its path.

It was Gavelek's idea to stay and fight.

A lot of ideas were bounced back and forth. One of them was to abandon the compound, get out of the Cygnans' way. But there was no guarantee of safety in that. Maybe they could avoid the main force, but what of the scouts? And who could say what the objective of the main force was? It might have pursued them wherever they went.

So Gavlek decided they would stay.

On his order, the drills and pumps were shut down. The pipelines were closed off. All hatches were locked. Any holes in the compound structure were plugged. There was a fence around the compound, a solar collector shield that turned the rays of 61-Cygni into energy for operations. It wasn't intended as a defensive perimeter. But with a little ingenuity, it was turned into a barrier that surely even the massing Cygnans couldn't hope to penetrate. Gavlek had the maintenance crews run high-voltage cables to it from the central fusion generator. There was enough juice in it now to fry gravel. The only breech in it was the drive coming in and this had been covered with metallic netting and likewise electrified.

If the Cygnans got through, they were going to be pretty crispy.

An hour later, everyone was waiting.

On the screens, they could see the approach of the hive. The grasslands fell at their approach. The mowers couldn't have hoped to be this thorough. They cut a swath nearly four miles wide. According to Urmanski's scanners, the actual army was nearly five miles long.

"I think what we're seeing," Stemick said, "is a migration of the entire colony. I'm not convinced they mean us any true harm. We just happen to be in the way. Like driver ants on Earth, they're just on the move and anything in their path is going to be destroyed."

"Including us," Walker said.

But Gavlek did not accept that. "There's no way they can breach that fence. Just no way. It's sixteen feet high. Unless they're really good jumpers, they're toast. You didn't find any wings on that one, did you, Stemick?"

He shook his head. "But I believe it was a soldier. There's no telling about the others, the workers, drones, queens. Who can say?"

Isley had been in a few bad spots in his time, but never anything like this. Never anything that left him feeling so damn helpless, so damn frightened. Because he was scared shitless and he would have been the first to admit it. There was something instinctively abhorrent about great numbers of insects. Something that set the human mind on edge. Ant colonies. Hornet nests. Beehives. Just seeing all those damn things congregating and wriggling, it set the skin to crawling. And it was much, much worse when the insects in question were eight, ten inches in length.

"Here they come," Urmanski said. "Less than three hundred yards from the fence and closing."

"I see 'em!" Walker said, face pressed to the windows.

Isley joined her.

The barrens were collapsing. As if the Cygnans were armed with chainsaws, the great, tightly-packed fields of grass stalks were falling like tall timber. Then they were gone and the swarm pushed across the road at the fence. They showed no fear, no hesitation. The scouts moved directly before the colony, antennas waving and feeling and snapping like bullwhips.

"They can sense the energy in the barrier," Stemick said.

"Well, now we'll see how intelligent these bastards are," Isley said.

The scouts came at the fence with tight, economical jumping strides. The first dozen hit the fence and there was a snapping, popping sound as the electricity reduced them to burning cinders. But more followed. Waves of them attacking, soldiers and scouts throwing their bodies into the voltage as if they could overcome it by sheer numbers. Their little blackened bodies clung to the fence like burning marshmallows. There was smoke and fire and arcing electricity. Those in the compound shielded their eyes from the blinding flashes.

The compound was equipped to do many things, but it was not made to filter odors. And right then, it was filled with an acrid, burning stink like seared meat and scorched hair. It filled the comm room in a nauseous, pervasive mist.

"Look at them bastards, will ya?" Isley cried out, fascinated as he was repelled by their numbers, their ferocity. "Christ, they're insane!"

And it seemed that way.

Thousands of buzzing and hopping bodies crowding for space at the fence. They hit it with everything they had, inundating it with sheer numbers, going right over the top of each other, crawling over burning corpses, attacking the mesh with their mandibles. A creeping, writhing, wriggling mass, more piling up all the time until you couldn't even see the fence any more. In fact, with all the fireworks and smoke, you couldn't see much of anything. But you could smell that hideous, incinerated stink and hear *them*. Oh, yes, you could hear them just fine. A buzzing, whistling, piping wall of deafening noise.

Those in the comm room were covering their ears at the din.

You could hear the anger, the rage, the torment of the Cygnans.

But they were not about to give up.

And Isley was thinking: *They're not intelligent, they can't be goddamned intelligent. Intelligent creatures don't act like this, they don't attack in waves and die and keep dying.*

It reminded him, if anything, of wars he'd read about in history class. Human wars on old Earth. Human wave attacks. Bodies piling up so deep the second wave had to go over the top of the first and so forth.

Trembling, shaking, wanting to scream and maybe even needing to, he felt something cool and damp touch his fingers. He knew it was Walker's hand. Their fingers found each other, interlaced together tightly like mating squids. There was solace in holding hands. When the world—your world—was coming to an end, what else was there to do?

About that time, the lights started to flicker as if all the fixtures were loose.

"Urmanski?" Gavlek said.

Urmanski looked like he wanted to cry. Maybe he was crying. "The generators, Skip...they're not made to put out this kind of juice. They're overcapacity now."

And everyone in the room knew what that meant. They knew very well. The fusion generators would shut themselves down and it was only a matter of time now.

Outside, in that flashing and arcing lightshow, the smoke cleared a bit and the fence was gone. It was covered in the burnt, sizzling bodies of the Cygnans. Thousands and thousands of them with more pouring over it every moment. It began to sag and then collapsed completely. The lights flickered again and died for real this time.

And the swarm poured into the compound.

The only lights inside the compound came from the sunlight streaming through windows and skylights of which there were many. With the generators down, it began to get warm in there. Without the air conditioning going and the air circulating, the sun heated the compound's metallic shell like a tin plate on hot asphalt. The atmosphere quickly got stuffy and thick.

At Walker's side, her hand hot and sweaty in his own, Isley watched the Cygnans flood forward, a twitching, droning sea of insect frenzy. So many. So goddamned many. It reminded Isley of maggots on a dead cat, a busy canvas of worming, slinking, industrious motion punctuated by the monotonous, ceaseless droning wail of soldiers and workers and drones. He could feel the flesh at his groin creep, move in prickling waves up to his belly. His throat was as dry as a cave. He had to remember to blink, to breathe, trapped in that web of unspeakable horror.

The Cygnans assaulted the compound's main structure and everyone within drew tight into themselves. Had they been able to fold up and slide into a crack, they would have done so. Because the Cygnans were massing by the thousands, the hundreds of thousands, engulfing the building like antibodies ingesting a disease organism. And the same thought was on everyone's mind: *How long? How long before they get in?*

"Christ," Walker said and Isley had never heard such a tone of quiet desperation in her voice before. "Dear Christ, I can't stand it!"

You could hear them on the metal walls and roof, their clawed feet like thousands of pencils tapping and tapping and tapping. It was a sound that went right through everyone in the dim, shadowy compound. That constant, hollow tapping. It made some whimper, others scream.

It wasn't long before Cygnan bodies were pressed tightly against the windows and skylights. They were pulsing and scraping and clawing and biting and stinging, trying desperately to breach the shell of the intruder, to get at the soft internals that made it live, made it a danger. With the blazing sunlight hitting them, their orange-red abdomens seemed to glow like sunsets—salmon, vermilion, scarlet, and coral. It was like candlelight flickering through crimson carnival glass, making the Cygnan bodies appear to be transparent, made of gelatin. Yes, beautiful almost, but so deadly and soon enough the light began to fade as skittering bodies heaped atop one another and a dire, twisting blackness fell over all and everyone.

Urmanski was whimpering pathetically.

You could hear others shouting in the corridors, crying, laughing in desperation.

"You better do something, Skip," Isley told him. "People are panicking here. You got fifty odd people trapped here and they're losing it."

And you couldn't blame them because the sound of all those mandibles and spurred limbs working and seeking, trying desperately to find a way in was enough to crack open minds like hot chestnuts. The shell of the compound was humming, vibrating now with an awful, lunatic noise. It was like having your head thrust in a beehive. You could not escape the droning racket.

Gavlik's face was red and puffy, beaded with sweat. His lungs sucking stale, dry air. "What do you want me to do? What the hell do you want me to do?" he yammered, moving forward, then back, then in a drunken circle. "Can't you hear them? Can't you *feel* them? They want us! God, how they want us! In my head! *Ahhhh, God, they're in my mind, in my mind! I can feel them!*"

And Isley could, too. That central, relentless, irresistible hive intelligence worrying at the edges of his will, pulling, pushing, tearing, wanting in, trying to make him do things he did not want to do.

The walls were beginning to groan and creak now. Like an aluminum beer can in a crushing fist, they were beginning to give under the weight, under the force of those murmuring, creeping bodies.

Gavlik ran off and Isley smelled something foul and realized Urmanski had shit himself. He was insane now, pressed into some gibbering, frightened childhood corner from which he could never hope to escape.

But he was the lucky one.

Isley and Walker ran out into the corridor. Emergency lights had come on and bathed everything in a moonish, surreal glow. Shadows leaped and hopped. Crewmembers were attacking each other now. Hitting and being hit, stomping and being stomped. Some were trampled under the boots of marauding, screaming gangs that turned on one another after they worked a victim to his or her knees.

Isley was hit by a wall of bodies. He saw Walker go down, try and drag herself through a doorway. But hands yanked at her, boots slammed into her body, her head. Isley tried to make it to her and collapsed under a bevy of hammering fists. But as he went down, he knew, he knew, all right.

It was the Cygnans.

This wasn't simple mob mentality at work, something bred of horror and despair and madness. It was those insects, their minds channeled into a single, devastating thought: kill, maim, kill. They were inserting their primitive, barbaric wills upon the minds of the men and women in the compound. Working them into a lather, taking them back to a darker, uncivilized time when the hive had to be purged, cleansed.

Crawling on his hands and knees over the broken bodies and shattered faces of friends and co-workers, Isley caught sight of Stemick. He was using a cutting torch to melt the lock on the main door. In fact, he already had.

The lock hissed and fell away and the door blew open and a tide of Cygnans washed in, inundating him. They were everywhere, scuttling and wriggling and hunting. They were on the floor, on the walls, moving over the ceiling in a lethal progression. They fell on the crewmembers and gave each and all a taste of their venom.

Isley, shrieking madly himself now, saw a man with an even dozen Cygnans on him get stung repeatedly. He dropped and went into rabid convulsions. Blood and saliva flew from his mouth and his body snapped and convulse like it was being electrocuted. His head bashed violently into a concrete step until his skull came apart and a gray slop of brains splashed over his face. A woman came stumbling forward, countless Cygnans up underneath her coveralls, looking like some throbbing tumorous growths there. The insects dropped from the ceiling, vaulted through the air, fell over people en masse like tarps. The corridor was a deafening wind tunnel of buzzing and trilling and thrashing bodies and airborne insects.

Isley caught sight of Gavlik.

He tried to run with a blanket of them on him. They began to sting and he threw himself violently against a steel bulkhead, shattering his jaw, his teeth spraying from his mouth like dice on a table. And then he was down, too, legs shuddering and arms slapping and body twisting. And it was like that for everyone.

Isley saw that the insects had abandoned one of the windows.

He broke through it with a hammer and dove out into the

suffocating heat of Cgyni-5. The bodies of the attackers went to pulp beneath his weight. And he saw, really saw. There were so many that they were three, four feet deep on the ground. A living, chitinous carpet of insects.

There was no escape.

But as he ran forward, screaming, trying to break his way through...the sea parted. Yes, the colony opened and let him into its body. Soldiers reared up on their hind legs, barbed mandibles clicking and snapping.

He could feel the communal mind in his head now, like needles and knives ripping through his will, his sense of self. He could see nothing but Cygnans. The greatest army ever assembled. And he was caught within their numbers. Seeing things no one ever had and no one ever would. It was a profuse, innumerable dominion, an infestation of creeping, crawling, droning, whirring insects. And then, as they continued to part, to press at him from behind and push him forward, he soon saw why.

There was a gigantic ball rolling in his direction.

A huge, rolling, peristaltic ball composed of workers, all hooked together via mandibles and claws and armored appendages. The ball rolled forward and then it stopped. The frenzy of interlocked workers began to melt away like snow on a roof and beneath, beneath—

Yes, the queen.

She was the size of a collie. A huge and bloated representation of her hive. Legless, her abdomen swollen with millions of eggs, she rubbed her mandibles together with an awful jangling, hissing sibilance. Unlike the others, she had eyes. Immense triangular orbs the color of green stained glass. They looked not only at Isley, but right into him and through him.

His mind was a puny, trembling thing under her gaze.

His brain exploded with white light, with white noise, with thrumming waves of agony. His freewill was stripped away like meat from bone and what it left behind was another empty vessel for her godless, black sentience. She filled Isley and destroyed every possible vestige of refusal, of free thought, of willpower, of defiance. These were unacceptable mutations purged by the hive. Obedience was the mantra of the colony and Isley was one with that now.

From somewhere, from some distant alien world of dementia, a voice was speaking. But not a human voice. A buzzing, droning voice like thousands of hornets attempting human speech: "*We are peaceable...we are one...you and yours built these structures in the ancestral migratory path...it could not be allowed... not during the festival the time of rebirth the time of life of filling and rending and seeding...now run off to a place that waits for you a secret and quiet place...*"

And Isley did.

For that was the world, *his* world: the grasses and those who tended them.

Something snapped in him with a wet, pulpy sound and then he was running through the colony and wanting only to see those grasses, those high yellow grasses. And then he did and burst through them as they slapped against his face and cut his hands and shredded his coveralls and he kept running until he fell from sheer exhaustion into that yellow, dry, hot world of coveting stalks. He buried his face in the arid, crumbling soil. The stalks rustled now and whispered and pushed in closely it seemed, holding him, keeping him. And the barrens, that ocean of yellow living husks covered him and held him and erased his path, enfolding him in a secret dark womb of madness.

THE PUPPETEER

(Dark Animus #5, 2003)

It was in a tree-lined, autumnal park that Kroff first found the puppeteer. First got his taste of genius and lunacy and the ethereal thread that binds them into one.

September had only begun to kiss a blush into the foliage and bring a nip to the air. A sallow moon cast wild, phantasmal shadows amongst the square-hewn hedges and bird-pecked marble statues. Kroff was new to the city, a habitual night-wanderer, a disciple of nightscape and archaic urban architecture. Many were the evenings that some fog-shrouded path had led him to desolate quarters, deserted churchyards, and abandoned neighborhoods. And this night, lost yet again in the grim tangles of concrete and brick, he blundered into the park.

It was lit up by pole lanterns and electric bulbs that swayed rhythmically in the soft breeze. There was a veritable maze of clapboard booths and green-smelling tents, narrow kiosks and canvas-roofed huts. People were milling about, children laughing in the moonlight. Vendors hawked roasted sausages and popcorn, balloons and rubber snakes. Clowns walked invisible dogs and jesters walked on stilts, juggling bottles.

Kroff took it all in, loving the absurdity of it. Like some Medieval fair.

"Excuse me," he said to a tall man with a bulbous red nose, a clown that had never quite taken. "Could you tell me what all this is?"

"Is? Is, dear boy?" He laughed with a roaring sound, that was somehow unpleasant, unnerving. "Why this is a festival, of course. The Greater Puppet Festival to be specific. Make your-self at home. Linger here and linger there, but above all enjoy yourself. For this night comes but once a year."

Kroff was a little confused. Greater Puppet Festival. Why not? Nothing wrong with it, surely. But Kroff's watch told him it was after two in the morning. What sort of festival went so late? Or did it start late on purpose?

He lit a cigarette, smelling fried foods and sweat, linen and candle wax. Other things. Some too sweet, others far too sour. Some pungent and some acidic. A wild fusion of odors, each demanding that he follow it to its source.

"Makes one giddy, doesn't it?" the red-nosed man said, looking about him, seeming almost confused with the frolick-ing, bustling activity assaulting them from all sides. "Oh...here *they* come. I better go."

Kroff was about to say *who?*, but he never got the chance.

Bald-headed harlequins in diamond-patterned costumes and flour-whitened faces dipped about him. They came sin-gly, in groups of three or four. They jumped and danced and swayed. They rushed in from either side, a perpetual motion machine of white, grinning faces.

Distorted faces.

Because that's what Kroff was thinking as they charged about him holding hands and locking arms, encircling him in a snare of dancing paper-doll images and pressing white faces: they were *distorted*. Their teeth were very yellow, very long. Their lips red as rubies. And in the ashen moonlight—eyes too large, too bloodshot, the left orb often substantially larger than the right or vice versa. Their faces looked rubbery, fluid. The skin more anemic than powdered.

But then they broke off, scattered like leaves before a gust.

Crowds brushed past Kroff, turned him forward, then backward, completely around. Children raced through his legs. Something else passed over his head. There was music every-where. Strolling minstrels plucking lutes and harps, weaving melancholy textures with clay flutes and dulcimers.

It was all like some mad renaissance festival.

But the man had said *puppets*, hadn't he?

The Greater Puppet Festival.

Puppets happened to be one of Kroff's few passions in life, other than nightwalking. So he mingled about, catching occasional glimpses of hunched forms slipping behind tents. Forms that seemed to have too many limbs or not enough. Others that were joined at the hip.

He went from booth to booth to booth, more intrigued and excited by the moment. Here were puppet plays and garish puppet theater. Giant puppets worked from within. Shadow puppets and glove puppets. Rod puppets and finger puppets. Punch and Judy shows. Indian leather puppets and Japanese *bunraku*, Vietnamese water puppets and Malaysian shadow figures. Kroff watched a Medieval epic portrayed with armored Sicilian puppets brandishing battleaxes, pikes, and mace. He saw gruesome examples of French Grand Guignol and German *Theater der Grisly Marionetten*, in which war and plague and starvation were symbolized by horrid, skull-faced moppets and drifting wraiths leaping through charnel yards of heaped bones, all with requisite Teutonic surrealism.

And as he watched, puppets and marionettes moved about him, bumping into him, crowding him, leaping away on strings he never saw.

Then the red-nosed man was at his side. "Sometimes... sometimes I'm not sure which are puppets and which are people," he said, dropping this mystifying commentary then fading off again into the crowds of people and dolls and manikins and things which seemed to be all and neither.

Kroff moved about, positively dizzy, trying to absorb the festival inch by inch.

Voices spoke and faces leered, dummies pranced and harlequins laughed. It was all unsettling, shocking, and, yes, *amazing*.

But true shock and amazement had not been encountered as yet.

That came when he discovered the wonderfully intricate Czech marionettes, manipulated by masters of the school. He watched plays which were sometimes hilarious and other times appalling. And then, in a tent set beneath the spreading, craggy limbs of an old oak, he found genius.

Frightful, morbid genius.

On a twelve-foot stage adorned in plush red velvet, a marionette play was under way. At least…Kroff *thought* they were
marionettes. But on closer inspection they appeared to be dolls.
Dolls roughly the size of human infants, but swollen, obese little things with bulbous heads, black demented eyes and chubby
fingers. They waddled and crawled and squealed. What he saw
of the play was…*disturbing*. The grotesque little creatures had
crushed down one of their own and were ritually dissecting it
with nipping fingers and nubby teeth.

Kroff watched, transfixed.

Were they puppets? Yes…no…possibly. But like none he had
ever seen. They were manipulated by an unseen puppet master
and manipulated with the greatest dexterity. One would have
almost believed they were living things, that the howls of agony
from their dismembered peer were actual cries of torment. That
the stuffing and sticks were some arcane anatomy and bones
being picked and plucked and sorted through.

But as disgusting as it all was, it was the puppets that held
Kroff's attention. They did not seem to be fashioned from poly-
foam or clay, latex or wood. What material could create such
a ghastly semblance of human flesh? And was it sculpted or
molded?

The tent was soon crowded and Kroff was shut off from
the stage by a gang of rotund men, so he did not see the final
denouement…but he *heard* it. The sounds of biting and chewing
and sucking. Feeling dizzy, his belly filled with squirming life,
he slipped out of the tent, noticing with some apprehension that
the faces of that cheering, jeering crowd appeared to be *painted*
on.

It took him some time before his breathing was normal after
that, before cold grease quit bubbling in his stomach. And then
he asked one of the Czech puppet masters.

"That tent…that show," he managed. "Who…who is the
master of those…*marionettes?*"

The man smiled with a plastic grin. "Why that's Herr Obis,
of course. Who else could it possibly be?"

And then Kroff knew, maybe as he had known all along.

Obis. Of course.

Kroff made his way from the Greater Puppet Festival, not looking behind him as he sought fresh air and consuming darkness. He did not take notice of the misshapen carnival puppets that followed him, whispering and bobbing, slowing dissolving into shadow.

He knew of Obis, of course.

No true aficionado of puppetry and toy theatre had not heard that name. Had not been captivated by the man's technique or secretly offended by his creations. Obis had once been called the Puppet Master of Prague...and no slight compliment was this in a city famous for its legions of marionettes and the astounding masters that worked them. He was to puppetry what Einstein was to physics: a revolutionary, a virtuoso, a messiah of strings and dolls that had redefined, reinvented the ancient form. In Obis's supple, magical hands, puppets did not just dance jigs and slap one another on scale-model stages, they performed ballet and opera, complex dramatic works.

Obis's puppets and presentations were legendary.

Some of his early masterworks were kept in the special collection at the Munchen Stadtmuseum and at the National Theatre Museum in Vienna. Others were locked in glass cases like priceless antiquities in the Musee de la Vie Wallone in Liege and the Muzeum Loutkarskych Kultur of Prague itself.

To call Obis's works mere puppets was to demean the master himself.

For what other puppets could walk and talk, sing and dance and frolic with no evidence of manipulation? Obis's only true criticism was that his puppets were often quite loathsome and degenerate in appearance, but were claimed—by him at least— to be mere expressions of the sin and corruption in all men. Symbolic, then, of the timeless struggle of good and evil, life and death, sanity and madness. Regardless, his puppets—though amazing feats of engineering in their own right—were notoriously repellent and profane in appearance. And his plays and operettas were, at best, elaborately staged *contes cruels* and shock theater featuring casual disembowelment and decapitation, cannibalism, incest, torture, a cornucopia of lurid practices that quite often left his audiences feeling faint and sickened.

No one in Paris, Bremen, or Hamburg would soon forget Obis's depiction of the Spanish Inquisition or the Roman arena, his characterizations of the Sawney Beane clan or the pastimes of Gilles de Rais.

It was said that Obis lost control.

That there was no clear dividing line between his creations and the man himself. That he often referred to his puppets as "my children, my children". His apparent insanity and aberrant behavior soon drew not only students of puppetry and the curious, but throngs of degenerates searching for new decadent thrills. Obis's rare shows were instantly sold out and, given the subject matter, it was only a matter of time before reformists and zealots had him banned in nearly every city in Europe.

Not that any of this bothered Obis, of course.

He was a recluse who lived in a decaying mansion in Prague's Medieval quarter with his puppets and was only too happy to retire there. When his name did come up, it was generally whispered and this as a warning of the high price of genius. For his name became synonymous with certain heretical practices. Obis, they said, was something of a sadist, a wizard, a student of arcane lore...the likes of which did not make for pleasant conversation.

To Kroff's knowledge, Obis had not been heard of in over thirty years. A master of the old school, his works had been largely forgotten in the shadow of cinematic triumphs in puppetry.

And now, by chance or Fate, Kroff had located him.

For regardless of technological advances, Obis's mastery of the form was the altar before which all such endeavor paled.

It took some doing on Kroff's part to track Obis.

After weeks of fruitless searching, he contracted the services of a private investigator. And to his surprise, the results came quite quickly. Not only was Obis found, but he was living in the city. Kroff had to put off a visit as his mother took ill and passed away, leaving him a moderate inheritance which would

free him from the specter of employment. He considered himself temperamentally unsuited to labor of any sort, so his mother's death was a blessing. Being without her was not unwanted.
For at best the old lady had been domineering and intrusive
and, at worst, vindictive and hateful. The funeral arrangements
were made and dispensed with and a feeling of peace and sat-
isfaction fell over Kroff.

With no further hindrances, he went to see Obis.

The neighborhood in question was one that Kroff would have
discovered sooner or later in his nocturnal jaunts, a centuried
and squalid run of tall, slanting houses falling to ruin. The
streets were narrow and serpentine, often ending in vacant lots
or feeding into cramped alleyways that themselves terminated
in barren, walled courtyards. The sidewalks—when in existence at all—were frost-heaved and broken, replaced by decaying planks that soon gave way to footpaths beaten through
weedy lots.

As Kroff paused to light a cigarette and get his bearings—no
easy thing in that sullen, moldering neighborhood—he gazed
about, fascinated. The entire district should have been bull-
dozed decades before. It was cramped and constricted, dirty
and crumbling, and quite possibly infested by rats...if the
scratching and skittering sounds heard from shadow-clustered
cul-de-sacs and bricked passages were any indication. It was a
grim, phobic garden of concrete and stone and brick. The vegetation was oddly withered. The trees denuded and suggestive
of hunched, gnarled shapes.

Just the sort of place that would attract someone like Obis.

Kroff's private investigator had, among other things,
gleaned some very colorful rumors from the locals...when
they would speak of Obis at all. Bits of ephemera concerning
the man and his suspect activities, wild tales concerning grave-
robbing, witchcraft, and necromancy. He was oft-referred to
as "that old witch Obis" or "Wizard Obis", his residence called
"that damnable house of dolls" by more than not. There were
other stories, of course, mostly concerning the dolls or puppets
which could be seen looking from the windows of his abode

after dark...pale, abominable things with mad staring eyes that watched passers-by with more than casual interest. And then there were the disappearances of several local children.

Kroff was of the mind that Obis inspired fantastic exaggerations wherever he went. That his mere presence subverted reality.

Finally, then, Kroff found what he had come to see: the residence of a certain Mr. Obis.

It was a high, crooked house on a crooked street of similar such edifices. All of them seemed to be constructed of some dirty, mottled stone much like stucco. They were pressed together so that there was scarce enough room to walk between them. Doorways slouched and gambrel roofs leaned, tall chimneys sagged and windows were numerous...some shuttered, some filthy, others broken or boarded, but all set into curiously askew frames like paintings that had been carelessly hung.

Kroff stood staring up at Obis's house, the others crushing in to either side. There was not a straight line to be had. Everything—doors, windows, balconies, ridgelines—all offset, warped even. Perhaps on purpose. It was more than a little disconcerting.

As he climbed the cracked steps to knock, he noticed that the doorway had been bricked over. And not recently. He moved around to the far-left side through an arched passage chiseled into a stone wall. The passage seemed to cut straight through that tall house itself...but above, no roof, just starlight. Though there were no steps, the path meandered downward until Kroff was beneath street level. To either side rose high dirty brick walls set with occasional red-painted doors, but no handles to open them with.

The path ended at a door. Surely it led into a cellar. It was oddly narrow, a single barred window near the top. But it had a knob and the door itself was open. Kroff went in, found himself in a cramped corridor smothered in darkness. It smelled of dust and rotting cloth. Moving by feel and calling out to the puppet master every few feet, he continued on, realizing that the corridor was moving upward at a gradual angle. He could hear sounds in the murk around him...scratchings and skitterings, more evidence of an infestation of vermin.

No matter.

He arrived at an immense chamber. It was lit by moonlight coming from skylights cut into the roof, more than three stories above. The chamber was perfectly round, easily fifty feet in circumference and completely hollow. He was reminded of an observatory. There were no doors set into those curving walls, no exit or entrance but the one he'd passed from. A rickety, steep staircase clung to the walls, going up and up, corkscrewing around and around, then seemingly terminating near the skylights themselves. On the second and third floors, there were tight balconies before angled doorways. From the second-floor balcony, there was a shaft of light beneath a door.

Kroff called out the name of Obis, his voice coming back down at him and not as a single voice but as many just out of sync with one another. A mocking, echoing clamor.

The shaft of light above widened until the door was thrown open.

"Who is down there?" a voice called. "What is it you want here?"

Kroff announced himself. "I saw you at the park one night, Mr. Obis. The show you put on."

Obis was a rawboned thing standing on the second-floor balcony, backlit by the room he had vacated. "Yes, yes. The Greater Puppet Festival. And you wish to see more? Ask questions? Of course. Come up then, don't loiter down there of all places…"

Kroff found the staircase and started up, clinging to the rail, not caring for the heights below him. The stairs made a complete spiraling circle of the chamber before they reached the balcony, so that as Kroff got closer to Obis, he got farther away. And then, ultimately, he came around. He was glad of the light and the warmth from the room, for all the way up he had a most unpleasant sensation that he had not been alone in his climb.

"Come in, yes, do sit down," Obis said. "And stop staring, please."

The door was shut—and bolted—and Obis gestured to a wingback chair before a small hearth. He was terribly thin, wizened, his hair sparse and white like a dusting of new snow.

"I can't tell you what a pleasure this is," Kroff said, beaming.

"Pleasure? Pleasure, you say? Hmm. We'll see, won't we?" Obis could have been seventy or a hundred and seventy. His spectacles were square-framed, his nose hawkish, his eyes beady like steel balls in oily chum. "Would you like some tea?"

"Yes, yes, I would."

Tea served, Obis sat across from Kroff, brushing his hands against his denim apron as if he were trying to wipe something off them.

Kroff was amazed that he was actually with the puppeteer. That he was having tea with him. The room they were in was high-ceilinged, the walls oddly bowed, crowded from floor to ceiling with wooden shelves. And on them...ancient books, heaped manuscripts and rolled diagrams, carnival masks and carved marionette heads and limbs. A jumble, really. Everything piled and scattered in a mad profusion.

"I've been a fan of yours for many years," Kroff said. "When I saw that festival in the park—"

"Yes, yes, yes. Why don't you ask me what it is they all ask me? It's why you came, isn't it? You've come to hear about my puppets." Obis said this matter-of-factly, as if it was all too obvious. He spoke with no discernable accent, though he was reputed to have been born in Czechoslovakia.

"I suppose I have come for that."

Obis nodded. "No reason to be ashamed or shy, my boy. For there is a fascination to my creations, isn't there? To puppets in general?"

"Yes."

"What is the attraction of puppets? Have you ever contemplated that? What is it that draws us to them or them to us? Is it simply that they are toys that move or is it something more?" Obis wanted to know. "Something we prefer not to think about? Hmm. Yes, they are like *us*, but they are not *us*. Imitations. Copies. Reproductions, certainly. Caricatures at best...showing the race in all its absurdity and horror. Do you agree? Dolls, puppets, marionettes, mannequins...they are but wood and wax and vinyl, bits of string and yak hair, gears and cogs within…not flesh and blood, not living. But on the other hand, not truly *dead*. For something that has never lived cannot truly be considered dead, now can it?"

Kroff sat there, sipping his tea, lighting a cigarette, wondering what the hell this was all about. "No, of course not. But a dummy is just a dummy."

Obis nodded. "Except when it is *not*."

Kroff stared. "I don't understand…"

"Have you ever wondered if that mindless assemblage of wood and wire and cloth that you manipulate via strings may be something else? That perhaps inside its cold, wooden clot of heart…it may be *conscious*? That perhaps it is simply waiting to be born? Sleeping now, but ready to wake at any moment…"

"No, I never thought—"

"Of course not, why should you? Such talk is madness. And you're not mad, are you? No"—he giggled—"no more than I am, or my puppets upstairs or below or disassembled upon those shelves."

All that was written on Obis said he was *peculiar*, but being with him in that huge, awful house populated by dummies… well, Kroff was beginning to wonder if it wasn't something more. For he couldn't help the odd, apprehensive feeling stewing in his skull that the moment he had entered that bleak house, he had fallen off the edge of the known world. That he was trapped in a nightmare (Obis', perhaps), lost in the dream-tangles of the man's dementia. That, try as he might, there was no way out. That he would never again find the banal, boring life he had left behind.

"Yes," Kroff said, all his rehearsed questions falling to ruin. "Well, I suppose I should—"

"Quiet," Obis said, looking concerned.

He held a finger to his lips, cocked his head to the side as if listening for something. Kroff just sat there, his cigarette paused at his lips. He heard nothing at first, then…well, it sounded like a muted shuffling from the stairwell outside. Like someone— and perhaps more than one—had just passed the landing and were going steadily up. But, *creeping* like an errant child not wishing to be heard.

"What...who was that?"

Obis looked at him, his eyes huge and unblinking. There was something in that look—shining red-rimmed eyes like mirrors reflecting vast depths—that made the flesh crawl at the back of Kroff's neck.

Obis smiled. "Nothing. Nothing at all."

"I heard someone..."

"You heard nothing, my friend. It is an old house. It makes sounds. Odd sounds. Just ancient timbers settling, nothing more."

But Kroff was not so sure. There had been a marked stealth to those noises.

"Please, have more tea. I'm afraid I haven't been much of a host." Obis poured, his hand trembling slightly. "You wish to know of me? You wish to know why my puppets are like no other? Then let me tell you a story. Let us reach back through the years..."

I am an old man (he said) and so it will come not as a complete surprise that I fought in the First World War. Ha, then we called it merely the World War or the Great War. No matter. What I will tell you of happened in Silesia, a province of the Austro-Hungarian Empire. After the war, Silesia would be divided up between Czechoslovakia and Poland...but you did not come for a history lesson, eh? No matter, my unit—all brave Czechs and Moravians—had been shattered by the British, cast to the four winds, as it were.

Alone, I wandered for days, the rain pounding down, my arm in a sling. It was badly damaged and poorly set, splinters of bone thrusting through the flesh. Shrapnel wound. The dressings were foul and rank, blood-stained, the pain immense. My uniform hung in rags. I had not eaten in days. The lush forest had been turned into a lunar landscape from the shelling, dips and hollows sluicing with mud. The trees were blackened and burnt, the limbs blasted free. They rose from the waterlogged sludge like pillars, like monuments to the grim deeds of man. I was in terrible shape—hungry, feverish, drenched to the bone. I was on the verge of death, I believe, when I saw the house.

What sort of house, you ask?

Dear God, how shall I describe that place? Though part of it lay in ruins from the barrage, the majority was untouched. I had never seen a house like that before nor since. It stood on a hill, surrounded by skeleton trees, a cross between an abbey and a gothic mansion. The roof was high and jagged, the windows arched and made of dark stained glass. Architecturally, it was a busy place, an insane hodgepodge of styles and movements that had no business being brought together...Romanesque and Medieval half-timber, Gothic and Colonial. A collection of wild angles and asymmetry, diverging lines...a surreal tomb of towers and leaning walls, rectangular stone blocks and jutting spires. It was tall and low, squat and narrow. A madhouse that seemed to be slowing sinking into that sea of mud.

The rain pelting down, shivering and shaking and weak, I pounded at a huge oaken door. It was opened immediately, but by no one that I could see. I stumbled into that asylum, into that candle-lit morgue of flickering orange light, crawling shadow, and half-glimpsed things. There were narrow stairways which seemed to lead nowhere, winding corridors that led into sloping galleries, spiral steps and passages that ended abruptly...or led into others which had no egress. Yes, a claustrophobic maze that seemed to reinvent itself by the moment. A place where windows looked not to the outside, but into other rooms which could only be reached by trapdoors, if at all. Yes, a madhouse designed by a lunatic. Not a house as you or I understand it, but a *fevered dream of a house*. That is as close as I can come...like a house as it would be in a nightmare, something straight out of German expressionistic cinema.

But it was much worse than that.

For it was crowded with shapes and forms that I soon saw were dummies...mannequins and surreal puppets. Grotesque, unpleasant things that withered the mind just to look upon them. But I could have expected no less in such a house. The corridors were thick and clustered with these disproportionate, gaping, staring phantasms: clowns and soldiers, dwarves and burlesque queens, dandies and peasants, lunatics and harlequins. They were all around me, flickering candelabra and tall tapers painted them with a wild, leaping illumination, making them move as if they were caught in some grim shadow-show, some malevolent dance macabre...

As I stood there in shock—dripping wet, half out of my mind from desperation, starvation, and the horrors of war—I kept hearing sounds. Shifting and rustling, muted susurrations. I couldn't account for it...there was motion and activity and I thought I would scream. I stumbled this way and that, getting farther lost in the labyrinth, crying out, helpless, the eyes of those dummies following me from room to room.

Then I fell into a small ell, sweating and shivering. The walls were decorated in heavy velour tapestries. There was a small table with candlesticks burning, casting a soft golden glow. Next to it was a mask. A half-face thing one associates with a masquerade, except this one was flesh-colored, lumpy.

"Put the mask on," a voice echoed out from somewhere. Not exactly male nor female. Perhaps a man mocking a woman or a woman mocking a man. Regardless, it was high and strident. "Please put the mask on."

I did, my fingers trembling so badly I could barely accomplish it. The mask was slightly moist, as if it was made of skin... skin that was still perspiring.

A shape came into the room. I was certain it was a living mannequin. But no, it was a tall woman dressed in a shapeless cloak and high leather boots. Her hands were gloved. A tumble of red-blonde hair hung over her shoulders in ringlets. But her face was covered by a mask, a white distorted thing that covered everything but her mouth and chin. It had narrow Asian eye-slits and a thin wedge of nose. Her own flesh was nearly as pallid, her lips black as those of a corpse.

She looked upon me through that mask, her eyes dark as pitch. "Please sit down, Herr Obis. You need to rest."

I had not told her my name, but somehow, she knew it. Just as I knew her name was Madame Yorda. I was too delirious to be certain of anything. Perhaps we *had* been introduced...but by whom or *what*? She brought out a serving tray of hot coffee, biscuits and jam. She moved with an odd, loping motion. I was ravenous. Despite the insanity of the house and my host, I ate

with my good hand and kept eating. The coffee was marvelous. She gave me cigars and a dark, sweet schnapps. Despite the
pain of my ruined arm, I felt warm and oddly safe there. The
war seemed centuries away, a lifetime gone.

I thanked her for her hospitality, told her who and what I was.
Begged her for shelter for the night which she happily granted.
She was kind, though humorless and strangely detached. Sitting
there, my stomach warm with schnapps, a cigar in hand, the
tension gradually bleeding from me, I was struck again by the
idea that this was not a lady before me, but perhaps an imper-
sonator. And that shrill, abrasive voice...it was like no voice I
had ever heard before or since. Empty, grating, it had more in
common with grinding metal than a human voice. It reminded
me of a Victrola recording...scratching, dusty, skipping.

Madame Yorda went on in some detail about who and what
she was. She claimed, at one time, that she had been the greatest
puppeteer in Silesia, nay, all of Prussia. This I doubted, for my
family were puppet masters since antiquity. My father's people
were some of the finest puppeteers in Prague. I had never once
heard the singular, obviously Slavic name of Yorda mentioned
even in passing and my family knew all the greats, they often
dined with us when I was a boy. Of course, I did not mention
this. It would have been rude, impertinent, yes?

Regardless, Madame Yorda went on in some depth of her
accomplishments in that grating voice which made me cringe
for it had the same tonal qualities as fingernails on a black-
board. Most discordant to say the least. Well, Madame Yorda's
end had come, she said—referring to herself in the third person
quite frequently—in Breslau. There she had been involved in
something called the "Theatre of Grue", of which I was familiar
with in only the most rudimentary sense: my grandfather had
spoken of it. I had assumed, from the way he talked, it was but
a memory. But Madame Yorda spoke of it as though it were yesterday. Anyway, her end came in Breslau.

"It was my puppets, Mr. Obis," she told me. "They dis-
obeyed me, sought to destroy all that I was. Heaven only knows
how long the revolt had been planned or how deep the roots of
insurrection indeed were..."

She was mad, of course. She told me that that night in Breslau, her puppets moved out into the crowd, that all their frustrations, lusts, and jealousies were loosed in a campaign of murder and mutilation. It was a horror. There was a panic as the puppets fell upon the theatre-goers in a swarm. A mass exodus, a frenetic rush for the doors...people were crushed and trampled. The doors had been locked, you see. And it was the puppets' doing. The theatre went up in flames and hundreds perished.

"They blamed me, of course," she said. "Called me witch and heretic and murderess. It was revolting. I was dragged naked through the streets, whipped and beaten and confined to the prison for the criminally insane in Olmutz. Do you know what such places are like, Mr. Obis? Dozens and dozens of us were crowded into cramped, dripping, vermin-infested cells, we slept and ate off straw filthy with our own waste. Rats provided our only true source of sustenance. We were beaten, violated, starved. The warders were sadistic, the inmates murderous, the treatment barbaric...yes, that is where Madame Yorda died. At least, the important parts of her. Ultimately, I was released, broken and crippled. The State yanked out my soul with dirty fingers, spit on it, then put it back in, told me to go live a productive life..."

Eventually, she told me, she came here to the family residence, poured herself into her work, the likes of which crowded every room and passage.

I was exhausted and I suppose I drifted off, inexcusable as that may seem. I had a vague memory of being washed and placed in a fine feather bed. I only know that I slept and slept, possibly for days. Upon waking, I recalled terrible nightmares involving my arm. But as I opened my eyes and realized where I was, I became aware that there was no pain in my shattered limb. I held it up...there were no bandages, no sling. Although it was stiff and a bit cold to the touch, it was perfect. Not so much as a bruise or a cut. I had the most inexplicable feeling that the limb was not my own. Yes, I could move it, feel with it, do anything with it a hand and arm could do...*yet*, that disagreeable, frightening sensation persisted that something altogether alien had been grafted to my body.

Insane?

Oh yes, but insanity held a terrible influence in that house. Even had I slept for weeks, there was no way my arm could have been so miraculously repaired, revitalized, remade.

I climbed from bed, dressed quickly in my threadbare uniform—which was clean and pressed, though faded and patched now. I made my way through that house of damned puppets, searching and searching until I came to a low doorway which hung awry in its frame. Beyond, was a set of stone steps.

I went down.

And what did I see in the cellar? To this day, I cannot be sure. It was a workshop of sorts. Full-sized marionettes dangled from exposed rafters, swaying gently. There were masks and puppet heads on the walls. Arms, legs, and hands set on hooks. Torsos. Long, low tables crowded with gears and pulleys and obscure machine parts. Armatures and dowels and glass jars of puppet eyes. Madame Yorda was there, of course. She was standing over a huge, steaming tub of grease from which came a fetid, wormy stench. There was something in that slop, something alive that made those foul waters quiver. I saw hands, then arms reaching up out of there, viscid things glistening with a foul jelly. Yes, something had been born in that vat, something Madame Yorda was helping up from the placental stew.

I must have screamed or cried out...and the entire room woke up.

Legs were kicking on the walls, arms swinging, fingers grasping. What I took to be a crate of wooden hands began to clutch and wriggle, dozens of them trying to crawl free like huge pale spiders. Eyes in jars were darting about with a macabre life. Faceless manikins and those missing limbs were alive, walking and crawling and dragging themselves about. One was a woman...human-like legs right up to the waist, but above nothing but an armless skeleton fitted with cogs and machinery, wires and creaking hinges. Things whirring and clicking and sparking inside her. No true face, just a set of livid, seeing eyes bulging from orbits, finding me and fixing me. Others in a similar state of incompletion waltzed from the shadows. Some were just walking legs or inching torsos. Arms dragged themselves off shelves. Heads and masks were whispering and screeching.

I ran back up the steps as that slimed, featureless thing rose up from the frothing, oily vat. It turned to look at me, though it had no eyes to see with. I had the oddest feeling it was meant to represent *me.*

I was mad. I knew it. I know it now.

The entire house had woken up, was screaming and hissing, rolling and swelling and clutching. Long arms and gnarled hands reached for me in the corridors. Puppets drifted along the ceilings, calling my name. Mannequins were dancing and swaying and marching. Everything was alive...rustling and whispering and swishing. Demented forms hobbled from secret, dank places. Legs hopped after me. Mannequins that reeked of the grave took hold of me, losing their grip as I yanked their limbs from sockets.

Then ultimately, all those dead mouths chanting my name, hands that were strong and irresistible snatched hold of me. Hands. Yes, hands hooked to arms that grew from the walls, but were savagely alive. A dozen took me, tangled me up like tentacles...gray, flaking arms.

Then I knew. In my mania and derangement, I honestly knew.

The puppets...marionettes...dummies, call them what you will. They were not puppets as such. Madame Yorda had assembled them from the raw materials of the grave, imbued them with some diabolic life. Yes, she had looted battlefields for the components which were all-too plentiful in those dire times. The dummies were made of corpses, assembled like inanimate puppets in the traditional fashion with wires and armatures, swivels and hinges and simple motors...but they were not puppets as such. That house was an ornate mausoleum.

Madame Yorda came limping through that carnival of deranged, lewd animation. "You are a puppeteer by birth, by inclination," she said to me in her squeaking voice. "You would have done well here with us. Did we not save your life? Did not Madame Yorda replace your arm? No matter." She pulled a glove off and the hand beneath was a metal thing with wires and pulleys that operated the fingers. She pressed it to my face.

"You'll not leave without taking something with you..."

I jerked as if with a jolt of electricity. And something... I do not know what...something in me boiled over, liquefied, ran like hot sap. Seized by hysteria, I fought free of those arms and threw my bunched fist at the face of Madame Yorda. Face? Hardly. What I hit was no mask and beneath it was no face. She was a dummy like the others. Her face shattered like brittle wax, hung like shards of glass from a black buzzing hollow beneath.

She began to shriek.

They all began to shriek and claw and shamble.

Yes, it was then I ran from that charnel madhouse of screaming grave marionettes.

Well, I won't go into the neurotic wreck I was for many years following that experience. Suffice to say I was institutionalized more than once. You see, I was not insane in the conventional sense. It was much greater than a mere psychological affliction which had taken hold of me, it was a delirium as much of the soul as the mind. I had seen things, witnessed things, learned things no sane mind could hold.

Yes, I fell back into puppetry.

But I was no common puppeteer. For something in me had died a horrendous death and something else had been born. Something from that appalling house controlled me, worked me as I had worked dozens of puppets. A man cannot come into contact with that degree of festering pestilence and remain unchanged. Yes, Madame Yorda had planted some dark seed within me and the flower it bore...dear God.

Suffice to say, I submerged myself into the Germanic schools of grotesquerie and the bizarre. Ravening aberration, both physical and mental, became the focal point of my creativity and my life.

I began to gain a certain notoriety and infamy for my puppet shows. For my creations were like no other...I assembled them from repellent items purloined from cemeteries and collected from mortuaries. I toiled for my art in graveyards and the noxious damps of the crypt. It was insane, yes, but I could not stop. The more of those little horrors I created, the more *they* made me create. My materials were plundered from caskets and burial pits, cast-off bits of lifeless clay, but yet, *yet*, a certain malignant life lingered in those bones and hides. A dirty wasting vitality, a perverse and decayed sentience. They were dead piecemeal, yes, but when brought together, gummed and stitched by my expert fingers, a collective spark emerged.

They lived en masse because they *wanted* to live.

Do you understand? *They wanted to.*

Obis was cackling about it all. "Those museums coveting my puppets, nothing but Frankenstein-ish mummies, the lot of them."

"Then...then your puppets," Kroff said, his voice dry, his face wet with perspiration, "they are...*cadavers*..."

"At one time, yes...but now? Now I am beyond such simple resurrections."

Kroff stared. He could not stop staring. Obis. Surely a genius but tortured by a seamless madness that was complete in its mania. Kroff knew it would be pointless to argue with the man or talk him down from his high ladder of psychosis. Obis was too calm about it all, discussed it almost matter-of-factly like it was of no more concern than the weather or taxes. He was convinced and that was that.

And the scary, unsettling thing was that Kroff almost believed it, too.

There was something pandemic about the puppeteer's delirium, a catching, spreading pathological nightmare. You could not be in that house or with that man for any length of time without feeling it—that brooding viral contamination entering you, weakening the fibers of your sanity.

"You doubt what I say?" Obis put to him, not offended. He sounded...*relieved* that Kroff did not accept any of it. And maybe this was reassuring to him, that there was someone who simply could not believe in the nightmares of his reality.

"It's...well, Mr. Obis, I—"

"You think I'm just crazy?" Obis laughed. "Certainly I am. But my madness runs far deeper than that."

He rolled up the sleeve of his left arm, exposing the smooth flesh there. It was shiny and hairless, too perfect, not so much as a freckle or blemish. "You wish proof, Mr. Kroff? Then observe." He produced a penknife and peeled the skin from his wrist— just an inch or so. There was no blood, just something glistening beneath like colorless neoprene.

"Would you call that an ordinary arm, my young friend? Hmm?"

Kroff was shivering. "And your puppets..."

"The ones at the festival? Yes, special, very special. The latest additions to my collection. I've modeled them on dead children taken from slabs and morgue drawers—"

"Enough," Kroff said. "I've had my fill. This is disgusting. I'll hear no more of it."

"A wise choice," Obis said. "Go out the way you came...do not stop, do not linger. And, please, do not come back."

Of that, Kroff had no earthly intention.

After the door was bolted, Kroff hurried down the stairs that wound along the high, hollow chamber. Suddenly, he stopped. Obis was crazy, yes, but those puppets at the park...they were something special. There had to be a unique mechanism to them. Kroff could accept nothing less. Now that he had dismissed Obis as a mental case, the house did not frighten him. Surely, it was weird and almost hallucinogenic in its dimensions, but just a house.

He wanted one of those puppets.

Common thievery and nothing more, but he justified it all by saying that he would examine one in private and if it had been created with illegal materials, he would turn it over to the police. This satisfied his conscience. Quietly, slowly, he went back up, passing the second-floor landing and hearing what he thought was Obis sobbing. He continued up, the stairwell spiraling around and around until he was at the third-floor balcony, the yawning black attic above. Wan starlight issued through the skylights set above those huge, crisscrossed rafters.

The door was open.

A blast of black, oddly warm and acrid air rushed out at him. His fingers clawed madly for a light switch and found one. Out of the corner of his eye, he caught a glimpse of something skittering into the shadows. A rat. The place was plagued by them. Even in Obis's room, Kroff had heard them scratching in the walls. Surely, it was only a rat. But his mind kept picturing something small and crooked running off on two feet.

He brushed that aside.

A single naked bulb swung slowly on a wire suspended from the high ceiling above. He was in Obis's workroom. Low windows looked out over the streets, a skyline of peaked roofs and lightning rods, archaic chimneys. A view right out of Medieval Europe. Prague. Surely, the skyline of the city, Kroff's city, did not look anything like that.

What city were those windows showing him?

But he dismissed that. It was dark. He was overwhelmed. That was it. He looked around the room, that place of creation. Yes, yes, yes, it was all here. Molds and casts hanging from the walls. Buckets of latex and clay, blocks of wax and coils of wire. Corkboards crowded with tools. Epoxy putty. Pipes and tubing. All the usual paraphernalia. The only thing unusual were the detailed, yellowed anatomy prints tacked above the bench.

But Kroff supposed a puppeteer had to understand anatomy, that sort of thing. Carefully, placing his feet softly so as not to give himself away with the creak of a board, he began investigating. There was a wooden crate of tiny, chubby hands. He picked one up, felt it in his palm...it began to squirm instantly as if reacting to his body heat. He tossed it with a scream.

It rattled across the floor but did not move again.

Imagination? Surely.

Licking his lips, he went to a door at the rear and threw it open. He found himself in a large auditorium of sorts and he was on the stage. There was a mannequin sitting in a chair with one of Obis's obscene little puppet dolls held on its knee like a ventriloquist's dummy. Kroff moved off the stage, discovered that all the seats were full. In them, perhaps thirty or forty of those bloated toddler-puppets from the festival in the park. They were hideous in the low, shifting theatrical lights. Cobwebbed and dusty, they were dressed in suits and fine lacey dresses that were patched with mold and fungus. And their faces...dear God, deformed, misshapen, like things sculpted from wax that had melted in the sun, pooled and ran, settled in all the wrong places.

Kroff, sweating and trembling now, artificial eyes boring into him, touched a fat little girl whose left eye was set significantly lower than the right, her jagged grin nearly reaching her ears. She was warm. Not hot, but simply warm and vital. Her eyes were set in black-rimmed pits, her disproportioned and abhorrent face coveted shadow. Her flesh was oddly soft, pulpy like rotting fruit...Kroff's finger sank through one cheek.

Filled with a panic he could not understand, one that was deep-hewn and superstitious, he took hold of a boy puppet and ran back up to the stage. The mannequin was staring at him, the puppet-doll in its arms smiling. Kroff made it into the workroom, heard shufflings and whispers and rustling sounds behind him. A high squeaking voice said: *"Mama, mama, mama..."*

But Kroff would not listen nor accept what was happening. He shut the door behind him, heard something like tiny fists pounding and clawing.

But it was only in his mind.

It had to be. Just like the fevered scratching in the walls, that sense of shadowy movement on the stairs as he made his way out of the madhouse of Obis.

For weeks after, it was the same.

Always the same.

Kroff wished to dissect the puppet-boy, discover its wonders, but he never did. At first, he was simply too revolted, then maybe afraid, and then...? Even he did not know. He grew to hate that profane, malformed little monster. He covered it with a sheet, but the sheet always fell off. He put the puppet in a locked cabinet...but it always found its way out.

He did not doubt that it was alive somehow, that behind those peering glass eyes there was something aware, something relentless, something mordantly hateful. Its livid eyes followed him around the room and sometimes its head was in a different position or the fingers unclenched. Always subtle, very subtle. But Kroff knew, God how he knew.

Just as he now knew that it was not simply some clever little puppet-boy in a dark, dingy burial suit.

Obis had not made it from cadavers, not entirely. Beneath was a standard armature of pipes and wire and pulleys, but over this artificial skeleton, the skin and scalp of a dead boy had been carefully stitched. Obis skinned dead children and sewed their skins intact onto his dummies. Kroff had examined the suture lines himself.

It was a warm and fleshy thing. At night, he could hear it breathing. Behind his locked door upstairs, he could hear it move about. The pattering of little feet, tiny fingers that scratched at his door. An occasional demented, childish giggling heard in the darkness.

And often, yes, often in the morning, the door was somehow open and Kroff was listless and fatigued as if he'd been busy through the wee hours.

And what was most disturbing were the tiny pinpricks at his throat.

And the fact that although he was getting thinner and paler by the day, the puppet-boy grew fatter, his complexion florid, his cheeks pink and round. Yes, the puppet was becoming a corpulent, well-fed blob.

Out of his mind after weeks of what he considered abuse at the fat, hungry fingers of the puppet, he went to see Obis. But the door was locked, the house dark and silent.

But if the house was a tomb, the neighborhood was alive.

But with *what?*

Children? Yes…or nearly. Skeletal stick fingers jumping and hopping and running and laughing. Their eyes were blue glass and their smiles painted on. A group of them were playing ball with a skull. A street vendor, his eyes festering pits of madness, looking much like a mannequin from the Greater Puppet Festival, manned a booth in an alleyway. He called out to Kroff, showing him his wares—bones, dozens of bones arranged on the counter. He grinned happily and vomited out a tangle of writhing worms.

"Raw materials, sir? Are you in the market for raw materials?"

Kroff ran off. There was a little girl sitting on a stoop, her face like a Halloween mask, anemic and drained. She wore flapping rags, grinned with a toothless maw. "Hey, mister, you gotta help me," she said. "My dolly, she's bad. You better talk to her. You better tell her she can't bite people, she can't suck their blood..." And then, from those moth-eaten shifts, an equally moth-eaten doll was produced. Its face white as cream, gray hollows under its eyes. As Kroff looked on in horror, it opened its eyes and they were tiny crescent moons. The doll grinned and showed its teeth. Long, sharp teeth.

The world had gone insane and Kroff with it.

Weeks bled into months.

Kroff was still trapped in that little house with the fat puppet boy. But it was worse now, far worse. Kroff was a wasted collection of skin and bones that shambled lethargically back and forth, back and forth. The puppet was an obese mass of chins and jiggling rolls. Kroff wanted badly to destroy it...but it would not let him or his madness would not allow it. Whenever he got close, its eyes would burrow into him, showing him awful things and making him remember other things that stripped away what was left of his humanity, his soul.

A few days before he had attacked the puppet.

He brought his hands to its flabby neck, wanting to snap its gaping head off. His fingers sank into pulsing, moist flesh... fungous and greasy. He screamed and collapsed, had the oddest dream that something licked his throat as he slept.

He no longer bathed and could not remember eating or the passage of days, could recall nothing but what those penetrating, morbid eyes told him. But there was something, something important. Something revelatory. For every afternoon he woke from heavy, torpid sleep, his clothes filthy, his fingers clotted with black earth.

Then one gloomy day he found a scalpel in the kitchen.

Needle and catgut in the living room.

It all pointed to something, something he had once known, something extraordinary...but what was it? What?

Dear God, what have I done? What have I done?

He wracked his brains, but the puppet's will was stronger than his own. But he would remember, regardless of how much it hurt. He spent all day thinking and thinking, his brain aching, his nerves frayed.

And then, just after sundown, it came to him.

The workroom.

Not the workroom of a man named Obis...*who* was this Obis, anyway? But the workroom of Kroff. For he had one, but his memories of it were stygian and obscure. At the rear of the house he hammered at the locked workroom door. He finally kicked it in, that gassy graveyard stench making him reel. Inside, shadows crawled like snakes. There was dirt heaped all over the floor, small caskets piled in the corner next to the coffin of an adult. But they were all empty, empty. The table was scattered with wire and tubing, needle and thread, and all those tiny, pathetic bones.

On his hands and knees, he could remember opening graves, making things with what he found.

But mostly he remembered the other grave, the cadaver he smuggled across town...yes, the making and unmaking, the stitching and sewing, slitting and peeling, gumming and knitting.

Oh, dear Christ.

Kroff—a dirty wild-eyed wreck—sobbed and whimpered, digging through the black moist earth, looping worms brushing his fingertips as whatever was still human in him went with a surging, snapping wetness.

The house was waking up around him, filled with shivering sounds and cryptic noises. Cellar doors opening. Attic hatches flung aside. Shadows moving, darkness flowing like liquid. Footsteps and breathing, squeaky voices and fingers dragged along walls like tenpenny nails.

Moonlight flooded the room, limning things best unseen.

A disjointed, buckled shape drifted through the doorway... dangling from invisible strings that made it jerk and dance. Arms moved on swivels and a hinged mouth opened and shut. It was a garish horror from a sideshow, a gaping mummy strung together with wire and catgut, connectors and string. A hideous, leering nightmare caricature that wore the shriveled, gray skin of his mother.

Kroff's mind was long gone before it fell over him, touching him and kissing him and licking his face. And when the child-puppets came in to embrace him, he giggled.

It was nearly a week later that the house was entered by the police.

They made their investigation but could not account for a great many things. And others, they did not want to account for.

So when the old man who called himself Obis showed to collect things that Kroff had borrowed, they did not interfere. He took his puppets and left…the children, the old woman, and the young man with the contorted face and mad staring eyes whom the police found dangling from the ceiling by wires.

THE LEGEND OF BLACK BETTY

(The Undead: Flesh Feast, 2007)

1

They told Oates it was the yellow fever that did his little Mandy in.

Half the county was laid low with it and the other half were remembering the 1878 epidemic of Memphis that had left over 5,000 dead. Even then, in that corner of Nevada, people were running scared…of each other, of sudden drafts, of the unburied dead. They were staying clear of what they called "plague-houses" and undertaking parlors, shunning cemeteries and coffin-makers.

"People are saying some crazy shit," Oates told Doc Rifer on the morning of Mandy's funeral. "Saying a lot of things, without actually saying them."

Rifer shook his head, stroked his white beard. "Pay no attention to that rot, Daniel. People around here are a lot of superstitious fools. Your girl went of the yellow fever, that's all and nothing more."

He said they were looking at an epidemic of the fever. That it was going to be plenty bad before they got it under control, that was for certain. They'd be closing the lid on a lot of folks before it blew over. But it *would* blow over. It just had to run its course, that's all. And Oates wanted to believe him, because Rifer knew his business and he'd worked malarial camps during the Mexican War and had been doctoring for well on forty years.

"I've seen my share of poxes and fevers and morbid disease, son, and what you have here is surely the yellow fever," Rifer told him.

Oates didn't know what to believe, not really.

Yellow fever? Sure, some were saying that and others were saying there was an epidemic brewing, all right, but it was one of a spiritual nature. They weren't being much more specific than that; only that a lot of them had gotten into the habit of crossing themselves whenever it was mentioned. One thing was for sure, though, they were all bolting their doors and closing their shutters come nightfall. And it wasn't at all unusual to see things like crucifixes and garlic hanging over doorways of carefully-battened farmhouses.

"Your Mandy had the symptoms, Daniel," Rifer explained to him. "The fever, the chills, the jaundice, the vomiting. It was all there. Now there's a real smart Cuban physician name of Finlay who's saying the fever is spread by mosquito bites. And you know what? I'm in agreement with him. Now, if I were you, I'd be draining that stagnant crick back of your farm, for that's where the real danger is. That's where the fever mosquitoes are breeding. You never mind that horseshit about spooks and vapors, you leave that to the old women. Yellow fever, that's our enemy."

These were the things Oates thought about as they gathered on that windy hillside amongst the sunken graves and marble markers, the mounds of earth with simple wooden crosses pushed into them, leaning and canting every which way. Rich and poor were buried side by side here, sheltered by tall cottonwood trees, profuse stands of buckthorn and mesquite. There was a calm and serene beauty about the little cemetery, but it was not a place a man ever wished to come. Surely not for himself or loved ones and particularly not for a child.

He kept staring at the squared-off grave, the mound of black earth. That small pine box sitting next to it...and what was in there, oh Jesus, what was in there. Surely, all his hopes and dreams for the future. All the glory and joy and love he had ever known or ever would know was nailed shut in that goddamned box and now they were going to bury it, they were going to offer it to the worms. They were going to put beautiful little Mandy in that hole, of all the terrible and unforgivable things. *Mandy.* Mandy with her flowing red hair and bright green eyes, that delightful crooked smile and laughter like wind chimes. They were putting his precious girl down into that goddamned charnel and they were burying the best parts of him along with her.

He was trembling now, his eyes wanting to spill tears. Holding them back was almost physically painful. He swallowed, then swallowed again. *Why don't they put me in that fucking grave with her, because I'm just no good without her, there just ain't nothing left in me—*

Be strong. You got to be strong now.

Oates sniffed away his grief, adjusted the black sleeve garter at his bicep and put his arm around Elizabeth who was shaking very badly. She was not a particularly strong woman, either emotionally or physically, and this was just more than she could bear.

"Just hold onto me," he kept telling her.

But Elizabeth seemed impervious to his presence. Her face was pale and pinched, her eyes red-rimmed and swollen like wounds beneath the black mourning veil. She was not crying anymore. She waited there wavering in her black dress and bonnet, her mind sucked into itself. Oates held her close and she felt light and insubstantial as if she were nothing more than a bag of sticks. She barely seemed to breathe.

Good God, he found himself thinking and not for the first time, *just let us get through this. Give Elizabeth the strength. I can't bear to bury my wife and my daughter…*

Reverend Fisher clutched his prayer book, said, "I am the resurrection and the life, saith the Lord: he that believeth in me, though he were dead, yet shall he live: and whoever liveth and believeth in me shall never die."

"Amen," those few gathered said.

The preacher's words were like knives and spears punching into Oates; he had to tense himself to take their impact. But they cut, God how they cut, slitting him open and making all that was left drain away in hurtful rivers. He felt completely empty inside. He squinted his eyes shut, trying to be strong, trying to find his center, and when he opened them, he was still there, still in that damn cemetery burying his daughter. There weren't but six or seven people there besides Elizabeth and himself. All the friends they'd made through the years had not showed, afraid of catching what they thought Mandy carried. And those that had come were standing well away from the casket, pressing handkerchiefs to their mouths and noses, fearing they might breathe in some pox oozing from the box itself. Only Doc Rifer and Reverend Fisher were unafraid.

"We brought nothing into this world, and it is certain we can carry nothing out," the reverend said, pressing his missal to his chest. "The Lord gave, and the Lord hath taken away; blessed be the name of the Lord."

A few people were sobbing now, making muffled sounds beneath the cloths covering their mouths.

Elizabeth had stopped shaking. Instead of leaning against her husband, she stood up straight and tall, her lips set in a grim line. Beneath the veil, her eyes were bright and sparkling like she was seeing something no one else could. She reached one hand out as if to grasp that of her dead daughter.

Reverend Fisher said, "We commend unto thy hands of mercy, most merciful Father, the soul of this thy child, Amanda Catherine Oates; and we commit her body to the ground, earth to earth, ashes to ashes, dust to dust…"

Elizabeth had thrown aside Oates's arms and was walking over to the casket. There was fierce resignation to her and no one could have hoped to stop her. She threw her veil back and everyone saw that awful face, the mouth twisted like she was on the verge of a stroke. And her eyes…hot and savage and piercing.

"In there, in there, in there," she began to shriek, her voice rising up sharp and scratching above the droning words of Reverend Fisher. "Don't none of you hear what's in there? Don't you hear that? *Don't you?*"

Oates went to her, something shattering inside him now. The mourners stepped back and Fisher looked confused, still reciting the requiem for the dead but in a small, mumbling voice. Oates tried to get hold of Elizabeth, but she fought his hands away and dropped to her knees next to the box. The sound of her hands slapping flat on its lid were like thunder.

"Elizabeth," Oates managed. "Come away from there, come away…"

But Elizabeth would not come away. She pressed an ear to the box, listening for something inside. "Don't tell me you can't hear it! That none of you can't hear it! It's Mandy! Listen, goddamn you all, *listen! She's in there breathing! I can hear her breathing! Can't you hear the scraping of her fingers at the lid? Can't you—"*

People were shocked and horrified now. They were crossing themselves and looking on in abject terror. Oates and Doc Rifer took hold of Elizabeth and dragged her away from the box. She came away willingly, but she was small and hunched over, her head cocked to the side like she was hearing something the others couldn't. Her eyes were huge and mad, unblinking.

"Please, everyone," the reverend said, "let us gather in prayer."

But nobody was up to that now. They were all standing around in their Sunday finery, whispering and crossing themselves, looking too frightened to stay and too frightened to run. A wind blew and tree branches overhead rattled together, a wreath of flowers tipped over. A crow cawed in the sky.

And Elizabeth, looking completely deranged and pressing her hands to the side of her head, just overwhelmed with grief and, yes, maybe horror, said to everyone gathered, "You wait… just all of you wait…tonight or tomorrow night, oh yes, you'll see then…*what put my Mandy down will raise her back up again and she will walk among us!"*

Then she shuddered and her eyes rolled back white and she collapsed to the weedy graveyard earth.

2

Oates came awake feeling the night around him.

Feeling it reaching out for him with black, gnarled fingers.

It was immense and coveting and thick, crushing him with its weight and wrapping dark ropes of itself around his throat until he could not breathe. He sat up in bed, gasping, a sheen of sweat laying cool and damp over his face. His whole body was shaking and his heart was racing.

He moved his hand to touch Elizabeth, but she wasn't there. No, she'd had a fit at the funeral four days before. She was under the care of her aunt over in Fallon. Oates sighed, licking the sweat off his lips. He brushed damp hair away from his brow.

A dream, that's all it was. He'd had some kind of nightmare. And why not? These past days, this past week or so, had been hellish. He was remembering it all now and feeling the heaviness of it trying to squeeze his guts out his mouth.

There in the darkness, he trembled and tried to breathe.

Christ, he hadn't felt like this since Antietam, when he'd woke in a hospital tent outside Sharpsburg laid low by typhoid fever. He could remember the fever and the chills and the vomiting, all those Union boys around him stacked up like cordwood, all dying of the miasma, drowning slowly in their own filth and bodily secretions. And the smell...good God, the stench of battlefield dressings yellow with pus, flesh gone to gangrene, feces and vomit and piss. Horrible, just horrible. Men moaning and whimpering, death taking a few more each night as contagion and trauma and despair laid them low. The orderlies taking them out wrapped in stained, graying shrouds. The sounds of shovels digging shallow graves and—

Enough.

By God, it was enough.

Oates threw his legs over the side of the bed, pulling from a bottle of Old Crow on the stand. He pulled out a tin box of hand-rolled cigarettes and lit one with a stick match. The flame made distorted shadows leap on the walls. He pulled off his cigarette, listening and listening and not really sure what for. But something was telling him it was important that he listen. He could hear the wind moaning out there, making the eaves rattle and the farmhouse tremble. It was a lonely sound. A sound of desertion and memory gone to seed.

And the more he listened, the more he was certain that it was not just a dream that had yanked him from slumber. There was something else. A noise, a slight disturbance, something. If you were to have listened as he did, you would not have heard anything. But if you knew that farmhouse like he knew it—he'd built it with his own hands, board by board and brick by brick—you would have sensed that something was not right. Maybe a door was open or a shutter left unlatched, but it was there. A sense that something was askew or just off-center.

So why don't you just go look for the life of Christ?

And that was a good question, because he didn't know why he didn't go and look. But it was as if something inside him refused to move. It wanted him to stay put, to hide and not dare breathe. Because, well, if he made noise, someone or something might hear him.

Nerves.

Just nerves.

He was alone at the farm. Elizabeth was completely unwound from the funeral and with her aunt. And Mandy? Well, Mandy was…Mandy wasn't there anymore.

She's dead…why don't you just quit pretending otherwise? Say it already: Mandy's dead. Your daughter is goddamned well dead.

The idea of that brought a wave of fresh agony rolling through him. Yes, she was dead. There was no doubt of it. She was in her grave up on the hill and his wife was on the verge of nervous collapse because of it. These were the facts that he was having trouble with. Thinking them was one thing, but accepting them and admitting them to yourself was quite another. There were things a man could do and things that just brought too much pain.

But it was too soon.

For the love of God, she'd only been gone a week now. Not even. And in that time, the mere act of walking and breathing had been overwhelming. The strength and volition it had taken to get himself and Elizabeth through that horror, the wake and the funeral, had wasted him, drained him dry as a peach pit. There was nothing left in him. Nothing at all. Every morning when his eyes fluttered open, he almost expected to hear Mandy singing or bouncing her ball or playing jacks on the kitchen floor. As if the whole thing had been some wild and terrible fever dream and he was going to be coming out of it any time now and one of these mornings, she'd come bounding in, grinning and giggling, that ocean of red hair flooding her neck and shoulders and—

Shut up, you idiot! Listen! You have to listen now. This is important.

So, Oates was listening, something inside his belly clenching like a fist. He did not know what he was listening for, but it was going to be bad. Real bad. And whatever it was…if he heard it, if he actually heard it…it might strip his mind bare.

Those were wild and irrational thoughts, yes, but deep inside he was feeling very wild and very irrational. There was a creeping sensation at his spine and his heart would not stop pounding. Though the night was not especially warm, a trickle of sweat ran down his left temple and rolled across his cheek like a tear. He was tense and terrified and he was not even sure why.

Just listen, then you'll know.

He heard it then. A sound like something had been dropped, something small. Maybe a pencil. Something that rolled a few inches across the floor. Then he heard another sound…a thud, then a creaking. And that made his guts fill with ice, because he knew that creaking: it was Elizabeth's rocking chair. But if Elizabeth was in Fallon, then *who* was rocking in that chair, back and forth, back and forth?

He got up, put his feet on the cool plank floor.

The creaking stopped.

Then started again.

Whoever was out there, he had the feeling they were now aware that he was aware of *them*. Shaking, Oates could not get it out of his head that all this was calculated to have a desired effect and that effect was absolute terror.

He was not a coward.

He'd been through the War Between the States, he'd rode shotgun on a stage, he'd kicked up his heels in some of the toughest mining camps in Arizona Territory…yet, whatever was out there, waiting in the darkness for him, filled him with a fear that was sharp and brittle, beyond anything he'd ever known.

Okay, somebody's here, so goddamned what? Elizabeth came home early or Raul Penchot had come over to see how he was or—

Stop it, you idiot! You know what's come calling is not that. What's come calling in the dead of night can be nothing good, nothing wholesome.

Oates pulled one of his Colt Navy .44s from its rawhide scabbard. It was loaded. It was always loaded. Cleaned and primed and oiled. You take care of your gun, his old man had said, it'll take care of you.

He pulled the Rochester lamp from its hook over the dresser. He lit it with a match and stepped out into the short corridor. He could smell the pine sap in the walls and something much worse. Whatever had come into the farmhouse had brought this other, noxious stink with it: the smell of rainy caskets and putrefaction.

In the corridor, there were footprints.

Quite a few of them and they were all small and familiar. The footprints of a child, one that had dragged itself through pasture muck and puddles of dirty water. From what Oates was seeing, this child had been standing just outside his door, clots of soil and black water dripping from it. There was a squashed beetle in one of the prints.

You can't be thinking these things, you just can't.

But he was. Those prints were telling him things that destroyed something inside of him, laid him raw on some primal level. They were like the prints of an eight-year-old girl, one that maybe died of the yellow fever like so many in the county. Except this girl she had—

What put my Mandy down will raise her back up again.

He could hear Elizabeth's voice shrieking in his brain, echoing down corridors and through empty rooms.

He was scared white now.

By God, what he was thinking, what he was feeling, and, yes, *knowing*…it was not good, not good at all. His breath would barely come and his limbs felt rubbery. There was a weight in his belly that did not belong there.

He cocked the pistol.

He stepped into Mandy's room.

The stink was worse in there. Whatever had come into the house had spent some time in this room. By the light of the lamp, Oates could see a dirty stain on the bed coverlet like somebody filthy from the fields had sat there. Elizabeth had packed away those precious few toys of Mandy's...the wooden blocks and spellers, the flaxen-haired dolls she'd made for her, the rubber ball and crayon box. Sure, they were all packed away, but there on the floor, amongst the dirty prints and stink, Mandy's jacks were all laid out as if she had been playing with them.

And maybe she had.

As he came out of the room, sweating and shaking, he realized something that he hadn't before. Something that he should've thought of right off. The dog. Boots, their old hound... he wasn't barking. Goddamned dog, he barked at anything. The moon slid behind a cloud and he barked. But right now, out in the yard...it was dead quiet.

Where the hell was that damn dog?

He followed the prints into the little parlor and there was Boots. Blood was splattered right up the walls, dripping off the arm of the loveseat. Looked like a calf had been slaughtered in there. But it was just the dog. He'd been eviscerated, gutted right there by the hearth, his jaws wide and foaming and red, his viscera pulled out in a tangle of snakes. His throat had been torn out. From the trail of ichor smeared across the floor, Oates figured the dog had been killed outside and then dragged in here.

He was still warm.

Elizabeth's rocking chair was still moving. The seat cushions were black with dirt. A loop of the dog's intestines was tossed over one of the chair's armrests, just abandoned there like a scarf someone had been knitting. Whoever had been sitting in the chair had been playing with it, gnawing on it, just waiting and waiting, covered with dog blood and hairs, smelling the stink of slaughtered dog and maybe enjoying it.

The prints were black with blood now. Oates followed them to the steps leading to the loft above. He held up the lantern, expecting to see some smiling white-faced wraith staring down at him, but there was nothing. Only those bloody prints that led up but did not come back down. Whoever had made them was waiting up there, behind the door.

Oates let out an involuntary groan at the idea of it.

It's up there. It's waiting for you.

As he climbed the narrow stairs, he could hear breathing. Yes, it was waiting for him with teeth and claws or a purloined knife, but it was surely waiting and there was no love in its heart…just a riven, unspeakable blackness that it had brought out of the grave with it.

Do what you got to do, son. That ain't yer daughter waiting in the darkness. Can't say what it is exactly, only that it ain't human. It's just something that came out of its crypt with murder in its heart. Cold, walking meat. Meat pretending to be a little girl…

He couldn't take it much longer.

There came a point when even stark madness was better than the things you saw in your brain. The graying faces and dead eyes and pale mouths swimming in for a kiss. No, sometimes it was better to look insanity in the eye and be seen.

When he got to the top of the steps, he could hear a voice humming behind the door. A scratching, sibilant voice that was like Mandy's, but not exactly. More like Mandy being impersonated by something that had been gargling with glass shards and cemetery dirt, chewing on meat.

Oates grasped the brass knob.

It began to turn in his hand and he gasped.

The door swung open and Mandy was standing there, mildew grown green and thick at her throat and down the sleeves of her dirty burial dress. Her eyes were yellow and reptilian, glaring with a stark madness. An earthworm twisted fatly in her hair. Something black was smeared all over her pale, bloated face. She reached out with shriveled fingers, rank earth dropping from her in clots, a vapid grin on her face.

"Dad…dee," she gurgled.

Oates felt something like a scream shattering in his head. He took one flailing step back, words coming to his tongue that made no sense even to him. Mandy stepped forward stinking of hot, boiling carrion. He could smell her breath…cold and offensive with the smell of dog bowels and dead things she'd been chewing on.

"God forgive me," he said and brought up his Navy Colt.

And pulled the trigger.

3

Two days after he'd buried his daughter's remains for the second time, he came out of the madness that had shaken him like a wet dog. There had been fever and nightmares and a cool acceptance of insanity, but now, like a storm that lays waste to the countryside, it was passing.

Oates couldn't remember much after he put that bullet in his dead daughter's head. Just some weird confused mess of him wrapping her in a blanket and carrying her back out to the graveyard, putting her back in her ruptured coffin, filling in the grave with his bare hands, crying and cackling beneath a full moon. Then coming back to the farmhouse, cleaning up the mess she had made...the dog's remains, the muddy prints, that which had sprayed from her skull when he pulled the trigger. Then drinking whiskey and sometimes screaming his throat raw, falling to the floor and pounding his fists.

Now all of it seemed distant and unreal.

Mandy had come back from the dead and there was no getting around that. Like Lazarus, she had kicked her way out of that box and come calling.

But it wasn't Mandy.

He knew that like he knew his left hand. Mandy was sweet and caring and loving, but what had come out of the grave wearing her skin, well, it was something else entirely. Something born of hate and filth and degenerate evil. It had been no more human, no more capable of love and compassion than a leech sucking the blood from your leg or a jackal gnawing on bones it had pulled from a tomb.

But how to explain it?

How to take something like that in and keep standing, not fall down and scream yourself mad? There was only one way to do it and Oates found it: hatred. Bitter, unrelenting hatred that burned like sulfur in his belly, seething and consuming until his very soul was blazing hot and white. This was what would get him through the weeks to come and this was what would feed him and keep him alive. This was what would put him on the trail of whatever had done this to Mandy.

His madness evaporating in the burning light of vengeance, he made himself a hot bath and scrubbed himself clean, shaved and pulled on a pair of striped trousers, a cotton shirt, vest and frock coat, high-shafted trail boots. Then he made some coffee and drank it from a tin cup out on the porch, thinking and remembering and plotting. It was morning and the air still carried a chill. He stared out over his alfalfa fields and corn, the barn and cribs beyond. The countryside was beautiful. Green and lush and rolling, cut by stands of cottonwood and aspen. In the distance, he could see the mountains rising up, looking purple and red in the early morning light, the slopes green with juniper and pinion pine.

Yes, it was fine land, rich and healthy and vibrant. Beautiful.

But beneath that beauty there was a horror that was real and wasting. For there was a malignancy chewing at the belly of Churchill County, something that had fastened itself like a parasite and was sucking the blood out drop by drop. Oates did not know what it was, but he could sense it there, whatever it was, growing fat and full on purloined life, something insidious and ravenous that had slipped up from the slimy cellars of hell with diabolic intent, stuffing its guts with the bones of men and women and, yes, children.

Such a thing could not be allowed to exist.

He knew it wasn't just Mandy. He could think of two dozen others that had died in the past month, people he'd known and worked and drank with. Farmers and storekeepers and miners. Just common, ordinary folk that had been put into their graves by a contagion that was like no contagion that could be imagined. Now, Doc Rifer was saying yellow fever, but the epidemic facing the county was surely not yellow fever. Maybe it mocked the symptoms of the black vomit, as yellow fever was sometimes known, but it was surely something else. Doc Rifer was a good man, a wise man, but there were things even beyond his scope, beyond the ken of all mortal men and this was surely one of them.

Sitting there, Oates pulled out one of his home-rolled cigarettes and lit it. He pulled off it, letting his mind drift off. Yes, quite a few that he knew had perished of the fever and quite a few more than he did not know. People in that county were basically simple. Farmers and miners and retailers, they understood basically what they could hold in their hands. Most went to church and most said they believed in the Lord God, but he knew that sometimes faith was not so much deep-felt as a matter of tradition. If it's what your parents did and what your neighbors were doing, then you would do it, too. True faith was exceptionally rare, regardless of what people said or pretended. The people of Churchill County were a good sort, hard-working and mostly honest. They did not let religion nor superstition steer them any more than was necessary, they worked the land and raised their families and drew their strength mainly from the good earth itself. They had very little patience with the unknown and the unseen.

But now, that had changed.

People were clutching crucifixes and Bibles, sleeping with prayer books under their pillows. They were hanging garlic and St. John's wort at their windows, nailing horseshoes over their doors and sprinkling salt at their thresholds. Many were inviting Reverends Fisher and Shockley from the Congregational Church to come and bless their homes. And quite a few had even asked Crazy Bob, the tent show revivalist, to do the same. Oates did not see this as a deep conversion of faith, but as a symptom of the disease which was taking root all around them. For here was a disease, an ailment, something intangible that Doc Rifer could not get under his brass microscope or separate in a test tube, and it scared them. They were afraid of shadows and vapors and knocking at their doors in the dead of night. There were vague whispers, some of them not so vague, concerning the dead that would not stay dead.

Oates had dismissed it all, spooks and ghost stories and witch-tales, but now he knew better.

But he wasn't about to hide from any of it. There was something evil afoot and it would not be vanquished by hiding and praying and making Indian sign outside your door and hanging charms about. He was going to hunt it down. He was going to get his hands on whatever was responsible and crush it beneath his fists, feel its bones snapping and its vile blood running out in creeks and rivers.

With that in mind, he went in the house and began to make plans.

In his bedroom, he looked at himself in the mirror, something he'd been afraid to do, fearing the acute physical change that grief and madness must have left upon him. His dark hair had gone gray at the roots and his mustache was flecked with silver. There were deep-etched lines at his mouth and eyes that had not been there a few weeks previous. The face he saw looking back at him was intense and angry and resolute, the face of a man that had been pushed too goddamn far and was about to start pushing back.

Amen to that.

4

Throughout the day, he made the rounds on his dappled mare, doing that which pained him, but had to be done. He visited farms and ranches, cabins and far-flung mining camps in the hills talking with laborers and farmers and hard-rock miners, just about anyone who had lost a family member or friend to the fever. Some would not speak of it, but a surprising number of others willingly invited Oates into their confidences, speaking of the fever, the burials, and what had taken place afterward. He heard horror stories that day, but he listened and accepted and they gladly shared these things with him when they learned what he had been through and that he planned to run this contagion to ground, to burn it out at the roots.

The stories were pretty much the same.

Kin was buried and several nights later, they showed up, pounding at doors after midnight, slaughtering animals, opening graves and feeding on what they found inside. Quite a few that witnessed these things went mad. A few had been murdered by their newly-risen wives and fathers, brothers and sisters. It was all insane and incomprehensible, but the pattern was there for eyes that wished to see.

Those that died of the fever were returning from the grave.

And not as haunts that tapped at windows or moaned in the night, but as malefic, predatory things, ghouls that fed on the dead and cannibals that preyed on the living. Oates had put a bullet in Mandy's head. That had put her down and this seemed to be the accepted method.

Aim for the head every time.

He heard all manner of tales that day. Things about the walking dead slipping into houses and biting kinfolk or simply lying in their old beds or sitting at supper tables and saying the most awful things. Secret things they could not know. But what was most interesting was that the name of a town in the desert called Crowley kept coming to the fore. Something had happened there that nobody really wanted to talk about and it all had to do with some negro whore called Black Betty that had supposedly raised the Devil.

These were the things Oates told Doc Rifer about that evening in his book-lined study. Rifer argued with him, of course, but not for long.

"I'm going up to Crowley, Doc, and I'm going to burn this blight out or die trying," he said. "You can believe all this or not, but I plan on running this evil to ground and there ain't a damn thing you can say to stop me."

Rifer didn't bother trying. "Crowley. Yes, I've heard about that pest-hole and more than once. Place is deserted now, Daniel. If you plan on going out there, you might want to stop by a little village called Compton on your way. It's maybe three or four miles this side of Crowley. You want to know about that place, Compton would make a good beginning."

"Was planning on stopping by anyhow," Oates said.

Rifer swallowed. "Daniel...have you ever heard the term 'zombie'?"

"Not that comes to mind."

"It's essentially a superstition from the West Indies, Haiti, and Guadeloupe. People there believe that a witch doctor of sorts has the power to raise the dead."

"Maybe that's what we got right here. Maybe that Black Betty came from there. Don't know and don't honestly care, Doc. Because I know where that bitch is going and that's straight to hell."

"Be careful, Daniel."

"I will." Oates went to the door, paused. "If I wasn't to come back, please take care of Elizabeth."

5

Oates did not see himself as a savior, some messiah coming down to ride herd on the Devil. He was just a man, no better and no worse than any other man. Only difference between himself and the others was that he had had enough. This sickness, this fever, this plague of sorts had been allowed to dig deep and fester. And if it hadn't, maybe Mandy would have still been alive. Maybe and maybe not. Now its roots were running deep and it would be no easy matter to cut it out, but Oates figured it was time somebody got their knife out and that somebody just happened to be him.

The day he rode into Compton on his mare, he was riding about as high and randy as any man a week on the trail. He was blown with desert dust, his teeth full of grit. Those that looked at him as he came in quickly looked away, maybe not liking the gleam in his eye that was like gypsum winking back yellow moonlight.

Compton wasn't much.

A few rows of tall brick-fronted crackerbox buildings with false cornices, some plank shacks and log houses set in-between, a couple dirt roads intersecting the lot. Oates saw a tent-roofed saloon, a couple bunkhouses, a boarded-up dance hall and lots of signs weathered illegible by the wind-driven sand. He saw the finger of a church steeple in the distance, but other than that, not much. The town was dying a slow death out in this dry, suffocating desolation. There'd been a gold mine and refinery up in the hills at one time, but that had played out a few years before and now Compton was anemic and looking for a deep grave to crawl into.

He kneed his mare to a walk and pulled reign outside the saloon, tying her off at the hitch rail out front. He stepped out onto the warped board sidewalk, pulling his sawed-off American 12-gauge from the saddle scabbard. A couple Mexicans were sitting out front, eating peppers from dirty jars and smoking thin brown paper cigarettes.

A kid came running up, stopping just before Oates and giving him the once over. "Ya'll want me to water and hay your mount, mister?"

The kid wore a grimy sodbuster hat and corduroy trousers with holes in the knees. Oates wasn't sure if those were freckles on his face or spots of dirt. But, then, that was this whole goddamn town...nothing but dirt and dust every way you turned.

"Be obliged," Oates told him.

"She'll be down at the livery yonder when you need her, mister."

Oates went into the saloon, the rough-hewn batwings creaking on leather hinges. Inside, it wasn't much. A few beaten-looking men were sipping beer and playing hands of Seven Up and five-card. A round, greasy man behind the bar was mopping sweat from his brow. He didn't even ask Oates what he wanted to drink.

And that was the feeling he was getting from the rest of them, too, and maybe that whole goddamned town as well: lethargy, inaction, and stagnation. They were sticks of furniture, inanimate things watching the dust settle and the flies buzz. Like wooden Indians standing outside cigar stores waiting for pigeon shit and little boys to scratch their initials into them.

No, he did not like the feel of Compton. The town was doomed, filled with ghosts of what was and what could never be again. And these men were content with that. Just worms sliding through its carcass.

"Whiskey," he said, setting his shotgun on the bar, hoping the barkeep would tell him to put his gun someplace else, because the way he was feeling, he just might've.

Sure, this is Compton in the last stages of fever, he found himself thinking, *slowly going to dirt and rot. The good men are all gone or dead, and this is what's left. Weak-eyed, gutless scavengers. That's why Crowley has been allowed to spread its contagion, because these shitters either don't give a damn or they're too goddamned scared to do more than drink and piss and sleep.*

The stink of apathy and cowardice bubbled like molasses over a low flame. A real low flame. As Oates drank his whiskey—kind of gritty as if it was full of sand like everything else—he took in the atmosphere of the place which wasn't far removed from an alley privy: close and crowded and dim, stinking of sweat and silence. The men slouched over drinks and gripping oily dog-eared cards with grubby hands were just an extension of the saloon itself. None of them would even look Oates in the face as if maybe they were afraid of what they might see in his eyes and what it would tell them about themselves.

He sipped his whiskey, pulled out a cigarette and lit it. He leaned against the bar in his dusty wool pants and gray vest, sweat-stained shirt and pinch-crowned Stetson. He had his Colt Navy sixes set in low-slung gun belts, butts forward. Usually, in a place like that, the kind of hardware he was carrying would have attracted some attention, mostly the wrong kind. But here? No, just blatant disinterest. *Welcome to Compton, stranger. Sit a spell and have a slug of whiskey. Please excuse us while we don't give a high-stepping fuck.*

Oates drew off his cigarette, still trying to make eye contact with someone. No dice. Seven men and not a stick of curiosity to be had.

"Gentlemen," he finally said. "Name's Daniel Oates. Got me a spread outside Stillwater up north. Reckon you've been through there, you hung your hat in Nevada Territory any length of time. Here's to you and yours. Round of whiskey, barkeep."

There were a few grunts of assent from those gathered. Not much else. The bartender passed out the whiskey and the men drank it with all the enthusiasm of bored cats lapping up milk. Again, disinterest in just about anything.

There was one with a spark in him, though. An old party

with a tangled white beard and a dirty flannel shirt. He sat in the back well away from the others. He actually looked at Oates beneath his Southwestern sombrero, nodded, and tapped the blackened stem of his corncob pipe on the table. "Thanks kindly, stranger," he said.

Oates flicked the ash off his cigarette. "Now that we've made acquaintances, maybe one of you would like to tell me about a town near here. Deserted, they're saying. Some kind of funny business about it. You know the place I mean? I'm guessing you do."

"Crowley," a voice said.

One man swore under his breath and left his whiskey untouched, went right out the door. Another followed quick on his heels, grumbling and kicking a stool out of his way. That whittled down Oates's new acquaintances to a lean five. And other than the old man who kept watching him with a surly grin, the others just plain pretended he did not exist. Or maybe that he was a bad stink that would clear given time.

"Yep, Crowley would be the place I'm thinking of, boys. Been hearing some funny things about what went on there and what might be still going on."

One of the men playing five-card laid his hand flat on the table. He stroked a well-waxed mustache. "Ain't nobody in Crowley, mister. Was some silver veins near there, but they's all dry now. Just as dead as Crazy Horse's left nut."

A few men grunted at that. Maybe it was supposed to be laughter.

Oates nodded. "Don't say? Not what I been hearing at all. Folks is saying some mighty peculiar shit went on up in Crowley. I think I heard something about dead people that don't wanna stay dead."

Mustache laughed at that, but it was tinny, off-key laughter that sounded awful pained. "Shit, boy, only Lazarus ever did come back other than the Messiah hisself."

"Well, I'll tell you, what I'm talking about here has little to do with Jesus and the saints and everything to do with the Devil." Oates took a drag off his cigarette. "Now, question is, are you boys gonna sit there and dance a jig with me, take turns blowing smoke up my ass, or are you gonna start telling me the way things really are?"

"I think," Mustache said, "you ought to get on your horse and ride back up to Stillwater. I'm figuring you ain't gonna like Compton much. Because Compton ain't Stillwater. And Crowley? You'd best just leave that lick of hell alone, hope it leaves you alone, too."

Oates crushed his cigarette under his boot. "So that's it, eh? The lot of you are just going to sit here holding them goddamned chairs down while that cancer breeds on your doorstep?"

"Sometimes, mister, sometimes it's best to walk around a rattler rather than trying to stomp it," Mustache said. "Some things got teeth. Some things tend to bite if you interfere with their ways."

There was logic there, Oates figured, but not the sort he cared for. Sure, you might not get bit if you kept your hand out of that den of rattlesnakes up in Crowley. But on the other hand, sooner or later, those snakes might decide they needed more living space. Maybe another town.

Oates said, "Okay, boys, I'm done greasing you. I came here looking for men to ride with me on Crowley. Men who'd had enough, men who were ready to burn out that graveyard up there. But I'm guessing you boys are not those men."

"You guessed right," Mustache said. "And the last god-damned thing we need is for some stranger to be riding up there and stirring things up. So, do us all a favor, and go on back home."

"Well, friend, I'd dearly love to do that, but my home ain't exactly much of a home anymore," Oates said. "See, this epidemic we got in the county, it ain't just thick here in Compton. It's everywhere. People are catching some sort of fever, dying, and then a few nights later they're climbing back up out of their graves—"

"Shut up," Mustache said. "You just shut up with that crazy talk."

Oates shook his head. "Nope, don't plan on it."

"Then I'll be leaving, because I don't have to listen to this."

Oates pulled one of his Colt Navy .44s. He brought it up

fast and without hesitation. And he put it right on Mustache. "Now, I don't consider it real friendly of you to walk out in the middle of my story. In fact, I think it's downright fucking rude. So either sit your ass down or they'll be sweeping bits of your skull out the door come morning."

Mustache sat down. He was pissed-off and reckless right then, but he wasn't wearing a gun. His friends were, but none of them liked the idea of drawing on Oates. You'd been around enough hell-for-leather mining camps, you got to know when there was murder in a man's eyes and there was no doubt of it with Oates.

"So, where was I? Oh yeah, now that fever's spreading. Nobody knows how. Maybe it's the hot dry wind that's been blowing. Who can say? Only thing anyone can figure for sure is that it's blowing straight out of Crowley." Oates took another slug of whiskey. "Now, a couple weeks back my Mandy Catherine got sick, real sick, you see? Fever and sweats, skin gone yellow like the camp fever took her. Vomiting black blood and just wasting away until she just couldn't fight it no more. So we put her in the ground, we put my little girl in the ground. Eight years old and we put her in the fucking ground—"

"That's enough!" Mustache shouted, standing up and making for the door. "I won't listen to this! You can't make me listen to this!"

Oates didn't hesitate. Burning up inside and just sick with the memory of Mandy, he pulled the trigger and put a slug right through Mustache's back. It threw him up against the wall, leaving a glistening spray of blood and tissue in its wake. He staggered two or three steps and went face-down.

"You killed him," the bartender said. "You killed him."

"Yes, I did. Same way I'm going to kill the next man that opens his piss hole and interrupts what I'm trying to say." Oates lit himself another cigarette. "Okay, so we put my girl in the ground and a few days later? Well, a few days later she comes home. Decides to kill our old hound and then sit in my wife's rocking chair and chew on the guts. Now ain't that a pretty fucking picture? How can such a thing be? That's what I asked myself. But I didn't have any good goddamned answers until

I waltzed into this stinking shithole. Then I knew. God yes, I knew. My daughter died because you goddamn ass-sucking cowards were too damned afraid to take care of business! Too damned afraid to get some iron in your pants and ride up there and set things to right!"

"Don't you think we wanted to?" one of the others said now, his eyes sick and scared. "Don't you think we all wanted to go up there and burn that snake pit out? That we're all just dog-sick of hiding behind locked doors when the sun goes down and jumping every time a stick snaps out in the yard or there's a knock on the door? Do you think we like that?"

Oates leathered his Colt. He'd had enough. "I'm guessing you must. Well, good day to you all. I can't honestly stand the sight of you people anymore, so I'm riding up to Crowley. You can expect me by nightfall. I'll be bringing Black Betty with me, on account she's real anxious to make your acquaintance."

With that, Oates stepped over Mustache's corpse and went out into the blazing sunshine. He'd barely made it down the road before someone came up behind him. It was the old man from the saloon. "You looking for them what eats folks, eh? Well, then, you're gonna need some help."

6

Pumped hard with attitude and about as ready as he figured he'd ever get, Oates went over to the livery and got himself a fresh mount, a coal-black gelding rippling with muscle. Once he'd transferred his double-rig saddle and bags, he mounted and started riding out.

Weeds—the old man—was with him, of course, riding on his gelding.

And once he started talking, look out, he was like a leaky faucet you just couldn't turn off. Try as you might, you just couldn't put a kink in his hose. As they rode out of Compton, the words flowed and flowed out of the old man. It seemed there wasn't anything he hadn't done or hadn't seen. He'd cut trail with Jim Bridger in the Rockies and hunted buffalo in Kansas, been a Confederate sharpshooter at Gettysburg and laid track for the

Union Pacific line, panned for gold during the California rush in '49 and fought the Bannock in Idaho back in '78. And that didn't take into account getting drunk with Wild Bill Hickok, fighting the Comanche in Texas, or how he helped corner Sam Bass and his gang at Round Rock.

"Yes sir, I would suspect I've done just about everything and been just about everywhere," Weeds said, seemingly proud of himself. Then he frowned, spit tobacco juice over his left shoulder. "'Course, stranger, there are certain things I've never had much interested in doing, certain holes I'd prefer not to be sticking this old pecker of mine if a choice is offered. I'm figuring Crowley is one of them places."

"Maybe you ain't up to this, old man," Oates said. "You turn back now, I won't think any less of you."

"Turn back?" Weeds looked like he was ready to start swinging. His hand actually went for the Remington Army .44 in his holster. "Son, now you listen to me and you listen real good. I might not look like much and maybe you think I'm full of more shit than a greenhorn's pants, but get this: I don't tuck my willy between my legs and run. Never have, never will. I've ridden hard since long before you had hair on your little balls. I've been beaten and shot, hanged and stabbed. A Kiowa war party tried to roast me alive one time and when I was an Express rider, I pulled arrows out of my ass like quills from a porcupine. But I didn't back down and I didn't turn tail. I've pissed blood by the buckets and grinned whilst I did it. Now, I don't know, not really, what we're riding into, but I'll be at your side. I'll fight with you and I'll die with you and if we make it back out, I'll get drunk with you."

"Okay, old man, don't get your dander up."

"Don't get my dander up, he says. Shit and shit."

Oates almost smiled at that and he hadn't smiled in a long time. "Okay, old man. We should be riding into Crowley within the hour if your calculations are correct—"

"They are."

"—and before then, I think you better tell me what I need to know. You can start talking anytime now."

Weeds cut another chew from his plug and worked it

between his jaw and gum. "Well, stranger, I know most of it, I'm thinking. Maybe more than I care to know. See, about ten years back, Crowley had itself a couple silver mines run by the Silver Horn combine out of Utah Territory. Had a pretty refinery up there, the works. There were near on five thousand people squatting in Crowley and then things went to shit. I'm not sure which happened first. Maybe the veins dried out or maybe that hoodoo bitch Black Betty blew in on a storm of disease and misery." Weeds shrugged, studied the hardpan desert that stretched as far as they could see. "All I can say is that it was about that time things started getting a little funny in Crowley."

Maybe "funny" wasn't the right word for something that was damnably disturbing, demented, and just plain spooky. Black Betty was a prostitute out of Baton Rouge, came to town in a wagon with a dozen alley cats, bought herself a hotel and turned it into a high-dollar brothel within six months. Black Betty christened it the Dark Star, maybe on account of her skin color and the fact that she'd once worked for a cathouse called the Star of India in Baton Rouge. No matter, it wasn't long before Betty and her crew of meat-eaters were turning greenbacks by the buckets and pissing gold coins.

But there was always talk, funny talk about Black Betty and her girls and how they passed their time in their off-hours.

"Some of it was pretty damned crazy, stranger, I'll tell you that much," Weeds told him. "Horseshit about them girls practicing root-lore and witchcraft and herb-doctoring. Even heard a few tall ones about devil-worship and the like. No matter, maybe some were concerned about that shit, but men in general didn't stop going to the Dark Star to get a taste of that imported kitty up there. And weren't none of it cheap, mind you. Most of them alley cats in Black Betty's stable would cost you four or five hundred Union for a slap and a tickle. But that's a mining town, ain't it? When money's being pulled out of the ground, prices tend to inflate."

One of the worst stories that filtered out of the Dark Star came from a fellow named Harnes or Harmes, Weeds couldn't be sure which. He was some dandy out of Georgia with money to burn. Thought he'd come west for some hunting and some hell-raising. He was a regular over at the Dark Star. One night after hours, so he claimed, he slipped down into the cellar, said he heard chanting down there. He got down there and saw Black Betty and her sisters of the flesh standing around naked by candlelight singing some song that tore something loose in his mind. Or maybe it was what he saw…some fellow nailed to an upside down cross like a sacrifice. The girls were all painted up with funny letters and symbols.

"They were using that poor bastard's blood, stranger, doing a little finger-painting," Weeds said. "Any of that true? Hell knows. The town marshal was this idiot name of Rawley Cook, just some hot gun on the payroll of the mine. He went over to the Dark Star for a look-see but didn't find anything to support that Georgia cracker's allegations. It was probably bullshit, anyhow…but then, I knew Rawley and he was dumber than a dog turd on a doily."

Well, Weeds said, things went on and on as they do. He couldn't exactly say if there really was any truth to the devil-worship business, but there *was* something he had seen with his own eyes, not that it honestly amounted to much. But all those girls at the Dark Star, they all wore a funny necklace or amulet around their throats. He said it looked like a crescent moon with a snake coiled around it. A very odd thing and quite a few people had commented on them. But they were always commenting on something about the Dark Star. Things like the voices you might hear in the room next to your own that sounded like they came from some old hag speaking a language that didn't sound natural or the fact that Black Betty ordered an awful lot of livestock for her and her girls. Livestock they butchered themselves.

"Just between you and me and the sweat on my nuts, stranger, I'll be honest as a Christian coming to preach and admit to you, here and now, that I did not care for those girls. Don't look at me like that for chrissake. I mean, sure I liked to look at 'em because these were some sweet imported candies… but something about 'em, well it just left me cold." Weeds fell silent like he was thinking over what he had just said. "There was something funny in their eyes. Something that got down inside you and just didn't want to leave. Looking in their eyes, I don't know, but it was like staring into the eyes of a cow skull in the desert, you know? Nothing in there, nothing warm or human exactly, just this sense that whatever was *supposed* to be in there had been picked clean."

He admitted that it didn't make much sense. About all he could say was that those whores were hollow where they should have been full. Something inside them was gone and something else was living there. He likened it to hermit crabs you'd see on the beach. They'd steal snail shells and the like, crawl inside and set up housekeeping. The girls were like that... just shells. Wasn't nothing inside them, so something else had slipped in there, but something that just did not belong.

Oates listened and did not judge. It all sounded like some high and happy horseshit, but after what he'd seen and knew to be true, he wasn't about to laugh any of it off. Devil-worship and storybook witches flying on brooms? Well, sure, why the hell not?

Weeds kept talking as they made their way across the salt desert. The sun was blazing overhead, nothing the eye could see below but sand and rocks, some stands of giant cactus, yucca plants and agave. Now and again some greasewood or creosote brush. They saw a few sidewinder rattlesnakes, some spiny lizards skittering amongst the rocks, not much else save for turkey vultures circling high above looking for something gamy to peck on.

Weeds wiped sweat and flies from his face, said, "Now I suppose I should tell you about one of Black Betty's girls, the one they called Georgia Peach. Now she was something...blonde and blue-eyed with tits that would make your mouth water. She was a real Fancy Sal, that one. She was some kind of European treasure from across the pond and couldn't speak much of the King's English, but with them looks, nobody cared. Least, not at first. Georgia Peach was a real dainty dish, stranger, and if you wanted to jump that stuff it would cost you a grand. And there were plenty that paid it."

She was real popular, despite the high prices. Mainly it was mining executives that could afford her, some of the ranchers from up north. But eventually some real strange things began to be said about Georgia Peach. She was fine to look at, but you had to be careful if you touched her. She got pretty wild in the hay, Weeds said, and stories circulated about her biting men and scratching them up bad. There was a dirt-evil streak in her and you could see it in her eyes, that hunger that made you feel like a joint of meat pulled from a roaster. It came to a head of sorts when it was claimed that Georgia Peach slit some miner's throat while he was putting the business to her. One of his friends came in and saw her chewing at the wound, licking at what spilled out. People said it wasn't the first time. That Georgia Peach had slit more than one throat.

"Leastways, that's what was being said, stranger. Do I believe it? Yes sir, I do. Why? Because I don't claim to have seen it or known the man she slit, but I *did* know the feller what came into that room and discovered the crime." Weeds wiped tobacco juice off his chin. "Feller's name was Lyle Denehew, a hardscrabble miner that struck the mother lode. I saw Lyle a few weeks after his friend...some investor out of Detroit...was killed. Lyle told me all about it. Said he heard a funny sound next door. Him and his lady were all finished up, said he heard something like rain strike the wall, then a gurgling sound. For some reason, it set on him wrong. He went next door and stepped inside. Saw it all by candlelight. That friend of his was right on top of Georgia Peach and she still had those long legs of hers wrapped around him and was grinding into him. And that would have been fine, but there was blood all over her...splattered up the wall and her mouth was at his friend's throat. Even when he came in, he could hear that she-devil sucking at his throat.

"Lyle said something went cold inside him just looking at that horror. Georgia Peach saw him and pulled her mouth away from his throat, had a razor in her hand that looked like it had been dipped in red ink. She pushed Lyle's friend off of her and he hit the floor with a thud like a hundred and fifty pounds of cold Texas beef. Then Georgia Peach? Well, she slid off the bed, just soaked with blood. Her arms were covered in it, her tits and belly, her face. When she grinned...and she did grin, Lyle said, like a hyena with a mouth full of carrion...her teeth were stained red, bits of tissue hanging from her mouth like confetti…"

It was a repellent, hideous story, but Weeds saw it through. His friend Lyle ran out of there, wearing nothing but his britches and never came back. When the marshal got there, stewed on Mescal, he found a lot of blood, but no body and no Georgia Peach. Bed was soaked red, spirals of blood sprayed over the walls. The window was wide open and the sill had bloody prints on it, but that was about it. It looked like the body and what dragged it off went right out the damn window two stories up.

"Did they ever find her?" Oates asked.

"Oh yes, she showed a few days later, claimed ignorance of the entire event. Black Betty was tight with the Silver Horn execs who controlled Rawley Cook, the marshal, and the whole thing was swept under the carpet. And Georgia Peach? Well, stranger, no jury would ever have convicted her. Maybe she was some kind of bloodsucking witch in the sack, but out of it, just as fine and beautiful of a lady as you could imagine. Those blue eyes would have melted anyone."

But it was hardly at an end.

Georgia Peach was taken off the market by Black Betty. Maybe so she'd stop killing men and maybe because Black Betty was afraid somebody might decide to put a stake through her heart. One of the rumors circulating was that Georgia Peach was locked up in some room in the attic and fed raw meat, but Weeds said that was probably just a story. Who could say? But one thing was for sure, the girl liked to wander about town in the wee hours dressed in a cloak and folks were always afraid of meeting up with her on some lonesome road. People didn't see much of her, but when they did they said she was awful pale and those eyes of hers were enough to melt nail heads. Whenever she was out, a couple of girls went with her.

And then, one night, she slipped out on her own.

"Here's what happened, stranger: Georgia Peach had a real nasty reputation by that time, folks saying she was a hell-witch and a ghoul. Some squatter's kid went missing and people were pretty certain who'd gotten the boy. Kid's window was open and, well, people figured some evil wench in a cloak had slipped in there and taken the kid away. Maybe up to the grave-yard yonder to have herself a midnight feast. They never did find the kid's remains. Which is probably a good thing.

"Now, one night Georgia Peach got out, was walking around town by herself and she met up with some friends of that Detroit investor. Lyle claimed he was not among them. They took her to a barn somewhere and took their turns raping her. Yes sir, raped her harder than the U.S. government raped the Sioux Nation. That's the story that was told, anyhow. But, all liquored up and out of their heads, these boys got carried away even further. They took a couple axes and chopped that bitch up, sectioned her like a Christmas hog ready for the spit. Then, apparently, they bagged her up and took her parts over to the Dark Star and dumped 'em on the porch. Stuck her head on the newel post like a Halloweeny pumpkin.

"And that, my friend, set off the mother of all firestorms. See, Black Betty loved that girl. Loved Georgia Peach like she were kin. And the girl's murder put her right over the edge. Black Betty was this tall, leggy negress with a butter-soft Louisiany accent that would make you shoot your load right in your pants. Tall and high-titted, all that dark hair hanging down the middle of her back, and green eyes, green eyes like fine emeralds sunk in sweet chocolate. I saw her only once and despite those looks, she was not the sort of dark meat a man would want his busi-ness anywhere near. Not if he favored it, that was. On a good day, those green eyes would make your knees weak and make your heart pound. But on a bad day? That look of hers would strip the meat from your bones."

Black Betty, story had it, was not just some fancy chocolate whore out of Baton Rouge, but some wicked witch that had been run out of town for casting the evil eye and bringing the plague, all manner of things. It was said she liked to lay around nights wearing nothing but a necklace of animal bones and reading to her girls from rotting leather books written in Latin.

"Well, Black Betty was beside herself. Rawley Cook, never exactly sober, made an investigation and decided the same one that had killed that Detroit investor had killed Georgia Peach.

Utter horseshit and everyone knew it, but it looked fine on
paper. Now Black Betty, she closed up shop, shut the Dark Star
down for mourning and it never did open up again. People said
she nailed it tighter than a pine box. The girls were not seen outside of those walls. You could see lots of candlelight in the windows at night like the girls were going up and down the stairs
and from room to room in a candlelight procession. That only
fed the wild rumors of devil-worship and witching and all that
pagan business. Black Betty wasn't trying to discourage it either,
on account her doorstep was decorated up with all manner of
spooky voodoo shit. There were these garlands strung from
the porch overhang made out of the boiled white vertebrae of
rattlesnakes with dozens of little rodent bones sticking out at all
kinds of crazy angles. Those garlands were set with the skulls
of cats and rats and you name it like crazy skeleton sculptures.
When the wind blew, those hanging bones rattled and clattered.
There was some kind of decoration over the door made out of
a wagon wheel of cow femurs with a big gape-jawed wolf skull
sitting right dead center. Lots of pelts, wax-and-feather gris-gris,
and dried plants hanging about. Pots of some smelly concoction
simmering away night and day. Goddamn porch was looking
like a witch doctor's hut from what people said. It scared the
shit out of everyone, but there was no law against it.

"Now that much, stranger, is fact, but what else was being
said was surely bunk. But people have good imaginations,
don't they? And particularly with how the Dark Star was decorated. Well, what they were saying was that something was flying over the rooftops at night. Something bigger than a man
with wide outstretched bat's wings and a head like deformed
vulture's skull with curled back horns. Folks claimed it would
swoop about in the moonlight and maybe it did. They said this
monster or devil, whichever you want, was roosting in the attic
of the Dark Star, snatching away folks in the dead of night and
lining its nest with their skin and bones. That you could hear it
screeching and roaring up there at night. They were also saying Black Betty had called it out of hell to hunt down those that
had killed Georgia Peach. Six men disappeared in a two-week
stretch and that devil-bird was then no more seen."

It was getting deeper all the time, Oates thought. He had to accept the walking dead because he'd seen it. But witches and flying devils and what have you…he just didn't know if he could buy into that. If any of it was even remotely true, Crowley was most certainly the town the Devil built.

Weeds said that what happened next was just as weird.

One night during the dark phase of the moon, Black Betty climbed up onto the sharp-peaked roof of the Dark Star and started chanting things and calling out words into the sky above. Whatever she had been saying scared the piss out of everyone and people locked their doors and bolted their windows. Saloons emptied and churches filled. That night, as she screamed vile words into the wind from her high perch, things happened. The clouds boiled black in the sky and Crowley shook as if from an earth tremor. Windows shattered and lean-tos and tumbledown shacks fell right over. The cross high up on the steeple of the Congregational Church fell right off and was found the next day completely melted like somebody had tossed it into a blast furnace. But the very worst thing was that the graveyard up on the hill shook and rumbled like an empty belly. The gates fell off their hinges and tombstones fell over, graves were blown open and the marble vault of some rich miner was desecrated. The iron doors swung wide and a half-dozen coffins were spewed out into the cemetery, what was in them scattered in the weeds and bushes. Weeds said it was like that sepulcher couldn't hold down what was in its belly and decided to vomit it out into the grass.

"I'm surprised by this point," Oates said, lighting one of his cigarettes, "that the people of Crowley didn't go on a witch-hunt and burn Black Betty."

"Maybe they wanted to and maybe they just didn't dare," Weeds said. "Things settled down for a few weeks and I suppose people were hoping it had passed, but it hadn't passed. Black Betty was still holed-up in the brothel and she stopped ordering livestock, but instead wanted all the fresh meat she could get. And it was an awful lot of meat from what people were saying. Now, stranger, about that time the fever began. People started getting sick and dying, the mines ran dry and

Crowley was just a coffin waiting for its lid to be thrown shut.

"Somewhere around then, this whore from the Dark Star was found wandering in the streets with nothing but a blanket wrapped around her. She was filthy and scratched up, just out of her mind, gibbering and drooling and pointing at the sky. She was just plain struck mad. They got her over to the doc's and she was the whole time talking to people no one else could see, listening and answering questions that were being put to her from God-knew-what. The doc shot her up with some morphine, but that barely calmed her. She didn't know what her name was or where she had come from. She kept ranting that there was a plague on the town. When asked about the Dark Star, she said all the girls were dead, that they'd been given to something. Then she'd start rambling on how they were walking around and eating meat. And when asked about that contradiction, she'd say that, yes, the girls were all dead, but something else was living in them, spirits or something without souls. Things that had been waiting centuries to be born..."

Rawley Cook and the doc went over to the Dark Star, ducking and stepping lively around them bones, and talked with Black Betty. She said the girl was not one of hers. Cook later said Black Betty was looking thin and drawn, seemed to be having trouble breathing, smelled like bad meat. When she told them that all her girls had the fever, nobody had any interest in going in there to look around.

"Now, if things weren't bad enough what with the mines closing and the fever making the rounds, something else happened. Something that was witnessed by some very reliable people, stranger."

"And what was that?" Oates asked, almost afraid to.

Weeds looked suddenly sick as if he'd bitten into something rancid. He wiped his mouth and then wiped it again. "On near sundown, but the sun still bright enough where you could see plenty fine...Georgia Peach comes walking right up the road. Sounds like horseshit, don't it? But it's true enough. I knew three people who saw her. Del Whipple ran a smithy shop there, good friend of mine, he saw her same as the others. Del said he almost lost his mind. A couple of folks took one look at what was dragging itself down the road, maybe making for the Dark Star, and plum fainted dead away. You couldn't blame 'em. Georgia Peach had come down from the cemetery maybe, kind of pulling herself along, sort of dragging one leg behind the other. Del said she was naked, gray and blotchy like tombstone marble, all puffy-looking, had this dark fungus-looking stuff growing up from her privates and onto her belly, down her throat and onto her tits. But not so much that you couldn't see that she had been stitched back together like a rag dolly what lost its limbs and stuffing. Black stitching held her arms and legs on, ran from her business to her throat to keep her goodies inside. Her head was threaded to her neck and it hung off to the side like her neck was broken. And her face...yeah, there were stitches running over it like branching lightning, her nose set off to the side, one corner of her lips drawn too tight so that it was up on her cheek. She didn't have but the one eye, the other being a socket packed with graveyard soil. Her hair was full of dirt and worms, flies all over her, maggots dropping from her mouth like rice.

"Del said she stank like spoiled pork, a dirty smell that made your stomach jump into your throat. She was making a funny hissing sound that could maybe have been breathing or that wrecked throat trying to speak. He said that one eye was wide and staring, just insane and bloodshot, and when she put it on you, it made your guts run like sweet jelly. Sure, she was a walking corpse, rotten and stinking and wormy, but there was something in that eye. Something black and deranged and *aware* that knew things and had seen things that would make your mind go to sauce. Del told me that Georgia Peach looked at him like a spider might look at you if it was smarter than you and hungry and you happened to be caught in its web.

"Well, most people ran off, but Del and a few others stayed. They put their guns on her and she laughed at them and that sound was enough to turn your hair white, make you want to crawl under the bed and suck your thumb. Just a scraping, shattered-glass sound coming from that throat full of dirt. Del admitted to me that he actually pissed his pants. Undertaker Clem was there and she looked right at him with that one good eye and the blood drained from his face. She started talking in this awful scratching voice, telling everyone there things she couldn't possibly know. Terrible stuff about how Clem had been doing things perverted and unclean with the bodies of certain females that had come into his parlor. She talked like she'd been inside those corpses when he was...well, humping on 'em. Then she started talking about Clem's daughter Margaret who had passed of the fever a week before. Said how she had dug the child up and chewed on her pussy and bit the tongue out of her mouth, how Black Betty herself had made a shawl out of the girl's skin and had salted her death mask and hung it on the wall.

"But it wasn't only Clem that Georgia Peach...or the thing inside her...directed her ire against. She told another fellow there how his father had been raping his kid sister years before, how he made her suck his cock and swallow what came out. That fellow ran off screaming. Then she turned on Del, told him...told him in his *dead mother's voice* why she had committed suicide when he was five years old. And it wasn't because Del's infant brother, Joshua, had died of the crib death like everyone thought, but because she had lost her mind, gotten tired of his constant crying and pressed a pillow down over the baby's face until it stopped making noise and stopped moving. Del was crying like a baby himself when he told me that part. He said that witch said other things, but he would not...*could not*... repeat them.

"See, stranger, what was living inside of Georgia Peach's shell was not human, it was just black and dirty and foul, something without a soul just like that crazy whore had said. Something that was never meant to live, a filth that was never meant to be born. It had seen the other side, torn through the veil of death, and it knew all the tormented secrets of the dead. Things no man should ever, ever know."

Despite the sun burning down above and that salt-dry air that sucked the moisture right out of your skin, Oates was chilled. Cold right to his marrow and the sweat that beaded his brow was like ice water. "What...what did they do with her?"

Weeds laughed without a trace of humor. "They were out of their minds with what she'd been saying, so they killed her...if you can kill something already dead. They opened up on her, blew her to fragments right there in the street until she stopped moving. And then...then the worms started coming out of her, just boiling out of her with hot-corpse gas, thousands of fat maggots—"

"All right," Oates said, swallowing down his stomach. "That'll do."

But Weeds was far from done.

He told Oates how the fever was taking people and no sooner had they been put in the ground, then they rose back up again. At night, there were dozens of them in the street knocking on doors and scratching at windows, all wanting to be let in. More and more walking dead all the time, screaming out terrible things in the darkness, opening graves and eating what they found inside, gutting livestock and murdering folk that were fool enough to be caught out after dark. Entire families disappeared in the dead of night and sometimes they'd show up a few days later pounding on the doors of kin, wanting to be let in. There was one woman they called the Screamer who'd lost her child. She wandered the streets at night in a shroud, crying out for her lost child. Rawley Cook, drunk and out of his head, went after her one night to kill her and she looked at him and said something to him that made him put his gun in his mouth.

"Around that time, people dying and nightmares walking the night, Crowley depopulating itself, a posse went into the Dark Star to burn the poison out. There was no one left alive in there," Weeds said. "Not a one. They couldn't find Black Betty, but they found the other girls sure enough. Down in the cellar, they were all laid out in open shallow graves and every one of them was grinning. The posse dragged a couple of the girls out and chopped their heads off, but it all sickened them and they ran. And that, stranger, was the end of Crowley. The mass exodus began, people running to get away from the fever and the shadows that crawled out of their graves after sundown."

And that's how it must have happened, Oates figured. People were scared, so they ran as far away as they could get. And that cancer had been breeding ever since, spreading through the belly of the county. Poisoning and consuming and eating what good meat was left. In time, if this wasn't rooted out, the entire county would go bad.

"Now all that I say to you, stranger, happened no less than ten years ago, but it has never stopped. A year ago, I buried my Alice in the plot outside my place in Compton. Natural death, her heart was bad." Weeds was having trouble with this. "I started having bad dreams right off. God, how I loved that woman. She was all that held my world together. One night, I woke up after midnight and the front door was wide open. I found a trail of filth leading into the kitchen. I had a smoked ham in there and something with muddy feet had gone in after it. It ripped it right off the bone and then vomited all that meat on the walls, the floor, you name it. About then, I heard something outside. A wet crunching sound and something like a slimy sort of breathing. I went out there and there's this boy, maybe fifteen or so, except that he's dead and most of his face has rotted off the skull beneath. He's all dirty and black either from dragging himself up out of the grave or digging in others. Because, see, that's what he was doing then and there. He had dug up my Alice and he was chewing on her. He had nibbled most of the meat from her throat and breasts. When I shot him through the head, there was carrion dropping from his mouth."

The old man was quiet for a time after that and it was just the two of them winding out toward Crowley, both having suffered and both having seen things that would forever blight their souls.

Finally, Weeds said, "So that's it, stranger. You know all I know. Maybe some of it's bullshit, but I don't think so. Now you might understand why those in Compton are too afraid to ride out here, why some of those boys have all they can do not to put their neck in a noose and jump off a stool. Now you know what we're riding into and what waits for us there. All I can say, stranger, is may God help us."

Way Oates was seeing it, there was nothing left to be said. They had guns and attitude and hate and not much of anything else. God willing, it would be enough. The table had been set and now it was time to eat lunch with the damned.

7

If Compton was anemic and looking for a grave, then Crowley had already found one...only some fool with a shovel had dug its moldering hide back up again, brushed off the dirt and worms and tried to pass it off as a town. But Crowley was not a town, not anymore. At best, it was a monument to things long past and gone to dust; and at worst, it was a cadaver, something gaunt and crumbling and fleshless and no resurrection was going to make you think different. Some things belonged above ground and some things belonged below and there was no doubt where Crowley fit in.

As they came in and Oates got his first real look, it made something in his guts twist like a corkscrew. For it was a dead, diseased place, bleak and skeletal blown by a wind of hot pestilence. He could smell the corpse-slime and dry-rot seeping from those close-packed houses and shacks and buildings and he had all he could do not to turn and ride back out again.

Remember why you're doing this, he told himself. *Just keep that in mind. Whatever's breeding here in the warm darkness and cellar-damps took Mandy from you. It started a chain reaction that has gutted your family, pulled out all the good stuff in wet loops, let all that you love and care about bleed dry.*

Sucking in a breath of gritty air, Oates let himself feel it all again...the hatred, the pain, the despair. He let all those suppurating wounds on his soul spill their vile fluids until that poison filled him and made him want to scream, to get someone or something in his hands that he could snap and rend, pull apart like a doll.

Easy now, just easy now.

Don't lose your head. Let the pain work for you. That's the way.

"Can you smell it?" Weeds said, drawing his Remington Army .44 from the scabbard and holding onto it so tightly his knuckles blossomed with white half-moons. "Dirty, black smell...Jesus, like things buried and other things gone to mold. Take a good whiff of that, stranger, then ask yourself if I made all that crazy shit up...go ahead, just ask yourself because the proof is in the pudding, only this pudding, I'm thinking, is made out of bone meal and bad meat."

But Oates did not need to ask himself that.

Because he knew deep in the papery rustle of his heart that Old Man Weeds had not made up a thread of that business. He only reported what he had seen, what he had been told, and the conclusions his wily old brain had arrived at. Maybe Weeds acted like some half-ass Sagebrush Willy, but he was tough and he was smart and his brain was firing just as smooth and pure as a steam calliope. It didn't miss nary a note.

And Oates?

No, he believed there was an evil here, a darkness that was invidious and infectious that was reaching out for their throats even then. The horses knew it, too. They were getting skittish and whinnying. They knew bad when they smelled it and this place was about as bad as bad got. Maybe some people called animals dumb, but they were never dumb. Not really. A horse could sense things long before a man could. Maybe it couldn't tell you what it was feeling, but it recognized badness for what it was. And, unlike a man, a horse had no problem turning its tail and galloping away. It could live just fine with that.

Oates felt it getting stronger by the moment. There was a blackness here and a malignance and he could feel it moving up his spine like a snake.

So, yes, Oates believed.

Riding his mare, he looked over the town. It was a close-packed collection of high brick buildings and narrow wooden structures fronted by plank sidewalks, lots of shacks and shanties squeezed in-between. There was a rusting cannon in the town square, livery barns and rooming houses, a cinderblock jailhouse and plenty of taverns. Up in the hills above, you could see the old hoist shacks and towers and derricks from the mines, all of it looking decayed and stripped like the exoskeletons of immense insects sinking into the mounded earth.

Maybe Oates didn't like the feel of Crowley or what waited there, but there was something that was sitting on him just fine and that was the fact that the old town was a fire-trap. Way it was pressed together like that—crowded and leaning, some buildings sharing common walls and when there was an opening, a privy or a tent-roofed hut was jammed in place—it was going to work out just fine. If you lit up one building, the entire place was going to go…and especially with that hot wind blowing.

"Well, stranger, we'd best make for the Dark Star," Weeds said. "Ain't nothing else to see in this graveyard. Whole god-damn place has gone toes up."

As they rode, Oates became aware of the buzzards circling overhead, how they were sitting on hitch posts and roof over-hangs, spreading their wings. They knew there was death here and they were waiting for it to show itself.

The Dark Star was a high two-story structure set between a gambling hall and a rooming house, sagging and boarded up, weathered a uniform gray from the onslaught of the sand-driven wind. A sign creaked on posts, but it was unreadable. The roof was sharply peaked and Oates had to wonder how Black Betty had stood up there that night screaming words into the sky. A dozen buzzards were roosting up there now, cawing and picking at each other's feathers.

The porch was much as Weeds had described: lots of bones dangling overhead, many more having fallen, scattered over the planking. They were all yellow and ancient, some of them going to powder. Oates filled the deep pockets of his old, thin army overcoat with shells for the 12-gauge and Weeds carried his Remington .44 at his hip and a Hood double-barrel shotgun in his fists.

Oates let the hate fill him as they went up the steps and stood before the bone-latticed door of that mortuary. Using the barrel of his American, he knocked that grinning wolf skull aside and grasped the brass knob. A funny tingling went right up to his elbow. His fingers actually recoiled from the touch like they had come in contact with the lid of a casket.

"Locked," Oates said.

"Step aside," Weeds told him.

He put both barrels of the Hood up against the latch and pulled the triggers. The lock and knob were blown right into the foyer with a lot of wood. The door swung open of its own volition.

Weeds broke open the Hood, cast aside the spent and smoking shells, jammed two fresh ones into the chamber. "That's
how you do it, son."

Oates figured if anyone hadn't known they were coming
before, there was no doubt of it now. Old signboards creaked
down the street, dust devils whirling up the boardwalks.
Nothing out there but wind and sand and nothing inside but
death and silence. To him, the town in general and the Dark Star
in particular reminded him of things embalmed, things salted
and mummified and blown dry in the desert. As he stepped
inside, he felt a murmur of terror spread through him.

"Hey, you dead ones," Weeds called into the foyer, "we
come to do you a hurt."

True to form, everything was dry and splintered inside. The
fancy wallpaper was hanging in dirty strips, holes chewed in
the wainscoting by mice. The hardwood floors were warped,
the ceilings bowed. Dusty sunlight filtered in through shattered
windows and gaping holes in the walls themselves. They could
hear pigeons cooing from somewhere above.

"Where first?" Weeds said, licking the salt off his lips.

"The cellar," Oates told him. "Let's take care of what's down
there first."

Weeds knew the way and Oates had to wonder how many
times that randy old goat had been to this place. They followed
a corridor until it split and there was a door right in front of
them. Its panels were filthy like generations of dirty hands had
been touching it. An old, rusted iron catch was twisted to the
side.

"Wait a minute now," Weeds said and took off down the
hallway. He came back with a kerosene lantern. He scratched
a match off his boot and lit it. "No sense feeling around in the
dark whilst something might be feeling around for *us*."

Down the stairs they went, the individual steps creaking
and sinking beneath their weight, but holding. The stink was
awful down there, noisome and dry and nitrous. The floor was
dirt and it didn't take them long to find the shallow graves.
There were about a dozen of them, only half of which were
occupied. The whores were resting inside them, hands clasped

over their bosoms. One of them had decayed down to a skeleton and Oates didn't figure she'd give them any trouble. They were all dressed in fine white burial dresses of lace and silk that had gone to gray and rotting rags much like what they covered.

Weeds held the lantern over one of them, black shadows crawling over the cadaver. She was emaciated and threadbare, gray, leathery skin stretched over a framework of sticks and pipes. There were great holes eaten into her face and throat. She had no eyes. Spiders had spun webs over her face and woven cocoons in her eye sockets. Her jaws were sprung wide as if in a scream.

Oates had a hard time believing that something like her could actually move or walk. She looked like a mummy, something from a tomb and he told Weeds so.

"Well, let's see," Weeds said.

He handed the lantern to Oates and picked up a shovel nearby. Maybe it was the same one that had been used to dig the graves years before. Breathing hard, his jaw set, he took the shovel and pressed the blade to that corded deadwood throat. He looked over at Oates one more time, swallowed.

"Do it," Oates told him.

The old man sucked in a breath of air, brought the shovel up and then down with everything he had. The blade sliced right through the neck with a sound like an axe into kindling... a crackling, snapping sound. The head was severed just that easily.

"Not so bad," Weeds said, wiping sweat from his brow. He picked up his shotgun and took the lantern from Oates. "Maybe that's all we got to do, just lop them heads off and—"

The head moved.

It actually *moved*. The mouth hooked into a sneer, the teeth chattering together, a dry sibilance of air blowing out as if it were trying to talk and they were pretty sure it was. With each scraping gasp, a little puff of dust came out from between the shredded lips. Blackened, eyeless sockets fixed on them and they could almost believe that they could see.

Weeds made a choking sound in his throat.

Then the body came alive, arms coming up, hands whipping

about and trying to grab something they could tear and rend. The body thumped and writhed in the grave, legs kicking and torso thudding up and down, up and down. Oates brought his 12-gauge up and pulled the trigger, blasting that leering head to fragments.

The body shuddered, went still.

Oates was breathing hard himself now. He felt locked up and immovable. Yes, he had seen his dead daughter walk and that was horrible beyond imagining, but this...this was somehow worse. Like seeing a window dummy come to life or a scarecrow begin to breathe. It was absolute madness.

"C'mon, stranger. Just hold the light."

Trembling now, Oates took the lantern from the old man as they went to the next grave. Weeds did not hesitate. He put the barrel of his Hood to the dead woman's forehead and pulled the trigger, blowing that skull to fragments like a shattered vase. One of the hands twitched, but that was about it. Then to the next one. He pulled the trigger.

That was three.

They went to the fourth and the corpse sat right up, its fissured face looking over and up at them. The eyes snapped open in the head, black and shining things like spills of oil. The butt of his American against his hip, Oates aimed and fired one-handed without even thinking. The buckshot almost tore the dead whore in half. Her breasts and upper chest literally exploded into a rain of debris and something like plaster dust that hung in the air in clouds. She screamed at them, thrashing and clawing and trying to rise, but crumbling even as she did so. Finally, she collapsed back into the grave, snapping her teeth and staring up at them with a consuming malevolence, a hatred born in the blackest gulfs of non-existence, fingers like sticks and twigs scratching at the earth around her.

Oates fired again, the living head spraying apart with something that hit the far wall like gravel.

The other two were pulling themselves up from their sunken graves, one dressed in a raspberry taffeta dinner gown with pearls at the throat and the other in a sky-blue bustle dress. Both garments were decaying like their owners. But whereas the others were mummies from sandy tombs, salted and cured things that crumbled as they moved, these two were rancid and moist, their ruined faces furry with grave fungi that hung like garland from their throats.

Both Oates and Weeds were about to start shooting, but something was happening.

Something weird and frightening that they could feel along the napes of their necks and along their spines. The earth beneath them trembled and split open in dusty crevices and the dead began to rise in earnest. Somebody, somewhere, had sung a song of resurrection and that parched soil heaved and ruptured like ancient wounds tearing open and, dear God, what was spilling out. What was seething and oozing from the ground all around them. Fingers broke the dank, dripping soil, followed by hands and flyblown faces. Yellowed and ruined eyes studied the cellar. Lungs filled with dust and insects gulped in the hot wind. The dead rose and hissed, helped the weaker from their beds of dirt.

They were rising everywhere, dozens of them.

Hands were breaking that crust and looking for legs to grab and worm-holed faces were looking for ankles to bite.

It was utter pandemonium as the dead continued to rise, first a dozen then twice that, a profusion of the living dead, clawing and shrieking, faces rotted to pulp looking to steal a kiss and others shrouded in webs looking for hot meat and hotter blood.

Oates and Weeds stumbled back to the stairs as the earth around them lifted and bulged, mounds breaking open and grinning faces gnashing their teeth. Weeds kept shooting until his shotgun was empty, then he pulled his Remington Army .44 and blasted away until the pistol was hot and smoking in his hand. Oates jumped over a heap of rising cadavers and tossed the lantern. It struck the wall and vomited a rolling wake of flames across the floor. But still the things pulled themselves up and out, ever forward. Creeping things and spidery things, faceless things and hungry things. But the very worst might have been those undead babies, crawling things thrown together out of slime and bones, faces boiled down to unformed skulls.

Weeds led them up the stairs as Oates filled his shotgun and blew zombies in half, in quarter, in pieces. They were shrieking and wailing, living skeletons and limbless husks.

But the flames were rising.

They had climbed the walls and tasted the old beams and dry planks and found them to their liking. Everything was so dry and splintered, it caught instantly, flames mushrooming everywhere. The cellar was filled with smoke and shadows and screaming mouths.

Oates had nearly made it to the top when Weeds above him grunted and fell into him, a hot spray of blood splashing into his face. Weeds was dead. There was a hatchet buried in his head and he slipped past Oates and tumbled down the stairs to those ravening and clutching things below.

There was nothing Oates could do but vent the scream that had been building in his throat for so long. Weeds was engulfed in a sea of putrescence. His body floated for a moment or two, then sank, coming apart as mouths bit into it and greedy fingers tore flaps of meat from him in a grisly feast.

But Oates didn't have time to think about any of that or register the horror of it that would haunt his dreams for a lifetime.

For standing at the top of the stairs was a woman.

She was dressed in a black brocade dress with a high neck made of cream lace. Which was probably a good thing, because she had no head to speak of. White, hooked fingers reached out to him and he brought his 12-gauge up and gave her the final round. It threw her back, splattered the wallpaper with black blood and rancid tissue. Oates dove up there as she came forward again, tripping over him and thudding down the stairs.

He threw the door shut after her.

The rusty latch would barely move in his hands. He could hear them coming up the steps, slithering and drooling and rustling, things dropping off them, flies vacating them in clouds. Finally, as the first three or four marble-gray hands reached around the lip of the door, the latch came free. He kicked the door shut and slid the latch into place.

The dead pounded and hammered with fists that were hard like stumps and soft as rotting apples.

The air smelled not just of putrefaction, but of smoke now.

The Dark Star was going up fast.

Oates, his mind shut down now, a white silence breathing in his head, pulled his Colt Navy .44s and raced down the hallway.

He made it to the stairs and saw a little girl with a tumescent and bloated face waiting for him. She had no eyes, her flesh gone to a soft mucilage like hot wax eager to melt from the skull beneath. She held a baby in her arms...or something like a baby. It was more skeleton than flesh, a creeping bag of bones that only wanted to be held. It grinned up at him with white milk teeth, reaching out its rotting hands for him.

Oates fired one of his pistols.

The first round knocked that baby from the girl's arms and scattered its moldering bones like dice. The second round splashed the girl's face from her skull and cored the brain beyond. She fell straight over like a fence post.

Then the stairs.

More tricks and more treats.

Another zombie was coming down to call on him, but this one was regal enough to give you pause and take your breath away. This cadaver was that of a man who'd really been something in life. He was dressed in a purple velvet clawhammer coat with long tails, matching trousers, and pointy-toed lizard boots set with rhinestones and gold inlay. There was a pink silk cravat at his throat and a silver watch-chain at his belly. Atop his head was a high stovepipe top hat upholstered in that same garish velvet.

His face was just as ruined as the others, but even this had an almost patrician charm to it. He had no eyes. He moved gracefully down the steps, tapping a cane before him with a golden wolf's head on top. The skin of his face—what there was of it—was leathery and gouged like a well-worked barber's strop and the color of a new moon. The mutilated musculature beneath was stretched taut and bloodless over a finely proportioned skull.

"Mr. Oates," the mouth said with a voice like wind blown through a catacomb. "The dear lady herself waits you upstairs. A real gentleman never keeps a lady waiting, so—"

Oates couldn't help himself.

As a peal of demented, almost girlish laughter bubbled up and out of him, he put a .44 slug right into that high-stepping cadaverous dandy before him. Then he put another and another. The dandy's head came apart and he rolled down the stairs, coming apart in a dusty heap like an ancient parchment.

The smell of smoke was getting very strong now.

Oates could feel the heat welling up out of the cellar.

There wasn't much time.

Black Betty wants to meet me, he thought, *and I sure as hell don't want to disappoint the lady.*

He ran up the stairs and went from room to room until he came to a bedroom that must have been fine before the mice ate the stuffing out of the fine silk pillows and shifts, before age had faded that fine cherry woodwork, and before spiders had spun webs from the canopy of the bed to the feather mattress below.

There was something on the bed.

Something that rose to face him.

Here was the mother of whores and devils, that hell-witch and conjuror and flesh-eater. Here was Black Betty, a thing of blight and burnt offerings, mummy dust and cerements and graveyard earth. She was dressed in a faded and worm-holed silk reception gown with a long bodice and finely pleated sleeves that must have been khaki once, but were now gray and black. She drifted forward like a wraith from a plundered tomb, smelling of mildew and bones and organic rot. Her breath was like carrion.

Oates let out a yell and put two bullets in her that didn't even slow her down.

She still had that long train of lustrous black locks, but it was now attached to a tanned, charnel scalp. Her face was an atrocity. It looked like it had been picked by buzzards…pecked and nibbled and chewed. The ebony skin was hanging in flaps, great holes eaten through it so you could see the accursed yellow skull beneath. As she came forward, Oates saw that her dress was ripped from breast to crotch and that her abdomen was split open…and inside, things rustled and scratched and squeaked.

She was filled with nesting, slat-boned rats.

Pistols in hand, he dove at her even as she came to meet him. She took hold of him, trying to crush him against her. He battered her face with the butts of his Colts and she threw him down with a strength he was helpless against.

Then she jumped on top of him, straddling him and holding him down, that decaying face swimming in for a kiss. Rats poured out of her, clawing and biting and nipping, and Oates screamed as he felt teeth sink into him, those greasy gray bodies flooding over his own. Black Betty's jaws opened wide and a tongue like a bloated black worm slithered out and licked his lips. Then, a chlorotic grin on her embalmed face, she spoke in a powdery and broken voice: *"Now you're getting what you came for, Daniel Oates. You are having me as I had your daughter and, oh how we enjoyed her...how we enjoyed that sweet little cunt, how we licked her and tasted her, fucking and sucking her pathetic little soul until there was nothing left but sinew and bone and salty meat, but even then, we chewed and feasted and loved that little sweet—"*

And Oates, though he was certainly half-mad or maybe completely mad, interrupted her by saying, simply, "Fuck you."

Then he stuck the barrels of his Colt Navy .44s right into her mouth until she made a gagging sound. He pulled the triggers, blasting her skull into shards, all that filth inside vomiting up and out in a cloud. The rest of her went quickly. Her skin blistered black and fanned out with cracks like candy glass. She went to rags and dust and squirming things, the rats melting away into clods of fur. She was nothing but filth and worms and broomstick limbs attempting locomotion.

Then just a heap of rot.

Oates brushed her off him and stumbled into the hallway. The corridor was thick with smoke. Flames were climbing the stairwell. He turned back into the room, kicking through the dirty glass and seeing the porch roof directly below him. He knocked away the rest of the window with the barrel of one Navy, and jumped out, hitting the roof and rolling off. He thudded into the dirt street and found his feet, immediately going face-down.

But he got up again.

Weeds's horse had broken the tie rail and bolted.

But his gelding was still there. He untied him and climbed onto leather. All around him, as the sun set, they stumbled out of doorways and climbed through windows, slithering from crawlspaces and attics and dark, webby places.

The walking dead.

In shrouds and burial suits and dirty dresses, they stepped out to greet the night and not a one of them did anything but stare as Oates galloped past them, making for the desert beyond.

Even an hour later, in the cool saguaro country of the Nevada desert, he could see where Crowley was behind him in the darkness. It was a glowing orange conflagration that flickered and blossomed like a fire flower, consuming and wasting and spreading.

The town would be wind-blown ash by morning.

By the time Oates reached Compton, he was ready. Ready to pick up his life and hold his wife against him. Ready to begin mourning his Mandy properly.

BONE MARROW STEW

AFTERWORD

When I was thirteen, I woke up one late summer night, crossed over to the window, and there beneath the glare of a full moon I saw a funeral procession: an old black hearse leading a silent motorcade of likewise black cars up the drive that wound along the lake. They drove very slowly and I stood there watching them until long after they were gone, my heart pounding in my throat. I can remember thinking one thing distinctly as all do who experience something beyond the norm: Is anyone else seeing this? I remember looking at all the sleeping houses, rooftops frosted by pale moonlight, and not a single window glowed with light.

The experience was surreal, dreamlike, and, yes, *disturbing*.

A funeral procession after midnight?

Could it be?

And if it was, *who rode in those cars? Or what?*

As disconcerting as the experience was, I also recall that it was fascinating. I wanted badly to run outside and cut across the vacant, grassy lot that bordered the shore drive and get a look at the occupants of those cars. What would I have seen? A bunch of loveable ghouls like Bradbury's Elliott family or the morbid kin of Charles Addams? Or would it be something far more sinister?

Now, many years later, the rational part of my mind tells me that it had to be a dream; yet, the nightside of my brain assures me that it wasn't. To this day I can make no sense of it, for as much as I try to convince myself it was nothing but a random nightmare, there's still that part of me that demands it was not.

My thirteenth year was pivotal in other ways, too, for it was that year I came across two books that would forever alter who I was and what I was and set me on the long trek to who I am now. The first was Robert E. Howard's *Pigeons from Hell and Other Weird and Fantastic Adventures*, which was basically a re-packaging of his Arkham House collection, *The Dark Man and Others*. Wow. From the first lines of the title story—still my A-Number One favorite horror story bar *none*—through such gems as "The People of the Dark" and "The Dream Snake" there was mounting frisson; I was absolutely transfixed. These were the kind of stories I'd always been searching for and in finding them, something deep inside me went from being passively potential to actively kinetic. It sounds crazy, but it was almost like some bizarre, inexplicable sense of déjà vu...as if I had *known* these stories before, loved them, forgotten about them somehow, then rediscovered them and loved them anew. It was an amazing experience for me. The dust had barely settled when I found the second book: *The Shadow over Innsmouth and Other Stories of Horror.* You might know this one. It was put out by Scholastic in 1971 and featured a weird *Nosferatu*-looking Deep One on the cover. For many of us of that generation, it was our first taste of Lovecraft. Though a few of the stories were not Lovecraft's best—"In the Walls of Eryx" and "The Transition of Juan Romero"—there were others that left me absolutely breathless, particularly the title story and "The Colour Out of Space." Unbelievable. And for me, a secret window into a tenebrous world of creeping eldritch shadows.

Those two books were, for me, world-builders.

Nothing I had read before or precious few things since grabbed me with such power as these two slim paperbacks. I still have them. I will probably be gripping them in my cold dead hands when the end inevitably comes for me...though I'll probably trade the Scholastic Lovecraft for a better printing, maybe a British Panther or an Arkham House edition.

Anyway, when I finally made a consciousness decision to

be a writer, I went through a series of phases that started in high school, I think, and lasted until I was something like thirty years old. I wrote reams of imitative stuff in the manner of H.G. Wells, H.P. Lovecraft, Ray Bradbury, Stephen King, James Herbert, Thomas Ligotti, Elmore Leonard, Edgar Allen Poe, Clive Barker, and even Jack London. I blatantly stole their styles and the styles of a dozen others. But somewhere during the process of harvesting other imaginations, I discovered that, slowly, I was weaning myself away from pale imitation into something that I knew was truly my own. This was a *Naked Lunch* moment that all writers know: when you truly see what's on the end of your fork or, in this case, when you hear your voice for the first time—a rudimentary shred of it perhaps—and decide you want to hear it again. And again. And again.

Through the years, I kept listening to it and the result is in your hands now.

It's probably arrogant and more than a little anthropocentric to consider the stories in this book to be my children, but in a way, that's exactly what they are. I took great care in raising each and every one of them before I sent them out into the cold, cruel world. Some did well, others were misunderstood, and many simply ignored. But with each I learned something which is the sign of good parenthood...and writing, I think.

With all that stated and behind us, let us now delve into the birth pains of my drooling, crawling brood. As a proud father— and sometimes *not* so proud—I'll be more than happy to introduce you to my little ones, my little monsters as it were:

"The Reign of the Eater"—This one was technically my first published story, though there are rumored to be others that I never received a contributor's copy for. It was published in a cool little mag called *Stygian Articles* back in the mid-'90s that also put out some of the earliest work by that mistress of the morbid, Charlee Jacob. This story was experimental. I was chan- neling everyone from Edward Gorey to Italo Calvino to Thomas Ligotti, ingesting the poetry of Wallace Stevens and Poe and putting my brain in the mindset of Graham Ingels's gruesome horror comic panels of the 1950s. When all was said and done,

"The Reign of the Eater" came dribbling out. It became the front piece for a book of equally weird stories I wanted to do called *The Book of Souls*. I wrote many of the stories, but only published a few in obscure magazines.

"Red Sea"—I was placing a lot of stories in Greg Gifune's science-fiction horror mag, *Burning Sky*, so I thought I'd take a crack at his dark suspense mag, *The Edge*. "Red Sea" was the result. I like reading accounts of survival, particularly at sea, so this one flowed pretty easily and Greg liked it.

"The Eyes of Howard Curlix"—My wife was having a series of eye surgeries and I wondered what would happen if your eyes mutated so that you could see beyond the visible light spectrum. At the time, I was reading articles about optical physicists freezing light for use in superfast quantum computers and the two ideas came together with a definite nod to Lovecraft's "From Beyond."

"The Chattering of Tiny Teeth"—Two of my favorite things: ghouls and World War I. All wars are hell, of course, but some are more unpleasant than others and World War I was an absolute nightmare...the flooded trenches, the rats, the lice, the pouring rain, thousands of rotting unburied corpses. I had fun writing this story and was excited when Jim Shimkus accepted it for the *Warfear* anthology. Then I got my copy. I read my story. I found something like 42 typos. *Damn*, I thought, *did I send it out like this?* I went through my file copy and only two of the typos were mine. I was pissed. No copyediting? WTF? I vented on the editors but the damage was done. Here's an example of the crap that went into the book (which I was told was the result of some sort of copyediting software):

My Copy: *"By Christ, what a bloody show they put on!"*
WARFEAR Version: *"By Christ, what a boldy show they put on!"*
Again, My Copy: *"The trees here were black and leafless..."*

WARFEAR Version: *"The trees here war black and leafless..."*
And again, My Copy: *"His mind, yes, maybe it went too."*
WARFEAR Version: *"His mind, yes, maybe it went tot."*

Well, you get the picture. A story I was very pleased with became a comedy of errors. Never have I been the victim of a more incompetent and botched editing job. Jim seemed like an all-right guy and he was as aghast as I was. Thankfully, the proper version of "The Chattering of Tiny Teeth" has now seen the light of day.

"Not Sugar, Spice, or Anything Nice"—Just a quickie I knocked out for *Dark Corners*, a little mag Tim Johnson put out for a time. I liked the idea of a little girl in her pretty Sunday dress and curls being evil incarnate, sewing the seeds of madness and destruction. Kind of a *Bad Seed* vibe to it.

"Pit Crew"—I can't recall much about this one except that I had been reading a lot of books about prison life and came across something about prisoners having to dig up a potter's field cemetery and move the bodies. How disgusting, I thought. I later used that idea—in a supernatural vein—in my novel, *Resurrection*.

"Long in the Tooth"—Again, like "The Chattering of Tiny Teeth," a labor of love. The theory that elves, pixies, brownies and that lot being highly romanticized cultural memories of our encounters with races of Paleolithic pygmies has always fascinated me. As does the idea of tribal or cult survivals from antiquity. Combine that with the idea of the English fens of Lincolnshire—atmospheric, lonely, desolate. I read some tidbit about a race of little people that had supposedly lived there once, the Yarthkins. Not good little elves, these, but savage little monsters by all accounts that seemed to fit with the idea of what had inspired the "little people" myths. The Yarthkins were said (in the folklore) to have disappeared with the draining of the fens. My scientific bent of mind right away said: *Aha! Habitat destruction! They went extinct...or did they?* This tale came of it: the last relict group of Paleolithic pygmies hiding out in the fens and shadows, a prehistoric race on the verge of extinction. It's in a direct line of descent from Arthur Machen's "The Novel of the Black Seal" and Robert E. Howard's "People of the Dark" and "The Children of the Night".

"The Resurrection Man"—One of those weird, nearly unclassifiable stories I was writing for *The Book of Souls*. I recall having a single image in my head, that of the living dead haunting the Paris Metro. Not shambling zombies exactly, but charnel things reveling in the very art of death itself. I figured they would only come out at night and their home would be *Pere Lachaise*, where else? And once that came to me, I knew the Lizard King would be their leader. It was published in *Black October* magazine and I was thankful, for most of those stories could never find a home.

"Little Miss Wicked"—This was one of the stories that appeared in James Cain's outstanding *Dark Animus* magazine. I appeared in every issue as kind of the writer-in-residence, thanks to the kindness of James. I was reading stuff about gangbangers in Milwaukee, particularly the Latin Kings who'd been decimated on a Federal RICO conviction. They left a lot of bodies in their wake and I thought, wouldn't it be interesting if one of their victims—a slight teenage girl in this case—was resurrected by black magic as a demon of vengeance? I wanted something different than Voodoo or Santeria, though. Then I read about Macumba and Soul-Eaters...

"The Architect of Pestilence"—I was reading some firsthand accounts of life in Appalachian coal mining towns in the late 19th century/early 20th. The abject poverty and hopelessness of company town life fascinated me, the outbreaks of infectious disease, lack of education, and grim despair of those people cried out. A lot of them were Welsh immigrants who imported their folk beliefs with them. It's intriguing to note that in these remote, cut-off Ozark and Appalachian towns of America many of the ancient, pagan customs of Europe and the British Isles lived on for many, many years after they were extinct in their native lands. Anyway, I thought it would be interesting if a charlatan snake oil salesman showed up in one of these backwoods mountain company towns, spewing his high-magical claims, never realizing until it was too late that these ignorant, simple folk he was selling bottles of alcohol, pine sap, and laudanum to knew of a dark magic beyond anything he could imagine. It seemed to me to be a very M.R. James kind of idea liberally sprinkled with Davis Grubb.

"Night and Fog"—I came across some old *Fate* magazines from the 1960s. Lots of great sea monster accounts. One of them was about some skin divers that fell prey to a long-necked sea serpent on a foggy night off the Florida coast. I took that central idea, moved it to Monterey Bay, California—a hotbed of historical sea monster sightings—and ran with it. For on moonless nights on the Bay, as the fog comes in off the sea and all you can hear is the foghorn calling through the mist, it's as if time has ground to a halt and it's all too easy to believe in long-necked survivors of the Mesozoic haunting the surf.

"Queen of Spades"—Another pale survival from *The Book of Souls*. I had little hopes of placing it when I sent it to Jack Fisher at *Flesh & Blood*, but he loved it and to my surprise it became one of the more popular stories to come out of that great mag. I liked the idea of children alone, no adults, sort of a *Lord of the Flies* vibe. It reminded me of the games we'd play as kids in the fields and woods in which we were trapped somewhere and had to survive against something horrible (that part was usually my contribution to the game).

"The Wreck of the Ghost"—William Jones of Elder Signs Press said he was putting together an antho called *High Seas Cthulhu* and wanted something from me. The basic premise, of course, were Lovecraftian stories set on the high seas, but light on the overdone pastiche elements—banned books and lists of unpronounceable gods, the usual Derleth clichés and worn-out Lin Carter gobbledygook bullshit. I knew right away I wanted to bounce something off *Moby Dick*. The tall ships and sea folklore are two of my fascinations like World War I. Basically, I replaced old Moby with a Shoggoth and delved deeply into shipboard life on a whaler.

"One Dark September Night"—When we were kids, in fact right through high school, our biggest thrill in the summer and early fall was sleeping out in tents in somebody's back yard or in the nearest vacant lot. Nothing finer than a night spent in a musty green tent eating and horsing around, telling stories and wrestling. Once the lights went out—signaling the parents were asleep—we snuck out and roamed the town usually into the wee hours. I could really write a book cataloging our adventures knocking on doors and windows in the dead of night, stealing bird feeders, raiding gardens, and sneaking around in cemeteries scaring the hell out of ourselves, but suffice to say, although we met some very interesting night owls we never ran across anyone like the Dark Man. For that I am grateful.

"Migration"—This was originally written for Greg Gifune's *Burning Sky* mag, but I knew it was too long. I wrote it anyway. Like most of the alien worlds I've created, I could see Cygni-5 through my mind's eye with incredible clarity—a dry, yellow world, silent save for the endless plains of high grass crisping beneath the alien sun, the drone of far-off insects. It would have been a great *Outer Limits* episode, I think.

"The Puppeteer"—This one's from James Cain's *Dark Animus* magazine again. When the idea for the story popped into my head, I began researching puppets in detail and was amazed by the variety of puppetry schools and the rich history of the art form. And let's face it, like mannequins, we all find puppets some-what disturbing. They're like us, but *not* us...living wood and wax, plastic and springs and cogs. Just dummies...but in their flat shoe-button eyes isn't there something unpleasantly cogni-zant and morbidly aware? In his unbearably disturbing puppet story, "Dr. Voke and Mr. Veech", Thomas Ligotti tells us: *"Think of it: wood waking up...aroused from a sleep that should never have been broken."* I need say no more.

"The Legend of Black Betty"—The Yellow Fever epidemic of Memphis in 1878 killed some 5,000 people and sent another 20,000 fleeing for their lives. I read about it many years before I wrote this tale. It stayed in my head, gathering wool, and one day it jumped out as this story. I remember thinking it would be interesting if the plague were something of a darker variety (though I'm sure to the poor people of Memphis in 1878, it was plenty dark enough). I saw the plague spreading west. Frontier towns like Medieval plague cities. I threw in witchcraft and Voodoo and lots of weird paganism to pull the story away from the unusual deadhead zombie fare. I could easily identify with the character of Oates riding the vengeance trail, determined to track down the source of the plague that did in his family (and brought his daughter back from the dead as a cannibalistic monster). Having my own daughters helped, for I could easily channel his hate. I wasn't sure who Black Betty herself was when I started the story, other than the obvious fact that I borrowed her name from the old Ram Jam song—*Bam-ba-Lam!*—but by the end I had her dead in my sights.

Okay. There you have it. If you've stayed awake through this little monologue, I hope these tidbits will tell you a little something about how ideas come to me and how I put them down. Maybe there's no real magic in writing short stories, but there is an art to it, I think, one that is ever-evolving and rarely linear. Ideas come from every direction and a big, juicy part of the art is knowing what to keep and what to throw. These people were real for me as I wrote of them and so were their situations. I believed in these stories and I hope, for just a little while, you believed in them, too.

ABOUT THE AUTHOR

Tim Curran is the author of the novels *Skin Medicine, Hive, Dead Sea, Resurrection, Hag Night, Skull Moon, The Devil Next Door, Doll Face, Afterburn, House of Skin*, and *Biohazard*. His short stories have been collected in *Bone Marrow Stew* and *Zombie Pulp*. His novellas include *The Underdwelling, The Corpse King, Puppet Graveyard, Worm*, and *Blackout*. His short stories have appeared in such magazines as *City Slab, Flesh&Blood, Book of Dark Wisdom*, and *Inhuman*, as well as anthologies such as *Shadows Over Main Street, Eulogies III*, and *October Dreams II*. His fiction has been translated into German, Japanese, Spanish, and Italian. Find him on Facebook at:

https://www.facebook.com/tim.curran.77

Curious about other Crossroad Press books?
Stop by our site:
http://store.crossroadpress.com
We offer quality writing
in digital, audio, and print formats.